SEYMOUR LIBRARY

Discard

FEB 21 2011

PITUS PESTON AND THE LOOSE END

PITUS PESTON AND THE LOOSE END

Everett M. Hunt

Copyright © 2010 by Everett M. Hunt.

Library of Congress Control Number: 2010910987

ISBN: Hardcover   978-1-4535-4574-4
            Softcover   978-1-4535-4573-7
            E-book   978-1-4535-4575-1

All rights reserved. No part of this book may be reproduced or transmitted in any form or by any means, electronic or mechanical, including photocopying, recording, or by any information storage and retrieval system, without permission in writing from the copyright owner.

This is a work of fiction. Names, characters, places and incidents either are the product of the author's imagination or are used fictitiously, and any resemblance to any actual persons, living or dead, events, or locales is entirely coincidental.

This book was printed in the United States of America.

fivecorners@hughes.net

To order additional copies of this book, contact:
Xlibris Corporation
1-888-795-4274
www.Xlibris.com
Orders@Xlibris.com

Contents

PROLOGUE 11

RETURN TO OMAN 13
EARTH IN THE NEAR FUTURE 16
JOHN CATCHES PESTON-FEVER 20
HINTS OF WAR 33
KEN'S SECRET 35
JOHN'S COMPETITION 38
THE ALMANACK DIARIES 40
PESTON HOUSE LEGENDS 46
PITUS AND ATOYE ARRIVE ON OMAN 58
AME'S STORY GETS VERIFIED 61
PITUS PESTON'S JOURNALS 69
COLCHESTER 1863 75
CORSTET 80
THE ALOVIS CONNECTION 88
ANOTHER PESTON SECRET 93
A LEGEND DIES 101
COLCHESTER 1933 104
JOHN LETS JOYCE IN ON THE SECRET 107
THE OMANS MOBILIZE 115
JOHN MEETS MR. OTT 120
BATTLE FOR OMAN PART I 160

THE BATTLE FOR OMAN PART II 166
THE BATTLE FOR OMAN PART III 169
NESGOOR 172
HABINE 176
THE MYSTERIOUS MR. OTT 179
HABINE 183
GOING HOME 189
A FUGITIVE 205
ARRIVAL AT JAR DEST BARG 234

PEREGRINATIONS OF PITUS PESTON

EPISODE III

This is a work of fiction. Names, characters, places and incidents are products of the author's imagination or are used fictitiously. Any similarities to actual events or to persons living or dead is purely coincidental. All rights reserved including the right to reproduce this book or portions thereof without consent of the author.

PITUS PESTON AND THE LOOSE END

Colchester, Essex, England 1813

It was clear that the spectacular escape of Pitus Peston and Calnoon Atoye Itah from the inn at Witham, County Essex, could not be explained, especially to the two witnesses. How could one explain seeing two men cornered in a room escape by diving through a hole in the air in a flash of light? An explosion would not explain it, since the only objects apparently destroyed were the two men. Not another thing was disturbed. There was not even the lingering smell of brimstone always attendant to such a calamity as a detonation of a bomb.

The two thugs under Rohab's employ who rushed after Peston and Calnoon stood in bewildered stasis for several seconds. Then as their senses returned to them they turned to Rohab for an explanation, but by this time he was no where to be seen.

"Blimey, Harry, what the bloody hell was that?"

"Never saw the like of that in all my two score years John," said Harry.

"It's sorcery," said John. "Magic of the darkest kind."

Harry sniffed the air. "Methinks I smells the Devil's arse in this room." John too sniffed. "I don't smell nothin'," said John, "but I felt a breath of heat just bye when we came in here."

"I'll be askin' the boss of it," said Harry. "If he knew 'em, he prob'ly knows of 'em to boot."

"Ye'll na' find 'im. Our Mr. Rowan vanished like a fart in the wind," declared John.

"C'mon, Johnny," said Harry, "We bess be vanishin' too, T'is bad luck to stand where Beelzebub has been."

"Bless the Virgin those two sorcerers don't know our names," declared John.

The two hurried out of the room and straight for Colchester Town from whence they came.

The next morning, in the upper room of a tavern in a town several miles away, Rohab sat in a chair brooding. Beside him on a small side table sat a glass of whiskey half full beside a quart bottle of the same that was half empty. He reached toward the glass, but his hand moved past it to a pistol lying beside the quart. He gently picked up the pistol and gazed at it slowly turning it over in his hands. His focus shifted from the close-up of the gun to the far wall of the room. On the wall over the bed hung a needlepoint sampler showing an image of the Bible flanked by crudely done cherubs with the slogan beneath; *SALVATION LYETH WITHIN*. He pondered this a moment then returned his gaze to the pistol.

So close was he in achieving his goal: Not the murder of Pitus Peston and Calnoon Atoye Itah, though that would have been a decided bonus, but his long desire of ending his exile on this backward planet, returning to his native Haldan. As he sat there still under the effects of a night of drinking, his feelings of frustration and alienation slid away under the aegis of his liquid companion, resignation filling the void in his thoughts.

His emotions flattened and it became as though he was watching himself from a place over his own body. He watched in detachment his right hand leave the barrel and his left hand move over the hammer. That curious left hand then cocked the weapon. It was a flintlock pistol, a single shot, with a lead ball the size of a silver half dime in the chamber resting there as if wanting to be released from its prison.

Rohab slowly gazed around the room and then at the gun. He turned the muzzle toward his face and looked down the black hole. The words on the sampler again came into his mind; "salvation lyeth within". Rohab grasped the barrel with his right hand making a fist around it holding it so tightly it began to tremble in his hands. His left thumb rested on the lock. All he had to do was to pull back the hammer and let it slip from his thumb hold. Just as he made the decision, there was a loud rap at the door.

"Breakfast is being served," called a feminine voice through the door.

PROLOGUE

The quest for Loma's Cube was over. The incredibly old and enormous database set near the galactic center by the Innovator, Aldit Hor, was found. Its purpose was to store the information of the past age since the `Big Bang' and save it from the universal `Big Crunch' of our Universe in its evolutionary end times. The Cube held the science and arts of sentient beings from seventy galaxies, and was meant to be seeded into the new order, that sentience might leap from this higher pedestal, to new heights. The travelers, instead of learning advanced godlike technologies, learned only of their planets' bleak futures, before the Cube was whisked away to a new hiding place. Following Hivik's ancient path, two ships were homeward bound. They had to pass through one more dimensional doorway, the *Hole of Gin-ash*, which would take them from the interior of the galaxy to the vicinity of Oman, a planet a hundred thousand light years from Earth. Three of the four were Oman citizens; Calnoon Atoye Itah, Ralent Kinar Zifan, and Doss Orban Bettan. The fourth was Pitus Peston, an Earth man, who was a friend and comrade of these men.

Their first task was to save what was left of Oman, a once highly advanced world, devastated by war, soon to be visited again by this scourge. The next was for Peston alone to prevent a similar fate on Earth because of something left there centuries ago by the Omans.

RETURN TO OMAN

"When we get through *The Hole*, we will be nearly home," said Atoye. "We will also be in enemy territory. How is the Orbiter holding up?"

"That cobbled up glass field transducer is breaking down," replied Pitus. "Every time I reach 0.8 luminal, it red-lines."

"That's not fast enough if we want to beat the competition," said Atoye. "Kinar," he called, "we have to replace that transducer with something more durable. Get some of those ruby crystals from the storage room and transport over to the Orbiter." Kinar got up from his seat. A moment later he called back to the helm, "Transporting."

He approached the bridge of the Orbiter. Orban was seated next to Pitus at the controls. When Orban saw Kinar, he got up. "No one travels alone. Atoye, I am coming over." He touched his transport amulet and was gone.

"I brought over the mold you used to replace the transducer in the Duster. Where do you want it?"

"Engine room," said Pitus. He switched on the computer helm.

"We're on auto," said Pitus through his com patch, "and on your heading matching 0.1 luminal."

"Right beside you," replied Atoye. "Arrival at the Hole in two hours."

"Plenty of time," said Pitus. He locked in the course and they left the bridge. The raw stones were placed in a crucible and a proton rifle aimed at them. Pitus shook his head.

"Hell of a way to treat quality gemstones."

"Do you want a necklace or a properly running ship?" said Kinar. A couple of short bursts melted the gems. Kinar picked up the crucible with his tongs and poured the white-hot liquid into the mold.

"We'll let this cool a bit and see what we got," said Pitus. He tapped his com-patch. "I could sure use a nice cup of resee while our transducer is cooling down."

13

"Orban just made some," said Atoye. Almost instantly, two beakers of the drink appeared beside them on the engine room floor, reeves of steam rising from them, filling the room with its pleasant coffee-like aroma. "Enjoy," said Orban. "It is the last we have." "I'm glad I asked when I did," said Pitus smugly. "I hope you two didn't expect to finish it off by yourselves."

"Of course not," laughed Orban.

"Of course not," mimicked Pitus. He sipped from the cup. "I'll miss this till we get back to Oman, Lucius," said Pitus absentmindedly. "Sorry, Kinar, I forgot where and when we were for a moment.

"I was Lucius for a long time on Earth," said Kinar. "I can now see those days in a better light. I miss them in some ways." He gazed at Pitus sitting at the orbiter's helm guiding the ship along beside the Duster. At last he added, "With all that you've been through, would you . . ."

"Do it all again?" interrupted Pitus. "There can be only one answer to that. I was born in an age where animal power dominated, where most people I knew never saw the world beyond their township. When I found Atoye's Star Duster atop that butte in Navaho country, I became the most traveled human in history. It will be centuries before another follows my lead."

"You may be around to see it," said Kinar, "if that corstet you took has changed your body as it is supposed to."

"I seem to have been altered," said Pitus. "That is the second major thing on my wish list after the travel. There is so many places to visit throughout this galaxy that I will need to live centuries to see it all. And I have to find *them* . . ." His voice trailed off in wistful thought. Kinar let this last utterance slip by without comment. The chances of Pitus finding and rejoining his lover Orinesse and their child were nearly non existent. When the Innovators moved, the distance could probably be measured in mega parsecs.

Footnote; The beings known as THE INNOVATORS in early Haldan and Calbres lore were quantum creatures who made their home in the space between subatomic particles. For them, a trip to an electron would be as a trip to another planet for man. Dwelling where they did made available to them all eleven dimensions, so this imagined journey would require no effort. They could bring time and space to them. They entered the trederact or third dimension by merely puffing up their miniscule dense forms into ordinary vacuous mater. In their quantum world, they traveled non-locally crossing the breadth of our universe with as little effort as we would cross a room.

When the universe implodes after gravity wins its battle with inflation, the Innovators just step out of it and wait outside its confines until it renews its endless cycle with another big bang. We are part of their great experiment, and the Stone of Ewanok, Stone of Solnah, Loma's Cube, or whatever various civilizations call it, is the record keeper of our existence.

Kinar instead turned the direction of conversation around to more immediate concerns.

"What will you do when we get back?" asked Kinar. "Do you plan to help us?"

"Whatever I can do, I'm at your service. If I survive, I will go back to Earth and snatch up that corstet before it kills off my planet."

"Atoye feels terrible about that," said Kinar.

"How could he have known it would survive in Earth's biosphere?"

"It was a foolish mistake to allow such a powerful substance to get loose on an unprepared world. I share equally in the blame with him."

"Nonsense," said Pitus. "The prediction made at Loma's Cube of man's abuse of it, only serves to reveal man's own share of any blame. People living for a thousand years would be an astounding benefit."

"Only if technology was equal to the problems it would create," said Kinar.

"Long life spans with no disease, vigor for centuries . . . overcrowding and starvation . . . war. It almost seems axiomatic when I think of it," said Pitus.

His first order of business was to help his friends reverse the disaster awaiting Oman. The prospect of survival seemed dicey, yet his mind leaped ahead of this to a strategy for saving his own planet Earth from the incalculable benefit of corstet. At this moment, a galaxy away, another was being led by circumstances that would mold him into either an ally or adversary . . .

EARTH IN THE NEAR FUTURE

John Hodiak phoned his competitor across town.

"What's with him," said John. "He always lets the thing ring, and ring, like he is always busy or something."

Carol, his pharmacy technician came from behind the counter.

"Maybe *he is* busy. Lord knows we aren't!"

"Hello, Deak's Pharmacy," answered a voice full of boredom on the other end.

"Hey Jacques, don't tell me you're busy, this Saturday night."

"Naw, it dropped right off after five. I haven't filled a single script since then. I was thinking about how nice it would be to be able to snap my fingers and be someplace else while I was waiting for the next customer."

"Someday," said John. "Want to quaff down a couple of spiritus frumentis after closing up?"

"Johnny, we're no longer pledging the frat. You can call it 'booze' like the rest of humanity."

"SF or booze," said John, "You wanna?"

"The concept is sound, but the timing is not optimal," said Jacques. "Later, maybe. I have to go over to Randall and return a couple of books before they get overdue. Save your money and I'll help you spend it later."

"I feel like spending a little tonight," John replied. "Otherwise I will go home and start fixing something."

"You just moved into the old Peston house, I heard," said Jacques.

"I'm renting it from my brother Ken."

"That is a really nice old place, you know."

"Oh is it?" replied John. "It has the virtue of being a place I can afford at the moment and just about everything within its walls needs replacing or repairing . . . including the walls!"

"Now, you're being a curmudgeon," said Jacques. "That place is special. It is as old as the hills, dripping with history; and mystery."

"You say that almost with a yearning," said John. "When I think of all the things that need fixing, its age comes off more as annoyance than quaintness."

"I did a thesis on the original owners back in college," said Jacques. You remember that first year in pharmacy school when you were forced to take History and despised it because you were only interested in learning about drugs so you could get one of these glamorous, high-payin' jobs."

"Please, don't remind me. Now the liberal arts part is the only thing I remember enjoying!"

"I read everything I could find about the Pestons and that house. Worked my ass off. Got an A for it, too. You might be interested in looking over some of the stuff I used for my research."

"I didn't realize I landed myself in the midst of so much history," said John jokingly. "Oh, and let's not forget the 'mystery'. What mystery?"

"Shut up for a second and I'll tell you," said Jacques.

"The Pestons were Welsh immigrants who tried to settle in New Hampshire, but were run out of there by Ethan Allen and his boys because they purchased the property rights from a New York agent. They eventually moved over here and built a log cabin, and later built the front part of the house you are in now. There are even a few legends about hidden gold and strange visitations by 'shades from the past'. It's a lot of crap-ola, but intriguing nevertheless."

"I like the idea of finding some gold, but not if some ghost comes along with it," said John.

"What interested me the most was something I could never find out. They had a pretty normal family except for a son named Pitus. He was some kind of genius or something, learning all the Indian languages in the area, and Greek, and Latin, and all that. I would like to know what became of him. He apprenticed to an apothecary by the name of Lucius Ordway for a while, but had to stop when Ordway packed up and left town. Then he got into the printing trade and was doing well, when all of a sudden he took off for the 'Wild West' and was never heard from again."

"Sounds interesting," John replied, "but see, this is just the kind of conversation that should be yelled at each other in a bar over a juke-box spewing out some honky-tonk. Unfortunately, it sounds like you're booked up for tonight. Perhaps we can get together at another time."

"Booked up for tonight," repeated Jacques. "Was that another of your puns?"

"Damn right," replied John. "I really can't help myself."

Jacques groaned, "My aching ass . . ." After a moment he said, "Later tonight is OK, John. I won't be long at the library and the boob tube doesn't sound appealing for this evening. You know, I get three thousand channels of ultra-high-def viewing and still there's nothing to watch. Dad used to say that when he was a boy he lived for the annual showing of the Wizard of Oz on one of their three channels they got on an ancient Philco television set. He said Gramp and he would set down to watch it and munch on treats that Gram spent half the day preparing in the kitchen for the grand event"

"And your point?" asked John facetiously. He knew there was a point and his friend would not spare him the hearing of it.

"I guess if there is a point to it all it's that we become drowned to boredom with choice. Anyway, I think Lorraine will give me a couple hours "shore leave" as long as I don't come home a drunken sailor!"

"That's more like it. I'll stop over to your place about seven-thirty." John fumbled the receiver as he was hanging it up and it fell to the floor. He picked it up by the cord and held the cord over his head.

"Don't hang yourself, it's almost quitting time," said Carol.

"I'm just straightening the damn thing. How a phone cord gets tangled by just taking it off and putting it back on a hook is a profound mystery to me. Do you suppose the Government knows how it happens and just isn't letting it out?"

"Wouldn't surprise me a bit," she laughed. She looked at John a second.

"What's the matter?"

"Why do you call him 'Jacques'," she asked slyly? "His name is Joe, isn't it?"

"Joe became Jacques five years ago while pledging Phi Del. It was during the scavenger hunt. We were at Round Lake searching for the 'Garter of Venus', which was our final treasure. We found it around a dock piling and were planning a celebration over a half-keg when Atwood Pierce put it on his head pretending he was Caesar or something. The damn fool stood up in our canoe. He was already plastered to the gills and fell in. When we got him back into the boat, the precious object was missing. We looked all around for it, but realized to our horror that it sank. We couldn't go back without it, and it looked like we were in big trouble. Joe suddenly jumped in and went down for it. I thought he was crazy. We were in over twenty feet of water with who the hell knows what was down there, but he went down a second time and then a third. When he surfaced the third time, he had it in his hand! I said he was a regular Jacques Cousteau. The name stuck, the rest is history."

"Somehow, it all doesn't surprise me," said Carol. She looked at the wall clock and gave a bland cheer. "Yippee, it's time to leave this joint."

"I'll let you out. I have to do the deposit, finish the drug orders, and get things ready for the boss tomorrow."

"The Gin-Ash partition is straight ahead," said Kinar. "I see its signature in the remote sensor."

"Slow down to 0.1 H again," said Atoye. "We'll want to stop and take a good look at it before going in." At a distance of one hundred thousand miles they got their first visual of the hole. At one thousand miles the two ships came to a halt.

The Hole of Gin-Ash was actually a planar surface created by the gravitational interference of three orbiting equidistant dense objects. It was transparent, but easy to see because the light from the whole area behind was bent, crowding the image of half the galaxy of stars into a small ellipse.

"Looks congested on the other side," said Pitus.

"You know it isn't, of course," said Atoye. That is 180 degrees of star light converged into one spot as by a lens. It is a wormhole without the tube."

"No turbulence," said Kinar.

"Perfect gravitational balance," said Atoye.

"It gives me a shudder," said Orban. "It is like the entrance to hell from Calbres middle period literature."

"A feather could float through that without harm," said Atoye. "Hell would be trying to go around it. The tidal forces outside that perimeter would shake anything to a vapor."

"There's no way to tell by looking through it where it opens into," said Pitus. "All the constellations are squeezed together by the distortion."

"We know where it comes out," said Atoye. "It opens into the Haldan sector, much too close to their home planet for my comfort. Are we clear on the plan once we get through?"

"Maximum speed all the way to beta-Argulis." replied Kinar.

"Good." said Atoye. "And if we get separated?"

"Wait at the old position of Nesook Barg for two hours, then head for Oman together or not."

"Then let's go in," said Atoye.

JOHN CATCHES PESTON-FEVER

It was half-past six when John left the drugstore. Closing at six o'clock on Saturdays was a relatively new thing at Bingham's Pharmacy. John liked it, especially in summer when there was three hours of sun left. There was plenty of time for a stroll up and down the main drag's bistros and arcades at Lake George with a bonus along the beach to check out "the scenery". Tonight, however, was too short for that, he had to get back home to change and grab a bite before going to Joe's and Lorraine's.

"I think I'll get something to eat here and wolf it down in the car on the way back home. That'll save a few minutes." He drove down Glen to South St. and parked a short distance from the corner. "Hotdogs with the works, maybe four of them and a big orange, that should make a decent supper," John thought as he crossed the street to the narrow storefront where the "best dogs in the city" could be found. He pressed down on the latch and pushed on the door.

"Hey, Frank, you fixed the door from rubbing."

"Got tired of hearing you complain," Frank replied. "Did you hear my bell? I had to put one on the door now that it doesn't rub the floor. Otherwise I can't tell if someone has come in."

"Same reason Bingham won't let me oil the spinners in the store," said John. "He said he wants to know when somebody is looking over the merchandise."

"How many tonight?"

"Four; with the works, and a Mission orange".

"You're too young to know about Mission Orange. They ain't made that stuff for fifty years."

"I can't put anything over on you," said John. He snorted a laugh. "I read about it in an old book. Gimme whatever is currently brewed with an orange flavor."

Frank stood a thin wispy 6 feet 4, his steel gray eyes complementing his ring of iron gray hair about his head. His face was likewise thin and covered with wrinkles gathered over the past sixty or so years. Frank had run the restaurant since the days when it was called the NEW WAY. Before that it was known by the locals as DIRTY JOHN'S. Frank renamed it after the originator because he liked the sound of it. The place, however, was anything but dirty. One could "eat off the floors" as the saying goes. John stood watching, as always, in awe as Frank started the culinary assembly line that made this place so popular. First, he opened the steamer and took out four rolls and laid them in a row on a piece of marble counter-top. Then with a long fork he reached into another compartment and stabbed a pair of hotdogs and filled the buns. Again he plunged his fork and the other two dogs were soon bedded. Then he grabbed an earthenware pot and dipped a large spoon into it dragging a small splash of sauce onto each one. The spoon, from thousands of dips in the pot over scores of years, had worn through at the front of the spoon's bowl making it look like a fat, two-tined spear.

"When are you going to retire that spoon?"

"Never! It's what makes the sauce taste so good," said Frank proudly. "My father used this same spoon when he took over the joint back in the fifties. He told me 'Dirty John' himself gave it to him. If this place ever catches fire, I'm grabbing this spoon and running. The rest can go to hell!"

Frank looked out the window and pointed across the street. "I could ask you the same thing about that truck of yours. How's that old thing run, out there? It looks like an old duffer on the public welfare owns it!" He laughed loudly and a mirthful contagion infected a couple of others standing close by.

"I'll have you know that's a classic 1949 Chevrolet Pickup Truck that was owned by a farmer who never used it to haul anything but baled hay. Nice clean box!"

"What every man needs!" said Frank. There was a guffaw from one of the booths and one guy at the bar blasphemed an "A-Men." Frank winked mirthfully at him and then turned back to John. "Gimme twenty-two-fifty before you forget and make me have to send the cops after you."

"Geez, Frank, didn't these once cost twenty-five cents each?"

"Yeah, back when Bingham's ol' man bought 'em from my ol' man. Back when that jalopy of yours was in the show room."

John gave a little sneer and ponied up the cash. With a "see ya later" he left. John pulled the door open on his *classic* and tossed the box of hotdogs on the seat while he used the catch on the truck's door to open the bottle of soda. "Best little church key" on four wheels. And with only 384,000 miles on it." he remarked as he popped the cap off the soda bottle. It had been decades since a crown type bottle cap had been used on soft drinks, but somewhere Frank got a hold of some pop in the retro style bottles. It looked sort of like a Mission, but it wasn't. He took a large draught from the bottle and let out a sigh of satisfaction. He then put the key in the ignition and stepped on the starter pedal. A little pull on the choke made it come to life. He proceeded down the street a short distance and turned around in a driveway and headed back toward Glen Street.

"I guess I'll go the short way tonight even though the paper mill stinks up Broad when the wind blows east." Twenty minutes later he was home; to his new, old home on the bank of the Hudson.

The few furnishings John owned were piled in the living room, which was the largest room in the house. There were two bedrooms in this early salt box up stairs along with a garret, and another small guestroom on the first floor. There was also a kitchen that had its last renovation apparently during the Carter Administration, a pantry, a dining room, a hallway with the staircase to the upper floor directly off the main entrance. There was a cellar, the floor of which was paved with large flat field stones. It was cool and rather nicely dry for a cellar. The only impediment of space in this large cellar was the enormous defunct coal-fired furnace standing in the center of the floor, something left over from the Roosevelt days.

"It would be nice to sleep in a bed tonight," John thought as he glanced over the pile of furniture and boxes clustered in the center of the living room. "Maybe when I get back from Jacque's I'll have some time to put some things in their proper places."

It was a short, pleasant ride over to his friend's house on Dix Avenue. The sun was still quite up in the sky, and the chill had not yet set in to announce the start of day's transition into night. This was John's favorite time of the day, when work was done, the heat of mid day passed; the smells of the flowers seemed more intense, and the songs of the early evening birds; all these disparate elements mingled forming a new substance that John could only describe as "restful pleasure".

Many thoughts about this and other things, John kept in some journals. He started writing his feelings and events in his life while yet a teenager, when a music teacher told him that Beethoven kept such a notebook on his person constantly, lest some fleeting thought carry away a musical phrase that his mind had conceived ere he could find a means to freeze it upon paper. Sometimes it was amusing to return to those little notebooks of a decade ago and revisit the thoughts of youth. Some opinions and viewpoints changed with the mileage of life, some remained intact over the years. The thoughts that still had relevance despite the passage of time were the ones about the woods and meadows he frequented as a young boy. Nature was John's first romance, though he rarely passed up an opportunity to supplement this allegorical love experience with real feminine companionship.

After a couple more minutes John arrived at Joe's house. As John was pulling into the driveway "Jacques" emerged from the garage and motioned for John to park beside his car.

"Come on with me down to the library so I can return these books," said Joe.

"I thought you had already done that."

"I planned this for your benefit. While we are at the library, I can show you where the Peston Family History is kept. You could give it the once over while I'm taking care of business."

"Why not," said John, "We can grab a couple of hotdogs at DJ's afterward." The two rode downtown in Joe's new inertial drive Eco.

The car was completely silent except for a soft clunk when it went into gear. The only sounds of movement were the tires crunching on the loose gravel of the driveway. "I doubt I could ever get used to moving down the road with no engine noise," said John.

"I like it," said Joe. "I can at last hold a normal conversation without shouting, as I have to in your old rattletrap."

"It's the sound of power," replied John. "It's good for the circulation of the balls."

"This has all the power I need," said Joe, "and my balls circulate just fine. He jabbed his finger at the dashboard. "This will go all the way to Buffalo doin' seventy without having to recharge the fly wheel." He tapped on an upholstered mound between them. "There's a two-hundred kilogram tungsten steel flywheel encased in as much carbon fiber, turning over at two-thousand revs per second, all afloat in a mag-lev bearing."

"If it let loose, we could be pureed," said John.

"I won't say it couldn't happen," said Joe, "but the case is a 2-inch carbon shield keeping us from it. A flywheel crash might scare the B' geezis out of you, but so far, no one has ever been hurt. It's the wave of the future, and that gas guzzler is on the way out, especially with gas being eleven-fifty a gallon. So just shut up and enjoy the ride." Joe then routed the conversation back to his original set of topics.

"There's a cave by the river a little above the paper mill," said Joe trying to stir up interest in John for the local history. "Supposedly some kids found a musket, powder horn, and a small sack of coins in there from the Revolutionary War. It all went over to the Museum. Ever shoot one of those things?"

"Once, a while back. They are a lot of fun to fool around with. Can't hit a damn thing with one, but they're fun just the same. Ken let me shoot his back when we were on better terms. I thought about getting one and joining one of those clubs that shoot black powder rifles up at the range on weekends. Never did though."

"Good excuse to have a few beers and shoot a little 'bull', whether you shoot the gun or not." said Joe.

"You know, Johnny, you'll just have to become a history buff, especially if you are living in one of the oldest houses still standing in the town of Ft. Edward."

"I don't know if I can get interested in that old stuff," said John. "I'm a futurist, believe it or not. I hope I live long enough to see commercial space travel become common. I'll be one of the first tourists to go to the moon."

"Well, for me," Joe said, "I think I was born too late by about 200 years. I feel my element is in the Colonial days when life was simpler. You couldn't blow up the world then, you just worked hard and went to bed tired of body, but rested of mind."

"It was hard then too," said John. "I wouldn't want an infection without antibiotics, or have to have surgery without anesthetics. A trip to Albany and back would take a week back then. Today, we could shoot down the North-way and be there in half an hour."

"As for me", John continued, "I look toward the future. I think I was born 200 years too early!" They both laughed heartily at their widely divergent opinions, realizing that they could do nothing to fulfill their separate dreams.

"We're a couple of damn-fool malcontents." said Joe. He made a quick turn on the last second of a yellow light.

"I suppose you believe all that stuff about visitors from outer space like you always see in those 'scandal sheets'?"

"Yes, I certainly do." said John. "I think the Government is keeping a lid on it, though. It would cause a hell of a stir if regular folks like us found out that there really is an "Area 51" and that we weren't the only ones around, like the theocrats say."

"I don't believe it." said Joe. "If anything, it could be our own military doing experiments with weird aircraft."

"But what if there are other planets that are inhabited," asked John. "Decades ago SETI claimed they received an artificial signal from the vicinity of Zosma, in the constellation Leo. They sent out a reply which should have taken twenty six years to reach them. If they received it and replied, it should be arriving within the next few years. "It excites me to think there are other civilizations to discover and exchange ideas. Maybe other cultures got over all the social problems, and crime and war and live in peace and prosperity. We could learn a lot of things from such a people."

"Maybe we would have to teach them things." Joe teased. "They might be instead like we were long years ago, before the industrial revolution. Hey, if you locate a world like that, get me a ride there. It sounds like just the place for me!"

"Like that old Star Trek XVI movie where they found this pre-industrial planet," quipped John.

By this time they arrived at the Randall Library.

"Here we are, Johnny. Now to find a place to park." Joe scanned the sides of the street.

"Even in the evening there's no place to put a car on this street. What a pain in the . . ."

"There's a spot right there, don't get so excited." said John as he sat up in the seat in a posture of watchfulness. "It looks like that other guy is going to get there first." "Like hell," declared Joe. He punched the gas assist. The two easily gained the parking space since they had the advantage of being on the same side.

"Oh, damn!" yelled Joe. "Somebody put his chopper in the middle of that nice big space. Why can't they park those things on the sidewalk and leave the curbside to the cars!"

"Probably because it's illegal to park a motorcycle on the sidewalk," John replied wryly. "Just because you seemed to get away with it down at School . . ."

"I had a special dispensation from the local constabulary." Joe said smugly as he turned back into traffic to make another pass around the loop. "You know that `garter of Venus' I had to retrieve from Round Lake?"

"Of Course," said John.

"I played a part in getting one of the patrolmen a date with the real owner of the sacred garment."

"Sue McIntyre. It was said to be hers . . . the girl most likely to be craved in the Class of 2017. You should've got the keys to the whole damn City for a deed like that!" exclaimed John.

"You could say I got better than that," smiled Jacques. "I caught that very same garter a year later at Sue's and Ted's wedding. Ted's cousin, Lorraine Fitch caught the bouquet. That was four years ago," he reminisced.

"There's a spot up ahead," said John pointing to a gap in the seemingly endless line along the street. In a moment they were parked. The two walked across the well-groomed lawn up to the main entrance of the library. Joe just waved to the desk attendant on his way to the reading room and called out "Hi, Joyce. John there needs your services," and he then disappeared behind a shelf of books.

"That's an interesting way of putting it!" She replied mirthfully. She looked sheepishly at John.

"How may I help you," she asked. She was an attractive twenty-fiveish woman with long brunette hair that would have fallen onto her shoulders had she not had it gathered behind her in a pony tail. John studied her in the second between her question and his forthcoming reply. "Nice looking, great hair, not even put up in a bun; I thought all librarians were plain looking with their hair all put up like the matron of a boarding house. I suppose that is an old stereotype that has long gone by the wayside. What a figure! At least what shows from behind the desk. Sexy voice too. No ring either. Well, well, well . . ."

"Oh, ah, yes," said John in a faltering jumble of words due to his temporary failure to disconnect his mind from his delightful reverie. "I'd like to look at the history written about the Peston Family."

"That would be in the Codder Collection," she said. "Just go up those stairs and it's the first room on the left at the top of the stairs." She reached into a drawer beside her. "Here is the key. Please lock it again when you are done."

John took the key and as he did so her hand brushed his. John felt the softness of her skin in this very brief moment of touch, and though barely enough to be noticed, conveyed much pleasure for all its brevity. He remained still after this shock of delight, perhaps a quarter second longer than he normally would have before turning for the stairs. It was long enough for Joyce to ask a question.

"I don't wish to appear nosy, but do you have a special interest in the Pestons? I only ask because I find that manuscript to be particularly fascinating."

"There seems to be an unusual amount of mystery attached to this thing." John replied.

"There is to be sure!" Joyce replied. "It is not attributable to any author that our research department could find. It's not signed, only dated, and story has it that it was simply found here one Sunday morning in 1883 by Mr. Wadsworth, who was the librarian at the time."

"Somebody probably wrote it here and left it by mistake. Then they couldn't remember where they left it." After a second John added, "That doesn't sound very likely, does it."

"Not really. He noted that it was not there the night before, and he found it lying on the front desk on Sunday morning when he entered the library for some thing he had left behind the previous night. He said it was probably the first time in the City's history that someone broke into a public building not to steal something."

"I don't mind stating my purpose." replied John. "I am living at the old Peston Place." Her eyes lit up at hearing this, but she kept still. "I rent it from my brother and I am poking along trying to fix it up. Jacques is the one who said you had the family history here and urged me to read it. To humor him I'll take a look at it."

"Who is this Jacques?" she asked.

"He's over" . . . John gestured in the direction Joe went upon entering . . . "I call him Jacques. It's a long, story. Joe Castro, I mean."

"Oh," she said, nodding her head slightly. "Sorry, I didn't mean to hold you up. I was just curious, that's all."

"No trouble," said John. He was glad for any excuse to continue conversation with her. She was attracting him spontaneously, and there was a delight in sustaining that normally brief moment in stating his business, which was not meant to persist past getting directions to the Codder Room.

"Then I'll tell you something else, Mr."

"Hodiak, John Hodiak".

"Joyce Benton".

"What else were you going to say?" asked John who suddenly felt the hoped-for sense that he was spontaneously attracting her.

"Well, there is a little legend attached to the history," she said. "It was thought by one of Mr. Wadsworth's staff that it was written by . . . ." She hesitated hoping not to sound overly mysterious about what she thought was purely a crazy, nonsensical rumor.

"Who?" asked John with a sense of being teased? "Who wrote it?"

"Pitus Peston, the one who disappeared at the beginning of the 19th century."

"He would have been an old geezer if he was still around in 1883!" laughed John. "That is some baloney peddled to build up publicity."

"Probably, but whether it is true or not, it created quite a commotion back then. There was a story in the Albany and Troy papers about it, and the Library of Congress sent an expert up here to examine the document. The one who examined it said the paper that the history is written on was at least 100 years old at the time. There was a small group of people who formed a sort of investigative club to try to sleuth out the puzzle. Then interest just fizzled out and the Peston Family History was stuck in with some other local history papers in the Codder Collection. It remained there undisturbed for decades until last year a reporter from the Post did a feature story on it, hoping, I think, to solve the mystery."

"Did he," John asked?

"No, he theorized a family member wrote it, but kept it anonymous because the family didn't like the publicity and he thought the author wanted to escape trouble from his relatives, as some of it is rather disparaging to the early Pestons. Some of those who have read it say they have an eerie feeling that it is more personal than would normally be expected from a person writing about people he could not have actually known."

"Have you read it, Mrs. Benton?"

"Yes, I have. It's Miss, not Mrs. Just call me Joyce if you like."

"John," John said with a complementary bow.

"Very well, John," She repeated with some relish.

"Now my interest is really piqued," said John, "Especially after all the background about this paper. Upstairs, first room on the left, right?"

"No, left," she laughed.

"Yeah, I got it," John said coyly.

By this time a co-worker came over to the desk.

"Ann, will you watch the desk while I help this man find some things in the Codder Room?" Ann looked at John a moment for an assessment. Then she gave Joyce a just-between-girls look of approval as if to say, "You better show this one the Codder Room as well as your best butt-sway."

Joyce came around the desk.

"Follow me," Joyce said as she beckoned to John with a wave of her hand. John followed her up the stairs, her perfume wafting to him, exciting his senses, adding another dimension to the view John had of her graceful form ascending the stairs. John felt himself becoming less interested in the history. She unlocked the door and pushed it open. Then she felt with her right hand for the light switch. It was a middling-sized room with a whole wall on the left side filled floor to ceiling with books, leather bound and cloth bound. Beyond a stack of filing cabinets was a large rectangular oak table with four worn Windsor type chairs around it. On the wall opposite the wall of books were shelves of folders, a solid body of them, all numbered on the spines, their solidity of appearance broken by a single twelve light window in the area right of center. On the right side as one entered the room were folio shelves filled with large art books, county and state atlases and histories and village plat books as well as miscellaneous folders lying flat. The whole room smelled of old leather and paper, that antique mustiness that Joe often referred to as "the fragrance of time-honored literature". John repeated this phrase, which caused Joyce to raise her eyebrows as though surprised, but then she smiled as one aficionado does to a kindred spirit. John was glad he said it for the response it elicited in her. "It might be time to become a history buff," John thought as he contemplated many repeat visits to the Randall Library and the company of one of its librarians.

Joyce went over to the phalanx of folders and directly pulled out the one marked "No. 37", and placed it on the table. "Happy reading," she said, and she started for the door. "Please shut off the light when you are done."

"Wait!" exclaimed John. He startled himself with the intensity of his own utterance. Now in this interminable second that he had just arrested in its flight, he succeeded in stopping her. He really did it now. Now he actually had to do what he wanted since he met her. He replayed in his mind his asking her out to a movie or dinner and she saying "yes". This same scenario played over and over in his mind as they talked at the desk down stairs, on the trip up the stairs to the balcony and again as they approached the Codder Room's door. And again as she reached for the folder and placed it on the table. He put off asking because the uncertainty of the result of asking filled him with fear. "Don't blow it now, Hodiak!" John thought, during this arrest of time in which his utterance now trapped him. "Say it!"

"Yes?" she said as she looked back, her right hand resting on the door jamb, feet frozen in the motion of going through the threshold, her face turned, slightly puzzled, toward him.

"When does the Library close," asked John, his voice nearly cracking as it exited through his parched throat.

"At nine. You have a full hour yet."

He felt his time had already run out, the second he held at bay broke over his wall and resumed its inexorable course. No time for searching her mood or scanning for a tell tale sign of likely success. He felt sick inside over the chance of failure, but was goaded mercilessly by the necessity of "now or never".

"Come see a movie with me at the Holomax," John blurted out. Her expression shown a mild surprise which John agonized over as it revealed no hint of how she would answer. He now presumed failure and the embarrassment that it would bring along with it.

"What's playing?"

"I don't know," John confessed. In the next infinite second that John had traversed before a response could be received, his heart vacillated between jubilation and despair. The relief resulting from triumph over his inertia of fear mixed now with terror at the expected decline of the invitation.

"Be here at half-past nine," she replied in a lusty velvet command of familiarity. She then left the room without another word.

John sat motionless, numbed with the wash of primordial ecstasy. As the second-fractions raced by, the realization of his success finally hit him as a shock wave from a blast. His pulse made three-fold cadence with the ticking clock over the doorway. His mind lent its full attention to the coming evening.

For several minutes he sat staring outward from his chair. Then his rational mind regained control and he swallowed his heart back down to its proper place. "I'd better look this over just in case she asks me what I think of it." He untied the large folder and from it took out the smaller one and placed it on the table. He opened a faded green folder and from its pocket protruded a small sheaf of printed pages, likely hand set, edge-browned and compressed, appearing to have had little attention over the years. The paper indeed looked far older than the time it could have been put to service. He held it up to the light and could see the chain and wire lines found in hand-made paper of two centuries ago. The reason he knew of this character of hand made paper was a course in lithography he took at Russell Sage in his third year. It was interesting and fun and he absorbed the technique of printing lithographs quickly. He aced the course. In the center of the sheet he noticed a water mark of what looked like a jester with a small emblematic A on his chest.

"Why would anyone use such old paper to print on?" John thought as he picked up a sheet and held it. "Now it is more than 200 years old and is more supple and strong in appearance than last year's newspaper. Best to be careful with this; tear a page and get strung up by the librarian." He began to read . . .

"BRIEF HISTORICAL REMINISCENCES OF THE PESTON
FAMILY OF FORT EDWARD, NEW YORK STATE.

`The first Pestons came to America from Wales aboard the ship *ANNE* captained by a Mr. William Edwards, and landed at Stratford, in Connecticut on the evening of September 21st, 1754. Here the family, consisting of Jeremiah, his wife Sarah, and a lad of 14 years named Rufus wintered till the following spring intending to settle on a tract of land in the township of Rupert, in the present state of Vermont, then part of the New Hampshire Grants. This tract Jeremiah purchased while at Stratford from a New York Agent who assured him that New York held unequivocal jurisdiction over the area in question and cautioned him not to `throw away good money to a Hampshire sharper' who would attempt to claim genuine authority.

Because of the heated dispute over the territorial authority of this region, and the ceaseless harassment given the Pestons by the New Hampshire settlers led by that villain Allen, who could not countenance these people to squat on good Hampshire lands without properly paying for it, they quit the location and removed to the West and located on a plot of land by the banks of the Hudson in Fort Edward, in the present State of New York. The loss of most of their savings through this unfortunate occurrence made the next several years difficult, but they managed to erect a small dwelling and a barn, making a go of it farming a 50 acre tract about a mile south of the present Village of Fort Edward." After several pages John found the following;

"During the hot, dry summer of 1787, Rufus and Caroline deliver of a second son who was given the name `Pitus', whose curious name is said to have derived by the following coincidence;"

"As a name had not been selected ahead of time, the imminence of the birth occasioned no little concern in the father who believed the Devil stood by eager to claim any newborn who was not given a proper Christian name with which to welcome it. The physician being at hand for this birth was engaged with the elder child in an attempt to calm his fears from the howling of the wolves, who, from the length of the drought and the dearth of game had lost nearly all fear of man from the increase of their hunger. The child amid whining and tears asked the doctor if the wolves would "get inside the house and `bite us'." The doctor, a Welshman, having a heavy accent to his speech said reassuringly that he `vood dnot led ze voolves pite us'. Rufus, overhearing this exchange decided to call the infant Pitus because the newborn's cries were louder than the sounds of the wolves without, causing the joy of the arrival of the new member of the family to force fear out of the house . . . ."

John continued reading the History, and a little while later Joe entered the room and seated himself. "I see you found the legendary History of the Peston Family."

"Sure did," John answered, "Now listen to this." John turned back a few pages and read aloud . . .

". . . the lad named Pitus had a great proclivity to acquiring the various tongues and made a pursuit of learning the several local native dialects. He was, according to a friend of the family (This is purported to be William Lester, a neighbor who also fled from the New Hampshire Grants under like conditions as the Pestons. He settled with his wife and two daughters a few miles south of the Pestons along the Hudson.) an exceptionally bright boy who seemed already familiar with anything someone was teaching him. He seemed at times, though, a wistful, melancholic lad, taking to himself much of the time, wandering the woods and roads sometimes for days on end, which exasperated his older brother and contributed, no doubt, to the great enmity between them. He was wont to wear the trappings of the local natives and remove himself to their villages, fishing, hunting, and living as one of their number."

One day in the late Spring of the year 1808, he and his older brother, Lloyd had an especially choleric exchange, where Lloyd declared Pitus to be a useless vagabond, and further demanded Pitus give up his rights to the farm as Lloyd determined he'd earned it by carrying his brother's share of the work over the years as well as his own. Pitus, though taciturn by nature, had a small part of his father's temper and impetuosity, and, signing off my third to Lloyd, told him what I thought he should do with it!" After this, Pitus packed a few of his things in a haversack and left his home, never intending to return. The argument so upset Caroline that she called him "not her son", an act she later repented, so I hear.

This ends what is known about Pitus Peston except for a statement from a Mr. Dixon who coincidentally met Lloyd in Albany in 1813. Dixon had returned from a hunting expedition in Upper Louisiana the year before and informed Lloyd that he briefly met a man who was introduced by the name Pitus who was heading south-west near the head of the South Platte in Colorado down toward the Ute and Arapahoe Country. Dixon said the man seemed rather in haste even though he had plenty of time to arrive ahead of the winter snows. Dixon warned him of the hostile nature of the Indians in the region for which he was destined, but he expressed no heed of the warning. Lloyd told Dixon that it was impossible that he could have seen his brother Pitus in 1812, since it was reported to him a year earlier by a neighbor that Pitus was taken captive by the Sioux and murdered. John stopped reading and looked up at Jacques across the table.

"Some guy!" said Joe.

"Strange, bordering on the weird," John replied. "Do you think the Indians killed him?"

"Probably." answered Joe. "Out on some scorching desert plain or mudflat lie the crumbling, desiccated bones of Pitus Peston."

"Yeah," said John, "probably. "What do you think he was in such a hurry for, anyway?"

"Gold, no doubt," Joe answered.

"Gold wasn't discovered out there yet." John replied. "No, it was something else." John turned to the last page of the manuscript.

"See this set of symbols?" John asked as he pointed the mark at the end of the page. "Could that be the signature of the author?"

"Looks like Greek." Joe said in the midst of a yawn.

"Not Greek," John said as he scrutinized the figures. "I don't remember any Greek letters that look like that." He looked up from the paper with a thoughtful expression.

"Joyce said comments were made about how first person-ish some of it sounds when read. Remember when I was reading to you a while back? . . . . signing off *MY* third to Lloyd, told him what *I* thought he should do with it?"

"Could be a mistake in writing style," said Jacques.

"Maybe, but maybe not," said John. Two sentences after that the author refers to the disownment of Pitus as `an act she later repented, so I hear'. This could be a clue to a more interesting story. The change from third person to first person narrative is just too obvious to be a grammatical mistake."

"Say, Johnny, you're really getting wrapped up in all of this, aren't you."

"Maybe."

"Well, there is no more time to delve into the mysteries of the past this evening. It's ten minutes to nine and we will be kicked out of here if we don't go pretty soon." The two returned to the main desk where John returned the key.

Ann was at the desk. She smiled a coquettish smile at John as she took the key and said, "Don't be late."

On the way back to the car, Jacques remarked, "Don't be late? What does that mean?" He gestured back at the library.

"I have a date."

"Not with her," Joe said. "Ann is married."

"That makes no difference to me," answered John. "Besides, I know she's our bartender's wife."

"I know Mike, and anyone messing around with Ann is courting disaster."

"Not in this case." replied John. "What I'm doing would be with Mike's blessing."

'You're pulling my leg . . . I sincerely hope," said Joe.

"It's Joyce. Ann told me not to be late for Joyce."

"You thought you had me going for a minute, you horse's ass."

"I did."

It was quarter past nine when the two returned to Joe's house. John immediately jumped into his truck and headed back to town.

HINTS OF WAR

"Where the hell have you been?" asked Pitus. "Kinar and I were arguing about whether to stay or go."

"I lost you in the Comara Nebula. Our sensors went down and we had to repair them. Orban has learned a lot of flesstics (electronics) in the past few days."

"I'm glad we didn't leave on schedule," said Pitus.

"I knew you wouldn't obey your instructions," said Atoye. "That's why we came here instead of going straight home. Listen," he added, "I have to tell you something that probably shouldn't be sent through space. You and Orban switch places and while I'm briefing you, he'll tell Kinar." Orban transported to the Orbiter. When he arrived, Pitus went to the Duster.

"What is the big secret?"

"Twelve stellar craft are apparently en route to Oman."

"Haldi?"

"Probably, though none of the vessels are of Haldan configuration. Half are Fornician and half Soluran if what I overheard is true"

"I knew the Fornicians were in bed with the Haldi," said Pitus, "but I thought the Solurans were neutrals."

"Anybody can be bought, apparently," said Atoye. "The traffic we picked up between them suggests an invasion force."

"Can we beat them there?" asked Pitus.

"No problem with that," said Atoye. "They mentioned a bivouac at Fornis to on-load troops and another at Haldan. That will take a little time. We are also traveling lighter than they are."

"Yeah," said Pitus. "No weapons. We're too light."

"Stay here," said Atoye. "I'll transmit the code word that Orban was given for us to proceed." Atoye sent the message and punched the Duster to H7.

"There is a lot of work to do if we are going to stop Habine's successor," said Atoye."

"We will need a lot more than the four of us," said Pitus.

"By now Kinar has been let in on the plan by Orban, and they are en route to Calbresan. We are going to Nesgoor." said Atoye. "I will fill you in on the way."

KEN'S SECRET

Carol answered the phone and after a few seconds handed it to John.

"Hello, Bingham's", said John absentmindedly, "Oh, I suppose you know that by now", he added sheepishly.

"No kidding," snickered Joe. "I need to scare up a third for a game of cards after work."

"I can't." said John. "I've got a pile of junk in the middle of my living room floor that's been there for almost a week. I'm still sleeping on a set of springs on my bedroom floor!"

"How about some help, then," offered Joe. "The cards can wait."

"Oh, I really hate to impose," said John, "Bring some beer or good booze when you come".

John arrived home at about twenty past nine. He changed into some clothes more suitable for the dusty, heavy "bull work" that lie ahead. Shortly, the doorbell rang.

"You've got a headlight out on the passenger side," said John as Joe and Lorraine came through the door.

"See, you didn't believe me when I said it was a little dim on my side", Lorraine barked. "He just repeated that it was "dim" on my side of the car on the inside. The smart aleck!"

"Boy, how do you put up with him?" John quipped.

"All right you guys." said Joe, "Let's get some work done. I want to be in the sack by midnight."

With the extra hands the work went along swiftly. By eleven o'clock the pile of furniture and boxes was reduced to three boxes of folded clothes and a small metal filing cabinet.

"Well, I suppose you can carry on from here", said Joe.

"I didn't notice much in the line of furnishings left in the house from previous occupants." Lorraine remarked. "I was told this place was loaded with antiques when your brother bought it last year."

"There was little left in this house by the time I got here to stay. Ken and Freda cleaned out the cellar and attic before they let me move in. They took out a set of ladder back chairs and a drop leaf table that must have been in the place since the original occupants lived here, and all the old crocks and jugs from down cellar. He probably sold them on *NU-bay* for a small fortune."

"You should have gotten this place instead of your brother. I think you got a raw deal," said Joe. "I say that even though it is none of my business. Perhaps I talk too much."

"It is no secret about the relationship I had with Dad before he died. Mrs. Simmons reminds me about how sad she feels about it and how she tried to convince Dad I was not the culprit almost every time she brings in a prescription to fill. It is a chapter that probably will never completely close, so I reserve enough energy every day to deal with it."

"Never mind, Johnny." said Lorraine. "We'll be your family". She kissed John on the left temple.

"It's nearly midnight, already. Let's be going, Lorraine. Tomorrow is likely to be a busy day at the store, and I want to be well rested."

"I think I'll turn in, myself even though tomorrow is my day off," said John.

On the way home, Lorraine brought up the subject of John and his father again. "I think it's rotten how those two took all the old things away from the house before John moved in. They must lie awake nights just thinking of stuff like that to pull on him. How could anybody believe he took that old watch from his father?"

"Remember ol' man Keenan?"

"The one who ran the bowling alley on Broad St.? What about him," she asked.

"Last year, before he died, he came in the store to refill his medicine. He seemed to be winning his fight with cancer then, but he got pneumonia, and that was the downhill slide. It was a Wednesday night, which is usually slow, but this time there was virtually no business at all for some reason. As he came in, I had just hung up the phone from talking to John. It was dead over to Bingham's too."

"Who cares about the business?" said Lorraine impatiently. Joe ignored her and continued his story.

"Mr. Keenan remarked that he was about the only one downtown that evening. He asked me if he missed a Terrorist Defense Alert or something. I mentioned that John's store across town was empty of people too and I couldn't account for it. Besides, they would've sounded the siren or something for a TDA, I told him. Then he asked me how John was doing, and made some more small talk. Then he said, `You're John's best friend, right?'"

"Yes." I said.

"'Then maybe I can tell you about something and give you something that can right a great wrong done to that lad.'"

"He told me that last summer, Ken brought in a gold watch to sell to him, because he was broke and needed a couple hundred dollars to get medical treatment. Apparently he told Keenan he couldn't risk his father finding out because the watch was originally Medwyd's, and he certainly didn't want Freda to find out, or there would be hell to pay for it. He said to Keenan that it was intended as collateral for a loan, and Ken was to buy back the watch and put it back before his ol' man ever knew it was gone. When Mr. Hodiak went for the watch and found it was missing, John got blamed for it."

"Ken, that snake! He let his brother pay for his own evil deed." said Lorraine.

"Looks like it," replied Joe.

"Why didn't Keenan go to Mr. Hodiak and set the story right, asked Lorraine?

"Keenan didn't find out about John getting blamed for the watch till just recently," said Joe.

"You knew all this and didn't let me in on it?" Lorraine asked with agitation.

"I have no idea how I'm going to tell him. It will open up old wounds and create new ones. I really didn't appreciate having all this dumped in my lap." said Joe.

"Are you going to tell John all this." she asked.

"I guess so."

"Need some support?"

"I won't know that till the time comes." said Joe. "I planned to settle the matter right away, but put it off for one reason or another. Then the 'ol man took sick and died so quickly that I lost my chance. Then when John went to hear the will read, and found out he got a lousy two hundred bucks . . .

"Oh God," said Lorraine, "He got the cost of the watch that burned him."

"Fate has a sick sense of humor," said Joe. Anyway, it just kept going from bad to really bad and I finally decided not to drop this additional bomb on the already smoldering wreckage. I'm mainly concerned that John will go ballistic and do something foolish when he is told. That's why I haven't said anything so far."

"Maybe you *shouldn't* say anything," said Lorraine. "Let sleeping dogs lie, as the saying goes."

JOHN'S COMPETITION

A well-dressed man of about forty entered the capacious study. He sat a leather valise on the floor beside the large rosewood desk and greeted the seated man deferentially.

"You have the items I requested, Gordie," asked the man at the desk?

"All here, Mr. Ott. We got in and out of there without a hitch. Lenny cracked the door and stood guard while I searched the cabinet. I brought the ones from 1805 to 1815 inclusive and all the 1880's. There are fifteen diaries. No one knew we were there at all, and by the looks of the cabinet, no one is likely to discover they're missing before I return them." He lifted the valise to the surface of the desk, popping open the catches in a single motion. Gordie reached in and pulled out a large clasped magazine folder and handed it over.

"Well done," said Simeon Ott. He pulled off the elastic band securing the folder and gently pulled the contents out onto the desk. He carefully untied the pack threads that held a neatly wrapped sheet of thick brown paper around each volume. Carefully, he unwrapped each book and laid it on his desk. The early ones were calfskin duodecimos, each about three-quarters of an inch thick. They were generic type blank books bound up to serve for accounts. The dates were written neatly on the upper spines of each one in ink. The latter ones were *Excelsior Diaries*, in roan leather with gilt stamped dates and ruling. They were expensive for their time, selling for a dollar and a half each. Simeon laid his hands on the books and nodded his approval. He opened a slide drawer in his desk and reached into it. His hand passed over a small handgun, lingering over it for a second before moving beyond to a cream color envelope behind it. He removed the envelope and passed it over to Gordie. "There's your fee plus the bonus I promised for your keeping your assignment a secret. They should be ready for reinsertion by Friday."

"Thank you very much Mr. Ott," said Gordie graciously. He placed the envelope into the valise and stood for a second holding it. Ott looked up from the diaries and Gordie preempted the question forming in Ott's expression with one of his own.

"I have been performing errands for you for some years now, and have never asked any questions relating to the assignments given me, but . . ."

"Why have I paid you ten-thousand dollars to sneak into a place and retrieve something in secret that I could just as easily have viewed for nothing by merely making an appointment?"

"Something like that," said Gordie. Ott smiled and looked down at the pistol in the still open drawer beside him. After a second he pushed the drawer shut. "I wish to keep the nature of my research a secret. Be here at nine on Friday evening to return the goods." Gordie smiled thinly, nodding his head, turned and left the study.

THE ALMANACK DIARIES

It was a hot Saturday morning and John was up early, awakened by the light coming through his eastward-facing window. "Lots to get done today", he thought as he was getting dressed. The clock beside the bed indicated that it was quarter to six. "Got to fix the gasket in that toilet, and put some mop boards around the kitchen. Should be something up in the attic I can use."

He filled the coffeepot and plugged it in. Soon the refreshing aroma of the brew filled the room. He poured a cup and sat at the kitchen table pondering how he would fill the day that lay whole before him.

"I would like to go down to the library and take another look at that Peston History. But I have to fix that toilet; just have to. Hardware store won't be open for another two hours, so I have to wait for the gasket. Guess I could start on those mopboards."

The light to the dark attic, or "garret" as the room was called in the days when the Peston house was new, hung from a rafter on a long chain. The naked light bulb was kindled by yanking on a string that dangled in the air. John groped in the dim light coming through the undersized door that opened to the garret stairs, catching the string after a few waves of the hand. A yellow glow bathed the unpainted sharply pitched steps that led to the room at the top. John liked to look at these old stairs, worn down in the middles from the feet of generations of Pestons, escaping being replaced probably because of their remoteness and continuous concealment. The marks of the hand plane were still visible on the edges. At the head of the stairs was another swinging "poor-man's chandelier", which John pulled on. In this poorly lit room which was quite large as attics go, were several small piles of lumber containing pieces of wood ranging in size from sticks of lath to great wide floor planks. John stepped over to one pile where there was a particularly large board. He opened his folding rule and laid it against it. "This damn thing must be sixteen feet long by . . . ." he measured the width, "28 inches wide!" He spoke aloud as he gauged the huge plank. "This had to have been sealed up in this attic when they put the roof on. Otherwise I can't imagine how it could have gotten here." He slapped his hand against it and simultaneously blew the dust away. "Quarter sawn . . . Looks like hemlock. Must've been a monster." John started counting the rings outward from the heartwood. The outermost ring at the extreme left side showed a telltale sign of cambium which meant that it was the tree's last year of growth before it was felled. "Two hundred and five rings! This part of the house was built in 1760, so that means that this tree was a sapling about . . . . the year, 1555. This thing was alive before Shakespeare!" Suddenly this board became a valuable thing to John. He pushed it back toward the wall and selected several other smaller boards noticing that they were planed smooth on one side and beaded along one edge. "Spare pieces of finished wood for mop boards. Well, this job won't be as hard as I first thought."

His desire was to get all this necessary work done early in order to be able to spend some time at Randall, and maybe see Joyce again. At a little past nine John drove to Tyler's Hardware to get a gasket for the toilet. Later on, after the dirty deed of replacing the gasket was completed, John declared, "That's enough for one day. The rest of it is mine." He remembered that he left all the lights on in the attic. He ascended the stairs and walked over to the far end where a light fixture protruded from a ceramic socket. As he reached for the string he was stopped by a buzzing sound. It was a pair of wasps flying against the bulb, attracted by the artificial brightness that exceeded the natural light coming in through the six-light window fixed in the apex of the wall nearby. John was no lover of stinging insects. He had a particular aversion to wasps, which were quick and possessing usually of a nasty disposition. And on this sweltering August morning, they were more than usually active. Standing back as far as he could, John stretched out his hand for the end of the string keeping a posture that would allow a hasty retreat in case the two humming little acrobats decided to divert their attentions to him. As he snapped off the light he noticed a couple of small bundles wedged in a niche on the wall. His curiosity overpowered his fear temporarily and he snapped the light back on. The two hornets were now darting back and forth at the window attempting to fly through it to the clear air beyond, but John paid little heed to them as he gazed at the bundles above his head. John thought he gave this place the once over pretty well the first time he came up in this attic, but then there was that ancient wooden plank. Missing something that big, certainly made it seem possible for him to also miss something this little.

These new artifacts had escaped notice because they lay out of the normal line of sight hidden behind a rafter near the northeast corner of the house, right where the top of the left-hand queen post met the tie beam. Even with a 100-watt bulb in the ceiling light there was only a dim reflected glow in this remote corner of the attic. It was a bona fide miracle that the bundles were ever seen at all. John took out a flashlight and poked the area first with an old curtain rod that he found laying on the floor. There being no inhabitants in the bundles, he cautiously reached for them and pulled them from the niche. There were two stacks each about five inches thick, of what appeared to be papers. John unwrapped a short swaddle of cloth that bound one of the bundles. The linen sheet fell to pieces as he unrolled the first layer. Underneath this the cloth was a little more preserved and it held up under the strain of handling.

"I had better take this down stairs where I can have a look at it," He hurried down to the kitchen. John placed the bundles on the table and sat down. As the inner layer of cloth was in better condition, he allowed his excitement to quicken the tempo of the unwrapping procedure. "Maybe it's of money left here by someone. There could be thousands of bucks here in my mitts!"

At last, the shrouds were removed revealing two stacks of almanacs sewn all together. He winced from dissatisfaction at the discovery that he didn't discover a month's pay in his attic. The sight of the old pamphlets quickly allayed his initial disappointment. The first six almanacs were British, the earliest being for 1749. The rest were American. John quickly leafed through the stacks. There was an almanac for each year in an unbroken sequence to the year 1780, continuing in the other stack through the year 1808 with another for 1883 apparently stitched on at the end. There were many different titles, as if it were an eclectic sampling of early American printing. Within the pages of each was sewn in a sheaf of blank sheets that were filled in with written manuscript text as to make a diary.

"Well what have we here," said John, excitedly. "From the dates of these almanacs, I can only conclude that they are from the original Pestons who founded this farm!"

John started reading and then stopped, and left the kitchen for a moment. He returned with a steno pad and a pen. "There might be something to make notes about for further study," he thought as he scanned the browned but still supple pages. He held a page up to the light. There they were; the same chain and wire lines he saw in the sheets of the family history. And lo, there along the fore edge was half the outline of the jester!

"Well I'll be . . . ," John said aloud, a canny smile on his face. The early manuscript notes, for the most part, while interesting and probably of historic value, were no wise as interesting as the last ones. The writing in these final almanacs was by another hand than the rest. It was a less neat hand with the look of being set down on the page in haste. While it was intriguing to ponder the possible reason for the last non sequitur being lashed to the unbroken series of almanacs he had before him, John nevertheless returned to the beginning of the group where the earliest writings were to be found.

The earliest manuscripts were from the hand of Jeremiah Peston. He was a prolific writer. In some almanacs there were as many as fifty leaves with text on both sides. He was also a neat writer, as the Irish would say, "he had a good fist". He also had a good sense for a story. The diary entries were more like short stories than the usual truncated groups of statements that make up "daily journals". There was even proper punctuation and conversational text as though all written at a single time for each literary vignette. John started to transcribe the writings filling in for smoothness of syntax in those rare instances where he thought it necessary.

John paused in his reading and sat back in his chair. He placed his hands behind his neck and pulled against himself by way of a stretch. He looked at the kitchen clock. "Two hours I've sat here!" John said aloud, "No wonder my backside is falling asleep!" He got up from the chair and went over to the counter where the coffeepot sat and poured him another cup. He stood there a while with his back propped up to the counter, leaning slightly forward sipping from his cup. The smell of the coffee and the mere activity of sipping it seemed to reverse some of the fatigue that developed from concentrating on the antique manuscripts. John knew that these almanacs were never seen by anyone other than himself. There was no mention of them in the "History" at the Randall Library, and the appearance of them when he found them indicated that they had not been disturbed for longer than the hundred and thirty plus years that had elapsed since the History was written. No, this was "virgin territory" in the lore of the Peston family. It was exciting to consider that what he would likely find within the pages of these almanacs on his kitchen table would be things that have never before come to light; that this would make him the premier authority of a subject rapidly becoming dear to his heart.

John returned to his chair and continued reading. In this next portion of text he found a couple of medicinal formulas, for chilblains, dry gripes, and several "cures" for livestock ailments. He continued reading throughout the afternoon and past suppertime, leaving the kitchen only to fetch a dictionary and a new supply of paper. After a while he sat back in his chair and clapped his hands together in an expression of glee. Although tired from staring over the dark pages of writing, a process that seemed to draw the very moisture from his burning eyes, the lateness of the evening would not deter his further plunging into the recorded lives of the ones who established the place he now called home.

The thudding bump made by a large truck going by the house caused John to awaken. He was no longer at the kitchen table, but in the living room seated in his rocking chair, and cradled in his lap was the bundle of almanacs.

"How did I get here," John wondered. He looked at the clock on the stand next to the chair and it was 9 PM. The almanacs were opened in an inverted position on his lap and he turned them over to proceed with reading. The place where he apparently left off was unfamiliar to him and he scanned prior pages to re-establish a memory of the text. He recalled reading about Pitus going off for days at a time with some Indian friends. They were young Iroquois men who, though friendly and familiar with Pitus remained aloof from the others of the Peston family. There were some allusions by Caroline to Pitus and to Lucius Ordway, the apothecary. Apparently Pitus and he were close. John wished that there was more about this. It appeared that Lucius Ordway was a colorful fellow.

John pondered over the life thus spread out before him on these ancient sheets, his mind darting to and fro amid the myriad things that were untold; what Pitus did while with the Indian hunting parties, what his world looked like, what he himself looked like. Did this young lad of two centuries past enjoy the same kind of things as the modern counterpart? "Was life really better back in that early day, being slower-paced, less full of stress?" John thought as he sat in his 21st century rocking chair. "I think not! It was probably as bad or even worse then. No cars, no running water, no . . . penicillin, no . . . Ether! It could've been good if you didn't get sick. Back then, if you hurt your leg bad enough, four guys held you down while the fifth one, armed with a saw, cut the damn thing off; and no anesthetic!" John gave a shudder as he imagined the scene. As he sat there he mused about other, more pleasant things, but mainly about what this man, Pitus Peston must have looked like. He imagined, as one often does about someone interesting, that this man of the 18th century looked like himself.

Suddenly, he bolted up in his chair. "Damn! I was supposed to go out with Joyce tonight!" He looked at the clock. "Too late to call the library," he murmured. He grabbed his cell phone and hit the speed dial . . . "Boy, am I in for it . . . at least, I hope I'm in for it." He sat back in his chair. "She'll understand when she gets a look at this." He said, holding the bundle before his eyes.

Joyce picked up and said, "You stood me up, you bum!"

"I know and I'm sorry," said John weakly.

"I'm too beat to go out anyway," she said. "Rachel wants me to head out early so we can meet for lunch."

"She all right?"

"Yes. She wants to drink chai and catch up on the details of my life. You know . . . girl stuff."

"Don't say anything bad about me, other than I deserve, I mean."

"Your ears might ring a little, but it will all be good."

"I'll see you when you get back from Worcester, then."

"Three days from now. Can you stand it?"

"Of course not."

"That was the right answer."

"Have a nice trip," said John. "I'll have a surprise for you when you get back."

"Oh yeah, what?"

"How could it be a surprise if I tell you about it?"

"How about a hint?"

"It is literary and you'll be thrilled."
"A lot of help that is. You're just telling me this so I'll come back."
"I must confess, I would like that a whole lot."
"All right then, it's a deal. I'll come back to you if you'll thrill me."
"I promise."
"Good night," she said.
"Good night."

PESTON HOUSE LEGENDS

"Hey, Johnny! I ain't seen you for a couple of weeks. Where ya been?"

"Oh, just busy tinkering around," John said as he slid on a barstool. "How about a glass of draft, Mike."

"Coming up." The bartender filled a glass from the tap and placed it in a mockingly genteel fashion on a coaster.

"Have you been to butler school or something? I had no idea that this was such a classy place!"

"Only the best for my customers," Mike laughed. "So, what are you 'tinkerin' with that keeps you away from your friends and a good cold drink?"

"Working on a sort of historical project."

"On the Pestons, no doubt."

"As a matter of fact . . . How did you know?"

"A bartender knows everything that everybody is doing. That's part of the job," said Mike playfully. He poked his finger under his chin in a posture of contemplation. "Let's see how many ways I know. Joe said something about it the other night when he and Lorraine were here. I asked where you were these days since I hadn't seen you and he said you were wearing a path between your place and the Randall Library. Then there's my Ann who knows everything that goes on at Randall. And she and Joyce are thick as thieves. You couldn't keep a secret if your life depended on it. I still had my worries though. With you away for so long, I was beginning to get afraid that you 'took the pledge' or something."

"I assure you I will never give up a good glass of beer. *THAT'S* my pledge!" Mike cheered and offered a high-five which made a loud smack as John accepted it. Another sitting at the bar a few stools away sat idly listening to the conversation. He looked over at John. "You're John Hodiak, aren't you? The fella' that lives in the old Peston place?"

"I'm renting it from my brother."

"Fred Ames."

"Pleased to meet you." John said shaking the man's hand. Ames sat back down in his chair. A smirk developed on his face. "You haven't seen any ghosts yet?"

"Not any so far."

"When I was a kid I heard the place was haunted."

"The only old shades I have seen are hanging on my windows." John replied whimsically.

"Well, it's just a lot of talk, of course," Ames mused, "but Father took it seriously, rest his soul." He moved himself and his beer to the stool next to John.

"A hell of a long time has passed since you were a kid, Fred." Mike quipped.

"Yeah," said Fred. "Seventy next month, and for that comment, I expect to be plied with your best suds when I come in."

"Hell, I'll throw you a party in the back room," said Mike, "with a quarter-keg!" Ames laughed. Mike just grinned. He was probably making plans in his head already.

"Who were they? John asked. "That is, who were the ghosts supposed to be?"

"As one story goes," began Ames, "the spirit of Caroline Peston was said to be heard wailing and carrying on over the death of her son Pitus. It seems that just before Pitus left home for the last time, there was a hell of a row between him and his brother Lloyd, which resulted in Caroline disowning Pitus and kicking him out. She was said to have that legendary Welsh temper which is fast to flare but just as fast to cool down. It didn't cool down quick enough, I guess, and Pitus took off. She pined over it and when he was reported killed by the Indians out west, her sadness over it ruined her health and she died from remorse."

"She's been quiet as long as I have been in the house." John said sipping from his glass. "Anything else?"

"Another story goes that Pitus himself has been seen around. The time was in the early 1880's. I remember being told those stories as a boy."

"When the Peston Family history was left in the library," John added.

"The official word was that a family member wrote it and slipped it in there in order to play a prank and maybe get some intrigue started. Probably to start a family legend or something. But that's not what my dad thought," Ames said with more than a little conviction in his tone.

"What else could it have been?" John asked.

"Come on, Fred," Mike said skeptically. He looked at John. "He's just pulling your leg. Next thing you know, he'll be having you sleeping at the hotel from all this ghost talk."

"I'm not afraid of ghosts." John replied. "I find all this very interesting. Please continue, Mr. Ames."

"Fred. Just call me Fred." Ames took a swallow from his drink. "My father was told a story about the Pestons when he was a lad that made him a believer in all this stuff. When my grandfather Micah was a boy, he was very devout about attending church every Sunday. His parents weren't pious folk and rarely ever went to service, so he went along with a family from town. It seems that one such Sunday, back in the early 1880's as old Miss. Lattimore was getting into her buggy, she saw someone. It really gave her a turn and when she saw him, he ducked out of sight. She sent Gramp after him, but he couldn't find a trace. It was thought she was having a spell when she saw the man, because she said it was Pitus and that he looked not a day older than when he left her long ago."

"That's some story!" John exclaimed.

"Well, that is all it is, I'm sure," said Fred. "But it leaves a little something unsettling in the mind, doesn't it?"

"Sounds like something for the Mystery Channel," said John. "Is there any more to tell?" John asked.

"Nothing more about that, but there is one more legend."

"Geez, said Mike, looks like Johnny here has hit the jackpot."

"That is an apt choice of words," said Ames. "Pitus' brother Lloyd had two sons. One named Tommy who fought in the Mexican War under Winfield Scott and was killed at Churubusco. Lloyd followed not long afterward, in 1849. This left Medwyd, the younger son who was living in the house during the Civil War, and was said to have been a miser. In fact, he was so tight with a buck that when his wife Ophelia died, he had her buried without a coffin or a stone to mark the grave. He just rolled her body up in an old rug and put her in a hole on the property. It was said that he had quite a stash squirreled away someplace around there."

"Surely he would have told of it to someone before he died, or left word of it in his will."

"He had no will and he died without telling anyone of it as far as is known. He was particularly nervous about the way the war was going in the beginning with the Confederates seeming to have the upper hand as they did in the early part of the conflict. Medwyd was convinced that the Southern Army would invade the North and confiscate all the money in all the banks. So he went to the bank and withdrew all his money in gold and hid it at home. Three months after this supposedly took place, he was killed while on a business trip in Pennsylvania. There was no knowledge of the whereabouts of the gold and it constituted the bulk of the Peston wealth. His two sons tore the place apart and dug up practically the whole back yard looking for the loot, but never found it. Eventually the money situation got bad and the Pestons lost the farm."

"Maybe that explains the strange clinking sounds I've been hearing from time to time. It's old Medwyd counting his gold!" John quipped.

"It's probably the water hammering in your radiator pipes." Mike replied.

"Mike, you have no sense of adventure, I swear!" John retorted. He turned to look at Ames. He seemed to be a credible fellow.

"That's some fascinating stuff. You seem to know a good deal about the Pestons."

"I only know about the things that I just told you. It has interested me mainly because of the way my family and the Pestons have strode the same historic path." Having said this, he looked at his watch. "I'd better swallow this last gulp and get home; it is getting on to my bedtime"

"It has been a pleasure to visit with you. I hope to see you again sometime," said John cordially.

"Same here. Goodnight." Half way to the door Ames turned around. "John, you're invited to my birthday party," he said smiling wryly at Mike. He then left.

Mike grabbed a dishcloth and swabbed down the bar. "You didn't know you were living in the midst of a legend, or did you?"

"What about that guy Ames?" John asked.

"What about him?"

"He seems to know a lot about the Pestons. It just strikes me a little odd, that's all."

"You afraid he's going to put a spade to your back lawn?"

"I think he'd be afraid of turning up Ophelia, but I'll be watching. I am sure all it would gain is a lot of yard work for me filling up the holes."

"Don't worry about him." Mike said assuredly. "I've known him since I was in knickers. He's got enough of his own dough to not bother going around trying to dig up more, in the literal sense, I mean."

"It's all an interesting story, but story is all it is." John replied. Behind this apparent skepticism, his mind was filled with many intriguing possibilities dovetailing with the other facts he already knew concerning the Pestons.

"I believe I will have another beer." John said yawning. "Then I better hit the road." Mike turned to draw the beer and then placed it on the bar.

"Say, Mike," John asked in a low, confidential tone of voice, "in my rummaging around, I discovered that this building was once the drugstore where Lucius Ordway and Pitus worked."

"It was?" Mike said pensively. "I guess that would explain all the jugs and old crap down in the cellar."

"Got anything good down there? I'm looking for some old stuff to replace the things that my brother and sister-in-law ransacked out of the house before I moved in."

"Maybe I got some stuff. You talking money or just B.S," Mike asked with a teasing smile.

"I'll pay if you aren't the one with the B.S," John said. "Can I go see it?"

"Sure." Mike hailed his assistant. "Ace, I'm going down stairs to see if I can peddle some of that old sh—, I mean relics of antiquity to Johnny here."

Ace laughed and shook his head. "Johnny, don't let him get all your hard earned drinkin' money for a bunch of old junk. Wait. On second thought, let 'im. We need the shelf space!"

The two descended the rickety wooden stairs down into the cellar. The air was a little stale but rather dry as cellars go.

"Jeez Mike, you got a hell of a lot of stuff down here!" John hunched down before a couple of large earthenware jugs and picked one of them up. He rubbed the grime off it with his palm. It was a Norton from Bennington with a blue slip decoration of a bird resting on a branch. He knew this was early nineteenth century and probably worth a small fortune.

"I like this one." John said in a subdued acquisitive excitement. "It's got character." He picked up the gallon-sized one next to it. "This one's still got stuff in it." He carefully wedged off the cork and sniffed.

"Whew wee!" John recoiled at the acrid smell. "Smells like vinegar mixed with kerosene!"

"Take a swig and see." Mike suggested playfully.

"No thanks! I'd rather spend a longer time upstairs rotting my gut than doing it down here with just one drink!"

"Hey," said Mike, Look at this." He reached for a wooden crate and hauled it out. He pulled out one of the unopened quart bottles and held it up in the light. "Ox-Cart Ale. Jeez, this wasn't made any more when I was a kid working for ol' man Keenan over to the Falls."

"Looks like you are all set for the Ames Party," laughed John.

"Damned if it 'taint so," He grinned. "And here's something else we can put out for the party," he added, pointing to the shelf above it.

"Falstaff Tapper," said John. "How old is that thing?"

"It was fresh about the time Richard Nixon was sworn in," said Mike.

"I got a hell of an idea for you," said John. "If you do have a party for Ames, set all this out dust and all and tell him it's for the party."

"Great idea," laughed Mike. "I bet he'd shit a brick!"

Mike pointed to a group of wooden shelves. As John approached them, he reached out to brush away the thick layers of cobwebs that made the shelf look like part of a giant cocoon.

"What have we here?" He said.

There were a score of glass bottles of varying sizes, some empty and others with their contents still inside. He picked up some examining their labels. "Bingham would like to have some of these, no doubt. He's got a bunch of this stuff around on his counter at the store." He picked up a four-ounce bottle with a good label and held it up to a nearby light.

"Hey, here's something for you to use in your love life, by the sounds of it."

"Let's see," said Mike, taking the bottle in his hands. "What does this say? `Cupid's Dart'! Well I'll be . . ."

"I'd like to know what's in that!" John laughed.

"Maybe I *will* take a swig of this one!" Mike declared nudging the cork loose. "See if it's got any kick left in it."

"Best not." John warned. "If it did, you might be more than Ann can handle."

"I'm already more than Ann can handle!" laughed Mike. He put the bottle back on the shelf. "So, do you want any of this stuff?"

"How much?"

"Gimme . . . two hundred bucks and you can take it all."

"Two hundred bucks," exclaimed John. "If I give you all that, I'll need to bum the beer upstairs from you."

"All this ought to be worth that much at least," Mike declared. "I'll throw the beer in with the deal."

"I guess you've got a deal, then." John said, He reached into his pocket and pulled out the money.

"Don't you carry a wallet?" Mike said as he accepted the cash.

"No, and I don't wear a watch, either." John replied.

"I'll tell Ann to tell Joyce to get you both for Christmas."

"You do that," said John. "I'll come over after breakfast tomorrow and load up the truck."

The next morning was Sunday and the bar was closed. John arrived with some cardboard boxes and bubble wrap bags from the drugstore. Ann met John at the door. "Heard from Joyce," she asked coyly.

"No," said John. "I don't expect to since she's coming back late today."

"Miss her?"

"Of course," replied John. Ann broke into a sly smile. "And even if I didn't, I would be careful not to tell you, because Joyce would hear of it faster than a New York second," he added smirking.

"I would not . . ." Ann started to say. Then she burst into a laugh. "Yea, we both have our eyes on you, so you better tow the mark." Mike came to the door. "Hey, Johnny, I know it's Sunday, but . . ." he said in a low conspiratorial tone, "You wanna glass before we start?" Ann looked at the two incredulously and pointed at her wristwatch.

"Aw hell, Annie," said Mike. "Its afternoon in . . . Tenerife."

"And Dublin to be sure," said John. "And that's good enough for me." John slipped past Ann into the taproom. Mike's partner, Arnold was at the bar doing some accounts payable. "Hello Ace," called John as he sat at the bar. "Hi, Johnny," he said, not even looking up from his bookwork. After a glass of draught Mike and John went down stairs and the two started loading. While they were doing this, John asked some more about the place.

"Is there an attic?"

"Yes, but there ain't much up there. That is, no crocks or bottles or stuff like that. Besides, I thought I cleaned you out of cash last night."

"I dipped into the cookie jar this morning just in case . . ."

"I remember a couple of wooden boxes . . . and a leather trunk, but that's all. There were some old books and papers up there in a back room, but some guy beat you to 'em.

"Who?"

"Just some guy who said he was a book collector. He came in the bar one afternoon last month and asked. He seemed to know about the place like you. He bought some old leather books on chemistry or some shit. He was really happy to find some papers in a box. I knew he was happy by what he paid for them."

"Damn," John muttered.

"After we get the cellar cleaned out, we'll have a look," said Mike. "I declare," He added, "You get on to something and you can't stop." It was not long before John and Mike got the shelves cleaned off and brushed down of all the cobwebs. They both stepped back to look at their cleaning job.

"Ace will like this," said Mike. "He wants a place to put the wine inventory. John squinted at the wall and tilted his head back and forth.

"What's the matter with you?" Mike asked. "You ain't gonna keel over on me, are you?"

"There are boards behind that set of shelves on the right," said John.

"I see 'em," said Mike, "What of it?"

"There's no reason to put boards against a stone wall like that, unless . . ." John drew the back of his hand back and forth before the boards. "I feel a draught," he at last said. You got a space or something behind here." Mike went upstairs for a pry bar. John gave the wall a closer look. There was definitely something behind those boards and it looked like the job had been done a long time ago.

Mike returned with a 3 foot crow bar and a long flash light. They jimmied the section of shelves loose and moved them aside.

"What do you thinks' behind there?" asked Mike nervously.

"Well they haven't found Hoffa yet," said John.

"You're a funny-ass fellow," said Mike. "Did you know?"

"I've been called similar on occasion," quipped John. "If we do find some bodies, they'll be nothing but bones," said John, "These boards have been in place for a hundred years or more." He pointed to a rusty nail head. "Square nails. These were made back in the eighteen hundreds."

"Mike put the blade of the pry bar behind the first board. "Here goes," he said and shoved the shaft of the bar against the cellar wall. The thick plank groaned and popped out an inch. He got a purchase lower down. At this next thrust, the board popped loose. Behind the boards was concealed a heavy wooden door hung on two enormous "holy lord" hinges secured to the door by hand-forged cut nails. The door was made to swing outward into the cellar and was secured by a simple latch mechanism. John cleared the floor in front of the door and looked over at Mike.

"You want to do the honor?"

"You open," said Mike, "and I'll look." He grabbed the crow bar like it was a club in one hand and held the flashlight in the other and nodded to John. John pulled on the latch and opened the door wide, watching Mike as he did so. Mike pointed the flashlight into the gloom.

"Jesus," he breathed.

"What is it?" asked John excitedly. Mike handed over the light and John looked in.

"Son of a . . ." His voice trailed off in wonder. "Do you think they're full?"

"God, I hope so," said Mike. John propped the door open with one of the boards revealing a recess in the wall eight feet wide by twelve feet deep.

"Hey, Johnny, I know what this was. It was a smoke house way back when the place was first built. Part of the chimney still stands against the wall behind an old bush. I took it for granted that the thing was built above ground." He looked at John quizzically. "I can't imagine why they boarded it up."

"I can," said John. "I bet before the Civil war this was changed into a wine cellar and then used for a station on the Underground Railroad. Things probably got hot and they had to board the thing up to hide it. Then it got forgotten." "Yeah," said Mike. They both stepped into the room. On each side and the back wall were wooden racks lined with wine and old style sealed brandy bottles. Some of the shelves had rotted away with small heaps of shards from the bottles that fell on the stone floor. Most of the shelves were sound and held a few score of various bottles.

John picked up a bottle that rested on the floor atop a heap of shards. "This one is whole and full," he said. Part of a label remained. "Old Edouard . . . grape bran . . . "Grape brandy," said John. The bottle was one of the crude free blown dark olive "black glass" types. "This stuff is probably two hundred years old."

"Mike pulled his keys from his pants pocket. He had a small cork screw on a fob.

"This is got to be valuable," warned John.

"There's a shit-load of it in here," Mike said with delight. "Let's have a sample . . . kind of a celebration of the discovery." The old cork came out in fragments, but there was soon enough passage to get the contents out. Mike took a pull on the bottle first. He swished the liquid around in his mouth and swallowed. A grin spread over his face. "Smooth as a baby's ass." He handed it to John who did likewise.

"I think this is the best two-hundred year old brandy I've ever had," said John. "You're gonna hate yourself when you find out what this was worth." John scanned some shelves next to the wine racks. There was a cluster of ancient whiskeys, that would likely end up at Sotheby's, and among them was something that didn't quite fit. John took it down from the shelf. It was a wide mouth green glass food jar full of something like flower blossoms. He held it up in the light. "What the hell are you doing in here," he said to the object?

"What is it?" asked Mike.

"Looks like an herb of some sort," John replied.

"It's not booze, so it's yours," said Mike. John pocketed the jar.

"I gotta tell Ace. He'll crap his drawers," exclaimed Mike. He went up into the taproom with the bottle. In a moment, Ace flew down the stairs, followed by Mike. His partner entered the room and emerged a minute later. "Mike, I think we can tear up the mortgage on the place!"

That afternoon John devoted little time to anything else than his new acquisitions. He heard the sound of a car turning into the driveway. He was annoyed at the interruption.

"Who the hell . . . ? Oh, it's Joyce," he said under his breath. "Great," he thought as he stood watching as she came up to the door. John answered the door and grabbed her in his arms. He then kissed her on the cheek. She responded with another on his lips.

"I thought we could go for a ride over through Salem and into Vermont to look for some old stuff," she breathed when their lips parted. "On the other hand, maybe not."

"Look what I've got here." John said excitedly. He flourished his hand across the dining room table over to the almanacs.

"Is this my surprise?" she asked in a tone of disappointment.

"I can't wait to see the look on your face . . . Sit here." John said as he set the bundle from the attic in front of her. Rather than ceremoniously unwrap the bundle, he gestured to Joyce to do it.

"What's in here," she asked guardedly. "It better not be something gross!"

"Nothing gross or slithery, I promise," he said. "You'll like it." Not quite convinced it wasn't some joke, she screwed up her face and carefully unswaddled the bundle.

"1749! Wow, where did you find these?"

"Upstairs in the attic. They were stuffed in between some rafters." When Joyce found the first diary section, she gasped with wonder. "This isn't the handwriting of Pitus, is it?"

"No, but he's in there. You are now looking at the part written by his grandfather Jeremiah."

"Geez," she breathed, "Imagine . . ."

"I've read through them. The first ones are by Jeremiah, who goes up to 1780. Then Rufus, his son, who was Pitus' father, took over till he died in 1802. After that, Pitus wrote in them till just before he left for the frontier."

"What is this," she asked, flipping the bundle over. "It looks kind of out of place; not like part of the rest."

"It is, though." John said mysteriously.

"Webster's Calendar for 1883?" How is this one related to the others?"

"Compare the handwriting in the 1883 with that of the ones between 1802 and 1808." She flipped quickly back and forth between the writing samples of the last few editions and this one of seventy-five years later. The astonishment on her face quickly evolved into a smile of delight.

"If this *is* his handwriting . . ."

"You know it is."

". . . then the Indians out west didn't kill him after all!"

"Apparently not."

"There is one thing then that puzzles me. If he did come back, why hasn't there been any further information about him after 1813? Surely somebody would have seen him, and there would have to be some account of it."

"Read the entries in the '83 almanac and you will find out something rather interesting."

She located the beginning of the diary section of this last almanac and started reading aloud. John then directed her to the place of particular interest where the answers to her questions were to be found.

"'17 April: I return to a place that is but the merest shadow of my memory. I went to Union Cemetery and visited Allan's grave. He died ten years ago at the age of eighty-four. He and most all that were my companions, Leander, Horace, and Gill; are all gone. The rest are wizened, and so addled by age, that they can neither remember me, nor hear of my amazing adventures. I have decided that I must no longer allow myself to be seen by any who knew me, for being seen would lead to questions, and they, to explanations and explanations would lead to condemnation.'

Joyce turned to the next entry:

'20 April: The passage of time has not matured this place. Wars continue and are presaged for the future. I feel my nostalgia waning and giving way to a feeling of aversion. These are my people in blood, but clearly not in spirit. The heavens must contain a paradise for he who seeks it.'

'22 April: I was careless today. It is likely that Ellen saw me. She was being helped into a carriage after service. I gazed at her and regretted a life not shared. I saw her look in my direction and stare at me. She called and waved to a lad who was approaching the carriage and he ran toward me. I dodged into a hay barn and secreted myself until all was clear. She is 95 years of age.'"

"This is really strange." Joyce said.

"Well, there is another piece of the puzzle that is a bit wild," said John.

"Rest assured you have my complete attention," declared Joyce.

"I was at Mike's a couple of nights ago . . ."

"I know, said Joyce, "Ann told me." John was derailed a second in his train of thought. He recovered, thinking, "Mike wasn't shittin' was he."

"Go ahead. I didn't mean to barge in," said Joyce.

"This guy named Fred Ames was two stools down the bar from me and overheard Mike and me talking about the Pestons. He came in on the conversation and told me some legends about this old house, one of which was about Ellen Lattimore seeing Pitus after church in 1883."

"Oh my God!" exclaimed Joyce.

"Ames told me Ellen sent his grandfather, who was a boy at the time, to go get him, but he searched the area and couldn't find Pitus anywhere." Joyce looked incredulous about such a wild story. "It is beginning to look like he actually did write the Peston history."

"He would have been nearly a hundred years old. Most people at that age aren't able to accomplish things like that without help."

"Ames told me that Miss Lattimore said Pitus looked the same as when he left her long ago which means he looked about twenty years old." Joyce shook her head.

John bent over her and thumbed open a diary page from one of Jeremiah's almanacs. "Hold this up to the light and tell me what you see." Joyce did as he asked. "It's laid paper," she said, "I can see the chain and wire lines."

"What else," asked John? Joyce squinted at the sheet again. "There's part of a watermark. Looks like a harlequin or jester."

"Next time you're at the library take a gander at the paper used in the Peston History." Joyce stared up at John in astonishment. John just nodded his head.

"I still don't accept that he came back here after decades without aging," said Joyce. "Read the next entry in the almanac," said John.

'24 April: I have gathered some needful things for my journey. I have learned that Kinar has left for the origin. We must find him in order to locate the second key. I shall return some day when all who knew me are gone. Perhaps in another fifty or a hundred years this world will be a place of enlightenment. I can then return openly and the miracles I have seen shall be common to all men. I will not leave as a thief in the night. I shall leave a token of my return, a relation of my travels where it may be pondered. In two great libraries I will leave my narrative. Should they survive till generations yet unborn are prepared to travel in my footsteps, they will know that I, in this time, have led the way.'"

Joyce looked up from the diary, searching John's face for the answers to what she now dared not believe.

"How could he do that? In fifty years he would have been 146 and in a hundred years from this entry he'd have been 196 years old."

"He must have had reason to believe he would still be around at that time," said John. "Something is starting to fall together," he added. "What it is though is not yet clear.

"Who is this Kinar guy and what is the key they were looking for," asked Joyce.

"Haven't a clue," said John. Both were silent a few seconds then John spoke up.

"There's a book left behind of his travels. We must find it!" It will doubtless show us his path through the wilderness and maybe tell how he managed to survive his captivity as well as answer all these other questions we seem to be collecting."

"He said 'two great libraries'." Joyce said. "I hope he meant American Libraries."

"That sounds like something up your alley. See what you can find out about it," said John.

"We have no title, but we have an Author, that is if he didn't decide to use a pen name."

"I'll put my money on the State Library in Albany." John said. "We could shoot down Route 9 and have it in our hands by tomorrow afternoon." Joyce was less optimistic. "I will try the State Library, but I rather think he meant the Library of Congress . . . . or maybe the New York, Boston, or Philadelphia City Libraries. They are the oldest and the biggest."

"Wherever it is, I will be," said John with conviction.

"Not without me, you won't." Joyce replied. John laughed. "I wouldn't dare go without you!"

Joyce seemed bewildered by all that they had thus far discovered. "Do you think he was really able to come back as he said?"

"The idea of it is kind of thrilling," said John.

PITUS AND ATOYE ARRIVE ON OMAN

Pitus and Atoye approached Oman from the antipodal side from Ralmat Continent in the center of which was Jartic Orz There was no knowing what eyes were there watching for incoming ships.

"It's dizzying to look out at the surface spinning by so close," said Pitus. "What are we going?"

"Speed 1247 knots, altitude 44 meters." said Atoye. "I have the computer flying this thing; couldn't do it by eye this close and this fast. We should not be seen unless we happen to pass within fifty miles of another ship."

"Why are we going to Cavin Gorse," complained Pitus. "If there's a hell on Oman, that's it."

You know why," said Atoye. "We can be confident that no one will find us there. We can make a secure base of operations from there and be within transport distance to either Kesst or Jartic Orz."

There is every kind of creepy crawly, venomous thing that any nightmare has ever spawned in those jungles," said Pitus. The monock can swallow a man whole, and would probably enjoy doing it, unless his prey happened to have been bitten by a loresst viper. Then the carcass would be toxic . . . ."

"We will have to be careful," said Atoye.

The nav com showed land coming up on the screen and the computer slowed the ship to one hundred knots. Atoye took over the helm. He landed the Duster in a wide purple valley. Atoye got up out of his seat and peered out through the dome at the landscape. "This won't do," he said at last. "I think we should hide the ship even here." He sat back down at the helm and lifted up gently to just above the ground. "Let's find a spot for the Duster where no one is likely to stumble upon it."

"In this place," said Pitus, "I think you could pick anywhere. Only a fool would wander around here on foot."

"I mean from the air," said Atoye. "When those ships start coming in, they might pass over this area just like we did."

"I almost called out to Junior," said Pitus. "I surely miss him at a time like this." Junior was the once holographic image of young Atoye who Pitus programmed into the ship's computer for navigation and sensing during the time he was restoring the Duster back on Earth. He was loaded with so much data that he became sentient. On the way to the galactic center searching for Loma's Cube, the Cube augmented this data so profoundly that it made the holographic Atoye go solid and enter our physical world. When the Cube was whisked away to unknown parts after Atoye and Pitus entered it, Junior went with it.

"I miss him too," said Atoye, "though he did occasionally get under my skin. We will just have to do for ourselves." He popped open a compartment beneath the nav-com console and took out a disc. "This is old, but probably still accurate for this place at least." He shoved it into a feed along side the screen.

"A high resolution relief map appeared on the monitor. Atoye manipulated the directional until he found Cavin Gorse. The program automatically plotted their position and an indicator pulsed on the map. Atoye studied the map a few minutes. "We are about fifty miles from some badlands," he said. Pitus peered down at the screen while Atoye worked the directional and zoomed in on the spot to a resolution of one hundred meters. "I see a canyon," said Pitus "It looks heavily grown with trees. If that hasn't changed since the map was burned . . ."

"We'll see in a minute," said Atoye. He plotted the coordinates into the computer and resumed the helm, lifting off to an altitude of five hundred feet. Shortly they were there hovering over the spot. There was a climax grove of teasto trees, which resembled hemlocks, except these were a deep shade of purple. Atoye floated down and tucked the Duster into a cozy niche under their boughs.

"I think I'll dispense with the usual search of the area," said Atoye.

"I'm with you," said Pitus.

"Make sure we are sealed up good and proper," said Atoye. "We don't want anything out there getting in here with us. A krait might not pose a serious problem to you, but I have the same type of immune system as the Calbres." Pitus knew what that meant well enough. The foul odor of a spume from one of those furry little creatures would wash off himself and may require some scented soap for a couple of days, but if it came in contact with Atoye, his system would immediately detoxify the chemical by copying it in his blood in a non-toxic, but still smelly version. This auto induction is the reason Omans or Calbres are petrified of these otherwise cute little squirrel-like mammals.

"Where to from here?" asked Pitus.

"The Annex at Kesst," said Atoye. "Remember what Lucan said about it?"

"He said there was a lot of everything stored down in the passages beneath the Hibber Institute," Pitus said.

"I'm hoping that means weapons," said Atoye.

"He also said there was no power down there," said Pitus. "That means no light or heat in what could be miles of passages."

"As long as we have this," said Atoye, fingering his transport amulet, "we can get back out. This was still little comfort to Pitus who was not fond of dark enclosed spaces.

AME'S STORY GETS VERIFIED

"Mrs. Higgins."

"Well hello, Joyce, John! What a pleasure! I was going to go over to the store for my heart medicine. You nearly missed me." Without a word, John raised a small bag before her.

"Thank you!" she said gleefully. "But I didn't expect you to deliver it. Hold on and I'll get some money."

"Don't worry about it. I put it on a slip at the store. Just come in when it's convenient."

"Have you got a minute?" she asked. "I bet you haven't seen the Museum before. It's really quite nice."

"I would like that." John said cordially. "In fact, we came over here for that very purpose."

"Something in particular?"

"We would like to see Ellen Lattimore's diary."

"Diaries," said Mrs. Higgins with emphasis. She was prolific. Oh my stars, I mean, as a writer." If she was prolific in any other way, I'm sure I do not know!" She laughed nervously. John merely smiled and raised his eyebrows.

"There's a bunch of them . . . One a year from 1805 till 1885, the year she died. Unless you have a specific thing in mind, you two will be here quite a while looking all of them over.

"I wish to see the one for 1883."

"That was the last year she wrote a diary," Mrs. Higgins said. "These were donated in the year 1998 by her great-great grand nephew who wrote in an accompanying letter that the old lady stopped writing them suddenly the year before she died. As she was getting out the material from a large cabinet, she looked puzzled. John read this expression as one of interest in the reason for his asking for that specific date.

"I am interested specifically in anything she had to say about women's' rights."

"She was an ardent abolitionist and suffragette years before her time," Mrs. Higgins replied. "She was acquainted with the Northups from Kingsbury. It has been said that she aided in the freeing of Solomon Northup, the free Negro who was abducted in 1841 while living at Saratoga. I'm sure you will also get something of good out of the book he wrote about his captivity, TWELVE YEARS A SLAVE. There's a copy of it at Randall. Joyce can get it for you."

By now she had the package containing the diary out on a large table. The diaries were all wrapped in brown paper secured with a piece of packthread. This package looked as though it had been left undisturbed for many years, possibly last wrapped by Ellen herself. John remarked to the curator that it looked like it was never opened.

"Perhaps no one ever requested to see the material and it was left alone all these years. I've been here five years and I'm only just beginning to work on a way to catalogue all this stuff.

"If you had a computer," said John, "you could put all this on CD's."

"If I had a computer, that is," she replied. "There are no funds for anything like that in a small town historical society. I will have to use this old method until that changes."

"Well, I'll leave you two to your studies. The Museum is open till five, but you can stay a while after that if you want. I usually don't get done picking up till six." Mrs. Higgins paused a second and her face lightened up.

"Joyce, how about a cup of tea. I know you like it. What do you say?"

"That would be very nice, Mrs. Higgins." Joyce answered politely.

"And you, John?"

"No tea for me, thanks."

"I didn't think so . . ." She left for her living quarters adjacent to the museum. In a few minutes, she returned with the steaming tea, which she placed, on the table along with a little packet of sugar and a little compote of cream. Then she reached into a pouch behind her and produced a bottle, which she planked down on the table in front of John. "Guinness," declared John. "Now you're talking."

"It's Bill's from out of the cooler in the garage, but he won't mind."

John thanked her and she left the two alone to read.

"If she saw him at all, it would be in this book on the same day or a little later than the date of his entry about it." John said in a near whisper.

"You look for that and I'll look in the early ones written while Pitus was still here." Joyce replied. "I'll get them for you," said John. He reached into the cabinet and took out two bundles bearing the dates of the earliest diaries.

"What do you expect to find in those years," asked John.

"They were sweet on each other; maybe they were lovers."

"People didn't write that kind of stuff in diaries, even back then."

"Of course they did, if they were honest, and reasonably sure that no one else would ever see them."

"S'pose so." John said. He pulled at the string on the first bundle. "That's curious," he murmured.

"What," asked Joyce?

"This string pulled easy for something that hasn't been disturbed for decades." He took up the second bundle and closely examined it. "Someone *has* been into these packages, and not long ago."

"How can you tell," asked Joyce.

"See the edge of this flap of paper," he asked, showing it to Joyce. "There is a line of lighter paper just ahead of the leading edge of the flap. This light area was protected by the outer flap from oxidation and light exposure over the years. Look closely at the knot. There are parts of the string exposed that were once inside the knot and protected from the elements. He pulled on the bow of string. "This knot pulled apart as though freshly tied."

"What could it mean," asked Joyce.

"Maybe nothing, or maybe something," said John. "Unfortunately, nothing quantifiable. There's no way to know just when the packages were opened, but someone has looked at these diaries recently. One thing it tells me is that we are not the only ones interested in Pitus." He got his steno pad ready for transcribing as did Joyce. John started reading and then stopped.

"Joyce."

"Hmmm." she uttered not taking her eyes off the pages of the first of the diaries. "Do you keep a diary?"

"Yes, I do. Why?"

"Just wondering, that's all."

She smiled at him. "Get busy so we can do this all in one trip."

The museum was quiet for a long time, there being few visitors, unusual at this time of year. It actually worked well for John and Joyce, avoiding distracting or probing questions. Suddenly Joyce nudged John. "Listen to this." She whispered.

"Why are you whispering? This isn't the library.

"I know that. But you seem to be whispering whenever you talk."

"I do not!" John retorted in a hushed voice. He then burst out into laughter. "I stand corrected." Then he said in a normal tone, "What have you got?"

"It starts here at June 10th, 1806:

'Today P P came by to deliver a prescription for Grandma Hall's dropsy. He didn't see me because I was upstairs looking through a crack in the door. He is not very handsome, in the usual sense; not like Capt. Jordan's son, Seth, but neither is he as full of himself as Mr. High and Mighty. I could see the kinds of things that were on Seth's mind the day he put his hands on Rachel Bentheen's bodice. She screamed when he stroked along the tops of her globes.

I do not care a row of shucks about what she says about it; I think she really enjoyed it.

Mother says that Master Peston is very ambitious and hard-working and he is very smart. I will admit that he is smart and likely to go far in this world, but in what way, whether by virtue or vice, I am not at all sure to say. Leastwise, I find that I feel for him in a curious way, though my friends would pester me mercilessly were I to make it known. I dare say that I would not flinch were he to touch me as Seth did Rachel.'

"See, I knew it!" Joyce exclaimed.

"Adolescent musings at the hormonal zenith." said John languidly.

"I'm not far enough along yet. You just wait and see." Joyce said emphatically. She looked over at the diary John had.

"Have you found anything?"

"Not yet." John said impatiently. "I checked for a week on either side of the date in the almanac entry, but there's nothing about it."

"Keep looking. There might be something later on that alludes to it." Joyce encouraged. She resumed her own reading. A moment later she again nudged John. "Here's something else." `12 July 1806: There was a party for John Norton, who turned 17 on Thursday last. Allan Dutton said it was a birthday party, but Martin `Bacchus' told me that it was all for the purpose of getting *in the airs* and he planned to bring plenty of kill-devil to stir things up. He was true to his word, and had not only a keg of rum, but also some segars that were said to contain hemp, which must have been factual for the way they affected some present. There was much gaiety at the sap house, but I observed no one was brazen or indecent. I think all became too soon ploughed to arrive at a requisite state of baseness.'

"Say, this is a colorful bunch!" John said, slyly.

"People have some nerve maligning our generation, I'll say," added Joyce. `There was one very singular happening that concerned P-P, which I will set down before I lose the details, for I was somewhat affected by the smoke in the room and remember it only as it were, 'through a glass darkly'. PP sat down soon after he arrived, and did not seem to be interested so much in imbibing in drink than in observing the rest of us who had had a head start on him. Master Norton was in the altitudes and was made to sit down lest he harm himself from repeatedly falling. Allan was sufficiently intoxicated to be quite gay. Martin, who we were all certain, like Behemoth, 'could draw up the Jordan in his mouth' showed little signs of his drink.

Joyce laughed, "This would make a fortune if it were published."

"I would give a month's pay to read Peston's side of the story," laughed John.

"Wait," said Joyce, "there's more."

'Pitus laughed boisterously for some time but soon grew silent. Anon, he put his head upon the table and fell asleep. Someone, I cannot remember who, dared me to kiss him. I feigned disgust at the notion and let the others egg me on, but I, in truth, rather relished the idea. I did the deed and he opened his eyes and muttered something that was unintelligible. Later Martin threw open the door and a thick pall of smoke fled the room as though it were a ghost. Then Pitus partly roused and uttered a vulgarity and in nearly the same breath called out 'Alditor' whom he later said was an angel he met in a great meadow. He also made mention of an 'Ita' who was someone he was trying to find. When he came to, Allan asked him if he had had a dream and what it was. He then described a walk or journey over fields and vales, and on a stone road that led him to a polished floor. He said that gossamer veils brushed over him until twelve had done so, and after this last withdrew, he was in a ruin of great antiquity.

He did not say what this place was, but passed on through it where he came to a low grassy glade with many paths winding through. He said that he could not decide which path to take. A soft voice urged him on. He hesitated, which made the voice more urgent. His continued stubbornness, or rather his fear to start down a path, caused the voice to change to one masculine and gruff, which commanded him to go. He still feared to start off and he wept. The tears washed his vision and faded all paths but one, which he took.

This path led him to another ruins, in one wall of which hung a shiny metallic plate upon which were scribed figures of an unknown language. Pitus said that though the figures resembled no known earthly tongue, he possessed a native understanding of them. The tablet had an incantation on it with instructions that said to read aloud the words and receive the wisdom of the ages. He pronounced the words and the heavens opened up above him showing the stars in all their nocturnal brilliance, though broad daylight and he knew them all by name.

After this he said he awoke. It may be nothing more than a crazy dream born of hemp smoke, but I could see that the experience changed him in some way. Since that day he is to me more alluring than ever before. I know not if it is the change; he is more thoughtful and pensive; more gentle-seeming, and this being the root of my attachment, or whether I am drawn to touch him in order to feel something of the immortal. He is but a man, but, I believe, a special one.'

Joyce sight read this entry aloud, thus learning of its contents at the same time as John. Both sat silent for a few seconds.

"What do you think?" Joyce finally asked.

"I think she was sweet on him." John replied and quickly winced, anticipating the swat from Joyce for his levity.

"Now tell me something else."

John hiked up in his chair and pondered a few seconds. "As intriguing as this all is, it doesn't shed any more light on the almanac entries. We won't be able to check the history at the library till tomorrow. So far, I'd say we are not very far off home plate."

"Well keep looking." Joyce said impatiently. "The entry I read was of an event nearly a week earlier. Maybe you will find something about her seeing Pitus in a later entry."

Joyce put down the 1806 and picked up one at random. It was the journal for 1808. She was turning the pages as though skimming for something else perhaps to confirm her suspicions about Ellen and Pitus. John was immersed in his journal when a shriek from Joyce caused him nearly to tumble out of his seat.

"Geez, Joyce, I'm not too young to have a heart attack!"

"I knew it," she exclaimed. "I just knew it!"

"What," asked John?

"They did it," said Joyce in a hushed tone of excitement.

"Who?"

"Ellen and Pitus."

"Did what," asked John?

"What do ya think," she asked incredulously?

"It? You mean it, the big IT," asked John? Now his voice was hushed. "When did they . . . ?

"Right after he came back from a trip to Albany," said Joyce. "He stopped at Ellen's aunt Rosalie's in Saratoga to get an interpretation of the dream. He stopped at Ellen's to tell her about it and . . ."

"Let me see." Joyce put her finger on the spot and shoved the diary over. John started to read softly aloud.

". . . PP told me what Aunt Rosie said about his dream. He said she was a fascinating lady, especially her hands, whose long slender fingers looked as if they could reach into the heart and pluck the hidden fruits . . . He was so poetic and grand, and yet so tender in his speech. I felt my breasts swell beneath my shift. Then he reached for my hands and took them in his. He held them there and then softly stroked them saying how they were like Aunt Rosie's . . . My heart hammered as his hand caressed mine. I shuddered and felt damp. I lost all sense of constraint and pulled him to me. Suddenly we were within the tall grass of the meadow. His hands sought me and I helped him gain passage. I could feel his readiness for me and I sought him likewise . . ."

"I can't read this any more," said John.

"Why not," asked Joyce?

"What do ya think?"

"You need a fan or something," she laughed?

"Something," said John. He blew out a big sigh and then picked up his stout and took a swig. Then with a little difficulty he continued his search. Ten minutes later he held up his hand to get Joyce's attention.

"I think I've got it!" John declared. "Listen to this."

`30 May 1883: 'What I saw last month and disbelieved, still haunts me. Perhaps if I set it down, I will be able to put it to rest. After Meeting on Sunday morning at half past ten on 22d April, I saw a vision that disquieted me very much. I know that it must be the addled brain of my old head that caused me to see what I saw. I had no more got into my seat in the chaise for the ride home than I beheld a shocking sight. About five-rod distance from me stood a man who was the very image of Pitus Peston. He was looking at me from beside the corner of Jenkins' Livery. When he saw that I had seen him, he disappeared behind the horse shed. I hollered to little Micah Ames if he didn't see that man with the red shirt and brown hat, and to take after him and see where he went. It wasn't long before he returned and told me he vanished without a trace. He had the look of a man in his middle twenties, and therefore I must either conclude that it was one of similar face, or that it was the spirit of Pitus who appeared to me to herald my own end times.'

"Bulls eye," exclaimed Joyce.

"There it is," John said.

"This is all too fantastic," said Joyce.

"Maybe that hallucination he had at the party is connected." said John.

"How?"

"It may be wild speculation," said John, "but maybe the place he described was one he later found . . . some kind of fountain of youth or something."

Atoye manipulated the map of Kesst in the computer. "There's the Institute," he said. He turned to Pitus. "That is what it used to look like."

"It was beautiful," said Pitus "like a crust of jewels."

"So it was," said Atoye wistfully. "Omans came from all over just to be in the plaza at dawn to see the show the sun made as its first rays played off the glass towers.

I was there once during the spring equinox. I went out into the plaza two hours before dawn. Any later, and I couldn't have made it to the center, which is the optimum location for the effect. Just before daybreak there were probably ten-thousand souls milling about the place. One could hardly hold a conversation with the person right next to you from all the noise. When the light from the sun touched the orb atop the Hibber Spire that all changed. You could have heard a pin drop. We all stood silently watching the light creep down the spire to where it joined the roof of the Institute. When the sun hit that roof . . . the colors . . . It was like being inside a rainbow. The whole place broke into cheers and clapping. It was enriching to the point of life-changing." Atoye stared off in a reverie. "Maybe it will shine again someday," he uttered softly. He moved the indicator a little. "Remember that street?"

"That looks like where we went after the Annex and where we found Lucan."

"That is where we will go," said Atoye. "Ready?"

"As much as I ever will be," said Pitus. Atoye locked the spot into the nav-com and stepped back into the center of the bridge. "I locked in both points so we will end up right here when we trans back." He keyed the luso stone in his amulet, and the aperture opened in a bath of white light. They both stepped through.

They stepped out into the narrow side street, a paved stone walkway beside the looming structure of the bombed out Institute. They both hurried through the doorway of the same shop they entered on their first visit to the ruined city of Kesst some months before.

Atoye slipped a small rucksack off his shoulder and set it down on the floor. He got down on one knee and opened it. From the sack he took a portable light attached to a denim-like cloth head gear and placed it on his head. He touched a tab on the side of his temple and the light came on with a soft white glow. From the sack he took another and handed it to Pitus, who placed it on his head and tested it. Also from the sack, Atoye brought out two small hand torches, giving one to Pitus. Atoye stood up replacing the sack over his shoulder and then motioned for Pitus to follow him. They went back to the place where Lucan was living in this former shopping mall and souvenir shop of the Institute. Pitus tapped Atoye on his arm.

"Where do you suppose Lucan is? I really expected him to find us like he did the first time we were here."

Atoye shrugged, "He knows his way around here," he said. "Maybe he doesn't want to be found." He scanned the hallway and listened. "Just the same, we could use what he knows to find our way around down there, so let's try to find him." They advanced down the long corridor that led through to Lucan's apartment and at last came to a plain metal door. Atoye tapped gently on it with his knuckles. There was no response. They looked at each other a moment and then Pitus grabbed the door knob and turned it. They both entered Lucan's living space. It looked as though a cyclone went through it. There was also a foul funk in the air.

"Not good," said Atoye quietly. "Lucan," called Atoye in a forced whisper. When there was no response, Atoye motioned for Pitus to search off to the right while he started checking the rooms on the left. It wasn't long before Pitus called out, "He's in here." Atoye rushed to where Pitus stood in the threshold of a small study. Lucan was prone on the floor, a large brisler burn hole in the center of his back.

PITUS PESTON'S JOURNALS

Carol answered the phone in a cordial businesslike manner.
"John, it's for you. I think it is Joyce," she whispered.
"Hello, Bingham's." Joyce laughed loudly.
"Oh, yeah, I guess you were aware of that already."
"You can't help yourself, can you," she said. "Guess what? The watermark does match the one in the almanacs."
"I knew it would." said John.
"So, Pitus wrote the Peston Family History and was around in 1883 to deliver it," said Joyce.
"This is heavy stuff!" exclaimed John. "He would have been 96 years old."
"He apparently didn't look or act that old." said Joyce. "How could that be? I mean, how could he live that long and be still as a young man? It's like you said about finding a 'fountain of youth' somewhere."
"Maybe he did," said John. There was some skepticism in his voice as he uttered these words. There was also an inward struggle to overcome this for the joy and fascination in the consequences of it being true.
"Maybe he learned some medicinal secret from an Indian shaman, or what is more likely is that all that hard living toughened him up," said John.
"Ellen said he appeared to be a man in his twenties at a time when he should have been in his nineties." reminded Joyce. "That's a little more than just being 'tough'."
"How about the book?" John asked.
"I haven't had an opportunity to check it out yet. I will tend to it later this morning after whoever I get to talk with has had a chance to have their morning coffee." Joyce quipped.
"When do you get off work today?" asked John.
"Five."
"Me too," John said with satisfaction. "I'll pick you up. We can talk about it all then. Best to keep a lid on it for now."

When John arrived at the library, Joyce was seated on a park bench near the main entrance. The loop around the little park next to the library was lined with boxwood shrubs pruned down to knee-height which allowed John to see her as he drew near. He paid more attention looking at her than at his driving, when a blaring horn snapped him out of his enchantment. "Sorry," he called out to the oncoming driver, who he was depriving of his half of the road. When he stopped he attempted to get out of the truck in order to be a genteel man, not so much from good breeding than from the power of fresh new love. By the time he turned the handle, to get out, Joyce had yanked the passenger door open and jumped in by herself.

"I really was going to get the door for you," said John

"Weren't you trained to keep your eyes on the road," she asked whimsically.

"I'd rather keep my eyes on you," he said.

"Right answer again," she said, and leaned toward him to give him a quick kiss. "There's a proper time and place for everything," she said softly. "I'll make sure that happens later." Then she glanced about the cab.

"Hey, you cleaned all the junk out of your truck!" John pointed downward under the seat.

"On second thought," she added, "I guess not."

"There's something I haven't told you. I got some stuff from Mike the night I was down there talking with that Ames guy. It was sitting down in his cellar. It's amazing that all those things were still there after so long, but they were, and now I have them. I also got to go up in his attic and found some papers along with some journals of Ordway's."

"Who was he?"

"His name was Lucius Ordway, and he was a druggist who settled here after the Revolution. Pitus trained under him for about nine months," explained John. "I haven't looked over any of his things yet, but plan on doing it tonight. I thought maybe you could help."

"Then take me home, first." Joyce said. "I need to change, and while I'm there I can grab some things to snack on." John waited outside while Joyce went into her apartment. She was not long in returning, but had two grocery bags filled with things. She had also exchanged her dress for a pair of jeans and a light colored shirt.

"Do you really think there will be much about Pitus in his papers," she asked as she seated herself. "That is, considering they were together for only nine months?"

"Any lead, even from an obtuse source is worth digging out. Besides, the papers and journals were practically given to me. It was the bottles and jugs and the old druggist's equipment that cost me the bucks."

"How much did you pay?"

"I gave him a couple of C-notes."

"I'll probably have to feed you till next payday."

"Looks like you could with all of that in those bags." John quipped. Joyce just smiled.

"There's something important, I fear that might be bad news." John said. "When I asked Mike about seeing the garret, he told me that some guy had already asked about papers. Said he was a book collector. Mike said the guy was very pleased with what he found."

"Competition," said Joyce, "Just like you suspected at the museum."

"We may be *his* competition. He saw Mike last month."

"It would be nice to know who he was. We might be able to strike up a deal of some sort."

"It didn't sound like Mike knew who he was."

The two arrived at the house and John politely opened the door to let Joyce in ahead of him.

"This place looks relatively neat and tidy." Joyce said with a little surprise. Then teasingly she added, "Where do I look for the pile of junk—under the couch?"

"Take a warning from Fibber Magee." John replied. He then pointed to the dining room table.

"There's the stuff I got at Mike's. It's mostly Civil War vintage or older. Some of it was doubtless handled by our 'legendary historical figure'. John said.

"I would like to think so, but I doubt it," said Joyce, as she idly inspected the objects on the table.

"What's this glass thing—looks like a funnel all stretched out."

"That is a percolator."

"Like what you make coffee in?"

"No, silly. No one would ever use it for that," he replied. "It is used to brew medicines out of plants and barks."

"I don't see why you couldn't use it for coffee," she murmured, as she carefully placed it back on the table.

"Speaking of our legendary figure," John remembered, "I ran across an entry in the almanacs that tells how Pitus got his name. It gibes with the account of it in the History at the library.

"There would have to be some sort of story connected with a name like his." Joyce smirked. "The poor Guy!"

"I think it's rather distinctive." John said.

"Coming from one who has a regular sounding name, I'm not surprised." Joyce replied smiling. "Maybe if you were named, *Pitus Hodiak*, you would have a different angle on distinctiveness," she giggled.

"With a name like that, he probably grew up with a keen wit and a hard fist!" Joyce continued looking at the items on the table.

"I wouldn't be surprised if your money was well spent," she said pensively as she handled the decorative Norton jug. John Spargo wrote a book about the

Norton Pottery in Bennington. It's an old book. The library has a copy. This jug is probably worth more than you paid for the whole lot."

"I checked it out in an antique price guide," said John. "If I was to put it on Nu-bay, I could probably get a thousand dollars. Then my noisy conscience would force me to split it with Mike."

"That's another right answer," said Joyce.

"On the chair are the books I got from Mike's attic." said John. "I wish I had the other things of Ordway's that guy took. Damn that Mike for not finding out whom he was!"

"You're getting flustered over nothing, I'm sure," said Joyce. "And it's not nice to curse your friends."

"I'm sorry," said John. "I didn't mean it like that."

"Don't worry about something you can't control," said Joyce. "It could be a hidden blessing. If what you fear is true, we are at least alerted that someone else is snooping around."

"I might ask Mike if I can see his attic again."

"Do you know for sure that there are no more things in your own attic," asked Joyce.

"All there is are boards and wood scraps. I've been using some of them up fixing the kitchen."

"Let's go take a look anyway." Joyce urged. They ascended the narrow stairs. John used a flashlight to find the cord of the ceiling light. It was nearly dark outside, and the artificial light was barely enough to allow one to see.

"Let's do this systematically." Joyce suggested. "We can start by clearing off a spot and then stack the boards neatly in that spot." She cast a glance at him and said wryly, "I realize this method of working will be totally alien to you, so I will supervise and you can do all the lifting."

"O.K. boss, do with me what you will."

"For now I'll settle for you moving around some lumber."

John started working taking advantage of any opportunity to steal glances at Joyce in the dim light. "She is pretty smart, as well as just plain pretty," he mused. Occasionally the scent of her perfume wafted toward him bringing forth an energizing, powerful desire in him. John found himself investing more and more enthusiasm in her than in finding any more artifacts.

"That smell excites me." John said.

"I know." Joyce replied, "It smells a little like old books up here; 'like the fragrance of time-honored literature'."

"You got that from me, didn't you?" John laughed. He confessed, "It's Joe's phrase, but he said I could use it."

"Is that what he said?" asked Joyce. "I'm the one who first said that to him! That's plagiarism!" she said playfully.

"The dirty dog," laughed John. He wondered how he would return to the subject of smells and attraction in the way he wanted to mean them. He remembered the promise in the truck, but he felt it was a good idea to keep a mood up.

"I don't mean that smell."

"Then what," she asked.

John thought any further looking in this ransacked attic was a waste of time from the beginning. He felt this more so now that he preferred to spend the time making love with her. He either built up the courage, or abandoned fear; it was anyone's guess, in order to plainly state his desire. The words reached the tip of his tongue when Joyce shrieked.

"What is it? Did you see a rat?"

"No," she said reaching down by her left ankle. "Books!"

"Books," John repeated. "Probably some old Byron or Shakespeare that Freda missed," he said scornfully.

"Let's untie the string and see." John gazed at the bundle. "Say, I've seen them before. Lots of times, actually. I thought they were some ends of boards tied up all together. I never thought to pick them up to take a close look at them. Neither did Ken or Freda, apparently."

"Well, wood scraps they ain't!" Joyce exclaimed. "They are journals. Manuscript journals!" She held the top volume from the stack up to the light with it open to the title page. "Take a look at this!"

"The PEREGRINATIONS OF PITUS PESTON . . . . son of a . . ." John's oath faded out into wonderment. "Do you think . . ."

"I think this is something other than the books he put in the libraries," said Joyce. "I will still check that out in the morning, but this might be even better!"

"We'll take these down to the dining room table where the light is better." John exclaimed, his excitement putting on hold his former yearnings. They wiped the thick coating of dust from the journals and spread them out on the table. Then John sat at the end of the table with Joyce seated across the corner from him.

"What do you want me to do? I'm here for you." Joyce said excitedly. The way she said it reawakened the arrested feelings he had in the attic when he smelled the fragrance she had on. "Why don't you start on the first Journal and I will start looking through the Ordway stuff." John suggested. As she took the volume I and started reading it silently, John gazed at her. After a moment she looked up from the book.

"What," she asked?

"I'm glad."

"For what?"

"I'm glad that you are here for me."

"Well, that's just an expression . . ." John then touched her hand and caressed it. She stopped speaking in mid-sentence, as she understood that it wasn't a mere expression to him. John then leaned toward her across the corner of the table. As he moved toward her, she moved toward him as well, and they met over the table's edge and kissed. It was a simple kiss; nearly the same as a first kiss often is, though this was not their first. She remained in this glorious affectionate kiss and brought her hand up behind his neck to hold herself and him there. They spoke no words, though volumes were exchanged through their eyes. He stroked her hair back gently. Another kiss ensued, a tender, sweet exploration of this growing affection. They rose as one from their chairs and moved out of the bright light of the dining room toward the sofa in the living room. The light from the dining room reached to where they now were, but it was greatly attenuated, a bathing of shadows, a private, cozy dimness. The faded light faded also the restraint of their passion, and unbridled, led of its own accord. Between kisses, Joyce stayed John's advance by placing her finger over his lips.

"We're not getting much work done this way," she said in a silken voice.

"Do you think we should return to the dining room," he asked.

"It's too bright out there," she answered.

John leaned back onto a pillow at the end of the sofa, holding her and guiding her down until she rested on him. He put his arms around her in an embrace and they lay there for a moment. He buried his face in her hair. It was a world of its own; a world of touch and smell and delight. In him at this moment seethed a desire for her, but he held it at bay lest he ruin this moment with brutish abandon. That chivalrous notion was short lived. He was by now just like Pitus was in the tall grass at Ellen's and he knew Joyce, just like Ellen of two centuries ago, could not help but know this. She moved over him which was driving him crazy with passion. They kissed hard and suddenly lost their purchase on the sofa. Joyce made a startled shriek as they fell to the carpet muffled by the kiss. John rolled onto his back pulling Joyce on top of him resuming their kiss. Joyce loosened the snap of her jeans and John slipped his hands through the gap on to her creamy skin.

Joyce raised herself from him a little and then kissed him once again. In the dim light John could see the soft, sleek form of her breasts showing through her clothing. He wished to have the experience of their satiny softness with a vehemence of desire. Joyce then lifted her hand, and, with slow and careful movements, unfastened the buttons of her shirt.

COLCHESTER 1863

"Good morning, Mr. Sloan," said Amiel Johns, assistant curator of manuscripts at the Holloway Institute. Arnold Sloan, BA, MA., PhD., B. Litt., Oxon., was the new curator of the museum. Rumor had it that Sloan was an ardent waste hater and financial fat trimmer. Amiel knew very well on what side the bread was buttered, so he made a point every day to establish a good rapport with his new boss in case the axe was scheduled to fall.

"Good morning, Amiel," Sloan replied cordially. He hung his topcoat on the tree in his office and poked his head out through the doorway.

"Amiel."

"Yes Mr. Sloan?"

"Thank you for the financial report you gave me Friday. I have reviewed it and would like to meet with you in my office at ten." Amiel's blood chilled.

"Yes sir," he replied. "Ten it is." He continued on to his own office. "Here it comes," he thought.

The Holloway Institute was a museum with a permanent collection of Egyptiana, some renaissance art and some various other antiquities, gathered mostly during the lifetime of Amos Holloway, an eighteenth century nobleman with a good eye for a bargain. The main body of the collection festooned the halls and galleries of Lochwood Manor, Holloway's baronial estate until his death in 1772, when it was removed by order of the baron's last will and testament to a location in Colchester. A foundation was established with fifty thousand pounds sterling to care for the collection. With the aid of a sagacious manager, William Atoss, who purchased the orchards down by the river and sold them back to the swelling town at an immense profit, the funds were augmented to an amount tenfold the original bequest, which allowed the means to acquire additions to the collection through the ensuing years. Good publicity made the museum a popular place, and the steady stream of visitors at an admission fee of two shillings kept the coffers well above the necessary mark. This, along with an occasional bequest from the British nobility, kept the Institute well heeled.

The real value of the Institute's holdings lay in its extensive manuscript collection, with letters and diaries, etc. from famous men of letters from as far back as the reign of Henry the Second. Scholars clamored for the privilege of examining the collections with only the cream of the literati gaining access.

Recent times, however, saw a slackening of attendance and revenue. The Institute's financial wizard, Atoss, was now an addled nonagenarian, incapable of lending his considerable expertise to the Institute's woes. Since new money was not flowing in as before, the only solution remaining was a belt tightening. The Institute's board of directors selected Amos Sloan for the job and he was determined not to fail them.

Johns did little that morning other than await with no small trepidation the meeting with Sloan, which would almost certainly not be pleasant. He knew he would be given the task of selecting the victims for the financial bloodletting about to occur. Johns arose from his desk at a quarter of ten and trudged to the head man's office. On arrival, Sloan bid his lieutenant be seated.

"In my short tenure as curator," began Sloan, "I have had to make myself something of an ogre to the staff. It is not my wish to do so, but it is a necessary evil in my leadership position."

"I fully understand, sir," said Johns, a tremble in his voice. With a start like this, he was no longer sure his own career would endure past the next five minutes.

"My predecessor, unfortunately, was an eminent scholar, but not a man of business, and a museum, just like any other institution needs to be run as a business to thrive." Johns was silent, but probably could not have forced any more than a squeal from his tightening vocal chords.

"I am going to have to make some hard financial decisions in the short term as pertains to personnel."

Amiel gulped. What was he going to do without a job? He had no savings of any size. His wife and three young boys would be reduced to beggary. Sloan looked at Johns a moment. He could see the fear in his face.

"It is not you to whom I infer when I speak of cuts," he assured Amiel. It took a few seconds for the angst to dissipate, and after a brief silence, Amiel managed to croak a "Thank you Mr. Sloan."

"You have an assistant," said Sloan.

"Mr. Rowland," asked Johns?

"How long has he been employed at the museum?"

"Oh, a long time, Mr. Sloan; years and years," said Johns.

"Records show that he was hired in 1814 as an acquisition agent, a position he still holds," said Sloan. "One would think he would have been curator after all that time."

"He never sought advancement," said Johns. "I asked him about that one night while we were out with some friends at the Spaniard." Sloan raised his eyebrows slightly. Johns hastened to explain. "That's an old pub down by the river. It has been in business since the reign of James. It is the haunt of riff raff off the ships, but safe if one goes with a party and thus it is not without a goodly bit of intrigue," added Johns, with a playful smile. Sloan smiled politely and nodded his interest mainly with the explanation of Rowland's motive for shunning a promotion.

"Well sir, he said it was not in him to be an administrator. He explained that his long suit was in ferreting out literary treasures for accumulation."

"Sloan glanced down at the documents on his desk. "Are you sure the hire date is correct?"

"Why would it not be," asked Johns?

"He looks too young," said Sloan. "For him to have been hired in 1814, he would have had to apply while still in knickers." Johns chuckled. 'It is rumored he colors his hair," he said whimsically.

"There is no birth date for him in our records," said Sloan. "Nor is there any past record of military service." Johns shrugged. "He is a good scholar and cataloger," said Johns, "and he has located for us many excellent acquisitions."

"Nevertheless," continued Sloan, I feel his position is a duplication of expense."

"He has an encyclopedic knowledge of literature," said Johns. "He knew where to locate invaluable collections of personal papers of many early seventeenth century writers. The Rabelais papers, for instance. It is as if he knew them personally. I realize that could not be so, but . . ."

"I will give him his due," said Sloan. "He seems to have helped the Institute greatly. The time for spending funds on acquisitions has flown for the present. He may be well connected within the literati, but still I fear he has to go. His murky past leaves some doubts in the minds of the board members." Johns seemed to know that he could not save his friend without risking his own hide. Sloan said, "That is all Johns," and Amiel said, "Very well, sir," and promptly left the office.

"A half hour later, Rowland sat in the same chair as Johns. Sloan started the conversation cordially, but it soon changed to a grilling. Rowland answered the questions mostly with lies. He had done this before and knew the inevitable result. If he hadn't gotten sacked soon he would have had to disappear anyway. He enjoyed working for the Institute this time as he did before under the kind leadership of Amos. Because of this, he remained longer than was prudent. The questions were polite enough; "Why Mr. Rowland, how do you keep your youthful look?" His reply was uniformly that he took his daily exercise without fail and he ate sensibly and that because of this, The Almighty graced him with a good native stamina. But he knew the question lingered in the minds of his friends and associates . . . "How *does* he keep his youthful look?" Rumors about him and his "hold on the fountain of youth" were circulating. Just last week, an elderly woman who knew him for nearly forty years made a comment that he looked no older than her son. This surely came out of her with some difficulty since she prided herself as one who was well kept for her years. If only he could change a little to reflect the passage of time. Currently he looked to be a man in his mid fifties, but there were persons in the town who knew him as an adult for that long. It was time to go; perhaps to America.

In the pre-dawn darkness, John extended his arm outward on the bed. When he felt nothing, the sense of being alone roused him out of his sleep. He raised himself and peered into the room. Joyce was nearly dressed. John lay back down and remained still for a moment watching her in the dim green glow of the radio's clock beside the bed.

"Where are you going," he asked huskily?

"I would like to stay, but I must work tomorrow, or rather, later this morning. Don't you?"

"I'll give you a ride home."

"I hope so, silly. My car is at my apartment. I came here in your truck."

It was nearly sunrise when the two parted. "See ya after work?" Joyce asked moving close to him for a kiss good-by."

"It'll be late." John said wistfully.

"Got to pull a 'twelver' today at the store. God! How I hate twelve hour days . . . but then I rather relish getting paid for them," he smirked.

"See you when you get done, then." Joyce said sweetly. John held her and then they kissed. "This will be a day of 90-minute hours! I miss you already."

"I feel the same way," she replied tenderly. "We both have to get ready for work, though."

With reluctance they separated, and John got into his truck. Joyce waved to him, and he started to leave, but then stopped and rolled down the window.

"Be careful with what you know." John warned. "It would be unfortunate if the 'competition' knew about us, whoever that may be."

"I'll be discreet." Joyce promised.

Ott sat at his huge desk in his study. Spread out before him were a couple of small stacks of letters and a leather-bound diary. He picked up the diary and opened it to a place he had previously marked. He turned and pulled on a servant's cord. In a minute there was a knock at the door.

"Come through."

"You called, sir?"

"We can stop looking, Gordon. The bastard destroyed them all," Ott said rancorously.

"That is unfortunate," said Gordon. "Shall I recall the team?"

"Let Green and Hopkins keep searching. There may still be something out in Arizona or Nebraska. Morse is retracing Peston's route in the East.

When he checks in on Monday, I will tell him there is nothing around here." He returned to the diary.

"Is that all sir?"

"For now," said Ott.

With hardly a sound, Gordon left, closing the door behind him.

"You realized what would happen if it had gotten loose, didn't you," Ott said to the diary as though he were speaking to its author. "There must be some trace. You couldn't have gotten it all. I will discover your mistake. I am too old to die so young." He set down the diary and picked up another. "If I had known the connection," he thought, "I could have settled this long ago when the clues were still fresh." He stared off into the depths of the study. "How could I have known, though? I spent the first sixty years of my life discovering that I wasn't becoming an old man." It is wearing off, I fear and I need a booster." He laughed. At two hundred and fifteen I find my joints starting to get stiff." He opened the next diary. "Agelessness has a way of creeping up on a person just as aging does."

CORSTET

Joyce knocked on the door and, realizing the folly of such a formality, proceeded to step inside. She found John in the living room seated in an overstuffed chair holding in front of him a small, wide mouthed bottle. From John there was not a greeting, not even a word to her, just silence as he sat, turning the bottle from side to side, gazing at its contents as though mesmerized.
"Hello." she said, expecting to receive a loving greeting. Instead, he continued to sit apparently spellbound by the object in his hand.
"Are you all right?" she asked, not a little puzzled at his behavior.
"Yes." John answered still in his trance. She drew close and joined him in staring at the bottle in his hand.
"What are you looking at?"
"The Philosopher's Stone, I believe."
"You don't smell like you've been drinking, but you sure act like it." She sat down on the arm of the chair and leaned to give him a kiss. He was brought back to earth by this gesture, and set the bottle on the table next to him. Joyce then slid off the chair arm and into his lap, putting her arms around him as she did so.
"Mmmm, you smell good." John said with distinct pleasure. "Feel good, too."
"You're not so bad, yourself," she answered sensuously. Rather than indulging in a scene of affection, the gravity of John's involvement with the bottle and its contents arrested her attention.
"That doesn't look like any stone to me, let alone a Philosopher's Stone," she said. "It looks like a plant or at least, parts on one."
John picked the bottle up once again and held it in front of her.
"It's more than that," he said with awe. If I am correct, it is also a botanical 'Holy Grail'."

"Now that certainly clears it up!" Joyce replied impatiently. "It is apparently a profound discovery. Are you planning to tell me something about it?"

"I found it in here," said John pointing to a folio size book. It was leather bound over oak boards fastened with brass clasps.

"This one miraculously escaped the clutches of our unknown foe. It was lying flat behind a bunch of Zane Greys. It is ancient."

"It looks medieval," said Joyce.

"Not quite, but it goes back to the sixteenth century. It pays to look under, over and around even the least likely places."

"You didn't find that bottle in there," she said playfully.

"I found this," he said, holding up a folded piece of paper. "It is a letter dated October 12, 1806 by Ordway to some fellow named Anton Calhoun. It isn't finished and there is no information where Calhoun was, unfortunately. Anyway, Pitus brought Ordway a plant specimen soon after he started working for him that he said was gathered a few weeks before while in Albany. It was a red and blue flower with red foliage. He called it 'corstet'. The letter reveals that he was familiar with the plant, but he seemed totally baffled by how Pitus came to have it. He described it along with details of where it was found and when it was harvested. He sealed up the plant with two seed pods in this bottle where it has remained to this day. The letter goes on to say that if this gift of longevity were to break out into general use, it would likely cause the death of mankind."

"I still don't get what you mean," said Joyce impatiently.

John lifted the first volume of Peston's journals onto his lap and opened to a marked spot. "This book tells of the start of his journey," John explained. "Sometime, it doesn't say precisely when, Pitus and his friend, Allan Dutton went to Albany to visit some relations of Allan's. There Pitus befriended one of Allan's cousins whose name was Gill-something, and traded a knife he had with him for an Indian beadwork sash that Gill had. On the sash was worked a picture of what appeared to be a scene of death and the afterlife, but the particulars were unknown to Gill. Gill apparently told Pitus that his great-grandmother knew what the picture meant. They went to see her and it was there that Pitus found the strange plants. Pitus snitched some of them and brought them home, and later on showed them to Ordway."

"Still, I don't see anything spectacular about it," Joyce interjected.

"Patience, my dear," John said pleasantly. "This is all necessary to put the events in proper perspective. Now we have to go ahead in time almost three years, after Pitus leaves home. One of his first stops on his journey was the old woman's cabin." John paused to catch his breath. Joyce was now resigned to hear the details of what promised to be a long story, but did so patiently.

"The great-grandmother was old, and I mean really old; well over a hundred, and still in reasonable health. Here's what Pitus Had to say about it.; I'll start where Gram said to Pitus that he reminded her of someone and he asked her who it was . . . ."

"'My Joseph. When you held that old piece of wampum in your hands, you had the same look in your eyes.'"

"You see," John explained, "He went back to see Gram, who was what the family called her. Her actual name was Lucy Dutton. The reason he went there was to try to find out anything more about the sash he had. As you will soon see, He was now on a journey to discover the meaning of the image worked into the beadwork. Joseph was Gram's husband, who originally obtained it."

He returned to the text: "'I have come to try to find out more about it and then journey to Louisiana to get to the bottom of the mystery behind it."

"Are you sure there is anything to get to the bottom of," she replied mysteriously. "You know so, ma'am." I answered, gazing at the old woman. "Will you tell me?" Gram approached the opposite side of the table and set a cup and small plate before me. She turned away and soon returned to the table with another cup of tea for herself. "Upon my soul, son, I do not know the meaning of the figures or of the picture taken altogether. That is to say, I know not other than what I was told by my husband. I will venture to say that it is a thing not of this world."

At this, Joyce looked astonished. "Now I know there must be a book out there somewhere that he got published. The text of this journal reads like a novel."

"Fiction or non-fiction," John asked rhetorically. He continued to read.

"'How do you know?'" I asked.

"I don't know for certain." Gram replied. "I just feel it inside. When Joseph came back with that sash, he offered it to me as a gift, but it so bothered me that I finally could not bear to look upon it. I would have thrown it out long ago, but I knew it would have vexed Joseph greatly for me to have done so. So I shut it up in that old trunk."

"Do you think your husband knew something that he didn't tell?" I asked. "Joseph? No, he tended to tell me anything that was of any importance all through our married life. In fact, I grew sick of hearing about that sash day after day. If he knew something monumental about it, he would not have spared my ears the hearing of it. When Jo returned with the sash, he also had a small bag of seeds . . . .'"

"Now, here it comes." John announced, one hand raised with finger pointing upward, the other hand following the text like a preacher expounding upon scripture:

"'Joseph was told to plant the seeds the very next season, without fail, and when the flowers matured in the fall, cut them down and dry them. He was told to brew a tea of the flowers and drink of it every day. Whoever gave the herb to him must have been young. Jo kept telling 'the boy' this and 'the boy' that. It was an Indian boy, I guess. It was all very odd."

"Those were the unusual flowers I saw when I fetched the water with Gill."

"So, you WERE the one," she exclaimed.

"I what," I asked, a bit apprehensive over an apparent accusation.

"When I went out back later in the afternoon on the day you and Gill visited, I noticed a bloom had been plucked. It worried me for a spell, but then no one came to see me about it as time went on, so I figured you'd lost it."

"I dropped it down a fissure in the rocks near my house. I never got to show it to anyone." I said. "Go on, what was so special about the flowers.'"

"He lied to her!" Joyce exclaimed. "Not only did he lie about telling about it, but he also lied about how many plants he took!"

"I don't know if it will excuse him in your eyes," said John, "but here comes the reason why he didn't want her to know he blabbed about the flowers."

"'The boy told Joseph that a tea of the plant taken every day would cure ills and lengthen a man's life. Joseph was a man who would believe almost anything you told him, and he did what he was bid. I told him I thought he was being humbugged. Now that," she said emphatically, "he didn't believe. I remember, he got cross with me over it and said I should tend to them as he ordered and keep still about it. I durst not go agin' him, and I raised them. They turned out to be so pretty; I grew fond of the things and took great care of them. I dreaded to cut them down that fall, but I obeyed Joseph's directions and hung them in the rafters of the wood shed. After they were dried, I pounded all the flowers down into a powder, and we both had a cup of tea brewed of them every morning. It is rather bitter, but you get used to it after a spell . . ."

"Did you feel any effects from the tea after you started using it?" I asked.

"I felt something, but I thought it to be no more remarkable than the stimulant effects of coffee. Joseph, on the other hand, had an attack of ague shortly before we started taking the morning 'toddy' as he called it. Two days later, he was up and about as a young man. I too eventually felt different."

"In what way?" I queried.

"There was a feeling of litheness and good will, as though I had been given back the last twenty years to live anew."

"You mean the herb acted as a stimulant imparting a feeling of well-being?"

"This was much more than a 'pick-me-up'," she answered with conviction. "It added strength of muscle and sinew. It enabled as well as invigorated. It restored!"

"I have had some schooling in the apothecary's art, and have yet to hear of a nostrum that can really do what you say." I replied. "Surely news of something like that would have circulated about."

"It was so profound in its effects on us that we dared not let out the secret to anyone."

"Something like this could have rid multitudes of the diverse evils that plague the body. Still, you kept it from general knowledge. Why?" I asked.

"Perhaps you may think it mean of us to have kept it to ourselves and not shared it," she said sadly. "You must consider, lad, that at that time, if we had placed this before the public, we would have been put to the stake as witches. The tides of superstition were strong in those years just before the goings on at Salem."

"Salem! The witch trials?" Joyce asked incredulously. "She was an adult at the time of the witch burnings at Salem, Massachusetts, and was still alive in 1808?" Joyce was obviously having more trouble believing what she was hearing the more she heard, but her initial mood of resignation had given way to an enthralled interest. "If it is any comfort," John said, "I find all this hard to believe myself. I will say though, and you'll have to agree, much of what we have found out about this Pitus Peston has been corroborated by more than one source."

"I'm trying to keep an open mind about it all." Joyce replied, but there was a latent skepticism in her voice that she could not deny. John shrugged and kept on his reading.

`"When I first met you, you said something that has always stayed in my mind. After you heard my name, you said you hadn't heard the like of it in all your 166 years. Gill told me you were 106, and I would have taken your statement as an amusing miss-speech, but you then made so much fuss over the supposed error that it awakened a suspicion in me. That wasn't a mistake after all!" I then looked straight at her. "How old are you, may I ask? I trust, under the circumstances, you won't think it base of me to inquire."

"I was born in 1638. Joseph was one of the firstlings of Massachusetts Bay. I was getting on toward 40 when I met Joseph. I was living with an aunt on a small plantation on the lower James River. It was an earthly paradise," she said wistfully. "Joseph was a dashing, handsome man down from the north on business, the nature of which I can no longer remember. He saw me in town and circulated word that he found me `interesting'. That's all it took," she laughed. "I was considered a spinster, the prospects of being married at my advanced age almost unheard of. Joseph was nearly sixty when we started courting. Some said we needn't have a long courtship. Time was not on our side. We were in planning of a date when Jo met a man who said he had proof that there were great quantities of silver in the interior. Joseph decided to go with him. He was gone for two years, and when he returned, he came not only without silver, but he had spent the small sum he had saved for our wedding and the purchase of some land for a farmstead. All he had when he returned was that shawl of wampum and a bag of seeds. The desperation he must have felt when his quest for riches failed was probably the main reason he held onto them for the long journey back home. As it turned out, it was a treasure beyond any silver or even gold. I had my first child, William, the next year.'"

"Having a first child at 43 is a bit old, but I suppose, not impossible." Joyce said. "My grandmother had children to the age of 45."

"Given the state of medicine and nutrition of those days, I wouldn't want to do anything medically risky." John replied.

"It wouldn't be you doing the risking." Joyce said wryly. "All the man did then was pace the floor or get drunk. Come to think about it that is one thing that hasn't changed!"

"Point taken," John replied. This was one time he knew that the best long term strategy in debate was to keep his mouth shut.

`"Having a child at my age was considered a remarkable thing. Some who were superstitious thought it even diabolical. Can you imagine that," Gram said indignantly. "A baby's birth a devilish thing? We were watched carefully, and finally, when Able was born in my sixtieth year, we were so tormented with accusations of being in league with the Devil, we had to quit our home in Virginia, and move on. As time went on, it became more and more difficult to keep away suspicion.

When young Washington marched on Fort Duquesne, Joseph was an extremely aged man, though he looked no more than a man in middle life. He took it on himself to go with him. I couldn't convince the old fool to stay home. He told me he had to `help push back the invaders'. What did he get for all his trouble was a cold bed under the stony Kanawha soil.'"

"Then she ended her narrative." said John, looking up from the journal. "After this, Pitus states that she provided him with a supply of this herb in an oiled canvas bag for him to take along on his journey."

`Having done so, she admonished me, "You must not tell anyone of this. I am too old to move again, and if I am found out, it will be to my peril. Even if you tell a little, and vow not to say more, your hearer will press you till you tell enough."

"Surely," I urged, "In these enlightened times, you shall not be harmed, but rewarded for bringing out a thing like this. No one cleaves to the belief in witches and sorcery any more." She would have none of my optimism, but charged me,

"Pledge to me you will safely keep my secret."

"I promise," I assured her, "I will be discreet."

"Now, you must start on your way. Much of this day remains. You should not waste it.'"

"You think that's the plant?" Joyce asked, pointing at the bottle on the table beside John.

"It fits the description by Ordway," he replied, holding the bottle up for her to see.

"I'm going to see if any of these seeds will germinate. If this plant can do what it seems to be able to do from Peston's account, it will make Fleming's discovery of penicillin pale to insignificance. This might even be a cure for HIV!"

"It has been a long time in that bottle, hermetically sealed or not." Joyce ventured. "I wouldn't get my hopes up."

"I read someplace that there were wheat grains taken out of Egyptian tombs that sprouted after being dormant for three millennia. I can't remember where I read it, but I remember I read it. If that is true, two centuries would be child's play!" Joyce sat back in the chair and rested her arm across the back of it. She appeared relaxed, but was anything but. "This is getting a bit big for just us, don't you think," she asked? "Shouldn't we get some experts in on it?"

"The authorities would either confiscate it, or some fast talking hot shot would bamboozle us out of it. We would not even be credited with the discovery." John replied. "No, this is going to be our private adventure of sleuthing the truth."

"Well," Joyce said nervously, "It might be a little late for that."

"What do you mean?"

"I looked into the Union List for the book, and I found an entry for a 'PEREGRINATIONS OF PITUS PESTON' published in 1883. There are two locations listed. One is as you had hoped at the New York State Library at Albany. The other is at the DLC."

"DLC?"

"Library of Congress. DLC is an acronym used in some book checklists. I called on Albany first and they had no records of it in their catalogue. The one I talked with is a friend of mine and she said she would check some more files and get back to me. That didn't sound very promising, so I proceeded to call on DLC." She then raised her eyebrows in an expression akin to having knowledge that the horse was out of the corral.

"Tell me what happened."

"I got some staff librarian who seemed long on procedures and short on brains. I went through the usual business of stating what I wanted to find out. When I named the title, there was silence for a few seconds. Not the usual silence like being placed on hold, but that deafening kind that means trouble. The person then asked me to hold."

"I don't I like the sound of this." said John.

"When she came back on, she simply said it was gone."

"As in stolen?" John interjected.

"That's what I asked." Joyce said. "Then the woman stammered a little like she was flustered, and finally said it wasn't available, but if I would give the name of the interested party, they would be notified directly."

"Do they usually do it that way?" John asked quizzically.

"No, they do not," she declared. "They always deal with the library that made the request. I repeated that the request was being made by the Randall Library in behalf of an individual. The librarian got a bit huffy and replied that she wanted the name and address of the individual who requested it from me."

"What did you say to that?"

"I said that it was all rather irregular and wanted to know why they wanted that information. By now, I had the notion that something was fishy."

"Certainly is," John answered, "Then what?"

"Some man got on the line and demanded to know who it was who wanted the book. I told him to forget it, and I hung up the phone."

"I'll bet they think I stole their damn book!" John said indignantly.

"I never found out if it was stolen or not." Joyce replied, staring blankly ahead. "Then you didn't give my name?"

"Hell no."

"Good!"

"Maybe good and maybe not so good." Joyce warned. "They have *my* name and the name of the Library. I expect I haven't heard the last of this." She slumped down in the chair and sighed.

"I'm sorry that I made trouble."

"Don't be silly." John said assuring. "How could you have known there would be any trouble from a simple inquiry?" He stared off into space, "Maybe nothing more will come of it. Hell, we're not talking about a Picasso. It's just a book, probably worth less than fifty bucks! If they try to cause you or me trouble, I'll write them a check and they can jam it in their ass, for all I care!"

Joyce went home early that evening. John sat with the Peston Journals. Though page after page was full of adventure, John could not help but worry about the librarian who wanted his name: someone who would doubtless help authorities who would come to investigate, search, interrogate; confiscate! At last, he could no longer sit idle while what could be a precious lead time ticked away. John knew a person didn't have to be skilled to break into the house. The back door opened with a skeleton key. All one needed was the will to break in, and plunder the journals, almanacs, and papers, or the mysterious plant in the bottle, the mysterious 'corstet'.

THE ALOVIS CONNECTION

"I wonder how Orban is doing," said Pitus. "I hope he got with somebody who can help and not get thrown in jail."

"I am confident Orban will be successful," said Atoye. "All he has to do is apprize them of what the Haldi are doing and they will instantly see the threat to themselves if not sooner at least later." He peered down the long dark corridor, his headlamp reflecting shiny streams into the distance as it bounced off the polished walls. They came to what looked like a pile of rubble. As they got closer, it took on a more ominous form.

"A skeleton," said Pitus. Atoye bent down to examine the remains. "A late veteran of the Thirty Minutes War," he said. "It looks like a Haldi but it might have been one of ours. It's hard to tell after all this time. There seems to be no wound holes in the clothing. He probably got lost down here in the dark and starved to death." They proceeded along down the hallway. "That way we came in was a secret passage Orban told me about. It put us down in the third level below ground," said Atoye. They ascended a flight of stairs. "This is the second sub-basement," announced Atoye. Before long another body appeared, its desiccated mummy prone across the corridor. "This one is Haldi," said Atoye. Pitus looked at the remains with no small unrest. It was eerie being down in this pitch blackness amid the dead. Pitus kept turning his light behind him as they moved along . . . just in case. Now they began to find more and more corpses. All of them were Haldi and all had brisler burns that appeared to be of lethal power.

"Presuming there was a skirmish here," said Pitus, "Why aren't we finding Omans among the dead?"

"Good question that I can't answer," said Atoye. At a junction of two corridors they halted. "Which way now," asked Pitus?

Atoye trained his light along the floor. He crouched down to take a close look at two sets of foot prints whose paths extended down the side corridor. "Not real fresh, but recent," said Atoye. They stood still a moment listening for any sound. The only noise was the sound of their breathing. "Let's see where these prints go," said Atoye at last. They came upon an open door in the side of the corridor. It appeared to have been forced. A set of metal shelves were lying across the passage. "One of these legs have been burnt off," said Pitus.

"Yes, said Atoye. "It was used as a pry bar to open this door, by the looks of it." They cautiously moved around the door and peered into the room.

"I think I know where Habine came by those books he had in the orbiter," said Atoye. "If Orban sees them he will know his secret vault has been plundered." They entered the room.

"Orban never got to see the books Habine took from here," said Pitus. "I knew they were special, so put them in a storage bin on the Orbiter. Let's see. There was Crolee Zem's translation of the Loma Epic which he probably wanted to determine where the Cube was located. Then there was Hivik's Atlas of Roolandoo which gave the worm holes and temporal rifts in the galaxy in order to get to the Cube at the galactic center. He also had the last three volumes of the Hibber's Izut, which I am guessing he wanted for the details about the Ori Mori who guarded the Cube. There were some more books, but I can't remember what they were about other than the one by Opiter Indel who wrote about the Innovators who created the Cube." He laughed.

"What's so humorous?" asked Atoye.

"All those books are still in the Orbiter," said Pitus. "Orban is flying around space with them practically under his Oman ass!"

"We'll tell him when he gets back," said Atoye.

The walls of the large room were filled floor to ceiling with book shelves, most of which were loaded with old style printed volumes. On several shelves were paper sheets in plastic sleeves containing the rune-like figures that Pitus immediately recognized as Nafrect, the ancient language of Haldan and Calbresan. He lifted one of the sleeves off the shelf and held it up to his light. "I take it these are not reprints," he said.

"Not if they're in here, I'll bet," replied Atoye. Pitus carefully laid it back down where he found it. In the center of the room was a large conference table. The coating of dust on it was disturbed with impressions of the books that were tossed on it during Habine's foraging.

"I shudder to think what would have happened if Habine had successfully opened the Cube," said Pitus.

"Oman would have been finished," said Atoye. "The advanced knowledge he could have extracted from the Cube's database would have made him invincible. His army would have rolled through the galaxy conquering everyone."

"That's what the Cube told us was going to happen," said Pitus. "This means, we screwed up the time line of our future as recorded in the Cube, and the hell of it is that we will never be credited with saving the Milky Way from endless tyranny."

"Living my remaining days in the comfort of a restored Oman will suffice as my reward," said Atoye. He continued moving his light along the shelves. I see the gaps left by Habine's plundering. Orban will be pleased to fill them back in whenever that will be. You know what he told me, Pite? He said he might move to Alovis so he can spend his time in that great library that Claddis deun amassed at the mausoleum complex."

"That sounds like him," said Pitus. "If that's the case, he won't be re-shelving those books here."

Atoye shined his light on an adjoining solid wall of identical looking books. "Pite," he said, "Remember when we first arrived here on Oman and you wondered at the bulk of the printed book form of the Hibber's Izut? Here it is." He panned the five tiers of shelves that were fully thirty feet long. "All this on disc would fit comfortably in your pocket. They both stood awestruck at the history within the room. At last Atoye said, "We have been here long enough. We have to see if there are any stores we can use in the coming fight."

They returned to the junction of corridors and headed forward from the direction that they came. The floor was littered with the bones of soldiers, all apparently Haldi. "I have a theory about all this," said Atoye. "I think someone, probably of high rank in the Haldi forces was looking for that archive. When he found it, possibly by mistake, he wanted to keep the secret to himself."

"You think some Haldi general or something killed his own men to silence them?" asked Pitus incredulously. "Why?"

"A lot of that stuff in there belonged to the Haldi at one time," said Atoye. "The Kinanenses probably stole it. Somebody wanted to preserve that archive in order to find the Cube and for some reason never got back there after the war to retrieve it."

"Habine plundered it and found the Cube," acknowledged Pitus. "What you say may be right. It might even have been a cause of the war in the first place."

"Our finding the Cube and its removal to some unknown place has made all that ancient literature useless except for historic entertainment."

They back tracked the foot prints they found and came to another flight of stairs. "This is going to come out at the Great Hall of the Annex," said Atoye. He gestured for quiet and proceeded cautiously. Another flight of stair laid ahead, the dusty foot prints tracking through the door to them. They ascended the stairs and crept down the hallway to the door at the far end. There was a small reinforced glass window set in the door, which dimly lit the near end of the corridor. Atoye switched off his headlamp and so did Pitus. They peered through the glass at the expansive gallery of the Institute's Annex.

It looked empty so Atoye motioned for Pitus to follow him. He reached for the knob on the metal door when Pitus grabbed his hand. Atoye was about to say something when Pitus pointed excitedly toward the glass. Atoye looked through the window to see someone carrying what looked like a grenade launcher followed by another who bore a heavy crate.

"The Haldi are here already," said Atoye, "and it looks like they are building up an arsenal."

"What can we do to stop them," asked Pitus.

"Nothing at the moment," said Atoye. "We will have to step up our timetable for defense. Let's get out of here." They hurried back down the corridor in the darkness until they reached the door at the end. They snapped on their lights and double-timed it along the path they came. At the third level below ground they halted.

"Where is the passage," asked Pitus.

"We must have over shot it in our haste," said Atoye. He started to retrace his steps, when Pitus called out to him in a hushed voice.

"Hold it, Atoye, I see a light." Atoye whipped out his pistol and hurried back to where Pitus stood. Pitus pointed to a door and then cut his light. "Put out your light," said Pitus. Atoye cut his light. In the pitch blackness, a sliver of neon blue could be seen coming through from under the door.

"Where have you seen something like that before," asked Pitus.

"Alovis B," said Atoye. He remembered the time not long ago when they were chased to the Oman moon, Alovis and stranded at the necropolis there by their nemesis Ickh Habine. Alovis A was the site of the original mausoleum for the Oman dearly departed in continuous service for nearly a thousand years. It was essentially a warehouse for Oman corpses cared for by the Worrik Deuns, a race of sextons who, over the centuries, adapted to the fractional gravity and were no longer able to live on the planet because of this. Alovis B was the new designs for a modern "loved-one friendly" facility complete with visitor amenities to accommodate the relatives of the interred who would make visits to the complex and pay lavish prices for lavish accommodations. The war caused a halt to the construction of the half-finished facility, and even the Worrik Deuns quit the place in search of new viable opportunities on similar planets in the region. When Atoye and Pitus traveled the four thousand miles from Alovis A to Alovis B to look for parts to repair their vehicles, a necessary move to make an escape from the moon possible, they discovered that the unfinished mausoleum was used as a cache for weapons and other materiel.

"When you went through the aperture in that room at Alovis B, you seemed to bear down on the pole we were both holding. Now I see why," said Atoye. "The gravity was three-fold on your end of the pole."

"There's only one way to make certain," said Pitus. He opened the door and they both entered the room. It was a small storage room, little more than a closet and would be unremarkable but for a gleaming electric blue door sized aperture right in the center of the floor. Pitus approached it. "No pole or rope to hold on to, so . . ." He stepped into the rectangle of light. In a moment he came back out. "Just what I thought," said Pitus triumphantly. Alovis B."

ANOTHER PESTON SECRET

"There must be some safe spot for all these papers and books in case someone comes around snooping." John thought. "Maybe I can hide them in the attic." He went up the stairs and stood at the top, giving the room a sweeping glance. He then walked about the floor considering a place under the floor boards. "Naw, it would be obvious that the boards were pried up." He thought of putting them in a wooden box and covering it with lumber. "That's a bad idea for the same reason. Besides, it will be a real pain to get at them when I want them."

He left the attic, and continued on down to the cellar. "Not the greatest environment down here," he said aloud as he sniffed the musty air. "I could get an air tight container; maybe one of those rubber trashcans, and put a false bottom in it. Put some junk on top of the sealed box of books and bingo . . . sounds foolproof."

He decided to look around since he was down there. The late afternoon sunlight coming through the two west facing windows made it bright enough to see rather well. As he walked along the wall, he stroked his hand along it idly, thinking about how he would design his trash-can hiding place. He came to a corner of the wall and followed along the other wall. Ahead was a massive pie cupboard. It was filthy with dust and cobwebs. John approached it and gave it a once over. "Gee, this might clean up to look rather nice," he thought. "It'll be a real bear to get it up those stairs . . . Probably the reason Ken and Freda didn't glom onto it."

He put his hand on it and gave it a shake to test its solidity. "There's a draught coming from this corner." he uttered. "But there's no window anywhere near this spot." He felt around the wooden structure and felt the draught quite strongly near the floor. "There must be a hole or big crack in the wall here: Another damn thing to fix before winter." He looked down at the floor. "Hey, what's this?" He examined the floor stones. "There are arcs scratched into these stones . . . as if the cupboard swung . . ." He quickly stood back up and grabbed the corner of the cupboard. A couple of sharp pulls caused the cupboard to swing out revealing the mouth of what appeared to be a tunnel leading out under the back yard! "Wow! My own secret passage like they have in an old castle!" He placed his foot within the mouth of the tunnel and peered into the light-less hall. "Blacker'n a coal miner's bugger," he said aloud. "I had better get a light. Who knows what the hell's in there!" He ran up the stairs and into the kitchen. At the same time, Joe pulled in the driveway.

"Oh, damn!" John gasped under his breath. "Hell of a time for anyone to show up." He looked out and saw it was Joe. John knew Joseph would revel in an historical discovery like this, especially since it was fresh and yet to be explored. He vacillated between wanting to conceal the discovery, and to show it off to Joe. He was at the door and was about to knock. John thought, "What harm can it do to show him? Besides, if I don't let him see this and he finds out about it, he'll be a long time forgiving me for it." Ere Joe could put his knuckles to wood, the door flew open.

"Jacques, I saw you drive in. Come on down cellar and see something really neat!"

"You got a sauna bath down there full of pretty girls, I'll bet," Joe said flippantly. Joseph made a quick study of John's face as he went for the flashlight in the kitchen. It was clear the excitement showing there was not from a mere pleasant novelty, but from something that held the promise of being truly great.

"You seem so excited that that must be it, or something like it."

"You'll see. Grab that gas lantern and follow me."

The infection of excitement caught Joe instantly. The two jaunted down the stairs in the manner of boys on an adventure. Joe inspected the opening and then extended his hand against the breeze coming through it. He then turned his attention toward the pie cupboard. He grabbed it and pulled. It moved easily as though it traveled on a small wheel. "This pivots on a style anchored into the floor," he remarked with fascination. "Where does this passage go?"

"I don't know." John answered. "I just found it ten minutes ago. I was going for a light when you drove in."

"Come on," Joe said excitedly. "Let's get this lantern lit and see what we've got!"

"What do you think this is all about," asked John. "Could it be something like a storage cave for weapons of something; maybe from the Revolution?"

"It would seem that your house was once part of the so called 'Underground Railroad'. That's my guess," said Joe.

"Fugitive slaves were funneled through here on the way to Canada," asked John?

"That is right on!"

"Let's go see where it ends up," John said. "There should be an opening out behind the house, but I don't ever remember seeing any door or mound out there. "Maybe it was filled in after the war." Joe answered.

"Here, you have the lantern, so you may lead. You can be my shield against anything that might be lurking in there," John said facetiously.

"Thanks a lot," Joe quipped. "I hope a crocodile comes up behind us and bites your ass!"

The two crept forward hunched down to half height, Joe with the lantern held above their heads, John cautiously scanning the walls with the flashlight.

"Keep a lookout for snakes, rats, and bats, Jacques," John said nervously.

"Don't worry, there aren't likely to be any . . . Oh, God! Look out!" Joe yelled as he jumped back. He would have been in danger of trampling on his companion had not John made a two-yard stride backwards on hearing Joe's call of alarm.

"Oh, I guess it was nothing," Joe said. The grin on his face scarcely allowed room for any of his other features.

"You touch-hole," John exclaimed. "You nearly gave me a coronary!" This oath only served to broaden the dimensions of the grin.

They proceeded along the passage and encountered no occupants of any sort in the tunnel.

"This doesn't appear to be lined with stone or anything . . . just shored up with timbers and lined with planks," Joe remarked. "Yet it's pretty dry in here. The wood looks to be in good shape, too."

"One hell of a wine cellar this would make, eh Jacques?"

"Leave it to you to think of that," Joe retorted. "Yes, it would be a beauty!"

At last they came to the end of the tunnel. Light was coming in through a rotted wooden and iron grate.

"We must be a good thirty yards out from the house," Joe said.

"Say, I know where we are," replied John, a tinge of disgust in his tone of voice. He turned the flashlight upwards, and there it was; the underside of the bench seat of a "two-holer".

"It comes out under the 'schmitt-haus', at the edge of my trees in the backyard," John said. "This other opening is the grate where they shoveled out the excess poop." "Well, you know why they did that, don't you," asked Joe? "They put the entrance here to make it unlikely that anyone would snoop around and accidentally find the passage way."

"That means we're not standing in plain old dirt . . . Deez-gusting!" John declared.

"Don't let it bother you. After all these years it is as close to dirt as it can be."

"Yeah, but the out house was likely in use at the same time the tunnel was," John answered.

"One of the prices of freedom," Joe replied. "Crap washes off—iron shackles and manacles didn't come off so easily."

"Manacles go on your wrists, Jacques." John said just to show that he knew something after all.

"Acknowledged," Joe replied. "You don't think they walked through that small grate, do you? I trust you get the point of it all."

"Of course," John said looking at his own hands and silently praising the time of history he was in presently.

"Man, this is a long tunnel. It must have taken a good while to dig this baby." Joe said as he held the light up to see into its depths. "Doubtless meant to hold a goodly number of escaped slaves." He turned to John with an expression of satisfaction.

"I bet the Washington County Historical Society would like a look at this."

"Oh," John said falteringly, "I don't think I would want it to get out about this place."

"Why not, for God's Sake," asked Joe with surprise. "You'd be in the lime light. Probably make the front page of the Post Star!"

"I'd have a whole lot of people tromping all over my place looking around, and a bunch of others bugging me to give them tours of it. I ain't got time for that sort of thing."

"It wouldn't be like that at all, Johnny," Joe assured. "Besides, this is an important piece of our local history. You can't deny the people at least the chance to read about it in the paper."

"Jacques, I want you to promise me you won't blab about this, at least for now."

"Why the hell are you acting this way?"

"Tell me that you won't disclose this. I'm asking you as a friend."

"OK ... OK ..., I won't tell a soul," Joe declared. "But it's under protest." He eyed John askance. "Tell me this much; what's the big deal?" Before John could utter a word, Joe spoke again. "Wait! I know," he said nodding his head. "You think there's something valuable in this tunnel and you don't want people traipsing around and stumbling onto it .... maybe something like ol' Medwyd's gold?"

"Why, that's redic ... absolutely right! Jacques, ya got me," John replied. "Now do you see why I am acting this way?"

"Well, it explains it a little," he said disappointingly. "I'll keep your secret .... on the condition that you tell me if you find anything."

"Gordie, Come in here please," said Simeon Ott over the intercom. In a minute, the butler appeared in the doorway of the study.

"What a fool I am," said Ott. "I've been spending a fortune sending people all over the country looking for a thing that is in a place I have already been."

He picked up one of Lucius Ordway's journals and thumbed through some pages. "Ah, here it is. Listen . . .

'The specimen Pitus gave me in the sealed bottle is like a two edged sword. Though it aided me in locating a cluster that has happily been removed, it serves to show that perhaps others have stumbled onto it. I must find Atoye, if he is still hiding in England, and learn if he remembers any other places where it might be. The pods in the bottle may have to go. For now they are safely hidden in the smokehouse.'

"The tavern in Fort Edward?"

"Right where I got these journals," said Ott. "I will pay the proprietor another visit."

Joyce opened the back door to John's house and walked in. "Anybody home," she called, more as an announcement than as a question. There was no answer, so she went through the kitchen into the dining room. The table that a day before was piled with bottles, books, and loose papers was now clean as a whistle. "His truck is here, so he must be," she uttered; slightly annoyed that he hadn't shown himself. A minute more of silence elapsed and the mild annoyance gave way to uneasiness. Returning to the kitchen, she noticed the door to the cellar way was left open. An assuring sign of the stairway light being on calmed her building apprehension a little. "Johnny," she called from the top of the stairs. There was still no answer. Again she called and silence was the response. There was the imagined sound of something falling onto the floor in the living room. Rather than cause her to think it was John, it engendered an icy alarm to ripple up her spine. She turned slowly to clear the area with the corner of her eye, lest some prowler or other fiendish creature be in the house with her. Though she saw nothing, her fear augmented rather than abated. She turned her eyes back toward the cellar stairs.

"Je-sus!" she screamed. "What the hell are you trying to do; give me a heart attack?" She slumped against the door jamb putting her hands to her face. John quickly came up the stairs and put his arms around her.

"I was afraid you were hurt or something." She said, on the verge of tears from her fright. In a couple of seconds, she calmed down.

"Why didn't you answer me, damn you," she yelled. "You had to have heard me. I called to you three times!"

"Upon my soul, dear, I only heard you call once. I then dropped what I was doing and came running."

"How could you not have heard me," Joyce asked. "I yelled your name loud enough to be heard fifty yards."

"I was way in the back," John said.

"She asked quizzically. "How big *is* your cellar, for Pete's Sake?"

"Real big," John answered smiling. "Bigger than you can imagine. Follow me and I'll show you."

Joyce started down the stairs after John with an expression mixed of bewilderment, skepticism, and curious expectation. "What have you got down here, a secret air-raid bunker?" she asked, glancing back and forth trying to get a preview of whatever it was she was about to see. "Better than that," John exclaimed. He led her along the wall in which the tunnel was sunk such that the cupboard blocked the view of the opening. "Are we going to go into that wardrobe to another world like in the C. S. Lewis book," she asked pointing to the cupboard? "Not quite that good," John replied. Finally, they arrived at the passage. John merely pointed and said, "I ran across this yesterday."

"You were in there when I came in?"

"Yep. Right to the very end."

"What is it, an escape tunnel or something?"

"Now you're getting warm," John replied. "Jacques says it is a 'station' of the Underground Railroad."

"Wow! That's really neat," she said in wonderment. "Is it safe to go in?"

"It's as sturdy as Gibraltar." John declared. "Come with me. I'll show you what I've found."

John led the way and explained what he was doing as she followed along. "There is a pile of dirt and rubbish at the end, most of which dates back to the Civil War, though I now and then find something that is earlier. It's really a blast digging and finding things."

"This is a long tunnel." Joyce observed. "Where are we going to end up?"

"Underneath the old outhouse in the back yard." Joyce came to a halt at this news. "What?" she asked scornfully. "You're taking me under an outdoor john?" She then burst out in laughter. "I'm sorry, Honey, I didn't mean to put it that way!"

"I'll bet!" John replied. They both laughed. When they settled down, he said, "It has been so long that anything down here has turned to soil." Joyce assented to the truth of what John said, but betrayed her real feelings in the careful manner in which she stepped along.

"You know, underneath an outdoor toilet is one of the best places to look for old bottles. It's especially true of old liquor flasks."

"Oh really," Joyce replied skeptically.

"Yes really," John answered. "The ol' man comes out to sneak a little 'nip' now and then where he can be in private and safe from the prying eyes of his temperance society wife. When he kills it off, he throws the empty carcass down the hole!"

"That might also go for the ol' lady, as well," Joyce added facetiously. "Probably more than either of us suspects!"

When they reached the grate at the end of the passage, John showed Joyce some of his trophies. "Here is a nice, honey amber pint flask." He tipped up the bottom and pointed. "That is what is called the *pontil mark*. That means that it was made before the Civil War, most likely."

"You don't have to tell me what that is." Joyce replied. "I learned all about that when I went to Sturbridge Village and saw the glass workers make bottles and drinking glasses."

"Then you must also know that pontilled bottles are usually worth a good deal of money."

"Some are. Especially the mold-blown embossed ones," Joyce said. "Bitters bottles, whiskeys made from odd colored glass, and cobalt blue bottles are usually worth a lot. Now, if you could find an historical flask . . ."

"Like this," John said? He held up a bluish-tinged half-pint sized example of this early nineteenth century designer booze bottle. Joyce shrieked with delight at the sight of it. The outline of it refracted the light from the lantern and glowed with a hypnotizing aqua sparkle. The glass was full of bubbles and the surface was thoroughly whittle-marked. She took it into her hands and feverishly examined it.

"No dings or cracks . . . It's perfect!"

"Gee," John remarked, you're really turned on by that thing, aren't you?"

"I used to dig for old bottles when I was a young girl," she said excitedly. I researched the old town plat maps and atlases to find the locations of the early dumps. I dug a lot of places dreaming of finding a beauty like this." She laughed, "I guess I should have looked at a few 'crappers'." She then handed the flask back to john. John could plainly see the pleasure it gave Joyce just to look at it.

"You may have it if you like."

"You're kidding! This is worth probably five-hundred bucks, you realize." John took her left hand and held it up. In his other hand, he held the flask. He then slipped the neck of the bottle over her ring finger.

"This means we're going steady," he said whimsically. His facial expression then turned more thoughtful. "Please take it. It would please me to please you as much as it appears to do."

"I accept." she said, as she clutched the valuable object. She then, slipped her free hand around his waist and drew him to her. She kissed him softly and then embraced him, whispering in his ear, "Maybe we could let all this go for a while."

The town of Nesgoor is situated sixty miles to the north of Kesst. It is a beautiful place, even though it was showing signs of neglect since the Oman war severely hindered the commerce of renewal and repair. There was no practicing plumber in the town, for example. Skilled craftsmen such as this or carpenters or mechanics could be found in Baluge, a former mining town three hundred miles to the east, but when they came they were punishingly expensive. These skilled laborers could make much more running black marketing operations dealing in nearly everything, now that nearly everything was scarce, so doing "regular work" was less desirable.

Nesgoor was also the home of Kinar's parents, Albeck, now deceased, and Drolanee, his mother, who still lived in the small mansion near the center of town. Kinar was one of the travelers along with Atoye who escaped Oman centuries ago, pursued by the Oman army because of an alleged theft of military grade drive programs Atoye loaded into his ship to give it more "kondec", as Atoye said, which is the Omanee equivalent of "zing."

When he and Pitus first returned to Oman some months ago, before Habine and the quest for Loma's Cube impinged on their visit, they bore the heartbreaking news that Kinar had died on Earth from smallpox. When it was later discovered that Kinar survived, Atoye and Pitus, along with Orban returned to Earth to rescue him. When the four of them returned from Earth, they made plans to break this news to her. To prevent a possible fatal shock of Kinar showing up suddenly in person, Atoye and Pitus paid her a visit to ease her into the realization that she would again see her son alive and well.

Drolanee's first reaction on seeing Kinar was to slap him, unloading all her grief, then as quickly, grabbed him and clutched him in an earnest tearful embrace. When this emotional reunion was over, they all sat down to discuss the impending trouble in store for Oman by the Haldi force assembling at Jartic Orz and at Kesst. It was decided Orban would go to Calbresan to make contact with Pire Al Linka, former ambassador to Oman to elicit aid from the Calbres. Atoye and Pitus traveled to Kesst by way of the cover of Cavin Gorse, that savage tropical subcontinent uninhabitable by friend or foe in order to protect their precious ship from falling into enemy hands.

A LEGEND DIES

It was Saturday, and John was off work, but Joyce had to pull 'desk duty' till five o'clock. He had been busy all that morning on a project and by lunch time, he had finished.

"There," John said. "That ought to hold my evidence safe and dry." He stood before a large wooden tool chest, in which he installed a heavy tin box. The inner metal box was lined with cloth bags filled with silica gel to ensure it to be moisture proof. "Down in this tunnel no one will find them," John thought. "Now that this is done, I can get back to a normal life of scholarly research," he laughed. He left the passage and closed the "door" in the cellar wall. "Actually," he thought, "it has been more than a week since Joyce made that call to Washington. Maybe the trouble I thought would come has all blown over."

When John reached the kitchen, he decided to brew a pot of coffee. He looked out the window and noticed that the earlier clear sky had become overcast. It was now becoming blustery and chilly. "Looks like a storm is coming," he thought. John made a sandwich and some soup for lunch. He was thinking about what he was going to do with the afternoon. The coffee pot sat on a counter next to the cellar stairs. He went to it for a cup to go with his lunch. As he stood by the cellar stairs, a blast of chill air rolled up into the kitchen. "Yipes," he shuddered, "That draught has to be coming from that hole in the wall down there. That tunnel will likely send me to the poorhouse this winter if I don't block it up." He returned to the table and sat down. "Great," he said scornfully. "I wanted so much to do some house fixing today!" He finished his lunch and moved over to the coffee pot for another cup. He stood at the top of the stairs sipping the coffee, trying to get up the ambition to either do the job or decide to say "to hell with it". Virtue triumphed over the curse. He slowly descended the stairs, all the while trying to figure out how he was going to do whatever needed be done.

He thought of several possible solutions that ranged from bricking up the hole in the cellar wall, to filling in the end of the tunnel beneath the outdoor "necessary". The idea of impairing the access to the tunnel from either end was unsatisfactory to John. He dreaded doing anything to it, but decided to frame a doorway at the far end of passage, a couple of yards back from the outhouse grate. The requisite lumber John found in the attic. There was even a solid hemlock door up there that he could use, keeping the cost of materials at zero.

He brought the lumber down cellar and set up a work place just outside the entrance of the tunnel. He found the job of framing a door to be not as hard as he thought. When he had completed the frame and hung the door, he stood back to have a look at it. "Not bad if I must say so myself," he said triumphantly. At that he pulled the half-open door back and gave it a ginger push to see how it fit. The door slammed in the frame with a loud bang. After the loud sound, the silence seemed augmented. John reached for the door to try it again.

"What the hell was that," he said aloud? He rapped with his knuckles on one of the wall planks. The sound repeated itself. There was no mistaking it. There is no other sound quite like the jingling of a coin falling. John then slapped the wall. There was no metallic answer this time. He rapped the board above it. This time there was a trickling that lasted five seconds. John ran out of the tunnel into the cellar and returned with a crowbar. He choked up on it like one would a baseball bat and started to swing it, but regained control of his wits. "No need going at it like a maniac." he said aloud. He could feel his throat tighten and his heart felt to be beating just below his collar bone. "Medwyd's gold! It has to be!" John thought. "What an ass I will feel like if this turns out to be a bunch of loose nails falling behind the boards!" He slowly pried the bottom board loose. When he pulled it away there was nothing. "Oh, hell," he called out chiding himself. "There's not even the old nail!"

Disappointed, John placed the board back into position and commenced nailing it back to the wall frame. The blows of the hammer caused similar "coin-like" noises behind the boards, harpies of failed expectations rushing to pick at his frustrated hopes. He finished replacing the board and started to raise himself off his knees. At eye level in one of the gaps between the planks was the round edge of a coin! John reached for it and flipped it out with his finger onto the palm of his hand.

"A half-eagle; Five dollars gold!" His heart returned to its 'northern home', but beating double its former pace. John flipped the coin over. "1827. It is certainly old enough," he murmured. "It's not a legend after all; it's fact!" He returned to the use of the crowbar, and though recharged with zeal, he maintained the presence of mind to avoid bruising the boards that they may be replaced without appearing disturbed. This time he started at the bottom and continued removing the boards upwards from the floor. When he removed the third board, he found six more gold coins and two copper cents. When he removed the sixth board a shower poured forth from a rusted tin box just behind it.

John began laughing uncontrollably in his joy. He wiped the water from his eyes and swallowed. He fetched a large plastic bag from the cellar and carefully collected the hoard. "There's got to be thousands of bucks here," he gasped. "Medwyd Peston, God bless your soul!"

Much was in the form of gold, but there was a lot of silver also, and copper cents and half cents. Some of the gold appeared to be foreign, but silver is silver and gold is gold no matter where it comes from. When he got the bag upstairs, he drew all the kitchen blinds. There was also a window in the hall that gave a line of sight to the kitchen table. This blind he also drew. As he was pulling down the last blind it occurred to him that his good fortune also brought with it a price of its own. "This, for all its goodness, is but another thing to fret over; like the journals." John said. "I'd better get this all to the bank, after I see what is here."

Having secured the kitchen from potentially prying eyes, he got a small basin and half filled it with warm water. "This is the first time in my born days I ever had money to wash." It was, however, a labor that tired him not! John didn't know the value of some of the foreign gold. He found a conversion table, in of all places, the old almanacs. He placed the coins in stacks by denomination and added it all up when he was done:

Gold	$950.00 approx
Silver	192.25
Copper	8.48 1/2
Total	$1150.73 1/2

"That's just the face value." I must find out the true value. This has got to be worth a fortune!" He rubbed his hands. "Wait till Joyce sees . . ." John stopped in mid sentence. An icy hoar frost of avarice came over him and clung to him as old cobwebs. "One of the neatest things to ever happen to me, and something tells me I shouldn't share it with a soul." He pondered what he should do with the coins. If I take them to a reputable coin dealer, I will have to tell where I got them. It is doubtful that the actual truth would be believed. Still, if I tell, it might get out that I found Medwyd's gold and the claimants would line up as far as the street with Ken and Freda at the head of the line! I will get a safe deposit box at the bank and keep it and my mouth shut," he decided.

COLCHESTER 1933

The Holloway Institute endured the passage of time and Mr. Rowland, now Edgar Rawlings, applied for his old position in acquisitions. His resume, necessarily truncated, was enough to land the position easily. He was now a Ph. D. in both American and English literature. He was given an office, and upon entering it, was delighted with the familiarity of it. He pulled the upholstered office chair out from under the desk and sat down in it. The metal chair creaked as Rawlings shifted in it looking around the room. Then, to his delight he spied his old friend.

"So, you are still here," he said softly. He turned to his right and placed his hand on the arm of the Jacobean chair pushed up against the corner of the room, its ornately carved back a thing of intricate beauty, almost completely obscured by an oak filing cabinet sitting on its plank seat. It looked as though this makeshift arrangement for the files of his predecessor was made years ago. Indeed, it was probably the reason the chair was still here hidden in plain sight because the seventeenth century piece was probably worth a thousand pounds sterling. Edgar's chafe at the former occupant's apparent disregard of such a treasure gave way to admiration of his sagacity. "I'll bet you were spoiling for a time you could sneak this out of here," Edgar murmured. "Too bad a heart attack foiled your plan." He got up and wheeled the cushioned office chair out of the way and cleared the debris off his old friend, restoring it to its former place of honor behind the desk. The hard plank seat was actually more comfortable to sit in than the modern cushioned one, the plank bottom expertly carved to perfectly fit three centuries of academic asses. His own rested in it once during the American Revolution. Now in this time just before another war would start up he was in it again.

Edgar nestled into the ancient seat and mused. His thoughts receded to distant times. He recalled his native land and his long exile from it. He thought of his youth and once again longed to hike up into the green hills of Puva. Where were his kinsmen? Why, after all this time hadn't someone from the old country come to take him back home? His reverie was cut short by a knock at his office door.

"Mr. Rawlings," asked a young man. "I am Steve Armstrong, your administrative assistant."

"Come in, Steve," said Edgar cordially. He stood and extended his hand in greeting. Armstrong was about 5 foot nine, with sandy blond hair and blue eyes, set narrowly over his roman nose. His complexion was tan, from spending long hours in the sun, which could be construed by his athletic build. He was academic by day and sportsman otherwise. Rawlings was just over six feet with a Middle Eastern look, dark brown eyes wide set above a broad nose and mouth to match. His hair was brown, of medium length, with the beginning of salt and pepper throughout. His build was solid; not someone to piss off in an alley.

"I'm pleased to meet you Mr. Rawlings. I hope we may work well together."

"Just call me Edgar or Ed," said Rawlings, "and I'm sure we will work fine together."

"Well then, Ed, I have something for you," said Steve. "There are some diaries."

"Diaries," said Ed? "Anyone we know?"

"The author is unknown."

"Then why would that interest the Institute rather than some used book shop?"

"They are a bit puzzling," said Steve. "Perhaps you should see them."

"Puzzling? How so?"

"They span two centuries but appear to be from the same hand. I don't know how that could be, but Jacobs analyzed the handwriting and he declares them to be authentic and from the same hand."

"Curious," said Ed.

"There is something else," said Steve. "The subject matter is unusual." By now the two men were heading toward the conservator's office which was in the far end of the building and down in the basement.

"You have my interest piqued," said Ed. "What else can you tell me?"

"There are names mentioned that are strange; names the like of which none of us have encountered before. Also, some passages are in an unknown language."

"Still more curious," said Rawlings, cracking a smile. "How often had he listened to a build up of the goods like this, only to find some quirky unknown with an amateur flair for a story?" He enjoyed the temporary excitement of anticipation and allowed himself to be sucked into it. "Go on," urged Ed.

"One of the place names is Haldan and one of the personal names is someone named Calnoon." Rawlings froze in mid step. He stared at Armstrong who said, "The names don't refer to any classical Greek or Latin that any of us can think of . . ."

Ed quickened his pace. Steve had to almost run to keep up.

"Do these names mean anything to you," asked Steve. "Apparently the answer is yes," he murmured. He rushed down the stairs after Rawlings. Steve caught up with Ed as he burst into the conservator's workshop. The restorer, Michael Doane had apparently stepped out of the room, but on the work table sat an eight inch stack of octavos in full calf and variously edge worn. There were seven books in all. He quickly picked the top volume off the pile and opened it. After a brief look, he put it back on top of the stack.

"I wish to examine these personally," said Edgar.

"Mr. Doane hasn't finished collating and accessioning them," said Steve.

"Doane can have them back after I have done a preliminary examination."

"Are they rare," asked Steve?

"Who found them and where did they come from," asked Edgar.

"I found them in a second-hand book store in London on Fleet Street."

"Are you familiar with the names, asked Steve?" Rawlings seemed preoccupied.

"Mr. Rawlings?"

"The names," Rawlings repeated absentmindedly. He came back to the present. "I am not certain," said Edgar. "I will have to consult some reference sources first." He picked up the diaries. "Please tell Mr. Doane, I have them and will return them to him shortly. I wish to assess their literary significance before committing the funds for restoration." He started to leave and looked back at Armstrong. "You said you bought them?"

"Yes sir," replied Steve.

"How much?"

"Twenty pounds." Rawlings pulled his billfold from his inner suit pocket. He handed Steve a bill.

"Fifty quid?' he exclaimed. "That's far more . . ."

"Rawlings stopped him. "I'll get that much fun out of translating them, to be sure."

"Blimey, sir, thank you," Steve said, and pocketed the money.

"I will be in my office the whole day," said Edgar. "Please clear my schedule. I wish not to be disturbed." He hurried out of the shop and back to his office. He shut the door and smiled with acquisitive delight. Then he said softly, "The reason none of you recognize the names is because they are not part of Earth's history. But *I* know." He sat in his old chair and pulled the stack of volumes to him. "Kinar's journals," he breathed.

JOHN LETS JOYCE IN ON THE SECRET

Joyce came to the house and found John peeking out through a window curtain. "Do you see them," she asked.

"Yes. Who are they, as if I couldn't guess?"

"They are likely from the FBI," Joyce said. They came to the library today and questioned me. They said I would go to prison if I didn't give them your name!"

"What did you do?"

"I gave your name," she said blankly. "They wanted the book that was stolen from the Library of Congress, and if I had it to surrender it. I told them I didn't have it, and if I did, had they thought me so stupid as to call the DLC and ask them if it was there."

"Did they get rough with you?"

"No. They barked, but couldn't really bite with the rest of the people around in the library. I think the logic of my last statement threw them a little. They stopped asking me if I had it, and switched to whether you had it or not."

"What did they ask you about me?" John asked nervously.

"You didn't tell them about any other of the things I had relating to Pitus."

"I was careful to answer only what they precisely asked. I never volunteer anything. Remember that when they get around to question you."

"What did they ask you?"

"They asked if I knew whether you had it or not. I said I didn't know absolutely, but since you were the one who asked me to check around for the book, I thought it safe to conclude that you did not have it, either."

"Seems like a dumb question." John said, still keeping his vigil at the window.

"Exactly what I thought," said Joyce.

"The way they ask questions in the beginning must be by a particular procedure they have to follow."

"What do you mean by that," John asked.

"The first questions they asked me, were so asinine, don't you think?"

"Dumb like foxes, probably," John replied.

"There was one guy named Dolph, who did most of the questioning. He is a thirty-ish, sandy haired, heavy set man. He obviously liked to throw his weight around, if you'll pardon the pun, but I think the other guy who was thin and Latin-featured was the real boss. You can tell generally who the boss is in those types. It is usually the one who keeps still." She looked at John and read the worry on his face.

"There were three other questions that they asked me, and when they found I didn't know anything about them, they clammed up and dropped me like a hot potato."

"What did they ask about?"

"Weird questions" she said shaking her head. "They asked me if I believed in intelligent life on other planets, to which I answered that I didn't know."

"What else?" John asked.

"This was off the wall," Joyce said in a tone of bewilderment. "They asked me if I had ever heard of an Indian named Kawa Hinga."

"Kawa Hinga!" John exclaimed. He then quickly composed himself, and turned toward the window, peering out once more. "They've gone," he said. "I hope they don't come back." He then turned to Joyce. John made no further comment about the Indian name. He was not sure whether to let her in on the specifics of its relevance. In his expression, he was communicating with her in spite of himself.

"There was a third question," John finally asked?

"Yes," Joyce replied. Her tone of voice changed from one of bewilderment to probing skeptical scrutiny. "This was the most obscure of all. They wanted to know if I had ever heard the term, OOO." John flinched. Joyce looked at him critically.

"OOO," she repeated slowly and firmly.

"I heard you."

"I know you did." she said. "It has no meaning to me, but it clearly does to you."

"Is it that obvious?"

"You're as opaque as cellophane."

"Would you like to take a ride?" John asked motioning as though the house was not a safe place to talk.

"Sounds nice," she replied louder than conversationally as an affront to the believed eaves droppers about the house. They left the house and John reached for the door of the truck to let Joyce in.

"Let's take a walk," she suggested.

"The truck, too," John asked astonished.

"Let's just say that I would do it if I were them."

They strolled along the River Road south along the edge of the Hudson.

"Update me." Joyce said.

"O.K," John replied. "I have finished the four volumes of Peston's Journals, and quite a story it is," he exclaimed.

"After Peston left Gram's he went out to Niagara Falls and then down to the town of Olean where he wintered until the Allegheny River reopened in the spring."

"By now he is on his trip to New Orleans," Joyce interjected.

"Yes. He traveled to Pittsburgh, where he met the botanist John Bradbury. He said he regretted parting company with such a 'capital fellow', but John's business lay to the north in the Wabash and Miami River valleys, and his own destination was Lake Pontchartrain in Louisiana. He traveled to Natchez, Mississippi on a freighter and there met a Frenchman by the name of Andre Benoit. Pitus continued on down the Mississippi with this Benoit fellow as his guide and later penetrated the uplands of the northern rim of the lake. There he found one of the last surviving Biloxi settlements. He showed an old sachem in the village his bead work sash, but the old man could tell him nothing about it. The sachem did, however, show Pitus a carved stone pillar that had a glass-like wedge embedded in the top of it. He didn't know it at the time, but the wedge was a direction indicator that pointed in the direction of OOO."

"What *IS* OOO," Joyce asked impatiently?

"It is, or rather, was the abode of the Gods of Oman," John answered. "Now, I know that doesn't tell much, but let me tell you the rest of it in capsule form."

"All right," Joyce agreed. "Just make it a small capsule, the better for me to swallow," she added facetiously.

"Somewhere down south he learned of another pillar supposedly located up in the Dakota Territory. He went to St. Louis and stayed there for two years, working as a printer, during which time, he explored the area as far as he dared by himself. Later, he went on a hunting trip with some trappers to the vicinity of the Osage Indian villages. He met an ancient shaman who not only confirmed the existence of the second pillar, but told him about seeing the gods in person, especially one named Calnoon. The old Osage man, who was named Kawa Hinga, which means 'the great old one', said he was the maker of the sash some 130 years before. He also told Pitus that he traded it off to a white man named Jo."

"Joseph Dutton, Gram's husband!" Joyce exclaimed.

"Precisely," John said. "The shaman also said that he gave away all that he had left of a plant that made men live forever. It was supposedly a gift of this Calnoon."

"The herb that Gram had; Gosh, that was stupid of him to do that!" she exclaimed. "Why would he do such a thing?"

"Calnoon was apparently still around at the time. Kawa Hinga expected to be able to replenish his supply when he and Calnoon next met. Unfortunately, it never happened. Some plot so far, is it not?" John said with animation.

"After this meeting with the Osage man, he returned to St. Louis awaiting an expedition into the northern Missouri so he could join it and have safe passage to the other pillar. This comes when Manuel Lisa pursued the expedition led by Wilson P. Hunt, who was trying to clear the Missouri for the fur trade and establish an overland trade route to the settlement of Astoria on the Pacific shore."

"Astoria is the title of a book by Washington Irving," remarked Joyce. "I will read it to see if there are any references to Peston in it."

"That is unlikely," said John. "He was a common oarsman and an interpreter for Lisa, and that's all."

"Still worth a look," said Joyce. "So . . ."

"Anyway, Lisa caught up with Hunt at the Aricara Indian settlements in what is now North Dakota. These were friendly Indians. This was also near the land of other Siouan tribes like the Crow and Blackfeet, who were hostile to white men. Pitus learned that he passed the pillar about 600 miles back down river. He tried to get released from Lisa's expedition, but Lisa wouldn't let him go. Then, while on a hunt for game to replenish the meat supply, he got caught by the Sioux. He escaped from them and went back down to the pillar on his own. When he found it, he sighted in the Oman home base by triangulation on a map of Zebulon Pike's that he copied. It was off Pike's map into unknown Spanish territory. He wintered in Santa Fe, and in the spring, headed to what appears to be Monument Valley in Arizona."

"He started a systematic search of the area for clues to the location of 000. He wandered around for weeks, but found nothing. Finally he saw a flash come from the base of a butte and found it to be caused by a reflection from a man-made object. On the top of that butte he believed he'd find the 'abode of the Gods of Oman'."

"Monument Valley is a big place," Joyce remarked. "I went there with my parents when I was a kid back in the nineties. There are hundreds of square miles of buttes and mesas out there. Did Pitus give any clue that would narrow down the possibilities?"

"I didn't see much from reading the journal," John shrugged. "I may find something with a second look."

"What did he find there?" Joyce asked.

"I don't know. The volume four ends with the discovery at the base of the butte. It doesn't even tell what the so called man made object was."

"Then what do you think?" Joyce asked.

"Maybe he found some ruins of some ancient culture; who knows?" John said sullenly. "I know only that the closer I seem to get to my destination, the farther it seems to actually be from me."

"Kind of like the idea that the more I learn the more I realize how ignorant I am." Joyce said.

By now the two were a half mile down the road. "We'd better get back," John said. "It will be dark soon."

On the way home John spoke of other things; the calm and glassy surface of the river; how it looked like a dark blue chasm that one could dive into and fall endlessly. The musky smells of the late summer weeds growing along the river bank filled the air with their essences. John glanced at Joyce as she was looking out across the river. The beautiful outline of her face and hair became with this smell that was all around, an indelible mark of delight upon his heart. For all the pleasantness of this experience, in his mind, ground the grist of uncertainty.

"There's another thing that concerns me," John said at last.

"Which is?"

"The Feds will be at my door real soon with a search warrant."

"What do you care? You don't have the book," Joyce remarked.

"No, but the warrant could read to include any related materials or a kind of material that could be interpreted loosely enough to include the journals and everything else."

"I don't think they can make out a warrant as vague as that." Joyce assured.

"Even so, these guys could grab anything they wanted and swear it never existed," said John.

"You're letting your imagination run a bit, aren't you, honey?" Joyce said with an exaggerated sweetness meant to calm John's fears.

"Maybe yes; maybe no," John replied. "I intend to take no chances."

They entered the house as it was getting dark. Joyce started to reach for the kitchen light.

"Don't turn it on just yet," John asked in a hushed voice. "Wait here a minute." He walked carefully into the living room. There he turned the television on, putting the volume up rather high. He then returned to the kitchen.

"I have a little job to do," John said. "Come with me to the cellar," he ordered in a mimic of Boris Karloff.

"All right, Master," she answered similarly. "Just don't wall me in down there," she laughed. After pulling open the cupboard they both entered the tunnel. John led the way and stopped at the spot where the gold was found.

"Here, hold the light on those boards, if you please." He carefully pried one of the boards off the wall and set it down.

"How did you know there was a hole behind that board," asked Joyce.

"I must be smart, I guess," said John.

"Not *THAT* smart," she retorted. She stood there staring while he removed the next board down. "I can feel the radiation from your eyes burning my nape!" John quipped. "I'll tell you about it in a minute. Hand me the journals and the other papers, please."

"Aren't they upstairs?"

"They're in that wooden box." John said pointing toward the floor beside her. "That's a hell of a place to keep books; in a wooden box in a dank cave!"

"They are in a reseal-able plastic bag with silica gel to keep off the moisture," said John. "Hostile environment or not, they have to spend some time behind this wall or risk being confiscated!"

The bag fit tightly into the opening. Joyce held it in place while John prepared the boards by rubbing the pried ends in the dirt.

"Clever," Joyce remarked.

"So are they, probably," John replied.

After the boards were replaced, he smeared the whole area with grime from the floor using an old floor mop.

"That will have to pass for being undisturbed for a hundred years." They left the passage way and closed the cupboard. Joyce swept dirt over the scratches the 'swinging door' made on the cellar floor.

"You catch on fast!" John exclaimed.

"I can be a devilish girl when I want to."

"We may need it," John replied.

On the way up the stairs to the kitchen, Joyce repeated her question.

"So, how DID you know about that recess behind the boards? What I really mean is what did you find back there that you obviously removed to leave that hole?"

"You want to see what I found in that hole, just come with me in the living room." When the two reached the spot, John grabbed the large mantle clock that was setting on top of the television. He kept the lights off and went with the clock and his companion to the kitchen.

"Draw the shades first?" Joyce asked as though she already knew that what was coming should be kept secret.

"Yes," John answered. While she was so doing, John set the clock on the kitchen table. The sound it made when it contacted the table told of a greater than expected heft. "Now you can snap on the light," John said.

"Heavy, for a wooden clock," Joyce remarked.

"My dear, you have no idea," he replied.

"Well, I see a mantle clock that I know wasn't in the hole," she said facetiously.

"Patience, my dear," John said, turning the clock around to get at the back of it. He opened the back where the works usually showed, but instead, a mini flood of coins gushed out. Joyce gasped with excitement as the precious river flowed. When it ceased, John picked the clock up and tipped it over the pile made on the table, increasing its size by half again.

"There's $1150.73 and 1/2 cents there in face value. According to the latest 'Red Book', it is worth a whole lot more than that." He stood up straight and extended his hand toward the pile. "This is Medwyd's Gold!"

"A legend has died and a rich man born!" Joyce announced gleefully. John's triumphant smile then faded away.

"What's the matter," she asked. "Did you hear someone sneaking around outside?"

"No." John replied. "I'm just perplexed in the midst of my joy."

"What is the problem? I don't understand," she asked impatiently.

"Where can I go with these gold and rare coins and not be asked where I got them?"

"Probably nowhere," replied Joyce.

"It is like finding a Van Gogh in your attic. Once you try to capitalize on your good fortune, everyone in the world finds out." John said mournfully.

"So what," said Joyce? "You found it. It wasn't stolen. What's the big deal?"

"Ken."

"Your brother?"

"Yes indeed," John replied. "He owns the property, and knowing him, he would have both hands out, and I don't mean for a share or for half. No, he would claim it all by virtue of prior ownership!"

"You could fight him in court."

"Then the lawyers would get it instead of Ken; same result to me!"

"Maybe you can find a private buyer." Joyce suggested, "Someone who wouldn't ask questions and who wouldn't draw suspicion from others."

"Does anybody come to mind," asked John?

"I doubt there is anyone in Glens Falls who could lay out that kind of cash, and not have it all over town before you get home with it."

"I'll have to find someone else somehow," said John.

Dan Henning, as he now called himself, entered the United States with a skillfully counterfeited passport back in 1989 and slowly insinuated his way into the heart of the FBI From this vantage point he was able, with the blessings of the agency to infiltrate the inner sancta of their vast investigative data bases. Eventually, with the internet, he had at his disposal the whole world for a searching ground.

When the Peregrinations were discovered by virtue of their theft from the Library of Congress, the specter of an old nemesis reared its head. If what he was reading from the interoffice traffic was true, it could spell his release from his long exile. Did this book written by Peston a hundred and thirty-six years ago, really hold the key to his liberation? He felt he must have this book at any cost of sweat or blood. "Blood," he thought. "How gratifying if the blood could be that of Peston himself. In the offshore banks he had hidden tens of millions, enough to finance the building of a ship to take him off this backward rock and to his long lost home. The book, according to the classified memos he intercepted, held clues to the necessary power system for a ship that could cross the galaxy.

The surfacing of the Peregrinations was perhaps propitious. Maybe someone had returned. He had to find out. He took on the case to recover the stolen government property, the book, the memoir of his arch-adversary. At first he met resistance from the agency. They felt it was a case worthy of local law enforcement. In order to get this opinion changed, he had to let leak information that the book had strategic content. He was then put in charge of tracking down the book before it fell into hostile hands. Meanwhile, he monitored Interpol, the CIA, NASA, and even SETI, searching for clues of an outside visitation. He learned the truth about Area 51; that it was a hoax, but he kept his vigil. It was now late spring in 2019, and though he could have had no idea of it, payday was fast approaching.

THE OMANS MOBILIZE

"Orban," asked Atoye, "Were you successful with the Calbres? How much help and when can we expect it?"

"It was a waste of time," said Orban dourly. "They have not changed their stance since the war. They are determined to remain neutral."

"Neutral!" exclaimed Atoye. "Nobody is going to be neutral once the Haldi get on the move. Aldit Horruma, what are they thinking?" He looked up from Orban and saw Drolanee standing in the threshold of the doorway. He quickly apologized for swearing in her house.

"Maybe the Qetterans will help. I will go to Qetterxilict," said Orban.

"You can't go there," said Atoye. "You'll end up in Beljeaun. We are still wanted by their immigration."

"The risk is worth it," said Orban. "There is much more at stake than my freedom or my life."

"Let's hope it does not come to that," said Atoye. "You are of inestimable value here."

"I spread the word around Nesgoor," said Kinar. "I found some of my old friends who want to help."

"We will need more than some," said Atoye.

"I spoke to the right *some*," replied Kinar, "By now a hundred know about it. By tomorrow, who knows? I expect to hear from Gastin Lenar Biet later this evening. You remember him? He was once a colonel in the army. He said he is itching to get back at 'those Haldi bastards'. We will have both fighting men and women in short order. The question is, what will they have to fight with?"

"I can answer that," said Pitus. "Alovis B. There are enough weapons there for our army."

"That's a long way from here," said Kinar.

"Yes, but we know a short cut," Pitus replied nodding at Atoye. He explained what he and Atoye found at the unfinished mausoleum and the aperture in the complex and its open connection under the Institute.

"That stuff has been sitting there for a long time," said Kinar. "We will need to get a few people who know how to get it working properly."

"There are Haldi at the Institute already," warned Atoye. "They obviously don't know what we know."

"We will have to act fast to keep that so," said Orban. He turned to Atoye and Pitus. "When we were being chased around the galaxy by Habine, I noticed that he never used a luso stone transport against us. I do not think he has the old technology."

"Come to think about it . . . ," mused Atoye. "That makes the Duster and our amulets priceless strategic weapons. "I'm glad you fixed that thing, Pite," said Atoye.

"Kinar," asked Orban, "Can you get in touch with Colonel Gastin and have him pick a few good omans to guard and assess the cache?" Kinar stood up. "I'll be back in a half hour with him and anyone we can scare up."

In the mean time, Atoye and Pitus prepared to trans back to the Duster at Cavin Gorse. "It is night there," said Atoye, "the time when the worst of the predators come out of lair and hole and slough in order to recycle some protein."

"Want me to go first," asked Pitus. He knew Atoye had previously set the return coordinates for the middle of the bridge of the carefully sealed ship. An error of a thousandth of a percent from a vector as large as theirs would translate into some yards one way or the other and if that put him even 6 inches outside the ship he would be probably doomed. But Pitus knew Atoye, and when the stakes were high, he never failed to come through.

"You flatter by your trust," said Atoye, "but if you do end up outside the ship, the light from the aperture will attract every monster within a hundred yards, and some of them are fast."

"We can't do anything here," declared Pitus. He keyed the amulet and stepped through. Atoye came through right on his heels casting his fate to the wind. Fortunately, Atoye was worthy of Pitus's trust. They stepped into the center of the Duster's bridge. Atoye fine tuned the Duster's transport to open into the sub-basement of the Annex. He had Pitus test it. "I expect you to end up in that long corridor on level three very near the door to the secret entrance. I took a reading there and loaded it into the computer.

"We will know in a second or two," said Pitus. He keyed his amulet and stepped through the rectangle of light and off the bridge of Atoye's ship. Atoye stood facing the center of the bridge, watchful, the seconds ticking away seemingly in slow motion. "Where the hell is he," Atoye grumbled. Then his impatience converted to fear. "I hope I didn't put him in some unknown spot in those endless galleries down there. If he gets disoriented . . ." Another several seconds passed. The tension was rising into the red zone in his brain. He reached for his own amulet just as the aperture opened and Pitus stepped back out.

"Another second and we would have crossed paths," said Atoye. "I feared you got lost."

"No problems with the passage," said Pitus. 'It comes out about ten paces past the room we want. The lack of footprints where I emerged got me nervous, but I luckily headed in the right direction and found familiar ground."

"I checked my figures," said Atoye. "They seem right." He pursed his lips. "We had better not take big chances like we did coming here to the ship," added Atoye.

"I don't think there is anything wrong with either you or the trans," said Pitus. "The other aperture probably affected ours." Atoye nodded agreement to the plausible explanation. Nevertheless, he filed the fact in his head. "Let's go back to Drolanee's," said Atoye. "Kinar should be back with Gastin soon." He started to key the amulet and then froze. "What?" asked Pitus.

"Do you feel a draft?" asked Atoye. In an instant both of them had their brislers out. They assumed a back to back cover formation and carefully swept the bridge. Atoye dashed to the control panel and yes, there it was; the seal on the cargo door was breeched!

"Do you think anything got in?" asked Pitus.

"Depends," said Atoye, "on how far open the door is. We had betted get there as fast as safety will allow." They moved quietly down the ramp past the living quarters rooms checking each door for its integrity. Finally they came to a grate beside the entry to the cargo bay. "There's your draft," said Pitus. He looked through it. The cargo door is ajar."

Atoye opened a panel beside the grate and pushed a button. The door started to close but stopped as though it had hit an obstacle.

"Something's in the way," said Atoye.

"It can't stay like that, to be sure," said Pitus. "It will have to be shut by hand, though going in there now doesn't appeal much to me."

"Me either," sighed Atoye.

"Wait," said Pitus. "We could take the ship up a couple hundred miles. The vacuum and cold would kill anything in there."

"It would work, but it would also be too risky," replied Atoye. "If someone is watching, we would show up on a scanner."

Pitus sighed. "Why does it always have to be the hard way?"

"I can go in," said Atoye. "I've done this sort of thing before."

"We'll both go in," said Pitus. "We can suit up for protection in case there's a krait or something else small but deadly."

They both put on extra-environmental suits and stood a moment before the cargo door. Atoye tapped his com patch. "I'll go first and you make sure nothing sneaks into the clean area around the edge of the doorway. Then I'll clear the inside of the cargo door so you can enter." This done, the two stood back to back with brislers set on "medium cook" setting . . . no need to burn holes in the superstructure when a lower setting was capable of dispatching anything that could have fit through the gap in the door. If they were outside, on the other hand, they would have their weapons at maximum and one in each hand. They slowly shuffled in unison in a rotation sweep of the cargo bay from floor to ceiling.

"Looks clear," said Pitus. He went to the door to see what was blocking it. Pitus jumped back and blazed away with his pistol. The creature shrieked and struck. It was a two-meter male loresst viper! It grabbed Pitus by the boot with its strike and Pitus severed its head with the brisler beam. For another two seconds the jaws of the thing clamped down on the boot, a stream of ichorous venom running down the side. By this time Atoye had raced to his side. "Did he get through your boot?" asked Atoye. His voice showed no small sense of fear. Fear was a well founded emotion when in the midst of such a creature as a loresst. Its venom is a potent cardiotoxin, and can stop a heart as fast as an intravenous bolus of potassium chloride in an unprotected victim. A corstet consumer like Pitus or Atoye could probably last an hour before its effects would show. Bradycardia would be the first sign, then a Q-T prolongation where the heart progressively lost its synchronicity. A ventricular arrhythmia would follow and descend into a fatal ventricular fibrillation before the heart stopped altogether. A big city medical center could save a victim of a loresst, but none remained on Oman.

"I'm OK," said Pitus, "The boot was harder than his fangs. Pitus nudged the snake's head off his boot with the muzzle of his brisler, and then kicked both the head and the body out through the door and pulled it shut. "Nasty stuff," he said motioning at the slimy green venom on his boot. It was still dangerous to an accidental touch. Skin penetration could put a healthy man down for weeks in an intensive care unit. He turned down the power of his pistol a couple of notches and trained it on the stain. A couple of shots burned it off the boot.

"I hope there are no more of those in here," Pitus said. He fired at the wall over Atoye's head and a bantula dropped to the floor. It was the size of a dinner plate with an abdomen the size of a fist. This was a small one, the bantula capable of reaching a meter across with its eight legs outstretched. This fearsome creature, the largest species of tropical spider, did have one redeeming quality. Its diet included kraits. To Pitus or anyone not Oman or Calbres, the krait is just a nuisance. It looks like a squirrel, but possesses a skunk-like defense mechanism. The smelly noxious liquor it shoots out at its enemies is acidic and can cause blindness temporarily just as a shot of mace in the eyes. This is not the reason it is feared by the Omans or the Calbres.

The immune systems of these people make krait exposure a serious thing indeed. During the race to find Loma's Cube, the villain Ich Habine came to this island in search of a krait. When he captured one, he took it to Calbresan and planted the creature within the palace of the Calbres Primate. The Primate's son Benin it Zor was spumed by the animal and would have been doomed had it not been for the cure Pitus prepared from parsley whose principle, chlorophyll, is not to be found on either planet. With Benin's treatment a success, Habine's plans for precipitating a war were foiled.

The chore of clearing the cargo bay of vile stowaways took another hour. The total kills included twenty more spiders and another viper. Thankfully there were no kraits probably due to the presence of the spiders. "Well," said Atoye snidely, "That was a nice delay." He motioned to Pitus, "Let's get back to Nesgoor."

JOHN MEETS MR. OTT

John rolled his window down in front of the large wrought iron gate and stuck his head out at a speaker in the wall.

"Who is it?" a stern and rough voice demanded.

"John Hodiak. I'm here to see Simeon Ott."

"What business do you have with Mr. Ott?"

"I called Wednesday about some coins. I'm the guy from Fort Edward."

"Mr. Ott is expecting you. You are late."

"I know. I'm sorry. I had some . . ." John's apology was cut short by a loud buzz upon which the entry gate rolled aside.

"Some classy place!" John mused as he passed up the drive. He patted the truck's dashboard. "Better enjoy this ride, old feller. Only Caddies and Rolls Royces use this driveway, I'll bet!" With a smug smile he added, "I'll put this baby right smack in front of the house in hopes it will annoy some tight-assed hot shot!" He pulled up behind a car parked in the driveway just in front of the front door. It was a Mercedes. He grabbed a small wooden box off the seat beside him and jumped out. A short tiled walkway lead to the front door.

"As John reached for the door it opened. He was greeted by a butler who could have doubled for a hit man. He appeared urbane enough to properly greet a dignitary, but looked capable of being more "versatile". John could easily see he was not to expect the dignitary treatment. He didn't expect it.

"Wait here," the butler said motioning to a large leather chair just inside the door. After a fashionable wait, Ott himself came out of a room at the end of the hall.

"Mr. Hodiak, welcome to my home," Ott said offering his hand. As John took it he gave him a "once over". Ott appeared to be on the thither side of middle age, with slight graying at the temples of a full head of hair. He was of a lean build with a thin and rugged face. He stood about 5 feet 10 in a posture that would suggest former military service. There was something, however, that was not quite right. Though a likely sexagenarian, his steel-gray eyes seemed old for the face in which they were set. This observation though long to describe, took no more than a couple of seconds, indistinguishable within the span of a greeting.

"Thank you. Some home it is!" John declared looking all around. Ott smiled cordially at the compliment. It spoke more of awe than from an appreciation of taste. Provincial though it was, it had the refreshing quality of sincerity.

They entered a library part way down the hall. Again the "fragrance of time honored literature" greeted his senses. In the middle of the room was a large glass display case.

"Wow! Look at the coins!"

"Do you know something of coins, Mr. Hodiak?"

"John, please, John. I know a little, that is, enough to know that this stuff is a bit out of my league."

"I have collected coins since I was a lad." Ott said proudly. "There are some very scarce ones in this case."

"Like that 1838-O half dollar," remarked John. He remembered seeing a picture of it in R. S. Yeoman's Red Book.

"One of twenty minted," Ott replied. "I got it from a physician who said he'd let me have it for nothing if I would tell him my age."

"Just for telling him your age," asked John incredulously?

"A small sample of my blood was also part of the bargain." Before John could reply, Ott said, "I paid $45,000 dollars for it."

Though a strange statement in which an intriguing story probably lurked, John took it for some mysterious B S meant to impress. He was mainly interested in finding out what he could get out of Medwyd's gold and let the comment slide.

"I don't think I have anything like that in here." John said pointing to a small wooden box under his arm. "Lord knows, I wish I did."

"Well, let's see and you'll soon know."

As Ott was examining the coins, John glanced around the room. While he was doing this, Ott was casting a glance now and then at John.

"Would you believe me if I told you I saw that coin struck?"

"What coin," asked John?

"That 1838 half."

"Of course not," said John. He raised his eyebrows, but otherwise kept his mind on his impending fortune.

Ott returned to the task of examining the Hodiak hoard.

"Most of this is common stuff worth about bullion price. The coppers and the silver are not of interest to me, with two exceptions, though many of the pieces are doubtless of great value. I suggest you keep them for your grandchildren." John slumped in his chair a little in disappointment.

"Now that's all the bad news." Ott said.

John perked up, though to what extent he should be excited he could not determine by the expression on Ott's face. Ott picked up three of four gold pieces he had set to one side.

"These are Louis d'or. They are in fine condition. It is hard to find them unclipped, or shaved down around the edges. I'll offer ten thousand apiece for these." John's breathing halted a few seconds. He gulped down his heart.

"And that one?" John said pointing to the remaining gold coin.

"Is worth twenty thousand dollars, which is my offer." John bit his lip, but sat still. He picked up a silver dollar. "This 1795 flowing hair dollar is in about mint state fifty, one of the best specimens I've seen in years. I will offer fifty thousand for this, which is a bargain for me, but probably better than you could do anywhere else without getting mired in a lot of publicity. The other item is this 1793 chain AMERI large cent. Ten thousand for this is my offer."

"I thought you weren't interested in coppers," said John.

"It would be a gift to a friend," replied Ott. "If you want to sell it all, that is, with the exception of the silver and coppers as I stated before, I will give you one hundred and seventy three thousand. I have some reference books if you would like to verify the values of the pieces." John almost didn't hear this. His pulse was now into three figures. He took a couple of cleansing breaths. Ott put a finger on the piece of paper he used to jot down the figures as he assessed the values of the coins. With a smile he slid it across the table to John. On it was a short column of numbers with a total of $173,000 at the bottom. He did this obviously for dramatic effect.

"No, no." John said. "That sounds fine to me." His apparent poise covered a jubilant spirit. Ott motioned for the "butler" to go for the money. Ott picked up one of the pieces of gold and turned it back and forth under the desk lamp. John sat staring at the paper.

"I take it you would prefer cash. It wouldn't do to have your brother Kenneth find out you located something of value in his house."

John flinched and it didn't escape Ott's notice. He smiled sardonically at John.

"May I ask you one question?" Ott asked.

"I thought we agreed to no questions on the phone," John said nervously.

"Perhaps you will indulge me this one."

"Perhaps."

"Is this Medwyd's Gold?"

"Who's?" John asked.

"Thought so . . . Another legend bites the dust!" Ott said grinning.

"I didn't say one way or another," John said defensively.

"Doesn't matter, really," said Ott, "I certainly have no reason to tell anyone." He looked down at another coin.

"Was it in the tunnel in the cellar?"

"That's two questions!" John exclaimed. He was becoming agitated by how much the balance of knowledge was tipped off center. Ott merely smiled. He returned to the coins.

"You know a lot about my situation," John said. "Do you take this much interest in all of your 'business associates'?" Ott smiled again.

"A 'business associate' is one who does at least a quarter million dollars with me." John smiled back at him. He deserved that, he thought.

"There are things about where you live that interests me more than Medwyd's hoard."

"For instance?"

"For instance, papers, diaries, journals, and related historical artifacts by any of the early Pestons . . . especially those of Pitus."

John shrugged but remained silent. He determined it was to be his turn to play the game, since Ott seemed to enjoy throwing out intimate Peston secrets to watch how he flinched at their hearing.

"Maybe you should visit the museum."

"Surely you must imagine I did that," said Ott.

"Anytime recently?" asked John. Having asked the question, he realized it might be a needless risk, given what puzzle pieces seemed to be coming together in his head.

"Recently," asked Ott? "That's a peculiar question. Why do you ask?"

"No particular reason," said John. "They have expanded the museum holdings in the last few years. It might be worth another look."

"Perhaps I will do just that," replied Ott. He re-directed the conversation back to John.

"I would pay well for Peston information; Perhaps enough to make you an 'associate'." John retained his poker face even through this. Ott, however, noticed a telltale sign.

"I have seen many a man's face who has tried to deceive me over the years. I read faces very well," he said blandly.

"Is there something in my face that you can read, Mr. Ott?"

"If you have something, I'm sure we can talk business." Ott then pushed four six-inch stacks of currency across the table to John. John picked up one of the bundles.

"It is all there . . . one hundred and seventy three thousand. Count it if you like."

John fanned a portion of one of the stacks before him. He quickly closed it like folding a hand of cards. This was a royal flush.

"I'll take your word for it." He stood up and shoved Ott's tally paper and as much money into the box as would fit. He filled his pants pockets with the rest.

"I would advise you not to deposit that cash in the bank all at once," said Ott. "Any deposit of currency of ten thousand or more gets reported to the IRS and the DEA. Stick it in a safe deposit box and funnel it in to your account over several months." He stood up from the table and the two started for the door.

"I will let you in on something else, Mr. Hodiak," added Ott. "I am a wealthy man who has the means of getting what I want."

"Understood," John said. "I will keep that in mind, should I find something." John then turned to leave. He looked back at Ott. "I will keep in touch." he said. "I dare say," John thought.

John went quickly to his truck and closed the door. "I guess now I can tell Joyce who the 'competition' is, and it ain't good."

John's conscience chided him out of bed at eight-thirty. "I can sure use this day off," he said aloud to his image in the bathroom mirror. "Besides," he added, "Who would want a prescription filled from a rich ugly son-of-a-bitch like you!" He laughed at the image in the mirror and imagined that the reflection returned the snicker. "Maybe a comb and a razor will improve matters."

Having put himself together, John foraged for something for breakfast. Afterwards, he sat at the kitchen table. "Having a day off with nothing to do is a bigger pain than pulling a twelver," he uttered aloud. "Nothing to do that is after I get all that dough in the vault of Glens Falls National." He recalled his earlier thought of how he said he could really use this day off. He shook his head. "I must be going bonkers. I don't know what I want." The phone interrupted this reverie.

"Johnny."

"Joyce, my sweet," said John pleasantly. "Are you making sure I'm not wasting my day by staying in bed?"

"No," she said. "I have something important to tell you, but first, how did it go yesterday?"

"I dare not tell you on the phone because you'll freak," said John, "but I think I need to get a will."

"I can't wait to hear all about it," Joyce said.

"Why are you talking in a whisper? Is this the `library thing' or are you in some kind of danger." John asked with some concern.

"Danger? On a Thursday morning in Glens Falls? You've got to be kidding," she replied facetiously. "No danger, but I want only you to hear what I've got to say."

"I'll be there in fifteen minutes," said John. He hung up the phone.

John found Joyce at the circulation desk. She went into an office briefly and returned with Ann. "I am now on break," Joyce said. They went outside and sat at a table in the adjacent park.

"One hundred and seventy three grand," John said triumphantly.

"Oh my God," Joyce gasped. "That's great!"

"Damn straight on that," laughed John. He kissed her and then hunched down.

"You haven't got all that money sitting around in your house, I hope," Joyce said.

"It's in a safe deposit box at the Bank," said John. "I also went to Chafee and Dillard."

"The lawyers?"

"Ken ain't getting it if something happens to me," said John. "I made you my beneficiary."

She slid her hand over his. "I have no desire to collect it," Joyce replied. "But I'll be glad to help you spend it."

"You're on," said John. "Now, you said you had some news for me. Is it good or bad?"

"I think it's good," said Joyce.

"O. K., shoot," he said.

"My friend from Albany called me about thirty minutes ago."

"The one at the State Library?"

"Yes."

"Does she know what happened to Pitus' book?"

"She said she knew, but couldn't say on the phone."

"What the hell is this," John exclaimed. ". . . couldn't say on the phone . . . It's like the plot of a damn spy novel!"

"I don't know what it is," Joyce replied. "I do think you had better be careful." She paused a second and added, "Maybe you shouldn't let it go any further. Take it to the authorities before you get in deep trouble."

"I haven't a clue what 'the authorities' would be at this stage of the game," replied John. "I can't stop now. This book is a hot item for some reason. I want to know why." John was a mixture of excitement and apprehension. He took a deep breath.

"What do I have to do?"

"Betsy will have lunch break at Winnie's. Do you know where it is?"

"Corner of Lark and Madison," John answered. "I had many a club sandwich there."

"She will be there at 12:15. Make sure you are too."

"Will do."

"Don't order more than a cup of coffee. You too aren't having lunch; you are going for a walk."

"I don't know what she looks like."

"You don't have too. She'll find you."

"OK, I just waltz in there and order a cup of java. How's that going to distinguish me from every one else?"

As she went into the details, John was beginning to realize that this was not a game. There was the possibility of big time trouble, maybe even violence if he and his opponents got too close together. He pondered Joyce's advice to tell someone, but he determined to go through with it nevertheless. Playing safe doesn't always prevent regrets.

John promised he would be careful, and then glanced at his watch.

"11:10! I'd better haul ass!" Joyce made him promise once again to be careful and then kissed him.

Two minutes later he was across the Hudson heading for the North-way. He got on at the South Glens Falls entrance and pushed his speed. At Wilton he passed a speed trap. He quickly looked down at his speedometer. "Seventy-seven . . . BALLS!" He shouted as he slapped the steering wheel, "He'll come after me for sure!" John slowed down to sixty-five and waited to see the multicolor strobe lights in the rear-view mirror. He traveled a mile further without any sign of the trooper. "He had to have seen me," John murmured. He looked back at the stretch of road through the large side mirror. "If he did, he would've had me by now." He smiled and blew a lungful of breath out of his mouth. As the alarm of the incident wore off, the needle crept back up on the dial, this time further than before.

A mile north of Clifton Park, he passed two police cars parked in a rest stop. He quickly slowed down. "They should have seen me blow by them. I was going like a bat out of hell. What gives here?" He left the North-way at Latham and headed south on Route 9. He was thinking about the situation as he entered the outskirts of the city. "I could have done a hundred miles an hour without being hauled over. Those bastards are tracking me. They must know!"

Once in the city he planned to shake any tail that was on him. He turned onto Clinton Avenue and parked near the corner with Swan. As he figured, a cab shortly came by. John hailed it and got in. "Take me to Trailways Bus Station," he said, tossing a folded hundred dollar bill on the front seat. "No change if you make it in the next five minutes." The cab driver earned his money and asked no questions. John left the cab and hurried into the station. A crowd of people were near a bus that was getting ready to depart. John wormed his way through them and out a side door. He looked at his watch. It was 12:10. He looked up State Street from the corner of Green. "Where the hell is a cab? No time for a cab, I'll have to run," he thought. State Street Hill is steep and long for a sprint. As he reached the Capital Building, fatigue took over making him cut down to a brisk walk. He looked around him. No sign of his being followed. He continued across the northern grounds to Lark Street. He managed to catch some of his breath by the time he reached his destination.

"Menu?"

"No, thanks; just coffee for the time being," John said. He picked up the cup and furtively glanced over the clientele as he sipped. He saw no woman sitting by herself at any of the booths. "I'm not late." He thought. "She must be here." Then apprehension built up as he began to think she was delayed for some reason. In a minute, he had convinced himself that she was caught and being interrogated by the cops and was probably telling them where he was! "I'd better get my ass out of here," he thought as he downed the last of the coffee in his cup. He placed two dollars on the counter and turned to leave. As he did, a young woman sat down on the stool beside him.

"I'm looking for Pitus," she said nervously.

"Betsy," he called out in hushed excitement. "I was about to give up on you." "Come on," she said. "Let's get going."

The two left the diner and started walking west on Lark.

"I'm not good at this cloak and dagger stuff," John remarked.

"Neither am I," Betsy replied. "My heart couldn't take much of this shit."

"I know what you mean," John answered.

"The hell you do!" She exclaimed. "You tell Joyce I would do this only for her and she owes me big. I don't know why I didn't have Joyce e-mail a picture of you. It would have saved a lot of trouble," she added. John looked at her puzzled.

"I got to the diner a few minutes early. I saw this guy sitting at the counter, and I went up to him and gave the password, or whatever the hell you call it. He smiled and said he didn't know anyone by that name. I felt like a jerk."

"What did you do?" John asked, a laugh trying to escape from behind the smirk on his face.

"I just turned around and went over to the phone booth and acted like I was making a call."

"Original," John replied, grinning. Betsy by now had lost the original aggravation the ordeal had caused, and was now laughing.

"Wait!" She declared grabbing John's forearm. "You ain't heard anything yet! While I was in the phone booth, another guy came in and sat close by. He looked like the description Joyce gave of you so I left the booth and sat down next to him." She hesitated, swallowing a laugh, trying to continue with her story.

"Then what?"

"I gave the password, and the guy looked at me a little queer. He said in a quiet voice that we shouldn't talk there but go outside. I was confident it was you by now. Then as he was getting up from the stool he asked me how much I charged for a quickie."

"You're bullshittin'!" John said.

"I said, what the hell do you mean by that? He then said, You're the one who wants to do business; I never heard it put that way before; 'I'm looking for a penis' . . . , but it all means the same to me!'" John howled. So did Betsy. After a moment they calmed down enough to talk.

"Penis Peston!" He started laughing all over again. "That poor bastard!" Betsy hushed him and said she had to get back to work.

"The book was sold to Allen French. He has a bookstore on New Scotland Avenue about a half mile past the Hospital."

"Hudson Valley Books."

"That's it."

"I know where it is," John said. "A friend of mine used to go there a lot."

"That's all the help I can give you," said Betsy. "It caused a lot of attention for the little it is. A friend who works down in the stacks who will remain anonymous caught wind that the Feds were interested in the book. He found it and wanted to get it out of there for himself. He nearly got caught with it and it scared him, so he dumped it into some boxes of stuff French bought with the intention of buying it from him after things cooled down."

"That was some chance he took," said John.

"He knows how most booksellers work," said Betsy. "If it isn't a Hemingway or a Steinbeck *first*, they'll just put twenty bucks on it and shelve it."

"How do you know he didn't already go get it," asked John?

"He's such a procrastinator; he probably won't think to go there for weeks. You, on the other hand, better go there right away. I don't know, but I strongly suspect that this information is not exclusive." She turned to leave. John watched her as she started away. When she reached the corner, she looked back. "Tell Joyce 'hello' for me . . . and she owes me a steak dinner!" John nodded and waved. She returned the wave and then disappeared around the corner.

John thought of retrieving his truck, but decided instead to take a taxi to the book store. "You want me to wait, Mister," The cab driver asked.

"I don't know how long I'll be," answered John. "I'll take my chances on catching another ride."

He entered the shop and started browsing. The proprietor looked up from his work.

"Anything in particular?"

"Just impulse buying at the moment," John replied.

"Say, I like that," the owner said. "You go right ahead!"

John looked all around and saw no one else in the store but French and himself. When he was satisfied that this was indeed the case, he approached the desk where the man was seated pricing a stack of leather bound books.

"Come to think about it, I have been looking for an autobiography by a rather obscure New York author.

"Moses Van Campen . . . O. P. Alderman?" The dealer ventured as a guess.

"No," John said. After a moment's hesitation, he said, "I'm looking for a book by a man named Peston; Pitus Peston."

"Interesting," said the dealer.

"Do you have such a book?"

"I had one two days ago. I sold it to John Rafferty over to Berkshire Books in Pittsfield, along with some related things. He said he had a collector who might buy it. I don't know about it being an autobiography, though."

"What do you mean?" John asked. His disappointment at missing the book was nearly crushing his will to enquire.

"I skimmed over it to figure out where to shelve it. It was set up in the form of a biography, but it seemed more like a late nineteenth century science fiction novel. Some Victorian hacker, no doubt, was attempting to emulate Jules Verne. I remember chuckling at the title. It was a delightfully quaint example of Victorian alliteration; PEREGRINATIONS OF PITUS PESTON. That and some handwritten stuff came from some crates that were gathering dust in the State Library. Some of the books hadn't seen daylight for decades. That was good, actually. It kept them in wonderful physical shape. Porcelain white pages, no foxing, nice supple bindings . . . unfortunately, there was not much of any literary significance that I could find."

John left the bookstore and started off toward the bus stop at the corner. "All this hurry and worry and the damn thing isn't even here," he muttered. "I'd better get over to Pittsfield and hope no one else has."

He was walking toward the corner, using his cell phone to call a cab, when a light brown car pulled up to the curb a little ahead of him. John watched it suspiciously as he approached. His suspicion was confirmed as the door opened and a well dressed tall man emerged and headed toward him.

"Mr. Hodiak," the man called.

"Who's asking?" John asked sternly, attempting to cloak his fear.

"Tom Flynn; FBI," he declared, holding a badge with a picture I D.

"Yeah, I'm John Hodiak. Am I under arrest for something?"

"No Sir. Just want to talk with you a few minutes." Flynn ushered John toward the car and they both entered it. As he got in, John looked forward. Behind the wheel another man sat turned sideways with his arm over the back of the seat.

"Would you like a lift back to your truck?" He cordially extended his hand in greeting. "No charge; it's on 'Uncle Sam'," he added smiling.

"In that case, I accept," John answered. "That is, if you won't make me put it on my 1040 form as unearned income." At this, the man laughed loudly.

"Dan Henning."

"John . . . I guess you know who I am," John replied. He felt awkward, but at some ease. It was likely the response the two agents desired from him. Henning then turned around and started off.

"You must know why we want to talk with you," Flynn said.

"I know you have questioned my girlfriend and you have been watching my house. You probably have my phone tapped too," John said indignantly. "All this over a goddamn book!"

"Book? What about a book?" Flynn asked.

"Come on, guys," John replied sarcastically. "You're looking for the copy of the PEREGRINATIONS that was stolen from the DLC."

"DLC; what is that, Mr. Hodiak?"

"Library of Congress. Everybody knows that!" John said facetiously.

"We want that book, Mr. Hodiak," said Flynn sternly. "If you have it, you had better surrender it to us."

"I don't have the damn thing! If I had it or knew where it was, I wouldn't have had Joyce searching for it." John then looked straight at Flynn. "You're not just after a hundred year old book, *are* you? What is the big deal about this book?"

"We were hoping to find out from you," answered Flynn. "We are just as curious as you about it. We have orders to retrieve it and return it to its proper place." "Bullshit!" John exclaimed. "We're not talking about a Shakespeare first edition here, or the Gettysburg Address! The value of that book couldn't be even half the cost of one of your airfares up here, let alone all the expense of having you two guys running around all over hell searching for it."

"Even if we did know, neither of us has the authority to disclose it to you," Flynn replied. He ceased asking questions after this. John was tempted to ask them about what they asked Joyce . . . who was Kawa Hinga and what was 000. John felt they knew well the answers to those questions and still others. He thought it likely that he knew still more about Pitus Peston than they. But there was something they knew that he didn't. Something big, something astounding, something that captured the attention of the U.S. government.

John kept still.

"There's your vehicle up ahead," Henning said at last.

"It has been an enjoyable conversation," Flynn said. "Perhaps we should talk again sometime." The car pulled up behind John's truck. Flynn started to get out opening the car door for John.

"Never mind," John said. "I'll let myself out." Without another word he stepped out of the car and shut the door. The agents left, heading down Clinton Avenue. John watched them turn onto Route 9 and head north. When they were out of sight, he got back into his truck.

"What balls that Flynn guy has!" John growled. "They're playing me for some kind of imbecile!" He headed down the street. "It's got to be something relating to that plant he got from Gram." John thought as he drove along. He thought of the small flat he set up under the grow light in the tunnel just two days before. "Imagine if that stuff really works! Something like that could alter the balance of political power! Powerful men would pay a king's ransom for something like that . . . or kill for it at the snap of a finger!"

John drove down to Broadway and headed for Menands. "I'll take the bridge to Troy and then circle back down through Defreestville, pick up Route 20 by Sand Lake . . . just in case someone is trying to follow me." It seemed a long ride to the Massachusetts border. His sense of urgency quick-stepped the clocks, making him fear that he would arrive after the shop closed, though he knew it was supposed to be open for two more hours. No sooner did he conquer this fear with the truth, than it visited him anew in the form of doubts that the shop still had the book at all. The fear of failure infected him with a sickening dread. The loss of something so important after getting so close was nearly a visceral hurt. As he now sat en route, he had not yet met with failure. He felt a strange comfort in not having yet failed as if it were a weird form of success. Yet his rational mind convinced him that he would soon prevail. This emotional mix made a pain of its own as he continued to overtake his goal.

He entered the city and drove north on Route 7. "I can't be *THIS* lucky." John said as he spotted the store within a few minutes of starting his search. He parked the truck on a side street and crossed the main drag to the bookshop. As he entered, the door sounded like DJ's old door with the bell attached to boot! He used the same scenario as at Hudson Valley Books. When he observed only one other person in the store, and this an unobtrusive customer, he neared the front desk. On the floor next to this desk which was piled three feet high with columns of books, was a large box. From it arose a stack that rivaled the stacks in the desktop, looking as though ready to topple over. This precarious literary spire seemed to tease him to touch it, which John did, managing to remove the top volume without causing a crash. He opened it to the title page and examined the title. It was a volume of Burns. He gently replaced it and looked around for the owner. His eyes fell upon a small plum-colored cloth volume, spine pointing up from beside the tall stack. John peered down for a closer look. The spine was decorated with a gilt figure that looked a lot like Merrick Butte with a comet coursing along above it. "That's it," he breathed softly, his heart now rising to his throat. He reached for it with a force that would have broken his arm had an invisible barrier stood between his hand and the object he sought. His hand gripped it and snatched it out of the box. John opened the book to the title page. THE LIFE AND PEREGRINATIONS OF PITUS PESTON FROM HIS EARLIEST RECOLLECTIONS TO THE PRESENT TIME. It was dated 1883; the place; Ton-ga Hin-ga, Arizona Territory. John chuckled as he read this. "He hauled a printing press out to that butte and printed it there, I suppose," he said.

"Beg pardon," a man said as he emerged from a side room.

"Are you Mr. Rafferty?" John asked.

"Yes, indeed," he declared. "Something I can help you find?"

"I believe I found it." John said triumphantly. He held the book up to show Rafferty who eyed it curiously.

"Did you find that in that box?" He asked, pointing down at John's feet.

"Yes."

"Haven't catalogued it yet, so I don't have it for sale."

John cradled the open book in his hands. "Could he be aware of what this is . . . that this is hotter than a two-dollar pistol? If he knew that the Feds were after this book or one like it . . . If he knew the trouble I went through to get my hands on this . . . I must leave here with this book at all costs." John thought. At length, John returned to the reality of the moment. A very important thing had to transpire at this time for his needs to be fulfilled.

"I like it," John said. "How much do you want for it?"

"As I said, I haven't researched it out yet. I don't want to sell it till I check it out."

"Come on," said John, "I'm not from around here, and I'd like to buy this book. Can't you decide on a price so I can have it?" John smiled. In his mind a less cordial dialogue ensued:

"I'm leaving with this book either by the door or out through that damn picture window, but I'm leaving with this book!" The bookseller looked at it and flipped through it carelessly and handed it back to John.

"One hundred dollars."

"One hundred bucks," John exclaimed! Then the bookseller reached for the book and John intercepted it with a pair of fifty-dollar bills. Then John started to leave through the door when he noticed the car that he remembered spotting in Rensselaer. He took little notice of it at first while he was driving through Scodack, but after a while he became suspicious. It seemed to be going his way. "Do you have a back door I can use to leave?"

"I have a fire exit, but what's the matter? You're not wanted by the Law are you?" "No, but that guy in that brown Chevy . . . well, I accidentally hit on his girl at Ralph's over in the city. I thought it was over with an apology, but . . ." John pointed to the car across the street. The man got out and started walking briskly across the street toward the store. He tucked the book under his arm. A second glance toward the car revealed another man who hurried past the first one. It was the heavy set man, and he was reaching into his jacket while he ran.

"You clearly pissed him off," said Rafferty.

"Those guys want something I have."

"If it isn't your testicles, then it's that book," he said cannily. "It *is* that book, isn't it? Maybe it is more valuable than I realize. I should change my mind about selling it."

"Mister, take your hundred bucks and live a nice long life." With this, John bolted for the back door, ran down a short alley and into the rear entrance of a shoe store. He calmly but quickly walked into the sales room and out a side door, slipping through a nearby hedge. He then crossed two back yards and ducked into a Salvation Army store.

"How much for this coat?"

"Five dollars."

He paid the clerk, not waiting for the receipt. He threw on the light coat and walked down to a crosswalk.

John reached his truck and fled the city heading north toward Vermont. Five minutes into his ride he passed a pair of Massachusetts State Police cruisers stopped along a siding of the road. He wasn't speeding this time, but the two cars pulled into line behind him.

"This doesn't feel good," thought John. After a moment he rationalized his fear partly away. What did he have that they could want? Then he realized that he had no receipt for the book. "If I get stopped, they may claim I stole the damn thing and I wouldn't put it past Rafferty to back them up." He passed a sign for a beer joint in Pownal, just four miles ahead in Vermont.

The moment of truth came shortly as he reached the state line. Up ahead were the strobes of three state trooper cars positioned to block traffic. When he got close he saw a cop motion for him to pull over. John quickly shoved the Peregrinations under his seat. He came to a stop near the trooper and shut off the truck. Then he rolled down his window.

"Good evening sir," said the officer perfunctorily. "May I see your driver's license and registration?" John got the documents and handed them to the trooper. The officer was examining them when suddenly there was a sound of a speeding car. The trooper dodged in front of John's truck. The car screeched to a halt. It was the brown car. Instantly the heavy set man jumped out and rushed to the truck. He flashed his creds at the trooper. "We can handle this from here," he said to the trooper. To John he shouted, "Get your ass out of that truck." He yanked the door open and would have grabbed John were it not for the other man, Flynn, who ordered him to back off. John stepped down on to the pavement. He drew a deep breath and let it out to calm himself. Immediately an ID was shoved in his face.

"Dolph, FBI."

"I'm not that nearsighted." John replied.

"Good." Dolph said. "Read this!" He flipped a folded paper against John's chest. Dolph barged past John looking into the truck while John examined the document. "This is a warrant for the seizure of a piece of government property." John announced. "I have no such property but my own here."

"We'll see about that." Dolph replied rancorously. He then approached John and shoved his finger at his chest. "If you don't help me find it, I'll find it myself and then I'll take you in for obstructing justice."

John turned back toward the other. "Mr. Flynn, please feel free to ransack my vehicle."

"We must do our job." Flynn replied. "The warrant is all in order. All we want is the book."

"This Warrant says, 'United States Public Property'. I say again, I have nothing that belongs to the U. S. Government."

"You have a copy of the PEREGRINATIONS OF PITUS PESTON." Flynn said sternly. "It is material that affects the national security. Whether it is the Library of Congress copy or not is immaterial. Have you read any of it?"

"I haven't had a chance," John replied.

"That is good for you, Mr. Hodiak," Flynn replied. "That simplifies things greatly." In the meantime Dolph rummaged around in the truck.

"At least you admitted that much," said John. "How could a hundred year-old book be a threat to national security?" Dolph called out, "I got it."

"You have no right to detain me and rob me of my property."

"Nobody's robbing anyone of anything," said Dolph acridly.

"You are, you prick!"

"Watch your tongue, boy," warned Dolph. "I might have to consider this as obstructing justice. Then I'd have to hurt ya." He moved menacingly toward John.

"I'll obstruct your mouth with my goddamn fist!" John shouted. The trooper who stood nearby rushed in with the intent to restrain John. Flynn held up his hand.

"Enough," yelled Flynn. "Sergeant, you're out of line! Mr. Hodiak, you had better consider the consequences of assaulting a federal officer in the course of his duty." Flynn then took the book from Dolph and moved toward the car.

"We have what we came for, Sergeant. Let us leave this man to his own business." Flynn returned to his car.

Dolph followed, but stopped short of opening the passenger door.

"You no-good punk, you belong in jail!" The trooper raised both of his palms. "Am I arresting this man or what?"

"No," Said Flynn. "As far as I'm concerned, Mr. Hodiak is free to go."

"So that's it, is it?" John declared. "Just chase me down with a piece of paper, take my property, and 'Good-by to you Sir'?" Flynn did not reply, but opened the door of his car and got in. Dolph entered the passenger side. He gave John a smug look as they sped away. "Drive carefully," said the trooper. He headed for his own cruiser. Within a half minute he was alone on the side of the road.

John arrived home two hours later. He rang Joyce's apartment, but there was no answer. Then he remembered Joyce was spending the weekend at her parents' house in Tupper Lake. He had to work the next morning, but decided to drown the dour mood he had with booze.

Next morning was Saturday and John arrived at the store a half hour before opening. Bingham was found sitting on a stool behind the prescription counter.

"Hello." Bingham said quietly, without looking up at John. It was odd for a greeting. Usually Bingham bellowed out his "hello" like a Ward Bond calling for the wagon train to start moving. He also hardly ever entered the store before ten o'clock on a day he wasn't on duty.

"What's up today?" John asked with a little apprehension. "They usually come late who pays them to come early." John added jocularly, trying to curve up the straight edges of Bingham's mouth. Bingham said nothing, but looked down to a sheaf of papers, pretending to be looking them over. John looked at him for a couple of seconds and shrugged. He then started scanning the shelves of medicine lifting bottles of pills and rattling them and scanning a thing or two on the tel-ex gun. A minute passed and John heard Bingham cough. It was a manner of gaining John's attention, to which John responded immediately. Bingham then tossed an envelope down the counter toward John.

"Here."

"What's this?" John asked as he slit the top of the envelope with the point of a pen. "Money," John asked? "It's a bit early for payday." He then saw a note among the money. He quickly scanned the note. "I'm fired? What the hell is going on here?" He exclaimed in a low voice mixed of bewilderment and rising anger.

"I think it's clear enough." Bingham answered sternly.

"It's clear enough what you are doing. I want to know why."

"I found out what you were doing with all the time off you took these past few months." Bingham declared as though scolding. "You've been traipsing down to New Orleans, and out to St. Louis, and some place way the hell up in North Dakota."

"I don't know how you found all this out," replied John, "but I don't see where it's any of your business either. That was vacation time I took and the rest was unpaid personal leave."

"Plane flights, hotels, rented cars . . . . all that costs money; more than you're making from me! Unless, of course you have been *SUPPLEMENTING YOUR INCOME!*"

"You think I've got my hands in the till?" John gasped. "I never stole a dime from you!"

"I didn't say that." Bingham retorted, "Though with what I found out about you, nothing would surprise me."

"What the hell is going on here?" John called out as though making an entreaty to a higher state.

"My great-grandfather started this store in 1896. Then my grandfather took it over after the Second World War and used up his life building it up for dad to take over when he did in 1975. It's been mine since 2000 and I'm not going to let it be sullied by the presence of a goddamn commie!"

"Who's a commie?" John shouted. "I'm no commie. Who told you this bullshit?"

"I was told you were an enemy of the state by someone who ought to know. From who told it to me, I didn't have to hear more."

"Who told you," asked John, practically yelling out the question.

"Get out you commie bastard or I'll blow your filthy head off!" He drew a small handgun from a drawer beneath the counter. John backed up toward the door. When he reached it, he tried to speak. This only made Bingham thrust the weapon at him, and John disappeared out the door.

All Sunday John revisited the last of Peston's journals looking for clues for what might be in the book Flynn took. He decided not to bother Joyce at her folks. She would be back early this evening anyway. All the descriptions of things Pitus found in the temple, though fascinating, shed no light on anything that would incite the interest of the United States government.

"Slanted desks with motley color decorations . . . printing press that remembered everything laid in its bed . . . what the hell could that mean," John wondered? The part where Pitus described the book collection of the god or probably the god's priest, Calnoon, filled him with envy. "Sixteenth century American imprints, for Chrissake," murmured John. Some of that stuff is probably no longer extant. If it is still out there in the desert someplace . . ." He looked over at his cell phone. "Oh damn! I can't expect anyone to call me with the thing turned off."

Late in the afternoon a car pulled into the driveway. John heard it and got up to see. "It's Joyce," John murmured. She came to the door and John let her in.

"I had a stimulating weekend," she said as she kissed him, "but certainly not like you had. I've been trying to get you on the phone all afternoon."

"What did you hear and when did you hear it," asked John?

"Ann called me this morning," she said. "Half the town's talking about it."

"They say attention is better than apathy, but I feel I could do with a little less attention."

"What will you do," Joyce asked? "I heard nobody wants to hire you and maybe even the Office of Professional Discipline will go after you."

"They have to prove before they can act," said John, "Or I'll sue their asses off their hips."

"Got any merlot," Joyce asked?

"From the moment I met you," said John. She made a smirk and slipped out to the kitchen. John followed her to the kitchen. He heard the rattling of glass in the fridge as he approached. He entered the kitchen as Joyce was pouring a large glassful of the wine.

"Perhaps you should distance yourself from me." John said. "Commie, for Christ's sake. Nobody's a communist any more. Even the Chinese gave it up."

"Stupid talk like that isn't going to drive me away from you," she answered. She looked straight at John with a stern expression. "Are you going to wallow in your own pity, or work on getting the truth out?"

"The truth?" John repeated. "If I told the whole story, the truth would bind me hand and foot!" He left the kitchen and went into the living room. He dropped into large chair. Joyce followed and pulled a small wicker chair against it and leaned over John's head. She placed her hand on his shoulder and tried to comfort him.

"I called Carol as soon as she got home this afternoon. She wasn't at the store yesterday, but she got an earful from Bingham today."

"Enemy of the state is what Ann said. I never heard such an irrational thing in my life," said Joyce.

"It may be irrational to you, but there will be a lot of others who will believe it, no doubt." John said sullenly.

"So, what about Carol? What did she say?" Joyce asked.

"We had quite a discussion." John said.

"It seems that a Federal agent paid Bingham a visit Friday afternoon, asking about me. He said he was investigating me on a matter that he could not disclose, but a matter that involved 'national security'. The agent asked Bingham if he knew what I was doing traveling to New Orleans and to St. Louis and the other places. When he said he had no idea about it, the guy implied that I was making connections with certain individuals in those cities and impairing the government's own efforts on an investigation of its own. He also implied that I had stolen government property and he would soon be taking me into custody."

"That book!"

"Yeah that book," said John pensively.

"Did you find it," asked Joyce. John nodded

"Betsy told me to go to Hudson Valley Books. The book wasn't there but I was told that Rafferty had it over in Pittsfield. On leaving Hudson Valley I discovered that the feds were following me. We had a little 'chat' and then they left me alone. Then I headed for Pittsfield. I thought the feds were following me, so I took 'em to hell and gone all over Rensselaer County. When I thought I was safe, I headed for the state line. I got to the shop and found the PEREGRINATIONS just lying on top of a stack of books in a cardboard box. The owner didn't want to sell it at first, because he didn't know how much it was worth. I gave him a C-note for it."

"That seems to be the going rate for Pitus Peston artifacts," Joyce quipped.

"So it seems," laughed John. "After I got the book I looked across the street and saw two men running toward the store. One was a man named Flynn whom I recognized from my Albany 'chat'. The other I didn't recognize. He was a big, slobby looking sort of guy."

"Dolph, Peter Dolph," Joyce said. He was one of the ones who questioned me. He can be somewhat of a prick. How did you get away from him?"

"I ducked out the back of the store and circled around to my truck right away. There wasn't anyone watching it.

"No body was watching it," Joyce said skeptically.

"So I thought," John said. "I started up Route 7 toward Vermont when I came to a roadblock by the Massachusetts state cops. Next thing, Flynn and Dolph blew in alongside and slapped a warrant at me."

"They got the book," said Joyce dejectedly.

"Afraid so," said John.

"What could be in that book to make the Feds so interested in it?"

"I cannot imagine," said John.

"Perhaps a big secret that would cause a lot of embarrassment if made known," ventured Joyce.

"Like Abe Lincoln had a mistress, or something," asked John. "That doesn't seem worthy of all the attention." He stared off into the room. "It has to be about what he found at the end of his last journal."

"It's probably that corstet plant," suggested Joyce. "Maybe he mentioned it in the book and the government wants to find it. Maybe they know you have more information about it and they are waiting for a chance to get it all."

"I have to get all the other stuff out of here. The tunnel is no longer safe. The Feds have probably detected it with infrared by now, and worse than that, Simeon Ott told me of its existence when I sold him the gold."

When Atoye and Pitus returned to Drolanee's, they found Kinar there along with Colonel Gastin and two others.

"All is set," said Atoye.

Gastin stepped forward. "I have information about the Haldi," he said. "There are a hundred in force made up mostly of Haldi, with some Fornicians and Jamborini as technical advisors. Half are at Jartic Orz and half are at Kesst."

"I can understand the Fornicians getting involved in this, especially if the Haldi promised to pay them well," said Atoye, "but the Jamborini? Jamborone was friendly to Oman."

"These Jamborini are probably renegades operating without the knowledge of their king," said Gastin. "My scout at Jartic Orz told me they are trying to get a cleaver operational in the hills behind the city."

"A cleaver," exclaimed Orban. "They must expect some trouble from space then."

"Let us proceed without delay," said Gastin. "We need weapons and to maintain the element of surprise." They left Drolanee's house via Atoye's aperture. They were all gathered in the bridge of Atoye's ship. Gastin looked toward the ramp that led off the bridge. "You had better get that," he said, pointing at a cavin grass spider crawling toward them. Atoye pulled out his brisler and blew it apart. "I thought we got all of those bastards," grumbled Pitus.

"He was hiding in the dark someplace, said Atoye.

"I will see that you have a place for your ship in Nesgoor," said Gastin. "You will be constantly infested with them and who knows what else, if you stay down in this hell hole. Just be sure to take it up a few thousand miles and depressurize for an hour or two. That should kill off any other stowaways," He stepped back from center and added, "Let us be going." Pitus keyed his own amulet and they all piled through the aperture.

They quietly filed down the corridor to the storage room. Pitus opened the door and the corridor was bathed in the blue light of the passage. They quickly entered the room and closed the door behind them, shoving debris in front of the door to block any telltale light.

The electric blue door-like passage stood before them.

"Just remember," Said Atoye, "Through this aperture is 0.3 omans, so don't get hurt." The three Oman soldiers nodded. Pitus went through first, followed by Gastin, then "Kol Astor Ket," said one of the two other Omans in greeting as he went through. "Claddis Zifan Deter," said the other.

"Are you related to Kinar," asked Atoye.

"We are first cousins," said Claddis who smiled. Atoye smiled and clapped him on the back. "Let's go," said Atoye and they both stepped through into Alovis B.

Once all together again, Pitus asked, "Is Kinar coming?"

"Yes, if he can pry loose from Drolanee," said Atoye. "She doesn't want to risk losing him again." He smirked, "Poor Kinar will have to live all that childhood he missed while on Earth." They entered the large storage room where Gastin, Kol, and Claddis were swarming over the crates and cartons. Kol had a brisler charger up and soon produced a fully charged pistol. "These are Sond and Gonnets, Kol said with obvious relish. "Best made on Oman." To the Colonel he asked, "Do we want to prepare them here on the spot?"

"Yes," said Gastin. "Set up an assembly line of chargers and re-crate the loaded pistols." He turned and faced Atoye and Pitus. "Who is in charge of this operation?"

"I'm no leader," said Pitus.

"We need someone with military experience," said Atoye. "From now on we take orders from you on this campaign." He looked to Pitus who nodded his agreement. Gastin now officially a colonel again said, "Very well. I will return to Nesgoor and make the necessary preparations and get a company of men up here to take the finished weapons back to base." He went to the other two who were feverishly setting up the charging line. They exchanged salutes and the Colonel hurried to the transport.

"I believe I just witnessed a miracle," said Claddis. Kol who was standing next to him nodded.

"Let me in on it," said Pitus.

"Gastin asked you for an appointment as our leader," said Kol.

"Given his experience and my lack of it," said Atoye, "it seems the logical choice."

"What would have happened had we refused," asked Pitus?

"The Gastin I knew while under his command," said Claddis, "would have killed you and took over anyway. Having said that," he continued, "you two must really be something to get such deference from a man like that." He smiled and immediately returned to his work.

An hour later, twenty men and women emerged from the transport. Some were wearing the uniforms of the former Oman army while others were in civvies. They too swarmed over the horde of weapons and obviously knew exactly what they were doing. Gastin followed done up to the nines in his orange fatigues, his breasts gleaming with his military medals. He went up to Pitus and Atoye. "I have re-activated my commission," he said, "and all these soldiers are officially in the New Oman Army with the ranks they had during their former service. I am appointing each of you to the rank of Captain in the NOA." He reached into his jacket pocket and took out two gold crescents, signifying the rank of captain and fixed them to Atoye's and Pitus' shirt sleeves. "This will do in the absence of a proper uniform." He then took a step back and saluted them. Atoye and Pitus returned the salute.

"Colonel," said Pitus. "Perhaps we should have a detachment do some searching for other sources of supplies."

"Take two men and see to it," he replied. Pitus went over to the charging line and took two who could be spared from the assembly line. They went to the engineer's office, which was up one flight of stairs and in the corridor off the unfinished main reception room of the mausoleum. Since the main reactor two miles up in the mountains was offline, he had one of the men bring a power pack off one of the weapons chargers.

In the office he set the power pack on a table next to the computer. "We need to power this up," said Pitus. "It holds the blueprints of this facility and could help us in our search." One of the men, who called himself Rabine, took out a knife and severed the cable to the computer, skinned back the insulation and wired it into the power pack. Immediately the computer came to life. The other, called Dathin, sat before the screen of the computer and began touching it rapidly. In a few seconds he said, "We have the schematic you wanted, Captain." Pitus was impressed. He nodded approvingly and he and Rabine came around the desk to look at the screen. There were three excavated levels beneath their feet. "This is our location sir" said Dathin, "and this," he said pointing, "is where the others are."

"Good," said Pitus. "We need to study this well."

"Rabine is good at visual memory," offered Dathin. Pitus stepped back and told Rabine to move in close to the screen. "Rabine, study the area left of where the others are working. Take good note of exits and entrances. We do not want to get lost down there in that."

"Aye, sir," said Rabine, and without a word, Dathin got up and Rabine sat down in his place. Rabine manipulated the image to show the three levels from all six aspects. In a couple of minutes he sat back. "I have it, sir."

"Give me the short impression, Rabine," said Pitus.

"There are three levels, with level two being the most extensive having twenty rooms. Level three has six rooms, but they run deep into the side of the mountain. The room at the end of level three is three hundred feet long by one hundred fifty wide and forty feet high."

"That's a huge room," said Pitus.

"Big as a hangar," said Dathin.

"Hangar," repeated Pitus. He thought a moment at what that could mean. "Let's go there first." They headed for it at double time with Rabine leading the way. After running through a seeming maze on level two they came to an elevator. Since the power was off, they took the nearby stairs down to level three. Here the plan was much simpler. They hurried down a quarter mile long corridor until they came to a set of double wide steel doors. The frame around them was gasketed. A pressure gauge was mounted into the wall and Pitus examined it. "Are you sure there is another room beyond these doors?"

"Yes sir," replied Rabine.

"This indicator reads zero air pressure on the other side." Rabine turned and pointed back up the hall. "Air lock," he said. Pitus looked back up the hall and spied the retracted sliding doors fifty feet behind them. "Little good they will do with no power," he grumbled. Just this side of the retracted doors was another single door leading off the corridor. They approached it. "What is in here?" asked Pitus.

"Ready room for the air lock according to the plans, sir," said Rabine. Pitus opened the door. He switched on a portable light. "One problem solved," said Pitus as he looked across to the opposite wall and spied six pressure suits hanging on hooks. "The other problem is how to close the air lock so we don't depressurize the whole facility when we enter the large room at the end."

Rabine went to a control panel just inside the entryway. "This is the control for the sliding door," he said. "There is an emergency power supply, but it is dead."

"Maybe this will help," said Dathin. He pulled the power pack he used in the engineering room out of his backpack. Pitus laughed with glee. "Well done, Dathin," he said.

"There is an Oman army slogan," said Dathin. "Never leave behind something that once served well."

"It's a good saying," said Pitus. Dathin opened the panel and connected the power pack. The board lit up with green and red squares. Dathin touched one of the greens and a hum was heard that lasted ten seconds and punctuated with a thud. The square then changed to red. Dathin turned to Pitus and grinned. "Go ahead red," he declared. They each put on a suit and left the room through another air tight door that brought them back into the corridor on the inside of the air lock. They returned to the double doors where Dathin lifted a clear cover off a toggle switch and pulled it. The rush of escaping air lasted thirty seconds and then the green light on the double doors turned to red. Pitus grabbed a circular handle on the set of doors and turned it two revolutions. There was a silent vibration of a sliding cylinder and the doors pulled free toward them.

They stepped into the enormous room. It was pitch-black in the shadows but bright where the sunlight came in through the other end of the room which was open to the outside. Pitus pulled a sealed-beam torchlight from a pocket in his suit and panned it into the lightless shadows and they were; Four J-7 orbiters and three fighters complete with missiles on their undercarriage!

"I knew it!" Pitus yelled triumphantly. His voice sounded a bit tinny through the communicator.

"How did you know such a treasure lie in this room?" asked Rabine.

"It was just a hunch, or maybe some powerful wishful thinking," said Pitus excitedly. "When Dathin said *hangar size room*, I knew it could be for only one purpose. I expected to find a fleet of hearses, which would have been good enough, but this!" he said with arms out stretched. They ran to one of the orbiters and entered it. Dathin immediately sat at the controls and initiated the power. It powered up flawlessly and they all gave a cheer. Dathin worked the controls and lifted the orbiter a few feet off the floor then set it back down. Another cheer came from the three men. "We have to get back and tell Colonel Gastin," said Pitus. Dathin shut down the craft and all three piled out of it and re-entered the air lock. When the pressure once again equalized, they entered the corridor and sprinted down it and up the flight of stairs to level two.

"Where do we go," asked Pitus?

Rabine pointed to an otherwise nondescript door and they entered a utility passage that brought them back to the place where the rest of the team were working on the weapons chargers. When they bolted into the room, one of the men shouted an alarm. An instant later a dozen brislers were aimed in their direction. Pitus held up his arms and waved the armed men down. All three pulled off their headgear. Gastin hurried up to Pitus.

"What have you found, captain?"

"We found a hangar down on level three, filled with space craft," said Pitus. "Four orbiters, J-class and three fighters." Gastin smiled broadly and cuffed Pitus delightedly on the arm. He looked at Dathin. "You have fighter experience."

"Aye, sir, I do," Dathin replied. He turned toward the assembly line. "I need six more pilots." He had them within five seconds. "Stop what you are doing and follow these men."

Later that evening the phone warbled and John answered it.

"Johnny! What the hell happened," exclaimed Joe.

"I got fired."

"You know damn well I know that much from the sound of my voice," he thundered.

"I was just trying to find the proper entry level of this conversation," said John.

"I'd say it should start with why you seem so flip about losing your job and the attendant bad publicity," Joe said impatiently.

"Bingham's been broadcasting about the thing, eh? Maybe I should sue him for libel."

"I didn't hear this from Bingham," said Joe. "I got it from three different phone calls from other pharmacists. One call came from Bill Cook over in Rutland."

"I've yelled myself hoarse, cursed myself dry, and kicked myself lame, and even sat down and cried a little over it all. I'm too tired to be miserable any more," John answered dejectedly.

"I take it for granted that you're no thief, and I know you ain't an enemy of the state."

"I'm not guilty of a thing, Joe. I'm a victim of a game of hard ball by some federal agents."

"What do the Feds want with you?"

"What they want, they got," said John. "It was a book. A book that I bought and paid for legally and they took illegally."

"A book?" said Joseph. "I don't understand; A book of names, a black book or something?"

"A hundred year old biographical book."

"Who's it about?"

"Three guesses . . ."

"Pitus," said Joe. "I can see that would be an interesting thing to read. Lord knows, I would gladly read it, but I don't understand how Pitus Peston's life story should stir the attention of the Federal Government."

"I had the thing right in my hands, dammit!"

"Do you have any idea why they want it," asked Joe?

"Before I could find that out the Flynn and his mascot swooped down on me," said John. Then John spoke in a lower voice. "Look Joe, I have more things relating to Pitus. I have some journals he wrote on his travels out west and some other papers. I want to show them to you so I will have a witness if the bastards find out about them and confiscate them all."

"Journals," repeated Joe. "Jesus, I'll be right there!"

Before Joe could reach up to knock at the door, John yanked it open.

"You always seem to know when I am at your door," Joe declared as he entered the kitchen. "I swear, if ever I actually have to rap on your door, I'm gonna think you're hurt or something."

"X-ray vision," John replied. "Hello Lorraine." She smiled in greeting and sat down at the kitchen table.

"X-ray ass," retorted Joe.

"Coffee's on." Joe poured a cup. Lorraine waved off an offer from John.

"Joyce will be over shortly," said John. "She's tending to a special project."

While Joe sat at the kitchen table, John brought out the almanacs, journals, and photographs that he made during his trips across the country of the last several months. He explained the itinerary of Pitus from 1808 when he left home to his final destination at Tonga Hinga five years later. He showed photographs that he took of the pillar at Lake Ponchatrain and of the other in North Dakota. He showed the others the almanac entries where Ellen saw Pitus as a young man 75 years after he disappeared. Two hours later, Joe's coffee remained untouched.

Somewhere along in the narration Joyce came in and quietly took a chair at the table. John glanced at her, she nodded a "thumbs up" and he continued the briefing.

John finished up by bringing out the box he found atop Tonga Hinga. Joe lifted the container. It was the size of a shoe box.

"This is some kind of plastic but not like anything I ever handled." He handed it to Lorraine who felt of it and nodded in agreement.

"You sure this isn't a piece of rubbish some rock climber left up there?"

"You said yourself that it isn't like anything you've ever seen," said John. "Me neither . . . and it's old. That is apparent from the look of it."

"Carbon fiber probably," said Joe. "You could drive a car over this and not break it, I'll bet."

"What was in it?" asked Lorraine.

"Something that dated the thing precisely," replied John. He handed her a tightly folded sheet of paper. "That's all that was in it," said John and it was sealed and clearly undisturbed for a long time." Lorraine unfolded the sheet and read it aloud.

"At the base of this monument lies a true friend, Martin Backus, who warned me of peril and gave his life in the process. 9 August, 1813."

"Martin was one of Pitus' friends from his early days who followed another man, Todd VanEps, who was tracking Pitus in order to kill him," said John. "Martin was ambushed by VanEps and shot. He was left to die but he managed to get to Pitus and warn him. He died in Pitus' arms while delivering the warning. I found a piece of a wooden marker half buried in the dirt over the spot. VanEps is also someplace around there, justice courtesy of Pitus Peston."

"Was all that in here?" asked Joe holding up one of the journals.

"That was in the fourth volume," said John.

"Who'd a thought it," breathed Joe as he swept a glance over the real life adventure represented on the table.

"I don't know what he found on the top of that butte," said John. "The final volume starts where he saw an object gleaming from the butte's base. He also describes how he managed to reach the top of the thousand foot high butte. That's a hell of a story by itself. When he referred to whatever it was, he said, the 'palace' or the 'abode of the gods'; cryptic bullshit like that."

"What do you think," asked Joe?

"I will have to answer that question with another question," said John. "What could it be that would cause the FBI to give a damn about it?"

A few nights later, Joe returned home from an errand.

"The watch is gone." Lorraine said. "Did you give it to John? How did he take the news?

"It is gone, but I didn't give it to John." Joe said. "I made better use of it."

"Like what?"

"This better not go past your ears." Joe said seriously.

"I have never told any secret that you have entrusted to me these five years we've been married." Lorraine said indignantly.

"OK, OK, Hon. I Know that. I just want you to know how important it is to keep a lid on it."

"I'll understand that when you get around to telling me what you did with the watch."

"I gave it back to Ken."

"For Pete's sake, Joseph," she said in disbelief.

"Wait a minute, dear," Joe said. "I found out that right after Bingham fired Johnny, Ken went over to the house and demanded the rent. It seems that John was spending all of his dough making those trips all over the place. He was two months behind, and with John being out of work, Ken saw a chance to get him out of there, for whatever reason."

"Because he's a prick!"

"Lorraine!"

"Well, what would you call a guy like that?"

"A prick."

"So, keep talking." Lorraine urged.

"I went over to Ken's last night and gave him the watch. I told him that Keenan brought it to me and filled in the details. I also told him that only the two of us knew about the affair and if that was to continue, I had better not hear that John is put out of his house."

"Good!" Lorraine said with satisfaction. "I wish I could have seen the look on his puss when you gave him that watch."

"It was quite a sight." said Joe.

The next evening, John was with Joe at the bowling alley on Broad Street. After a couple of games, it appeared that the place was getting a bit crowded.

"Let's go over to Mike's for a beer," said Joe.

"I can't," replied John, "I have something I have to do."

"What could be more important than good beer and B S," asked Joe. "Never mind," he added, "tell Joyce hello for me." Joe clapped John on the shoulder and started for the door. Outside John asked, "Where'd you park?" Joe pointed to his car twenty feet ahead.

"Where are you?" asked Joe.

"Half a mile that way," he gestured toward the back of the parking lot.

"Don't get lost," said Joe. He jumped into his car and was gone in a few seconds.

Half way back to his truck, John spotted a dark limousine idling on the side of the lot. He gave it a mildly jealous look and then returned his attention to his own humble means of transport. A dark and heavy set figure stood facing him as he arrived at his vehicle.

"Mr. Ott would like a moment of your time," the man said in a manner that denied any prospect of declining. The man pointed to the limo and they both started for it with John in the lead.

"Very posh," said John, when he entered the vehicle and glanced around.

"Thank you," said Ott with cordial indifference.

"I'm fresh out of Louis d' Ors," said John.

"You are such a smart-ass," laughed Ott, "but I like that in a person that is honest." He handed John a martini. John politely accepted the drink and sat back in the plush seat.

"I was wondering," said Ott, "if you had given any more thought to my parting offer."

"Stuff written by Pitus? I told you I haven't found anything like that."

"Come now," said Ott, "Surely you would not have gone through the trouble of retracing Peston's route if you didn't have something. In fact, without a considerable amount of information, it would have been impossible."

"I did a lot of traveling in the past several months," said John. "I don't see how anyone could construe anything from it. I was just visiting places of interest."

"That may be plausible for St. Louis, but Laplace, Louisiana? Mobridge, South Dakota? You even rented a camper in Albuquerque and drove into Monument Valley."

"What of it," asked John defiantly?

"Those are all places Peston went," Said Ott. "I also know you hired a helicopter to take you over the area. That must have set you back some, but probably not as much as getting permission from the Navajos to let you land on Merrick Butte among other places."

"If you know all this, why do you need my help," asked John.

Ott reached down beside himself and held up a book. "Ever see anything like this?" The look on John's face told the answer.

"There were two copies," said Ott, "This one and the one you had briefly which is now in the hands of the F.B.I. He handed it to John. "Take it with my compliments as a sort of reparation for your ill treatment by them." John took the book and set it in his lap.

"Have you read it?" asked Ott.

"The bastards grabbed it before I had a chance," said John.

"Interesting reading," said Ott. "It explains why he never went back to St. Louis in 1811. He never knew that he abandoned his own son."

"Laura," said John, recalling a mention of her in the third volume of PEREGRINATIONS.

"Laura Leigh Ott was her full name. She raised the child alone, never married, hoping that her lover would someday return. She died in 1824 of pneumonia and was buried in what is now Oak Hill Cemetery."

"Her last name was Ott," asked John incredulously. "Is that a coincidence or are you a descendant?"

"I guess you can say I'm a descendant," said Ott sardonically.

"What became of the boy," asked John.

"He left St. Louis on the *Belle Fleur*, a side-wheeler on its way to New Orleans. Quite an interesting story by itself and while particularly poignant to me personally, I am less interested in all that than in some other things."

"Such as," asked John.

"Corstet."

John sat with a sphinx-like expression, hoping that the discerning gaze of Simeon Ott could not penetrate to what John knew about the plant. He, or rather, Joyce, had planted twenty-two of the seeds from the pods in that bottle from Mike's cellar. Twelve of them germinated and were by now nearly three inches tall under Joyce's grow light.

"Mr. Flynn is not a fool," warned Ott. "He has to get control of both copies of that book in order to prevent the information from getting out to the wrong hands. He will be after that one as well. Any other Peston related materials will definitely be on his hit list whether stated in a warrant or not. So," continued

Ott, "you had better think carefully about how to keep hold of all the things you claim not to have. You can deal with the Feds or deal with me. The difference between us is that I will share what I have and Flynn won't. Another difference is that I will make you an 'associate'."

"What's in this book to make the U.S. government want it so bad," asked John.

"I wouldn't dream of spoiling that thrill for you," said Ott. He motioned to his driver who immediately got out and came around to where John was seated. He opened the door.

"Think fast," said Ott. "It is later than you think." John stood watching as the limousine pulled away. He went to his truck with mixed feelings of foreboding and elation.

Lorraine answered the phone, and after a second, handed it to Joe.

"Hello," he said

"Hi, Joe," It's John. I'd like to come over and talk with you a minute."

"I dare say. I can guess that if you're calling me 'Joe' instead of Jacques."

"I'll be right over."

"What's going on?"

"I'll tell you when I get there."

Joe opened the door and John walked on in without even a greeting. As he crossed the threshold, Joe passed him an Ice Blue Light.

"What's the mystery, Johnny?"

"I know why they want the book," said John excitedly. "Joyce and I thought the book would be about his travels out west."

"Yeah, so tell me so I don't kill you in frustration and never find out." said Joe.

"It's about a longer journey," said John. "It's an account of his voyage to another planet."

"What!"

"Oman is more than the name of a god's temple like he first wrote in his journals. It is a planet on the far side of this galaxy!"

"For Pete's Sake," Joe said dejectedly. "Just when this was getting interesting . . ."

"Don't you believe it," asked John?

"Do you," asked Joe? "I mean, really . . . it has to be just a novel. I was getting excited that he discovered some unknown place that we could have tracked down. Now to find out that it's about space aliens is quite a let down."

"There are some things in this book that are very convincing," said John who now held the second copy of the Peregrinations up before Joe's face. Joe grabbed the book opening it up to the title page. "I'd like to read this even though it's about aliens," said Joe.

"When you're finished with it you'll be a believer," said John.

"O K," said Joe. "I'm game. What is this 'convincing' stuff?"

"He describes propulsion methods that I have only partly heard of. That is, I know some of the basic science behind it, but he goes far beyond in detail."

John took the book and turned to a bookmarked place. 'The Omans long ago learned to make a forced singularity which is used in vehicle propulsion. By using an array of collimated light bursts onto a sphere of hydrogen metal, the hydrogen can be converted into a black hole. This singularity must be enclosed in a magnetic bottle sheathed in heavy metal, their favorite being pure gold, to prevent spontaneous evaporation. To get the singularity to a functional size, matter must be directed into it. The matter needed is equivalent to that within a medium size mountain, such as those of the Rockies, or an asteroid of at least 5 miles diameter. The field of the magnetic bottle is breached midway between the poles and the matter is directed into it. This process takes several minutes to accomplish with a resultant black hole the size of a plennum (proton) within an elliptical bottle whose long axis is 14 inches and short axis 10 inches. This unit is placed within an inertial damping field for handling and transport.' All this and there are even mathematical formulae and sketches." Joe seemed stymied by all the techno babble John just read. Then he remembered another passage.

"He described the planet that was just recently found orbiting Zosma in Leo. He couldn't have known about that back in the 1880's."

"I don't know . . ." Joe said with a latent skepticism.

"What about all the weird things we already know about Pitus." said John. "It all adds up."

"If it *is* true, then it's incredible."

"It sure as hell is."

"So that's why the government wants it?"

"It is proof of life on other planets. It's a story about a UFO," declared John. "And you know how they want to keep things like this hushed up." He handed the book back to Joe. "Can you read it tonight?"

"Probably," said Joe, "but why the rush?"

"I'm gonna copy it before the pricks steal that from me like the other one."

The next morning was Joe's Saturday off. John roused him out of bed at seven-thirty. "Geeziz Johnny," said Joe through a yawn, "Don't you ever sleep in on a day off?"

"All my days are off now Jacques," quipped John.

"I'm doing a little work on that," said Joe. "You may have to work in Vermont, but what could be more poetically just than earning *green* in the Green Mountain State?" John shook his head at the atrocious pun, but added a "thank you". Then he asked, "Did you read it?"

"Every word," said Joe. "I was up all night, but no regrets." He led John into the living room where the *Peregrinations* lay on an end table. He put the book in a paper bag and handed the sack to John. "This is the biggest thing . . . ever," he said. "You should go public with this. You would never have to stand behind a counter for the rest of your life."

"Probably spend the time in a cell," said John. "I need to let this entire thing cool down awhile. Maybe some day . . ."

Joe nodded.

"There's something else," said John. "Someone's been in my house."

"How do you know?"

"The books on my shelves have been monkeyed with."

"Ken snooping around, probably," ventured Joe. "Change your locks and the bastard can't get in."

"It was not Ken this time," John said.

"How can you tell that," asked Joe?

"When Ken comes in snooping, he musses thing up and leaves things around to make sure I know he's been there and that it's tough shit," said John. "This time it was done with care to prevent me from detecting them."

"Luckily not with enough care," said Joe.

"The books on my living room shelf are not smoothly faced." said John. "They look unkempt and random, but they are anything but. They are arranged according to a template I cut out of a piece of lath. When I got home I lined up the template to the row of books and they touched the inner edge except for two that were shoved back a half inch too far."

"Very clever," said Joe. "They didn't get any of your Pitus things, I hope."

"It's all safe so far, but I have to get it all out of there. It's too damn hot."

"Bring it over here," said Joe.

"That would put you at risk," John said. "They might also think of that."

"Whoever *they* might be," said Joe.

"Got to be Flynn and his Neanderthal sidekick," said John. "I'm probably right now in the sights of a long camera lens."

"Sounds like you better be quick about getting that stuff out of the house," Joe said.

After breakfast John called Joyce. This was her Saturday off too.

"Hello? John! Where in hell are you," She exclaimed? "Do you know there are federal agents still after you?"

"Yes, and that's why I can't tell you," he replied. "I got the other PEREGRINATIONS."

"I gathered that. The feds were here with a warrant for it less than an hour ago. They're looking for you, too!"

"It happens to be the stolen copy," John said, "but they stole the other one from me so I think we're even."

"It won't be yours long if they catch up with you!"

"They have no right to it! It belongs to me."

"I don't think they care a damn about that," Joyce warned. "They seem determined to get it regardless."

"Go to the place," said John. "I know why they are after it."

"Go to the place?" Joyce asked incredulously. "They will almost certainly be staking it out."

"Not THAT place," John said. "Go find a good dog; don't let yourself be followed." John soon arrived at D.J.'s. He parked the truck behind the bus terminal and walked over. "Hey Johnny," Frank exclaimed, "You looking for a nutritional breakfast?"

"No, Frank. Is there anything going on out back?"

"This time of the morning," asked Frank.

"Can I borrow the room a little while?"

"What's the trouble? You look all flustered."

"When Joyce comes in send her out back."

"Hey, I don't want the felt on that game table all dug up . . ."

"Frank the comedian," said John.

"What's going on," asked Frank more seriously?

"I have something somebody wants and it isn't theirs to take . . . at least not for a while."

"You got something those guys from Washington want," he said nervously. "I don't want any problems with the G-men. They'll have me audited or something."

"*G-men*," repeated John. "You've been reading those Mickey Spillane's again?" John grinned. "You won't have any trouble. They don't know where I am. Just send her back; please Frank, I need your help for a little bit. I'll owe you one."

"You'll owe me TWO for this!"

John sat down at the large table that was used for the weekly "poker tournament", as the players liked to call it. There were nights at this table that thousands of dollars changed hands, yet not so much as a dime was ever seen placed upon its surface. Sometimes personal property or services were bartered over a hand of cards. One week a high ranking state official "purchased" a small sports car from another at the table for the price of a pair of sevens. Sometime before this, ol' man Keenan "negotiated" a gall bladder extraction from a surgeon well known to John. News got out about it, but nothing official was ever said. Though many knew that gambling was going on there, the ones who were doing it had enough collective influence to ensure that they were not disturbed. This, in John's mind, made this the safest place to be, at the moment when times were hot.

He swept his hands over the soft felt surface of the table. "God, I bet it *would* feel great to . . ."

Joyce entered and ran up to John. She put her arms around him. "You damn fool," she called in a muffled shout. "You're going to end up in prison!"

"I think not," John replied coolly. The feds want only the books. They don't want me as extra baggage."

"Then just give them the damn thing! It isn't worth the trouble it has caused."

"Not a chance!" John said, "It is my book, I paid for it, or at least the one the Feds took. Too bad this is the one from the Library of Congress. I say 'tit for tat.'"

"Where did you get it?"

"The *competition*."

"Ott," Joyce gasped. "He stole it from the DLC," she added as though talking about someone robbing the alter at Saint Peter's. "He just gave it to you," she asked?

"When Joe and I left the bowling alley the other night, Ott was there waiting for me. He asked me if I had anything else about Pitus. I of course said no, but obviously didn't convince him. He handed me the book and warned me that the Feds would be after anything else that had Peston's name on it, and it would be far better to deal with him than them."

"Maybe he's right," said Joyce.

"I don't trust either of them," said John. "The Feds can be slippery, but they have to adhere to some rule of law. Ott may not feel so constrained. I fear him more than Flynn and Dolph."

"Only the Feds want that book," said Joyce, "and they'll get you eventually."

"I know that. It's a losing battle. Except . . ."

"Except?"

"I'm going to copy it before I give it up to them."

"How are you going to copy that whole book," asked Joyce? "It will take a hell of a long time."

"I guess I had better get going at it then." John said. "I'll get a motel room someplace and a digital camera . . ."

"No." Joyce interrupted. "I have a better idea. My library connections will come in handy for this little project. We will have to go to Burlington."

"What's up there?"

"Not so much what as whom." Joyce said. "A guy I used to date has a photography shop. He has all the equipment; Cameras, computers, the whole works. And he can do it fast."

"It's getting rather complicated, this whole thing," John said.

"Somebody's got to help you," she said affectionately. "You're too crazy to pull it off without a blunder." John smiled and touched her hand.

"No time for that sort of thing," she said softly. "Let's get away from here; away from all this heat."

"They will recognize my truck."

"We'll get a cab and then rent a car."

"Joyce! What are you doing in these parts?" Morris exclaimed as he stood in the doorway. "We were just sitting down to breakfast." He called out, "Laurie, come meet a friend!" He looked at John. "Two friends, I'm sure."

During breakfast, Joyce discussed the business at hand.

"I'm free for the day. I'm also sure that Laura will appreciate me being out of her hair." He cast a quick glance at his wife who nodded in mirthful affirmation. While Morris was looking over the job, he said, "This used to be an expensive business copying over a whole book like this. Now with the computer and digital photography, it's the time that's most of the cost. I hope you don't think I am gouging you by charging two hundred dollars."

"Not at all." Joyce assured him.

"Is this a valuable book?" Morris asked. "I mean, too expensive to just buy it outright?"

"Not really." John replied. "It's worth a hundred dollars."

"You are paying me two hundred bucks to copy a hundred-dollar book? I don't understand." John hesitated. He had no logical answer to his behavior. Joyce rescued the moment.

"John is just borrowing this book. There are only two known copies. His friend wouldn't sell it to him because it is part of his collection. He lent it to John for a time, and I hit upon the idea of having it copied." She gave John an elbow and smirked.

"So I won't risk losing a friendship by stealing it!"

"We will try not to bruise the binding, or your friendship." he said jocularly.

When the job was done, John took one of the two c-d's Morris had burned of the book's pages to a post office. He purchased a small priority box and mailed it to Joe with a little note of explanation. Then the two returned home. Joyce drove by the bus terminal.

"Truck's still there." John remarked.

"I'm sure it is being watched," said Joyce.

"Take this copy with you. John said. He took a felt tipped marker from his shirt pocket and wrote on the disk. He showed it to Joyce who sight read it; "Dolly Parton's Greatest Hits." It took only a couple of seconds to sink in. "You are such a wise ass," she declared. John grinned and put the c-d in an album of music discs Joyce had between the seats. "This is our insurance policy just in case the bastards force me to give them the original."

"Be careful." Joyce urged. She leaned over to kiss him. "Don't resist them. You can always get a court order if they take it, and the copy is the proof that it exists."

"I do care if they get the original," John said calmly, "But I'll not lament it overmuch so long as you don't lose your copy and Joe doesn't lose his. It interests me mainly for its content. Though," he said with awe, "The book has doubtless been in the hands of its author . . . . maybe even in outer space."

John dropped Joyce off at her apartment and went on home. He entered the house through the kitchen and turned on the light. He checked out the whole of down stairs to make sure that there were no visitors while he was away. He then went up stairs and turned on the upstairs bedroom light and drew the drapes. Returning down stairs, he snapped off all the lights but those in the front of the house. He went down into the cellar with a penlight, just bright enough to find and open the tunnel. He kept his larger light off until he got well into the tunnel. He groped his way along in the passage with the tiny light.

"Oh!" he called out, tripping over something in the way, falling down on the stone floor. He scraped his right hand in breaking his fall, both lights flying out of his left hand. He felt around for the light but gave up after a minute. He took out a book of matches and lit one. In the flare of the match he saw the large light, but also four of the wall boards strewn across the floor.

An electric surge of fear shot through him as he gained the flash light and turned it on. He was still thirty feet from the end of the tunnel where he hid the collection, but each step added to the confirmation that his hiding place had been ransacked. "Flynn, that bastard!" John yelled. "He stole it all!" He stood in front of the gaping hole where he had stashed his things. "How could he have known about this place?"

John ran out of the passage and up into the kitchen. In seconds he was in his truck racing for the Glens Falls. He parked by the Library and jogged across the lawn to the hotel. He forced himself to gather his wits before going in. He knew he couldn't force the clerk to give the agents' room number, so he devised a quick plan. The gift shop was still open, so he went in and purchased a gaudy looking birthday card with a teal blue envelope. He casually went up to the desk. "Would you see that Mr. Flynn gets this?" John asked. He handed the card to the clerk. He slowly turned away as if leaving. A well timed backward glance saw the card being placed in the appropriate mail slot for Flynn's room. "The old trick still works," murmured John. "How many old movies have I seen that in?"

As John arrived at the door to Flynn's room, it opened and Flynn emerged.

"Mr. Hodiak," said Flynn in genuine surprise.

"I don't give a damn who you are; you have no right breaking into a man's house and stealing his rightful property!"

"Get a hold of yourself Mr. Hodiak. Come in here," said Flynn quickly pulling the door open and checking the hall for bystanders.

Inside John wheeled about to face Flynn. "You got your book. The rest of it is none of your damn business."

Dolph sat in a chair watching the television, but jumped up at the commotion and hurried toward the two.

"And you," shouted John," are probably the one who broke in my house, you prick!"

"That's the second time you called me that," snarled Dolph. "I'm not taking it this time." He grabbed at John and missed. John lunged at Dolph and they ended up grappling on the floor just inside the door. They both got to their feet, when Dolph punched John on the mouth sending him reeling into the hall. Someone had reported the disturbance and a house detective appeared while John was getting back to his feet. The detective grabbed John with one hand while holding a gun on him with the other. "You're under arrest, mister. We are going down to the police station," he bellowed. Flynn quickly showed his badge and said there was no need for that. The detective would not back down. "This is my beat, agent Flynn," he said. "I don't allow fighting with guests in my hotel. If you want to talk to this man, you'll have to come down town." Dolph stood and brushed himself off. He smiled disdainfully at John. "Good enough for you," he said snidely. "I will get the full story," said the detective. "If there is just cause, a grievance will be made to the Bureau as well. With that the detective led John away.

John was processed at the police station and place in a cell for the night. Shortly, he was visited by Flynn and Dolph. Flynn asked the guard that accompanied them, "Can we go someplace where we can talk privately?" John and the two agents were directed to an interrogation room. Flynn sat down opposite John at a table while Dolph paced around the room.

"We haven't been in your house, Mr. Hodiak," said Flynn emphatically. His voice then took on a softer tone. "My name is Tom," Flynn said. "Can I call you John?" John nodded sullenly and looked over at Flynn. This change of attitude helped convince John that Tom was truthful, but even if this was so, John thought it would be foolish to disclose the full details of the stolen goods. Just then Henning entered the room.

"Good evening, Mr. Hodiak."

"It's John. We're all on first names now," he said bitterly.

"John it is then. I'm, Dan," replied Henning cordially. "We met in Albany, as you may well remember."

"What's going to happen to me?" asked John.

"Assaulting a federal officer is a serious offense," said Dan. "You could go to jail for a long time."

"Good place for him," said Dolph.

"If you had acted more professionally," snapped Dan, "we would not have to be here."

"The lousy bastard attacked me," shouted Dolph. Neither Flynn nor Henning acknowledged Dolph. "Act more professional," Dolph repeated derisively. Then he cursed and stormed out of the room.

"Good," said Dan, "That got rid of him." John snorted a laugh and sat back in his chair a bit more relaxed. Dan took a chair next to Tom.

"Tell us what was stolen, John," he asked. "I will be straight with you," he added, "If it is related to the PEREGRINATIONS; it is also likely to be material of interest to the United States." John looked at Henning skeptically. His certainty that the feds broke into his house was eroding.

"It's nothing really," said John. "Just some old papers Pitus wrote while preparing for his trip out West."

"If someone else has been in your house after something, then you could be in considerable danger," said Flynn. "You need to tell us all about it or we can't protect you."

"It looks like whatever they wanted they got," said John. Flynn looked like he was going to continue, but Henning stopped him.

"Is there anyone you can think of who might have known about Peston or any of his personal belongings?

"Anyone who knew would never betray me," said John.

"If the book is any indication," said Henning, "what you have accumulated could be worth stealing or killing for." Henning stood up. "Mr. Hodiak, I am going to ask you a rather incredible question. Before you answer, I want you to think about all you have learned about Pitus Peston."

"I'll answer if I can," said John.

"Do you have any information that might suggest that Peston will be returning, and if so, when?" Flynn stared at Henning. John shook his head. "How the hell could that be," he asked?

"Very well, John," said Dan. "We will be back here in the morning when you go before the judge." Henning used a phone in the room to signal the guard. In a moment he appeared and led John away to his cell. Outside the station Henning said to Flynn, "Go with somebody over to Hodiak's house and have a look. We seem to have another interested party and I want to know who it is if possible."

"I'll see to it myself," said Flynn. Henning nodded approval and turned to leave.

"Sir," said Flynn. "Peston was born two hundred years ago. How could he be coming back and if so from where?"

"I'm afraid that's beyond your clearance," said Henning. He then hurried off.

That night in his cell, John had trouble getting to sleep. This was not for the obvious reasons. He lay on his back on the cot staring up at the darkness. "Peston coming back? That's preposterous." He thought about Ellen Lattimore's sighting back in 1883. "Could that have been real? What if it *was* possible? Jesus, what could that mean . . . Does Henning know something?"

A little before nine the next morning, an officer came in and ordered John to stand. "We're going to see the Judge now," he said. The Judge arraigned John on simple assault, not assault on a federal officer. This relieved John considerably. The bail was set at five thousand dollars, which considerably took away that relief. He was processed, made a call to Joyce, and was then returned to his cell. By the time Joyce got to the jail John was on his way out.

"Oh, Honey," she cried as she hugged him. "Don't worry, I got the bail." She let go of him suddenly. "What are you doing out here. I haven't had a chance to pay the bail yet."

"Someone beat you to it," replied John "or I wouldn't be up here."

"Who?" asked Joyce? "Was it Joe?"

"Someone named 'John Smith'."

She puzzled at this, but then said, "As long as you are out of that jail . . ."

"I have my guess about it," said John. "I will get the money tomorrow and pay him a visit."

"Who was it?" she asked again.

"The *competition*."

"Why would he do this for you?" she asked.

"He wants me to be his business associate."

"They headed for home, but John decided along the way that he needed a stiff drink more than anything after his experience with the law. They went to Mike's.

"Hi, Johnny and Joyce," said Mike cordially. He placed a glass of draft on the bar for each of them. John took out some money and placed it on the bar, but Mike waved him off. "These are on me."

"Thanks Mike," said John. "I imagine you've heard all the poop about me."

"That's all it is," said Mike. "Joe and Lorraine were here last night, and I got the dope from them." He laughed. "Dope, get it!" John smirked and then smiled. "You're a good man, Mike," said John, "I don't care what anyone else says about you."

"What a coincidence," quipped Mike, "neither do I." He eyed John quizzically. "What are you gonna do now?"

"Joe's been talking to some friends in St. Johnsbury. He might be able to convince them to hire a subversive. In the meantime, I have a little put aside," said John. "I can't tell you how, but I can say it's not stolen."

"Good for you Johnny. And if you got a stash, then you can buy your own suds." Then he laughed. "Only kidding."

Mike went off to wait on some other customers and Joyce went off to the girl's room. John sat sipping on his beer. A tap on his shoulder rousted him from his thoughts.

"Fred, hello," said John. Ames slid onto the next stool.

"You seem to be a V I P," said Ames.

"Anyone can have my fame for a nickel," said John, "and I'll even supply the damn nickel."

"You must have found it,"

"Found what?"

"Medwyd's gold. I heard you were traveling a lot and wondered if you had gotten lucky."

"I'm sure you know all about it," said John. "Don't rub it in. The whole town is talking."

"I didn't mean it that way," said Ames. "I heard about you taking time off work to go all around the country and Simeon Ott was at the coin show in Saratoga. He told me he had recently uncovered some significant pieces. I just put two and two together . . ."

"Simeon Ott," repeated John softly.

"That's who you must have sold the coins to," said Ames. "He's got one of the finest collections of U.S. and European gold in the world. He was quite proud of the French gold he had just acquired. I was there looking for some colonial coppers and we bumped into each other.

"When did you see him?"

"Yesterday afternoon at the Convention Center."

"That son of a bitch," murmured John. "I was away all day yesterday . . . Of Course."

"So, tell me," asked Ames. "Did I get it right?"

"Yes, but keep quiet about it," said John. "There are some who I don't wish to know it." He thought a second. "Come over Wednesday after supper and I'll show you the rest. There are quite a few coppers."

"Wouldn't miss it for the world," said Ames gleefully. "I'll bring a copy of PENNY WHIMSY and a check book too," he added expectantly. John nodded and Ames left. He acted almost giddy.

Confident that he had Ames bought off with his invitation to a private showing, John called for another beer. Shortly Joyce returned. They both finished their drinks and left. John was ruminating in the car as he drove and Joyce picked up on it.

"You know who stole your stuff?" she asked.

"I thought Flynn was lying through his teeth, but now I know it wasn't the Feds."

"Ken?"

"Doubtful, though he's always around for what he can get. The cat will be out of the bag soon if not already." They arrived at John's house.

"You *do* know who," Joyce pressed. John nodded. "I'm gonna find out tonight if my suspicion is correct."

"It's Ott, isn't it? Joyce declared. "I'm going with you."

"Not a good idea," replied John.

"I have a stake in this too," she said.

"What stake?"

"You," she said. She quickly stifled his protest with a kiss.

BATTLE FOR OMAN
PART I

Pitus and the other seven pilots suited up and entered the hangar.

"I want each of you men to pick a ship and run through a complete pre-flight check. No one lifts off unless all major systems are red. Move out when I give the signal which will be three sets of five pings to your coms."

The orbiters were armed with particle beam cannons. The fighters had these as well, but were additionally outfitted with an array of low yield nuclear percussion devices which could be launched through tubes on the undersides of the hulls. The percussion bombs were tactical and had a two kiloton yield, sufficient to stall out any flessmic weapon or ship's drive within a two kilometer radius. Contact within half a kilometer would almost certainly inflict severe structural damage to an opponent. Pitus left the fighters to the experienced pilots and selected one of the more capacious orbiters.

He entered the vessel and sat at the controls. There was a master switch which allowed power to flow from the magnetic bottle enclosing the forced singularity, which was the main energy source, to the master buss. From here on, the miles of wiring and optical cables conveyed the power to the far reaches of the ship. Pitus pulled three times on the handle of the switch, priming it for contact. Once engaged it would be held in position by a powerful solenoid to prevent accidental disengagement. He heard the snap of the solenoid and instantly the cockpit was bathed in light. In front of him were arrayed three panels. Directly in front of him was the panel showing the ships systems status. There were but three green indicators here. These were merely switches to auxiliary systems unnecessary to the performance of the vessel. He decided to leave them in off position. The rest were in "go-ahead red." To his right was a small panel showing weapon status with steady beam for cutting and pulse beam for bolusing a wad of plasma of a million kelvins at a velocity of a hundred kilometers per second. The panel to the left was a three dimensional tactical screen showing all the objects within a fifty kilometer radius for the short scanner. A mere push of a button engaged the long range scanner, capable of tracking objects up to a light year away. The three panels were optimal. No problems here. He looked at the drive life indicator on the right side of the center screen. It showed thirty percent degradation of the main drive. He estimated by the linear rate of evaporation that the Orbiter was built a hundred fifty years prior, about the time on Earth when Oliver Cromwell came to power. "Still plenty of juice for the use," Pitus said aloud pensively.

A forced singularity, created by laser implosion of a quantity of metallic hydrogen, is not permanent like one found in nature. For one thing, a natural singularity, otherwise known as a black hole, is many orders of magnitude larger. Even a mini black hole in space the size of a thumbnail is likely to contain within its event horizon, one or more solar masses. This is a lot of tonnage; a nonillion metric tons' of matter is contained in the Earth's sun, for example. A ship able to use a mini black hole of this size as a power source would extend from the orbit of Earth to the orbit of Venus if constructed with the current technology of the Local Group of Planets. This power source would endure for millions of years. By contrast, the puny singularities in J-7 Orbiters as they were made at the Assembler at Jartic Orz before its destruction in the Thirty-Minute's War, contain a mere billion or so metric tons, the amount of matter probably in Mount Washington, in New Hampshire. Its size is smaller than a helium nucleus, and can be expected to remain patent for about five-hundred years (eight hundred Oman years) before it fizzles out. The containment bottle was the latest version of pre-war magnetic bottle a little larger than a football, permanently hyper-magnetized by flessmic induction. The one in Atoye's Duster, however, was huge by comparison. The Duster was an older line of vehicles using more primitive technology. The magnetic bottle was not football size, but as big as a refrigerator.

He sat back and stretched his arms and yawned. It might be a long wait. Then a realization struck him. "What the hell am I doing here," he said aloud. "I am no ronta sard (dog fighter)." He tapped his communicator patch. Kinar answered.

"Ask the Colonel to send down another experienced pilot," Pitus said. "I have an orbiter ready to roll and an idea to put myself to better use than fumbling over these unfamiliar controls in the heat of battle."

Meanwhile, Atoye, Orban, and Kinar were at the brisler production line, which by now was producing a fully charged weapon every fifteen seconds. There were two hundred of them ready to go, which Gastin ordered to be delivered through the aperture to Oman. Atoye left with the first delivery crew in order to set up a relay transport from Kesst into Nesgoor where the NOA was digging in.

The enemy was losing no time in preparation.

"Sir," exclaimed a startled Katun. "Where did you come from?" Ich Habine had little Idea himself how he appeared at the Annex of the Hibber Institute at Kesst. The last thing he remembered was that thousands of light years away in the galactic center, he and Pitus Peston were in mortal combat in the shadow of Loma's Cube. He recalled that it wasn't going well. Peston had a knife at his throat, but for some foolish reason, wasn't using it. Then the Guardian of the Cube lowered his sapphire blue staff and a white light enveloped him. Seemingly in the next instant, he was at the Annex.

"Never mind how I got here," he growled. "How long ago did I leave here?"

"Sir," asked Katun incredulously?

"You heard me," Habine demanded. "Answer the question!"

"Two months," replied Katun. "We thought you had been killed or captured."

Habine looked pensive a moment. "I must have been held in suspension some where for all that time," he thought. "No time to be concerned about it."

"Are the men in place and ready to take this damn planet once and for all?"

"There are a hundred and fifty here, Sir and as many at Jartic Orz finishing up the weapons preparation."

"Is that all," Habine asked?

"There are twelve ships on their way. Ten fighting vessels and two troop transports each carrying a thousand troopers."

"That is more like it," Habine said. "I won't have to kill you for treason after all for shirking in your duty. When will they arrive?"

"Late today," said Katun. "The commander, Manik Coo, transmitted from Pragoot Barg this morning. Plans are made for outfitting at Jartic Orz and then deployment of half there and half here. By tomorrow we can start our march to Nesgoor and Baluge at the same time the southern army goes for Calatan and Avesta. That should eliminate any threat from the Omans.

"Security?"

"Our intelligence assures us that the Omans are unaware of the impending invasion. Even if they did find out, they are unarmed." Habine yielded an uncharacteristic sneer which was his equivalent to a smile of approval.

"When can I go to Jartic Orz," asked Habine. "I want to be there when our allies arrive and also check on the progress with the cleaver. There may be no other space worthy assets than our own, but the Calbres may send some aid if they reverse their usual policy of neutrality. A couple of cleaved Calbres ships will put a stop to their interference. I want the *surprise* to be fully operational for whoever dares come."

The surprise, a canon of sorts, was the innovation of Calbresan. The device in its original form shot out a planar beam of high energy neutrons at a target at thousands of meters per second. It was created for the purpose of mining asteroids to harvest their valuable metals. Prospectors had these expensive devices rigged onto their ore boats and could cut a target asteroid into slices that would fit into their holds for transport to a refinery on some planet.

The cleavers, as they were called, made it no longer necessary for prospectors to leave a perfectly sound ship to land on an often erratically moving mass in the hostile environment of space to rig synchronous explosive charges around asteroids to both break them up and prevent their fragments from careening off into space, sometimes back in the face of the prospector, thus ending an otherwise promising career.

This Calbres invention was almost instantly seen for its great military potential by the Oman Army Corps of Engineers. They modified the original device to include a microwave frequency carrier wave, which allowed the plane of neutrons to travel a long distance before signal degradation caused it to dissipate. Add a few terawatts of power and you have a beam that can travel at fifty percent of light velocity and cut through practically anything in its path with surgical precision in a quarter million kilometer range.

This surprise cleaver, the only remaining functional example, was mounted in a mountainside facility on the outskirts of Jartic Orz. The power source extended a kilometer underground and took up the equivalent volume of two Empire State Buildings. Its twin mast antennae towered upward for two hundred meters and could vector a beam anywhere in a one hundred and eighty degree zone effectively protecting one half of the planet. Habine loved these high tech gadgets and reveled at their being under his control. If no enemy space craft ventured into the killing zone, it was likely that he would sacrifice one of his ally space craft just to see the damn thing work.

"The shuttle is unloading at the moment," said Katun. "It will be ready for return south in a half hour. He pointed in the direction of the vessel, and without further words, Habine headed for it.

It was a hard path through the thick briars that formed a barrier to the outside of the woods. John and Joyce pressed themselves through five more painful yards of the thorny thicket where they emerged into an overgrown pasture. Winding paths were beaten down by browsing cattle wending their ways around thorn apple trees and derelict pieces of farm machinery, some of which had been crumbling undisturbed for probably a century.

They cautiously approached a wrought iron fence, and seeing no one around, vaulted over it. The house was still a hundred yards away. There was no one to be seen this far out, but most certainly, as they drew nearer, that would change.

"We'd better watch it from here on in," whispered John in his mounting apprehension.

"Too late for that." A sharp voice pierced the night air. Then the muzzle of a gun prodded John's shoulder in the direction of the house. "I have them," the man said into a walkie-talkie. "Bring them up," came the terse reply. The two were escorted to a study. After they entered, the gunman motioned with his rifle toward two leather Morris chairs. John took a seat in one, Joyce in the opposite one and the man with the gun stood behind John.

The fragrance of time honored literature and polished wood mingled into a pleasant smell. John tried to recall his first experience with the sensation the time he met Joyce. He hoped it would make him feel better, but all it did was make him feel angry at himself for getting them both into the present fix.

"What the hell was I thinking, trying to break in here," he thought. "I have almost certainly lost any chance of dealing with this guy. He could have me thrown back in jail." They sat there, the only sound the cadence of the grandfather clock in the corner. On the half-hour it chimed with a cheerful incongruity. The further moments passing allowed John to dwell on his situation. The gun and the genteelly dressed brute that held it infused him with fear that he may be in greater danger than jail. Then there was Joyce. He would have to act and right soon.

Ott's entrance a moment later averted any contemplated action that would likely result in disaster.

"My guests usually come through the front gate," said Ott sternly.

"Did you expect me to just sit back and let you steal my property?" asked John with equal sternness.

"I admit it was an uninspired plan the way it was done," said Ott. "But you weren't cooperating and the likelihood that those buffoons would get their hands on your materials; well I was becoming desperate; very unlike myself." He strode casually around the back of the huge mahogany desk and sat on the near corner toward John. He acknowledged Joyce with a slight bow, and then he dismissed the guard, who moved back but did not leave. "Go along, Frank," said Ott, "Mr. Hodiak is a civilized man, sensible at least. We will have no more trouble." Frank nodded and left through a small service door at the corner of the room.

"Where are my journals?" demanded John. "You have no right to them and I want them back."

"As far as troubling you about what you found and spent your time and money discovering, I have no right. I am sorry for that," said Ott.

"Then give them to me and I'll be on my way," said John.

"As for the matter of trespassing, I think that makes us even." Ott got up from the desk and started pacing before the bookshelves. Joyce followed him with her eyes, but not quite. She stared at the leather bound books just past him on the wall. She could tell the binding styles of the seventeenth century. There were a lot of their spines sticking out at her. Ott glanced at her then moved knowingly to a shelf and plucked out a volume and beckoned to her. She eagerly left the chair and took the book. On opening it she gasped at a first edition of Nathaniel Hawthorne's *Tamerlane* with acquisitive wonder. "Help yourself," he said.

He then rounded on John. "As for the knowledge of what Pitus Peston did and what he discovered here and elsewhere, no one has a better claim to it than I."

"Don't tell me," said John. "You're a descendent of Peston, and you claim my property based on your descendancy."

I claim the right to know because Pitus Peston is my father!" There was the thump on the table where Joyce lost hold of the book she was examining. She was too nonplussed to apologize. She just stared at Ott.

"You might be t'other side of sixty," said John, "but his son? Pardon my skepticism. He laughed disdainfully at such a notion.

"Laura Lee Ott of St. Louis was my mother," declared Ott. "Journal three puts Pitus there at the proper time. He cured Roscoe Cantrell of hepatitis by the use of an herb called corstet. He was told by Pitus that an Indian shaman gave it to him and he must not tell a thing about where he got the medicine."

"We all know he got the corstet from Lucy Dutton and had taken it for more than a year by the time he reached St. Louis. He was seeing the young woman Laura Ott while he worked at Charless' printing shop. He was waiting for an expedition into the upper Missouri, and eventually the opportunity to join Manuel Lisa materialized. The night before he left for St. Charles to join Lisa, he 'staid with Laura', a nice Yankee euphemism . . . I resulted from it on January 17, 1812.

"You really expect me to believe you are the son of Pitus Peston," asked John?

"You are a poor liar, Hodiak, said Ott. I can see the wheels turning. Peston's journals tell some of the story and Laura Ott's diaries tell the rest. He pointed to a stack of three leather bound duodecimos on the corner of his desk. The corstet he took affected his DNA. Since you are a pharmacist, I am confident you can see how it might be the cause.

John shook his head.

"I also know Pitus took some of Lucy's corstet seed pods and showed them to Ordway, who sealed them up in a jar. "I've read all that you have on Peston and can safely conclude that the seed pods are still around." He turned toward a roll-top desk opened it, taking a bag from it. He handed the bag to John. "Here's your property," said Ott. "I want those pods!"

THE BATTLE FOR OMAN PART II

"The enemy force has been detected," said Katun. "They have just now emerged for Pragoot Barg."

The Pragoot Barg is a natural wormhole whose opening is some twelve light years from Oman. It connects this part of space with a location about the same distance from the star alpha Argulis. Oman History has it as always being there and before that, the ancient Haldan legend tells of its use by the shaman Ewanok who used it as a leg on his journey to our part of the galaxy nearly a million years ago.

During the search for Loma's Cube just a few months before the events now unfolding, the Pollex end of Nesook Barg collided with a nullity, the Omans' name for a black hole. The nullity absorbed the barg and it was obliterated. It was conjectured by physicists at Franook University at Laguna Mi, Calbresan, that conditions must exist at that part of space for which the presence of a wormhole or barg is inevitable. Hivik, in his Atlas of Roolandoo stated as much in the preface of his great work over two thousand omans ago. "The whole of Roolandoo is as though part some great celestial garment, in whose gatherings and pleats hide secret places unfathomable and beyond ken not unlike one's father's robes where hidden from all his outings lie delights to thrill his child's heart on his return." When it would reappear was anyone's guess; maybe in a year, or a century, or an eon.

The Oman Air Force, newly created by the discovery at Alovis B had been briefed on their mission. They were to intercept the enemy before they passed Alovis, the Oman moon. Pitus was made commander of the little fleet who passed on tactical instructions to the individual pilots. The instructions were in the short version, to use their wits and courage to attrite the enemy, concentrating on the fighter escort first and then to neutralize the troop carriers, in which ever order was possible so that none of the enemy touched on Oman soil.

The Oman craft moved out of the hangar and positioned themselves at random among the clefts in the nearby mountains to evade detection by the incoming enemy fleet. They were then to wait for the go-order from Pitus who awaited the enemy sighting on their approach to Oman in the cover of the Oman satellite. Then the free-for-all would begin.

Pitus addressed his fellow airmen. "There are more of them than us," he announced, "But not by much. In purpose, we do outnumber them. They have murder on their minds and we have survival on ours. We have mothers, brothers, fathers and sisters and friends," he said adding emphasis on each class of dependent, "who depend on us and Aldit horruma, we won't let them down!" A general cheer went up among the men. "Dathin, who are you going to let assault your sister Cassina?"

"No one, sir," shouted Dathin. "I'd kill them for the thought of it."

"Damn right," declared Pitus. He addressed each of the others by name. "Claddis, Rakan, Besoon, Horkin, and you, Billoc, and you, Tarpan, who freshly joined us; who is going to kick your ass today?"

"Nobody, sir," came the shout in unison.

"All right then," said Pitus. "I am taking that as a promise and you all had better keep it. Enter your ships and move to your positions. Wait for the order from me before engaging the enemy. Hit fast and hard. They do not know we are waiting. He dismissed the pilots and when the last one left the hangar, he started back for the weapon assembly area.

On his arrival, Pitus sought out Gastin.

"Colonel," he said. "With your leave I will return to Atoye's ship. I need to set the computer to home in on the squadron's blips so that any of the pilots who are in peril can be extracted."

Gastin eyed Pitus curiously, then gave an assenting nod. "When I first got the request to send down another pilot for your replacement, I was disappointed. I thought you were shrinking from your duty. Then I realized that since you are not Omanee this really isn't your fight. I sent Tarpan and made him squadron leader in your absence. Dathin explained to Tarpan your chosen role in this battle. He apprised me of it. You will have to put yourself continually in harm's way to guard the pilots in the theatre of battle, and in an unarmed ship."

"Hopefully not for long," said Pitus. "The enemy will be shooting at those who are shooting at them. All I will have to do is dance around the stray fire. Another thing, Colonel," Pitus added, "It really is my fight. If we fail to stop the invaders here, they will, in time, be at my home, and we won't be ready for them, I fear."

The colonel nodded silently, then said, "I did well making you a captain. For a man who claims little experience leading men, you have contradicted yourself admirably in action." He saluted. "See to your duty and Aldit watch over you."

Pitus stepped through the aperture to Kesst and keyed his transport amulet. He stepped through to the bridge of the Duster. He paused a moment to look up at the observation dome and sighed. The outer lamination was scorched when Habine hit it with plasma, when playing a cat-and-mouse game in the Alecon nebular gas shell at the galactic center. A crack ran the length of the dome. It looked worse than it was, however. The lower laminate would hold for space travel, but a single direct hit would finish it. The Duster was a civilian vessel, and though Atoye souped it up to give it enormous power and speed while he lived on Oman, there were no weapons of defense on it other than agility.

Pitus turned to his nav-com computer and sat down before it. He tuned the ship's transport to accept the frequencies of the com patches each of the other pilots wore. If there was a chance to save even one of the brave men who were Oman's front line of defense, then this would have to be it. He was startled by a brilliant flash behind him. Atoye came through.

"Gastin told me what you were up to, and I came to help out."

Pitus grinned. "Then the Colonel's blessing is already starting to pay off," he said. I was thinking how much better it would be with you at the helm to make this ship able to dodge the incoming fire." He got up to let Atoye sit at the controls. "Great to see you, my friend," he added, and clapped Atoye on the shoulder. Just then the voice of Gastin came over the com. "Stand by for the signal." Three sets of five pings came through the com. Pitus relayed the same message through his frequency to his squadron on Alovis. "Time to play the hand," said Pitus. Atoye lifted off and the Battle for Oman began.

Tarpan Juun Gidast, the squadron commander of the New Oman Army fleet, watched the depths of space in deep scan in the direction of Pragoot Barg. The backdrop of fixed stars stood in mute array before him. His position was atop an escarpment in the shade of a ledge. With the glare of Coolin behind him, he had a spectacular view. The dazzling beauty was wasted on him this time. He was looking for movement; some telltale shift in those countless asterisms shining at him through the void.

They were all at radio silence, so none of the others could pool their surveillance. It was, however, understood that the first one to sight the enemy would break the silence with a single ping to the others. Then the alerted pilots would wait for the right moment.

THE BATTLE FOR OMAN
PART III

The direction of enemy approach would be someplace probably within two star formations; Argulis, the Runner, or Zixophele the Maiden. The Maiden was made up of eight stars, six of which were first magnitude forming her body and arms. The remaining two of second magnitude represented her eyes. Argulis, the Runner, (not after Zixophele, by the way), comprised seven stars, four of the first magnitude and three of second. Looking at Argulis, one could easily envision someone leaping over a hurdle. Both of these constellations were in the direction of Pragoot Barg.

It was vital to keep a steady watch for any sign of the enemy by visual because the enemy, if sweeping with their own scans, would pick up any signal from the Omans even though hidden among the canyons and crevasses of Alovis. When the enemy, which was certainly Haldi, came into view, there would be mere seconds to calculate the vectors of attack and deploy.

On first sighting, they would have to rush the incoming ships by going superluminal and popping back into flat space in their midst relying on surprise to enable an effective ambush. This was to be accomplished by "boring the hole", an Omanee slang term used by competitive racers, equivalent to "pulling a hole-shot" in drag racing. This hole-shot was a million-fold in power scale to the maneuver done in a hot rod. The pilot pulled the throttle fully back without first releasing the inertial damper. The ship's engine revved, so to speak, into the green danger zone, possible for only a few seconds, before releasing the drive. An enormous light boom ensued as the ship went maximally hyper. If done properly, that was the only sign the ship would reveal. That usually was enough though, to blow any cover. The ship would disappear from tracking until it re-entered flat space. Once among the enemy, the ambusher tried for maximal kill.

Tarpan strained his vision at the two star groups until his eyes teared up. He looked down at his instruments and saw the blips on the radar, but still no visual. He wiped his eyes and resumed his gaze at Argulis. Between gamma and delta Argulis was a star, but there was no star between them. This was it! No sooner had he reached forward to alert the others than a ping came over the com. One of the others had also seen the stella nova in Argulis. The signal given, the seven interceptors were on their way.

The Haldi forces were clearly not expecting a reception. The attack was coordinated to make a minimum profile when the squadron came back flat. The Oman fighters manned by Claddis, Horkin, Billoc and Tarpan flew so close that they were practically touching. When the lead Haldi vessel veered into a defensive position, the group of Oman fighters split apart at lightning speed followed by Dathin, Besoon and Rakan in the orbiters, blazing away with their beam cannons.

The barrage took out one of the drive pods on a freighter which drifted off out of the theatre of battle. The Haldi fighters, of which there eight, were still in action and were like a swarm of angry bees. Claddis, a former Oman ace dispatched one of the fighters, as did Besoon. Now they were even, if you counted the two troop ships. The race was on. The untouched troop carrier took advantage of the diversion to hurry on its way to the planet. It was now on the other side of Alovis and moving into an orbital approach. The enemy fighter escort left the transport in order to keep the Oman fighters engaged while the troop ship made for the safety of Jartic Orz. Claddis discovered this ruse and broke off the attack to pursue the troop ship. His adversary followed in hot pursuit shooting plasma into open space as Claddis deftly dodged the bolts with his gyrating movements.

They came into view on the Duster's sensors, and it looked like the Haldi was closing when suddenly, it broke off pursuit.

"That's not like a Haldi at all," said Atoye. "A Haldi fighter pilot never lets an opponent get away. It's a matter of honor. He would rather die than..." Just then a shining blade of light leaped up from the planet's surface. It passed through the spot where Claddis was seen only a second ago.

"Cleaver!" Atoye yelled. "It got Claddis!" Pitus immediately keyed the amulet and a brilliant white doorway appeared in the center of the bridge. Through it tumbled Claddis, who rolled across the bridge and bumped up against the bulkhead. Atoye rushed to him. He wasn't moving. Atoye pulled him onto his back. A stunned Claddis opened his eyes. "I have never seen that done before," he gasped.

"I never did it before," replied Pitus.

"What happened to me," asked Claddis? "I was chasing that transport, taking heat from behind. The ship was at its limit, the whole console lit up green from end to end. Did I blow it up?"

"A cleaver got you," said Atoye.

"Aldit horruma!" exclaimed Claddis. "The flash came from behind my seat." He rose up off the deck and Pitus gasped.

"That was damn close," said Atoye. "The collar of your flight suit is sliced off as though with a razor."

"We have to warn the others," said Pitus. He sat at the com and sent a signal. Then he dropped the Duster down out of the cleaver's vector range.

"One of the transports made it to Jartic Orz," said Claddis. "When they unload, the ship will be sent up to retrieve the others."

"Then I see the next mission of the NOAF," said Pitus. "Our fighters will have to harass theirs to delay the rendezvous of the transports." Pitus again sent code from the com. "But first we will gather at Nesgoor to assess the worthiness of our ground troops, agreed Atoye?" Atoye nodded and took the controls.

NESGOOR

The fleet arrived at Nesgoor to find the place transformed into a military encampment. On landing Pitus, Atoye and Claddis were met by Gastin.

"We need to gather for a planning session," said Gastin. The pilots, Atoye, and Pitus entered a large field tent, along with now General Gastin and three of his aides.

Their meeting was brief, with the result that the pilots would do as Pitus suggested. The main objective was to further attrite the enemy spacecraft and prevent the other transport reaching the stranded one near Alovis. "Destroy the transports if possible," said Gastin.

"With what," asked Tarpan? Gastin called to one of his aides, a Major Bannik, who left the tent accompanied by Claddis. The general continued his briefing and shortly, Claddis and Bannik returned hauling a dolly on which was a missile.

Gastin pointed to the dolly. "Each of your fighters will be outfitted with one of these plessmic missiles. There were several stored at Alovis and they were transported here." These missiles were low-yield atomics, each with about a tenth of the brisance of the ones that would some day be used against Nagasaki and Hiroshima.

"Blow them out of space," Gastin said. "The rest will be up to us." He pulled a map down from a stand. "We have five hundred soldiers armed and ready to meet the force which almost certainly will be advancing to us from Kesst."

Atoye suggested that a detachment be sent through the passage beneath the Annex to engage the enemy in a surprise attack. This was readily agreed to and Pitus was sent forth to pick a hundred troops for the mission. He went to an unused warehouse which was serving as a barracks. When he asked for volunteers to go to Kesst and 'kick some Haldi ass' he had them in less than five minutes. Pitus tapped his com patch. "Atoye," he said, "Set up the aperture. We are ready as we will ever be."

While this was being accomplished, Pitus ordered his men to arm with a proton rifle and a hand brisler. From the Duster Atoye set the computer to open the aperture at Kesst and connected it within the barracks. As the soldiers moved into position, Pitus tore open some crates and passed two percussion grenades to each. "If you find that you cannot overcome the enemy, do your best to get back through the aperture. We will hold it open as long as possible." At this, the soldiers filed through the opening.

The transports were in docking position. Claddis knew as soon as the air lock was established the enemy troops would rush into the good transport. He sat a moment at a sufficient distance to remain undetected. This he knew was correct because of the absence of fire from the two massive ships. He armed the missile, the pulsing green warning light a signal that it was ready to launch.

He pressed the launch button but instead of recoil from the launching rocket there was only a clunk. Claddis cursed and pressed the launch button again. The clunk didn't even come this time, but an impotent click. The missile carried an impact detonator as well as a remote radio activated one. To ram the transports was no guarantee that the impact detonator would trigger. There was too much at stake to risk this. He looked as best he could at the partially visible missile in his ship's undercarriage, but could not see the jammed mechanism, let alone reach it to manually release the thing.

He knew time was running out, not so much for the loading of the troops, as it would take a considerable time to transfer a thousand troops even under good conditions. What was urgent was that he not be seen in a sensor sweep and picked off by a sharp shooting cannoneer. Surprise was still on his side, but how long was anyone's guess. He thought of his friends Rakan, Tarpan, Besoon and Pitus. He remembered as a youth the miracle of Kesst at dawn, and other things, and he yearned for them all. He sat ramrod straight in his seat and worked his controls to arm the remote detonator. The day-glow green warning light shown steadily inches from his fingers. He yanked the throttle toward him and the fighter rocketed toward the transports. Their blips on his radar slid toward the center of his screen. Then he could see them growing rapidly through his canopy dome. He was almost atop them. "Aldit Horruma, this is going to hurt," he said as he pressed the detonator. There was a flash as bright as a new born sun, and then it was all dark once again.

"Both transports are destroyed, said Atoye.
"That's fine news, said Pitus. "How did they manage it?"
"It was Claddis," said Atoye. His voice was flat and his tone was not missed by Pitus. "Aldit Horruma," moaned Pitus.
"He's still alive," said Atoye quickly. "He radioed me that his missile was jammed in its lock and that he was going to wait for the transports to dock and start loading before going in. I said I would give him an aperture, but the chances of getting him out of there were slim."

Let me guess what he said to that," said Pitus. "I'll ram this thing up their asses, by Jaka's Left Foot!"

"Almost verbatim," said Atoye. "He said he would flame their asses, but the rest is accurate."

"You said he isn't dead," said Pitus, "but not that he is all right."

"He took a lot of radiation," said Atoye. "Enough blew back through the aperture to scorch our hull. They have him stable, but he needs some serious help."

"Take him to Calbresan," exclaimed Pitus. "Take him to Presceene. She can help him. "Get me back onto the Duster and we'll run it to the limit." There was no reply, but an aperture opened and Pitus dashed through it.

Aboard the Duster were Atoye, Orban, and Gastin. "As long as that cleaver is up we won't be able to get away. We can't outrun it," warned Gastin. Orban moved quickly to the nav com. He keyed some code into the computer and the aperture appeared. As he went to it he said, "I will take care of the cleaver." He had a percussion grenade in each hand and a brisler stuffed in his belt. Before anyone could protest, Orban was through the aperture and gone. Claddis was brought aboard. His jump suit was charred and he was severely burned over half of his body.

"Jesus," Pitus breathed in his native tongue. In Omanee he said, "Claddis, you damn fool. What were you thinking?" Then he bent toward him. "Don't worry, my friend, we will get you fixed up. Stay with us." Just then the bridge was lit with a brilliant flash. A rolling thunder clap shook the ship. "Let's go," said Pitus. He took the nav com and bored a hole out of Oman.

When they reached the Port of Olix, and ambulance was hovering next to the pad. Presceene stood waiting for her patient. As they were loading Claddis into the ambulance Presceene came up to Pitus and Atoye.

"What is going on? How did he get radiation poisoning," she asked.

"The Haldi attacked Oman," said Pitus. "We are at war. We have given them a good thrashing, but it's not over by any means." She touched her communication patch. "Get me Pire," she commanded.

"He is in cabinet . . ."

"Good! Tell him the Omans are at war with the Haldi," she shouted. She waited until she heard Pire's voice then she ripped the patch off her blazer and tossed it to Pitus and ran to the ambulance. Pitus gave the short version to Pire who then signed off.

"Do you think they'll help us," asked Pitus?

"I don't know the answer to that," said Atoye, "but I do know we are needed back on Oman." The three men re-entered the ship, and for the second time, Atoye left Calbresan without clearance from customs.

"Atoye was at the controls of the Duster. Before him the whole console flashed in an ominous green cadence. They were going like hell was chasing them when suddenly; three battle cruisers came into view. Through the com came, "Calnoon Atoye Itah." It was a feminine, though stentorian voice. "Captain Leesat al Hinn, here."

"Calnoon Atoye Itah here."

"The Primate Labban it Zor has ordered us to mobilize in your aid."

"Aldit be praised," Atoye murmured softly. "We have General Gastin of the Oman Army aboard." Gastin approached the com. "This is Gastin," he said, "Welcome to our fight."

"I am the squadron leader, general," said al Hinn. "There are three frigates and two destroyers under my command. If you would give me your orders, I will deploy them."

Gastin first briefed the commander on the situation thus far and the Calbres commander briefed the general on the assets her squadron carried. The strategy unfolded as they proceeded. When the general gave his final orders he added, "You will necessarily arrive before us. I am just told by Calnoon that we will have to slow down or blow up."

"My engineer wants to know how you made that craft capable of your present speed," asked al Hinn. "It is far beyond its specifications."

"I will explain over a cup of resee," said Atoye, "after we have finished our job."

"He and I both look forward to it," replied al Hinn. She then signed off and the escort peeled off and vanished. They arrived an hour later to see Jartic Orz ablaze in its nighttime shadow.

HABINE

They ran up over Kesst and then to Nesgoor where they landed at the New Oman Army Headquarters. Gastin hurried into the command post ahead of the others. When Atoye and Pitus arrived they found Gastin barking commands to his aide who relayed them through the com to the troops. He then turned to his commanders.

"Jartic Orz is back under our control," he said. The sounds of bombardment could be heard in the distance. Kesst is still under enemy control, but if you listen, you can hear the distant rumble of our remedy to that. The enemy has been routed from the city proper and is being rounded up in the countryside. Another pocket of fighting is going on at Baluge. Just then a crackling transmission came over the com.

"Is that *tardsoon* Peston with you?" said a rancorous voice. Pitus froze and then the full weight of understanding hit him. "Habine," breathed Pitus. He was supposed to have been killed on Ensheedou at Loma's Cube. Pitus saw him vaporized by the Guardian after he and Habine fought hand to hand. The fight was to the death, but when Pitus beat Habine and refused to finish him off, the Guardian finished the job so everyone thought . . . The com was open in conference mode with two way pickup as a result of incoming traffic from the field. Habine heard Pitus call his name. "Is that really you, Pitus Peston? Yes, it is your nemesis Ich Habine Ing," the voice on the com replied. "I have called you out in true Fornician fashion," said Habine. "Will you answer me or will you cringe in your hole?" Habine then laughed disdainfully.

"I don't know how you survived," snarled Pitus, "but I will finish you when we meet."

"Good," replied Habine. "I can already taste your blood.

"You and your army are defeated," said Atoye. "Give yourself up and end all this."

"As though I were apt to do that," said Habine sarcastically. "I want Peston."

Atoye worked the com, "Keep him talking," he mouthed to Pitus, "I will locate him."

"Do not waste your effort trying to find me," said Habine. "I intend to tell you where I am. I have a special request that I am sure you will grant."

"No deals, Habine," said Atoye. "Surrender or we will come for you."

"Only one will come for me," replied Habine. "I want only the *tardsoon* Peston."

At this, the general's aide blanched. Twice Habine called Pitus the name given by the Fornicians which is so insulting as to end only in mortal combat between the caller and the called. This aide lived on Fornis for nearly ten years and knew only too well what calling someone a tardsoon meant. He wouldn't have done it with anything less than a rocket launcher on his shoulder. Outside of Fornis the "custom" had little emotional valence. Habine said it only to insult Pitus with a superlative. The hate was already firmly in place.

Kinar was with them in the command post and he spoke up. "Why would you think we would allow such foolishness?" he asked.

"Because it is part of the deal," replied Habine.

"No deal necessary, you bastard," yelled Pitus. "You say where and I will come!"

"No you will not," declared Atoye.

"Stand down Captain," added Gastin, "It is surely a trap and he will either kill you or hold you hostage."

"Oh my, Captain Peston," quipped Habine. "Well fear not, Captain, I will not make you a hostage. I already have one and this one deserves better than being abandoned after what he accomplished at the cleaver installation." He put the com patch close to the victim's lips. He stubbornly refused to speak and Habine gave him a kick. "Talk," he commanded. A gasp for breath issued from the prisoner, but still no word came from his mouth.

Habine stood up. "He won't talk, so I will do it in his behalf. I have the one you sent to destroy the cleaver, Mr. Doss Orban Bettan. He cost me plenty and will pay for it with his life unless you send Peston, the tardsoon to me."

"Orban," said Pitus. To Habine he said, "You harm him and I will take you apart piece by piece myself," shouted Kinar.

"Harm to him will be an empty word soon," said Habine. "He is not very well; all that radiation from blowing up my cleaver, you know."

"Do not come for me, Pitus," croaked Orban. "He will not let me . . ." Habine repeated his kick into Orban's ribs and the gasp came over the com.

"Come and face me, tardsoon," snarled Habine.

"Skip the tardsoon," said Pitus, "I don't care a krait's ass what you call me."

"Then come save your friend," said Habine. "I am sending my position and you can lock on it. You are the one I want."

"I'm coming," said Pitus. "He looked at the others. "There is no other way. "He will either kill Orban or he will die."

"How noble and clear minded," said Habine. "Orban is looking very bad, but I will finish him off if you are not before me in ten seconds." He began counting off . . . one, two, three . . ."

Atoye looked imploringly at the others.

"Six, seven, eight . . ." Pitus raised his brisler in one hand and keyed the amulet with the other.

"No," shouted Atoye, but he was not quick enough in his lunge to stop Pitus diving through the aperture.

"The air was still open and all could hear Pitus burst through to the other side. They heard a yell and a thump, and then silence as the link was broken.

"Get him back," shouted Kinar. Atoye feverishly worked the com, but could not re-establish the link. It was being jammed from the other end. Pitus came to in a few minutes to find himself bound to a chair, Habine standing over him.

THE MYSTERIOUS MR. OTT

"What are you going to do to us," asked Joyce.

Ott looked at his Rolex. "It's late. Perhaps we should continue this discussion in the morning. Gordie," he said into an intercom. A moment passed and his butler came through the service door with the other who had the gun.

"Yes Mr. Ott?"

"Mr. Hodiak and Miss Benton will be staying the night. They can stay in the guest house." He turned to his captives. "You will enjoy the guest house. Feel free to avail yourselves of the refreshments." John started to protest, but Joyce hushed him with a look that gave him hope that there was some sort of plan cooking in her head, whatever that could be under the circumstances. They were escorted to the guest house a hundred feet or so behind the mansion. It was elegant and sumptuous inside and Joyce could not suppress a gasp of awe. Gordon gave a short tour and then bid them good night. He paused a moment at the door. "Mr. Ott is really a capital fellow," said Gordon. "It is unfortunate to meet under such suboptimal conditions. I regret the necessity to inform you that there will be guards posted outside. This is necessary because he cannot risk you going to the Feds with the plant." He started to leave but popped his head back in the doorway. "I cannot recall a single instance where someone who provided Mr. Ott with something he desired did not prosper greatly. Fear not and have a good night." Then he left.

John slowly walked the room studying the layout. Joyce wandered into the bedroom. After a few minutes she returned. "There is a king size bed with a sixty inch plasma TV across from it."

"There's a bar stocked with Dom Perignon and Jack Daniels on tap," said John. "I've never seen 'Jack' on tap."

"The bathroom is half the size of my living room," said Joyce, "all done in serpentine marble. The tub is enormous and has a Jacuzzi. If the bar has some merlot, I could really enjoy it." John checked out a small refrigerator behind the bar. "It just so happens . . ." He took a glass off the rack and half filled it with the wine and passed it to her. "I'll fill the tub. Wanna join me?" John grinned in answer. Joyce disappeared into the bathroom and John sat down before a computer and switched it on. "I suppose if we are stuck here, he can't expect me not to check him out," he said softly to himself. The computer booted up and, as he had hoped, it was for guests' use and not pass-worded.

John typed SIMEON OTT into the search engine. The response came back with over one million sites. He added Glens Falls to the search. Now it narrowed to thirty two thousand entries, most of them because of the engine's splitting up the search elements. He checked out the first page of hits. One was a bar in Duluth called Simeon's Rest. Another one was Ott's Collision in Warsaw, New York. Still another was the web site of a lawyer in Prescott, Arizona. So far, no good. There were numerous Glens Falls hits that were unrelated and useless.

John sat back in his chair and closed his eyes from the glare of the screen. He was rousted out of a half daze by Joyce.

"I came out for some more merlot," she said. She was wrapped in a maroon terrycloth bathrobe. John saw her slide in behind the bar and duck out of sight. There was the sound of the fridge opening and a brief rattle of glass bottles, and then she popped back up holding the remainder of the merlot. She grabbed two fresh stemmed wine glasses off the rack and held them in one hand, the bottle in the other. Her robe was not tied and it slipped slightly apart as she came around to where John was seated. One of her beautifully sculpted breasts seemed to peek out from the edge of the robe. She smiled coyly with an inviting expression as she silently padded past him back toward the bath. John followed her with his eyes, and she apparently knew this when she bent over the coffee table. The terrycloth accentuated the shape of her bottom in this pose which lasted only a second. Then she vanished into the bathroom. By now John was like blue steel and temporarily forgot about the computer search. He got up and went for the bathroom also, pulling out his shirt and loosening his belt almost as a single move.

The tub was enormous and two-thirds full of water. The pleasant scent of bubble bath filled the warm moist air. In the tub sat Joyce with just her head above the suds. She reached a foamy hand outward and drew her glass of wine to her lips. "Come on in, the water's nice . . . I'll guarantee it," she cooed. John stepped out of his jeans and pulled off his shirt. A few seconds later he was undressed and stepped into the tub. John settled in so that just his head was above the water. Joyce had just taken another sip from her glass and set it back down. Then she glided over him and rubbed her slippery body over his. John enfolded her in his arms stroking her from her shoulders to her buttocks in long slow arcs. The sensitivity of her movement over him was enhanced in the warm water and his arousal was pitching higher and higher.

They kissed hard. Joyce reached down and put him up into her and kissed him once again. Then she groaned with pleasure and slowly worked him up and down in her. She suddenly tensed and gasped. John realized Joyce was coming. This sent him too over the edge. He stiffened for a few seconds, then pulsed as he released into her. After the last mutual spasms of joy, they held each other under the dying foam and rested. The air above the water seemed chill, though it was tropical in that bathroom.

"That was a big one," whispered Joyce into John's ear.

"It sure was," he replied softly.

Joyce moved off John and slid across the tub to retrieve her glass of wine. Then she came back to him and huddled close placing one arm behind him and one of her legs over his. He turned to her and kissed her nose and smiled. She pulled him to her and kissed him heavily once again.

"I know we are being held against our will," Joyce said, "Yet, I don't feel in danger."

"Don't be fooled," said John, "This is still captivity. We are expected to give him the plant. If we refuse, it will probably get nasty. If we fold small and let him have it . . ."

"So why don't we?" Joyce asked. "Just let him have the damn things."

"All six plants?"

"Six . . ." Joyce started to speak but John touched his finger to her lips to still her.

"Yes," He said emphatically. "All of them that I have growing in my root cellar; every one of them." He made a gesture that conveyed to her that the place might be bugged. She smiled. "Yes, give all six of them to him and be done with it," she said loudly for the benefit of the putative ears, "but not till the morning, it is too nice here."

In a short while, they left the tub and dressed into the night robes. Joyce got into bed after selecting a few magazines and John returned to the computer. He wanted another go at unraveling some of the mystery around the *mysterious Mr. Ott*. John mulled over his conversations with Ott over the past several weeks. Was there anything in those encounters that might yield a clue?

"What was that thing he said when I sold him the coins," John murmured.

"What dear," asked Joyce?

"I'm trying to think of something Ott might have said that I can use in a search," replied John. He spoke barely audibly, "Something about that 1838-O half. He said he saw it minted. That was just some B S, it had to be." He keyed in *New Orleans Mint,* and searched several of the hits. There was a lot of interesting history about the mint, but no links to Ott.

Belle fleur riverboat was the next thing John entered. The first site stated that the boat was one of three side wheelers of the National Ship Line, which plied a regular route between New Orleans and St. Louis from the late 1820's until the beginning of the Civil War. The *Belle fleur* was destroyed in a fire in 1849.

The next search was Laura Lee Ott of St. Louis, Missouri. This one stopped John cold. There was a genealogy site listing Laura being born in 1790 at Pittsburgh. She died in 1824 and was buried in the Old Cathedral Catholic Cemetery, at Walnut St. and Second Avenue in St. Louis. There was one descendant listed, a male child born in 1812 with the name of Simeon.

"Jesus," breathed John. Ott knew about Pitus and Laura and also about corstet. John began to wonder if the plant really lived up to the claims made by Lucy Dutton. Could he have just been talking to the very proof of the claim?

HABINE

"Habine, you bastard," snarled Pitus. "I had hopes you were dead. Why had they spared you?"

"It seems that the Ori Mori cannot do without me," Habine replied sarcastically. "History as it will unfold has an important place in it for me. The Guardian brought me back here and before he left I asked the same question as you; why did he spare my life? He actually replied to me that your Loma's Cube has me at the head of the new Lu-Janx Empire. It just so happens that that is my plan as well, which also means that you, not I, are defeated before you even start." He pranced a little in his glory. Then his haughty expression grew more contemplative.

"I am best known as an adversary who gives his opponent no chance," he said. "It is my way and it has served me well for almost three centuries." He saw the surprise in Peston's face. "Oh yes, I am not your average short-lived Haldi. I managed to get hold of some of the *Oman blessing*, in spite of their stingy closeness with it. If one can pay, one can have," he said, almost to himself. "Beside the clear benefit of living a long and healthy life, I recognized corstet as an asset to my ambitious plans. Why work hard at building an empire just to die and leave it in the charge of some buffoon who will almost certainly lose it?"

"Assets come in many forms," he continued. "Money and weapons are obvious examples, but above those is one that has no price." He looked intently at Pitus. "A brave man in possession of a great mind is treasure worth as far more than the heavens are above the Earth, to use your native expression. I have sparred with you repeatedly since you arrived and cannot deny your bravery and resourcefulness. Further, I know you to be a son of Ewanok by virtue of your blood. We are brothers whether you like it or not. I am moved by your dauntless courage and our ancient kinship to extend once more a place beside me in the grand venture I am about to undertake."

Pitus remained silent a moment. He didn't expect a deal. After all, Habine said himself that he was known not to give his opponents a chance. Now was he being given a chance to be viceroy in what would probably become a large and prosperous kingdom? Pitus recalled a similar exhortation when he and Habine were in the state house at Kazur-Oma on Calbresan just after the first Eye of Harnuk was found there by Orban. There too the offer was made but then it was a ruse to allow Habine to close in on Pitus to kill him. What was it this time? He was already caught and bound in a chair, helpless before his foe. Why the *chance*?

"Let Orban go," said Pitus. "You want me and now you have me. Send him back to the others and we can talk." Habine stared at Pitus a moment then pulled the amulet out of Pitus' shirt.

"No," gasped Orban.

"You need help," said Pitus. "I will not have your blood on my hands." Orban continued to protest, but Pitus stilled him. "Tell Atoye not to worry about me and to remember how we came here."

"How touching," said Habine. He held the amulet over Orban and keyed it, swallowing Orban in the light.

"See," said Habine, I am not the heartless fiend you profess me to be." He then took out his brisler and stepped behind the chair where Pitus was bound. Pitus clenched his teeth and grimaced at what he believed to be his moment of death. There was a chirp from the brisler and Pitus fell forward out of the chair to the ground.

Orban lay still a few seconds on the floor of the command center. He opened his eyes to see Atoye and Kinar bent over him. He repeated what Pitus told him and added, "Help him Aldit's Sake!"

A camp physician rushed to Orban's side and examined him. "He has plessmic poisoning. He needs treatment."

"Get him to Calbresan," said Kinar, whereupon he was loaded onto a stretcher and borne out of the tent.

Atoye repeated the words Orban uttered. "Remember how we came here." He looked at Kinar who shrugged. Atoye said it again as a question. A look of shock came over his face. "Permission to leave camp, General," said Atoye urgently.

"Where to," asked Gastin?

"Cavin Gorse."

"That hell hole," the General replied?

"Pitus' life may depend on it."

"Permission granted," Gastin said. Atoye bolted from the command tent, Kinar at his heels. Within seconds, they were in the Duster and aloft.

Pitus realized he was not dead and rolled over onto his back. Habine stood over him.

"Get up," commanded Habine. Pitus slowly stood to face Habine. "Last chance," he said.

"Never," shouted Pitus. He lunged at Habine, but his foe dodged the attack. He trained his brisler onto Pitus' chest. "Somehow I knew you would not." He scowled and tossed aside the weapon. "Let us have another go as at Ensheedou." Habine lurched forward and grabbed Pitus by the neck. They both fell to the ground at the force of Habine's lunge and they grappled in the dirt pummeling each other. Habine swung and caught Pitus on the jaw, knocking them apart. Both scrambled to their feet circling each other for another grip.

"I have been waiting for another go at you," snarled Habine. "Man to man, so to speak. You are no match for me. I will beat you to a pulp before I kill you." He made a grab for Pitus who made a pirouette, grabbing the chair in the middle of the maneuver. He brought the chair around at Habine who splintered it with a chop of his hand. Pitus could see the malevolent joy in Habine's eyes as they once again circled around each other. He laughed in his perverse delight at the prospect of defeating his foe in hand to hand combat. Habine snatched up a leg of the broken chair holding it by the foot and brandishing it, jabbing at Pitus with the sharp splintered end. Pitus spied the amulet on the ground to his left. He jockeyed around to it dueling with Habine with the upper part of the chair. Habine swung his club in a roundhouse move which made him teeter off balance. Pitus dove for the amulet snatching it up in a roll. Habine leaped for Pitus who delivered a kick to Habine which sent him spinning away to the ground. Pitus keyed the amulet and the aperture opened up. Habine fell through it and was swallowed up in the brilliant glow. The doorway immediately closed and Pitus was alone. He went to the com and called through it.

"Gastin," said the general.

"This is Pitus."

"What is your location?"

"I have no idea. You'll have to vector this signal."

"Stand by," replied the general. "Keep the transmission open." In a few seconds the aperture appeared and Pitus stepped through it to find himself aboard the Duster. Kinar rushed to him.

"We were heading to Cavin Gorse to pick you up before something ate you," he said.

"Glad you understood my message, especially since you didn't have to carry out my request. Orban; is he all right?"

"He will be," said Kinar, "when they get him to Laguna Mi."

"Where is Habine," asked Atoye?

"I shoved him into a tropical get away," replied Pitus. "He is probably trying to scramble up that tree we parked the Duster under. Shall we go for him?"

"Gastin will probably like to have a talk with him," said Atoye, "but I think Cavin Gorse will mete out proper justice before long." He sat back down at the nav com and punched in the course for Nesgoor.

"Seriously," said Kinar, "Gastin will want Habine for interrogation."

"He'll never talk," said Pitus. "He is too proud and above us in his own mind to ever submit to interrogation. Anyway, where he is, we probably couldn't get there quick enough to find him alive."

"Good riddance," said Atoye. "He would be a threat to us all even in the bowels of Beljeaun."

"I hope he is in the bowels of a monock," said Pitus. "You know what he wanted me to do?"

"Join him," asked Atoye?

"Yes," said Pitus. "How did you guess that?"

Atoye shrugged. "Look at what you've done. You found our ship, learned Omanee, repaired the ship with no prior training, cured a prince, and saved a planet . . . Horruma, if you weren't on my team, I'd try to recruit you." They all sat silent a moment. Who could top Atoye's statement anyway? Then Kinar succeeded.

"Were you tempted even a little," he asked?

"Aldit Horruma, Kinar, what a thing to ask . . ." Kinar started to defend himself but Pitus spoke up. "It's a valid question, and I want to answer it." He looked at Atoye seeming to enjoy the bewilderment written on his face.

"Think of it. I was offered, and I believe sincerely, a place as the galactic emperor's viceroy with power and wealth beyond measure. The only problem is that I would be second to a murderous unprincipled prick. There's no prestige worth that." Atoye's expression changed to that of one whose judge of another's character stood him on firm ground.

"It's settled then," said Atoye. "We go back to Nesgoor."

They reached the town an hour later and reported to headquarters.

"Gastin looks pleased," observed Kinar. "That can only be good."

"Mission accomplished, I see," said the general. The three saluted their commander and he returned the gesture. "Baluge is securely in our hands," he said triumphantly. "Now we have nearly a thousand war prisoners on our hands. That was one unforeseen result of this operation," he added less enthusiastically.

"Perhaps the Jamborini embassy at Laguna Mi could be of help," said Kinar. "There is no Haldi embassy, unfortunately."

"I have been in contact with both governments," said Gastin. "Alubic, the Prime of Haldan, replied personally, stating that any Haldi involved were not operating under his authority. There are two transports on their way to collect them. The Prime promised justice and the admittance of observers from Oman to verify their disposal. He was particularly interested in getting his hands on Ickh Habine Ing. I take it you don't have him."

"Pitus stranded him on Cavin Gorse," said Atoye. We didn't go to pick him up. By now, his protein should be recycling into the local fauna."

"Good enough," said Gastin. He looked at his chronometer. "It will soon be night there. I will not send men into that place after dark . . ."

"Any reply from the Jamborones," asked Atoye?

"The Jamborone Prelate is even more upset than the Haldan Prime," said Gastin. He first suggested we execute all their nationals who took arms against us. I persuaded him that we had better things to do than to set up firing squads and burial details to process hundreds of his countrymen. He replied, and I quote, 'I will send someone to retrieve our rubbish.' On a happier note, I also sent a dispatch to Laguna Mi to convey Oman's boundless thanks for Calbresan's vital contribution to our success."

The news of Oman's deliverance from Haldi conquest spread to the four corners of the globe. In virtually every town there were celebrations. Nesgoor held a review of the Oman Army troops. Baluge was awash in hearty drink and some of the brothels were said to have opened for gratis for any Oman in uniform. Still there was a lot of work to do. Most of Oman was in ruins. The great cities, the seats of manufacturing, global communication, and centers of learning were gone. All had to be rebuilt, literally from the foundations up. Fortunately, a vestige of the brain trust of the old Oman survived the war, and this resource was already beginning to form plans for rebirth. All the surviving representatives of the central government were recalled to Kesst, and in the remains of the Hibber Institute, they set up legislative chambers.

Calbresan pledged its aid and so did Qetterxilict. Freighters crammed with heavy construction equipment and those able to use them poured in from the heavens. It would take time, but now time was again on their side. Proof that the dangerous radiation caused by the Thirty Minutes war had dissipated renewed the confidence to also rebuild the population base. That first post war year a thousand infant Omans came forth and the collective spirit soared.

Pitus remained to do his part, and managed with his expertise to repair scores of machines and vehicles. Alovis was tapped of its pre-war riches with computer systems from the Alovis B Complex. The huge library of Alovis A was returned to Kesst where it was housed in the intact remainder of the Hibber Institute's Annex. The university was re-established in the underground galleries below the institute making Kesst once again the first center of higher learning in the new Oman.

It would have been easy for Pitus to have remained in this burgeoning glory, but the Cube's message returned to him. The loose end, corstet, was still on Earth, and if not retrieved before the critical moment, would spell catastrophe and the end of his native home. There was no way of knowing when the discovery would occur, but once discovered, would certainly be spread beyond all retrieval. Each day of delay now felt as urgent as if a bleeding man lay before him seeking help. Pitus called his old friends together to inform them of his obligation.

"I think I know the reason for our gathering," said Atoye, "and it has already broken my heart. Yet, I can speak for us all in wishing you God's speed in your mission."

"Aldit shed his blessing on your journey," added Kinar. Orban, who had recently returned from Calbresan after his long recovery stood side by side with Presceene, Ambassador Pire and Benin It Zor, the prince of the whole of Calbresan. Orban stepped forward with the aid of a cane and clutched Pitus in a taught embrace. Then he hobbled over to an easel upon which was something shrouded in cloth.

"I thought long and hard of what I was going to say to you in parting," he said in Perfect English. "I composed these words which will adorn the entrance of the New Hibber Institute for all time to come." He lifted the veil to reveal a brass tablet upon which was inscribed;

TO THE GENERATIONS OF OMAN

That Those Who Pass Into These Halls Take Heed
That They Tread On Hallowed Ground And That
They Strive Always To Be Worthy Beneficiaries
Of The Exemplar Of Courage And Ingenuity Of
Our Chosen Son PITUS AURELIUS PESTON.

Orban then stepped back and started a slow applause joined by Atoye and Kinar. Claddis, Gastin and Drolanee joined in as well as the Calbres delegation. Pitus' eyes welled up, his heart ready to burst. Glasses were produced s well as a quart size bottle of prellon wine. When all the glasses were filled Kinar called for a toast. This time Pitus held up his hand before the crowd.

"This toast is for Atoye and Kinar, who, in coming to Earth, made possible an otherwise ordinary life to become extraordinary. For that I thank you both with all my heart." He then saluted with his glass and took a sip in veneration of his friends.

GOING HOME

Pitus was given a J-7 for his trip back to Earth. It was roomier than the fighters, though not so fast. Atoye offered his capacious Duster for the journey, but it was decided that the cracked dome might not survive the trip through the bargs Pitus had to pass through on the way home.

Pitus wanted a short goodbye and softened the grief of parting with a promise to return as soon as his work on Earth was done. He could not use Nesook Barg. The merge with the black hole swallowed it up. It would return, because, according to the Calbres, that spot in space was such that a wormhole was inevitable. The question though was when; a year . . . a thousand years . . . an eon? The cosmos had its own time table indifferent to the evanescent span of a man's life. Pitus had to go home by another route.

"One more jump and I'll be in my own back yard," thought Pitus checking the nav com. He programmed the standard approach to the dimensional portal and sat back with just his thoughts as company. The last four days were very full. Following Hivik's Path across the Milky Way, a journey for light of over one hundred thousand years, Pitus in the orbiter was traversing in one hundred days. The path consisted of seven dimensional short cuts, three of which were natural wormholes, or lum-bargs, located in the dense region of the galactic center, and four noo-bargs, planar apertures manufactured a million years ago by the Innovators. This arrangement made travel to virtually any part of the Milky Way, or Caleeron of the Omans, a relatively brief journey. One path was made even into the nearly uninhabited Sculptor ostensibly to open up exploration of the neighboring galaxy.

The planar ports on the periphery were positioned close to the outer ends of the central wormholes and were extremely powerful, communicating with regions in the spiral galactic arms, thousands of light years away. The aperture nearest Earth, called Jar Dest barg, opens four light years from Proxima Centauri, a mere hop from the Teran solar system.

The ports themselves are made by a hexagonal positioning of charged spinning singularities which hold their positions by the perfect balance of gravity and unipolar repulsive gravitational fields. In empty space these structures are stable indefinitely.

Time is a variable when dealing with bargs. The time gradient is at a positive maximum at the periphery of the barg on one side and declines to zero at a point in the very center. Here the time flux reverses and the negative flux increases to maximum as one approaches the periphery of the opposite side. The calculations for time are complex and require a sophisticated computer running the nav com to target the desired time on the exit side.

Pitus sat searching at the nav-com. At last, the blip appeared on his long range sensor. "Jar Dest barg, there you are," he said. "At least, that's what you should be." He brought up the orbiter's cartography to check the location. "Since everything in the universe is moving, the charts may be inaccurate," he thought. Indeed, the revision log of the stellar charts showed an update every five years up until the time of the Thirty Minute's War. Almost a century in Oman terms had elapsed since the last revision. That would be about seventy Earth years. How much displacement could occur in that length of time was anyone's guess? Earth moves around the sun, which moves toward the star Vega, which circles the galaxy, which is heading toward the Virgo Cluster . . . That's a lot of vectors to track. Yet, seventy years in cosmic terms is damn close to nothing. The blip must be Jar Dest barg. He plotted the course to it.

In the mean time a temporal strategy was necessary. Since he could go to Earth in any time, when should that time be? The best time, he thought, would be when he first saw the plant at Gram Dutton's when he sailed down the Hudson on his first trip with Allan to Albany. "Clean out the patch behind Lucy Dutton's house and have done with it. But wait; that wouldn't do. Doing that would preclude his getting some of it when he visited Gram's two years later on his trip out west. He needed the supply she would give him to help him survive his perils on his way to find the ship in the first place. Besides, the pods were someplace in Fort Edward, where ever Lucius put them. These very pods were the likely ones that would be discovered later by some unknown person and propagated, leading to Earth's human demise.

Pitus cursed himself for not taking the opportunity in 1883 of searching for the remainder of the corstet while back on Earth with Kinar, Atoye, and Orban searching for Harnuk's second eye. Of course, the Eye was of paramount importance at the time and he was not to find out the importance of the corstet left by Atoye and Kinar until he visited the Cube. It was becoming confusing trying to analyze all these threads of time with precedent and consequence. In order not to interfere with himself, he decided to return to Earth at a time later than he had ever been; shortly before the disaster was to happen. If 2060 was the date society ended by nuclear war, then when was the pivotal moment when that chain of events began?

Pitus thought back to the time at the Cube when he was learning about Earth's as yet to be unfolded history. "Wasn't the discovery of the cure for diseases made in 2020? If this time, 2020, was the date it went public, then the real time of discovery was shortly before that," he thought. "Sometime in 2019 . . . If it was discovered in 2019," he conjectured, "then early in the year is when I must return to Earth, to insert myself into the timeline to fine out where and when the events took place" he said aloud.

"Fortunately the drive program in this J-7 is outfitted with a routine for temporal modification when traversing wormholes and space-time membranes," he said.

Civilian vehicles were hardwired to calculate the position of time neutral entry when using a wormhole or artificial time-space branes. This was law within the Local Group because of the obvious mischief that could be caused by re-entry into the past. The Accord of Laguna Mi, shortly after the technology of temporal membranes was developed, made it a capital offense to attempt time travel among the seven signatories of the treaty. Haldan did not sign the treaty, but also lacked the means of accomplishing the feat. Temporal travel outward was not prohibited for the selfish reason that no one cared if someone screwed up history in some far off place. Certain military craft were able to override the time neutral specification, the J-7 in particular, and this was the type of craft Atoye stole the programs from which made him a fugitive in the first place so long ago.

Pitus entered data into the nav com computer using a disc copied from the Duster's chronometer. The Duster went to Earth in 1883, so this was a hard data point from which to reference the interval of time to the Earth year of 2019. A problem of temporal travel is relativity. Entering a membrane at a location other than neutral is merely a scalar quantity with no reference point. Fifty years one way or the other is merely that, and of no practical use . . . unless *now* is a bad time to be in. Since he was at Earth at a particular time, he could 'set his watch' to it and make a meaningful alteration. With the chronometer set with the Earth's reference point, he could let the J-7's powerful computer do the rest.

Pitus halted a thousand miles from the membrane. The re-set overwrote the ship's original figure set at the date of assembly. This was like turning an automobile odometer back to zero, obliterating data, some of which was important.

One useful piece of information the chronometer held was the expected life of the power source. Since the singularity ran out over time, it was important to know how much reliable life was left in it. It wasn't the matter within the singularity that diminished. That was forever trapped inside the event horizon of the black hole. It was the spin of the object that provided energy, and this fizzled out as a result of it being tapped over the years of service. Once the singularity stopped spinning, it became inert and had to be replaced. A singularity had to be disposed of carefully. If it got loose, it could suck whole worlds into it. Special waste handlers gathered them up and journeyed to the galactic center and injected them into the vast black hole there. This was dangerous work and the handlers were paid as princes for the job.

Pitus never regarded the residual on the magnetic bottle when changing the chronometer. He felt confident that the power source had enough energy to get him to Earth and back to Oman. The life of an artificial singularity was a statistical thing since there was no way to send a signal to it and receive any information back. Pitus put aside any trepidation his mistake caused him. What were the chances that the orbiter would run out of steam? "Not very likely," Pitus thought. He entered Jar Dest barg.

He entered the membrane and almost instantaneously emerged into flat space once again. The only sign of passage was a brief flicker of the lights as he traversed the membrane. He checked the nav com for position. It showed him just where he expected to be. To his left the reddish orb of Proxima Centauri showed dimly. Pitus was used to seeing stars shine with a blinding brilliance as beacons in the blackness of space. This red dwarf star seemed more like a low wattage night light illuminating a lonely corridor. He could look directly at it without blinking. Saul, on the other hand, dazzled with white hot intensity, making it necessary even though four light years away to take only quick snatches of sight of it. He plotted the course for his home star and set off for it.

He passed Pluto not knowing its name, but slowed down for a quick orbital flyby. "Have they seen you yet," he asked, marveling at the huge crater that covered a third of the planet's surface. "That happened a long time ago," Pitus mused, "probably by something large and slow moving just as the planet was congealing. He left the planet and continued inward through the vacant orbits of Neptune and Uranus which were currently at opposition of his approach and continued on to the next planet in his path whose bright set of prominent rings gave its identity away. He passed close by the Saturnian moon, Titan, marveling at the bluish atmospheric halo. "I must stop on that when I return," Pitus mused. He recalled offering Orban an opportunity to test the ships newly repaired outward transport by going down to the surface when they last passed by here in 1883. "I could bring Orban a rock off the surface as a memento of the occasion," he said. Jupiter was nearly ninety degrees to the larboard, and would have been an interesting flyby, but the mission to retrieve the corstet seemed more pressing as he drew near home. He took the ship out of the ecliptic to avoid the treacherous asteroid belt between Jupiter's orbit and that of Mars. After clearing the belt he returned to the planetary zone. Ahead was the ruddy crescent of Mars. It was intriguing to see this planet in a way that could never be seen from Earth. Suddenly his com picked up a faint signal. He supposed it came from Earth, but when he vectored it he was shocked. The signal was emanating from the Martian surface! "Have they finally climbed out of their bottle," said Pitus, remembering having said those words to Allan over two hundred years ago on their boat trip down the Hudson to Albany. It was his first peregrination, significant for the tremendous effort it took to go the short distance or fifty miles. Since then he has traveled distances that could no longer be expressed in miles; unless the hearer understood the quantity of quintillion.

Pitus descended toward the Martian surface following the signal. "I better send the universal greeting to whoever is down there," he thought. "I wonder why I haven't been asked for identification." He watched for cities or at least outposts as he descended in altitude. "Nothing anywhere," he murmured. "Where the hell are they; underground?" The signal was stronger now but seemed to be emanating from a yet invisible point. "I guess I'll just have to drop down and take a look. Rather rude of them for not answering."

He landed on a rock strewn plain kicking up a faint plume of reddish dust as the orbiter came to rest. He knew the atmosphere was too thin to breathe and the temperature was something like minus 70 degrees outside. He put on a thin insulated suit and a bubble helmet and fitted a micro breather into his mouth. These were capable of supplying air for about thirty minutes. At the Alovis B mausoleum, he and Atoye found cases of them and more than once they proved themselves invaluable. He had two more in a suit pocket in case he ran out of air. If he needed one he would have to pop the helmet which would not be pleasant, but this was not a vacuum like Alovis. He could survive the maneuver. He set the airlock and after the inside air was reduced to outside pressure, he cracked the hatch and stepped out onto the Martian surface intending to greet whoever was making the signal. Pitus took several steps toward the gleaming source of the signal and stopped.

"What the hell," he said irritably. "It's some sort of machine." He looked about. "There must be a village or at least, a dwelling and some people nearby." He hurried up a small rise for a better vantage point. From a perch atop a barrel-size boulder he surveyed the area to the horizon for 360 degrees. "Nothing," he said. "Nothing at all." He turned his attention once again to the machine. It was a self controlled vehicle moving slowly toward his ship. Behind it stretching outward beyond sight were the tracks its small wheels made in the pristine soil.

Pitus returned down the rise and approached the device. The top looked like a flat onyx table. Around the periphery were lenses. "It must be a surveyor of some sort," he said looking closely at it. "Solar powered . . ." He crouched down in front of it and it stopped. Then the machine turned its wheels with a tinny whirr and started off around him. "Proximity sensor . . ." Pitus Smiled into the camera, the sun shining on his face lighting it up clearly. He waved at the lens and mouthed "Greetings; Pitus Peston at your service." Then he got to his feet and returned to the orbiter.

Once again in space, Pitus consulted the nav com. A bright star showed sixty degrees to starboard. It wasn't any star though. There it was, Earth! He set course for it and watched its steady glow augment until it became a bright blue disc. It occurred to him that he might be under surveillance. If they could send that cute little gadget to Mars . . . well there was nothing to do about it. His plan was to come in fast and minimize their tracking time. He came in over the North Pole, heading southward across North America at an altitude of twenty miles; speed, four thousand knots. The com was full of activity. "They have advanced some since I was last here," he thought. He dropped the orbiter to an altitude of one mile and slowed to three hundred knots. "By now they have me," he thought. "I'll have to put this thing in the woods and trans out." He passed over the north shore of Lake Huron when it happened.

The lights flickered. Pitus looked down at the console. The panels showed that the ship was on auxiliary power and green from end to end. "This doesn't look good," he uttered. Then the ship lurched and began losing altitude. He was over water now and in a dive. The mains were off line. He frantically worked the controls to divert whatever power was left to the thrust dampers. This helped slow the orbiter to one hundred knots, but it was descending at a steep pitch. He would not survive an impact with the water at this speed. He jumped up from the nav com and opened a wall panel. From it he took a softball-size flotation device that would open into a single man raft once activated, powered by a thumb sized magnetic drive capable of propelling it at twenty miles per hour.

Pitus tucked this under his shirt and returned to the com. He set the computer to guide the aperture to a place a few miles from the ship at an altitude of ten feet. He keyed the amulet and a brilliant white doorway shimmered in the cockpit. He was less than a quarter mile above the water with only seconds before impact. He dove for the aperture and came out in a stick dive into the lake. The water was cold. Pitus tread water and turned his head in the direction of the ship just in time to see it dive into the waves in a big splash. He pulled the float out of his shirt and activated the inflator. It took about two minutes to inflate, and by the time he was able to roll into it he was shivering violently, chilled to the bone. He activated the drive and headed toward shore five miles away.

He was not quite half way to shore when he saw a fast moving boat heading from the west directly toward him. Within minutes it was alongside, four men in protective vests poised with rifles pointing at Pitus. A fifth called through a bull horn for him to cut the engine of the raft. A ladder was dropped alongside and Pitus was ordered to come into the boat. While two of the border patrol soldiers snagged the dingy, two others helped Pitus aboard the cruiser asking only if he needed medical assistance. Pitus was puzzled at the manner of the two men. They spoke very slowly in exaggerated clarity as if they were speaking English to a foreigner. Pitus replied in English that he was cold, but otherwise in good shape. This seemed to ease some of the tension that dominated the first moments of the rescue, but it was quickly becoming clear that this was not only a rescue but an apprehension. If there was any doubt of this it was dispelled when his rescuers took him wordlessly below decks to a small room that could only be described as a well apportioned brig.

He was offered dry clothing in which he gladly dressed. It was an orange jump suit similar to the Oman garb he was already wearing. This, however, was made of cotton, unlike the thin polymer of the alien fabric. He sat down on the bunk bed in the room and remained their five minutes when the door opened and an officer stepped into the small room and sat down opposite Pitus.

"You spoke English to the rescue team," the officer said. "Is that your native language?"

Pitus pondered this a moment. He realized he was being tracked as he entered the Earth's atmosphere, and further, that his arrival was a breach to some national or even planetary security. Should he keep his mouth shut? Should he play a tack of an alien visitor, some 'take me to your leader' position? He thought this would serve nothing but to land him in some dungeon like Beljeaun on Qetterxilict. He had had enough of this with his first experience. The other plan would be to tell the truth, which would likely gain him the probable title of crackpot. Didn't Hibber the sage of Oman once say that when one told the truth, it relieved one of the burdens of having to remember what one said? Pitus decided on the truth plan and let it go where it would.

"That is my native tongue," answered Pitus. He glanced to his right at a mirror placed into the wall. There was no sink beneath it. On Calbresan there were such in the rooms where he, Orban, and Atoye were kept. The mirror in this case was a device for observation of prisoners.

"Am I a prisoner," asked Pitus? The officer hesitated. "Let's not use such a negative term," he said at last. Pitus shrugged. He knew this was the case.

"Where did you come from," asked the officer?

"May we start with an introduction," asked Pitus? The man blanched.

"I beg your pardon," he said. "I am Major Morris Pickett."

"Pitus Peston," replied Pitus and he extended his hand which the Major took for a perfunctory single pump. Pitus reclined back on his cot against the bulkhead. "Where did I come from," he repeated softly. "Where do I start, he added?

"Not from anywhere close by I trust," said Pickett. "We tracked you as a blip from the North Pole. Your heading was tentatively extrapolated back over central Asia."

Pitus knew they were planning to raise and impound the orbiter. They probably had a ship over the spot at this moment. With the power source gone the orbiter was no longer of use to him. "Why not just tell it all and see what happens," he thought.

"I came from Oman," answered Pitus. The Major glanced at the mirror and then back to Pitus.

"You've heard of it," asked Pitus, the motion of the major not escaping his notice. Just then the high drone of the ship's engines slackened.

"We have arrived at the base," said Pickett. "We will continue the discussion there." He got up and went to the hatch. "Can I get you anything while waiting to go ashore?"

"Coffee," said Pitus. "It has been years since I have had a cup." Pickett raised his eyebrows, but then smiled. "I'll have some sent in. Relax and I will return shortly." He then whispered something to a soldier standing outside the cell hatch and then left. In a minute the door opened and a uniformed man entered with a pot of coffee and a mug. On the tray also were three pieces of coffee cake. Pitus couldn't decide which smell captivated him more; the cinnamon of the cakes or the aroma of the coffee. It was like the time Kinar as Lucius Ordway shared it with him the first day he entered his apothecary shop as his apprentice. That was two hundred and fourteen years ago as the Earth turns. He picked up the mug. The insignia of the United States Coast Guard was on the side of it. Pitus eagerly grabbed the pot which was similarly decorated and filled the mug. He brought the mug to his lips and drew in a deep breath and closed his eyes smiling with distinct pleasure. He tipped the mug and drew in a taste. "Ah," he breathed, and repeated the maneuver. "This was worth the trip all by itself," Pitus declared, and jauntily raised the mug toward the mirror.

Pitus downed the mug of coffee and refilled it from the pot. He sat sipping for another five minutes. The feel of the ship told him it had docked, and very soon he would be led out of this place to where ever. He decided to show no will other than to cooperate. This held the promise in his mind of reciprocal treatment. After all, no one has been unreasonable so far. In fact, everyone seemed downright friendly. However, he was not so naïve to think he wasn't captive, a situation that might endure a long time. If it looked like it would be indefinite, an escape plan would be necessary.

The Major appeared once again and beckoned for Pitus. Topside he was led under armed guard off the cruiser and into a fortress-like building. Once inside he was taken to a larger interrogation room, complete with a central table, two chairs and a larger version of the dark wall mirror. He was left alone for ten minutes more, obviously under surveillance until the major returned along with a man and a woman. The man was probably mid fifties, thought Pitus, about six feet with a full head of short cropped hair completely gray. His eyes were narrow set and had that probing look to them. He was light skinned, probably Scandinavian and looked old enough to be the woman's father. She, on the other hand, was darker complected, with jet black hair. She had a Native American appearance. Pitus stared at her a moment, realized he was doing so, and looked away.

"I apologize for staring," said Pitus. "Your ancestry is American Indian. Not Siouan . . . southwestern though . . . Cheyenne? Navaho?"

"The young woman flushed slightly. She was clearly not used to being interrogated.

"I'm sorry," said Pitus. "I pray I did not embarrass you."

"I am not embarrassed at all," she declared. "My mother's side is Navaho as far back as the hills."

Another chair was called for and when it arrived all sat at the table, Pitus opposite the other three.

"Pitus," asked Pickett, "Is it O.K. to call you Pitus?"

"That is my name," replied Pitus affably. The major nodded.

"Your ship is being recovered," said the Major. "It may take some time. It is down four hundred feet."

"Catastrophic power failure," replied Pitus. "I didn't think to check the life expectancy of the drive bottle." Pitus said. He looked at the Major and then to the two others who sat next to him.

"Sorry," said Pickett. He motioned first to the woman and then to the man. "This is special agent Diane Morgan of the FBI and this is special agent John Billings of the C I A". Both nodded a perfunctory greeting at the mention of their names.

"Where did you come from," asked Agent Billings?

"From Oman," said Pitus.

"Your approach vector suggests central Asia; not the Middle East," said Agent Morgan.

"That's not the Oman I mean," said Pitus.

"There's only one Oman, as far as I know," said Morgan. There was a distinct edge in her voice. "I'll repeat the question," said Morgan and will expect a truthful answer." Pitus sighed. "If I tell the truth," he thought, "she's going to think I'm a crackpot."

"Oman is a planet on the opposite arm of Caleeron, or the Milky Way. I came back to Earth in an Oman built J-7 Orbiter."

"You really expect me to believe this bullshit," she shouted. At the same time she leaped to her feet and bent aggressively toward Pitus. Pitus had seen this before. Often in Qetteran or Calbres interrogations a team of two matched up against the prisoner, one a friendly cajoling sort who posed as a safe harbor from the other who was a nasty menacing prick. Usually the woman was the mild one and a hulking male was the assailant. This curious turn was amusing to Pitus, but he thought better of letting that be known at the moment.

"Yes," he replied. Morgan bent still closer over Pitus as if daring him to leap to his feet and challenge her. "Well I'm afraid I don't believe any of it, but you know what I do believe," she said rancorously? "I believe you attempted to fly through our defenses to do harm to the United States. If we find any nukes on that ship when we get it up out of that lake, you're life won't be worth spit!"

"I am here to save the United States," said Pitus, "and the whole world."

Morgan stood up stiffly and shook her head. "This just gets better and better," she mocked. "Now the truth comes out. We have a new super hero; Pitus Peston. She looked at him haughtily. "You have a bright red "P" under that shirt?"

"Diane, let it go a moment," said Billings. Please sit down. We will get to the bottom of this. He was perusing a short stack of papers delivered to him while Agent Morgan was doing her grilling.

"There is no record of your citizenship in any country, Oman or otherwise."

"I am an American," said Pitus.

"Not here," said Billings. "No Social Security number, no birth record either and I had it searched way back to 1930."

"You didn't go back far enough," said Pitus. Billings narrowed his eyes.

"You look to be a man somewhere around thirty or thirty-five tops," said Morgan. "How far back do you suggest we look?"

"I was born in Fort Edward, New York on September tenth, 1787." There was silence, at least for a couple of seconds. Agent Morgan threw her legal pad on the table followed by her pen. "I've heard all this bullshit I want to hear," she said to Billings. "You stay here if you want to, but I'm through." She stormed toward the door. "I'd put him in solitary for a few months. Then maybe he'll realize he can't pull this crap." She pushed noisily out the door. Pitus looked at both Picket and then Billings.

"You want the truth but are unwilling to hear it."

"Would you believe a story like this, if you were hearing it from me," asked Pickett?

"When you bring up the Orbiter, you will realize I am telling the truth." He looked toward the mirror. "Whoever you are out there," he addressed the unseen witnesses, "I tell you that the Earth is in peril. You have less than forty years left unless you help me do what I have come here for." He looked at Major Pickett. "I am done talking. Lock me up if you want. I don't give a damn!" Pickett threw up his hands looking at the mirror. "I guess we're done for the moment." He said to Pitus, "Your quarters are ready. They will be heavily guarded. Please respect my wishes and do not try to escape." Pitus nodded and stood up. Two armed guards came into the room and led him out of the interrogation room.

Outside he was led past the observers from behind the mirror. Agent Morgan was among them. To her he said, "You have those same intelligent eyes as he had."

"Who," asked Morgan?

"Hawk's Brother, my friend the skeptic. You have inherited that trait from him." Morgan stood her mouth agape as Pitus continued on to his cell.

"Billings stepped over to her. "What was that all about," he asked. "By the look on your face it wasn't more bullshit."

"I don't know how he found it out," she said. "My mother told many times the tradition of Hawk's Brother. He is my tenth generation grandfather." The bewilderment on her face was quickly overcome by her habitual skepticism. "Just some more bullshit," she said.

The quarters were not as austere as Pitus had imagined a prison cell to be. The dungeon in Beljeaun Prison on Qetterxilict was plain, cold and claustrophobic. This room was twelve feet square with a full single bed, nightstand with reading lamp, a writing desk also with a lamp and a television. An enclosed bathroom was just off this room and came complete with a shower. Pitus sat down on the bed. There were some magazines on the nightstand. Pitus pawed through them and selected one. "THE GOOD O'L DAYS," he read off the cover. Pitus turned through it till he stopped at a nostalgic article about old outhouses. He read only a few sentences before he stopped. "Whoever wrote this," he thought, "never smelled one or ever had to take a shovel and muck one out." He tossed the magazine back on the stand. The next one showed more promise. "OTHER WORLDS," he read off the cover this time. "Maybe they aren't so backward after all."

Pitus flipped through it glancing at artists' renditions of planets circling nearby stars, some of which Pitus knew were there, but the stories seemed speculative rather than factual. "I could write an article for this magazine," he said, "and it would be hard facts and none of this bullshit." He tossed the magazine back on the pile and lay back on the bed. He closed his eyes and soon drifted off to sleep.

Pickett entered the briefing room followed by Morgan and Billings. A woman stood at a projector. She saluted the Major as he approached and the Major returned the salute.

"What have you got for me, lieutenant," the major asked. He then introduced Lieutenant Lindsey Burke to Agents Morgan and Billings.

"This just came over from NASA," said Burke. "It occurred about twelve hours ago." She inserted a chip into the projector and explained.

"The Martian land rover *Olympus* landed near the equator last summer and has been heading toward the Martian south polar ice sheet. It reached sixty degrees south latitude at 2300 Eastern Standard Time yesterday, sending back nearly flawless video streaming. Watch what happens at 2305 . . ." She fast fed the timer ahead to thirty seconds prior to the specified time. She shifted her glance between the screen and the three spectators as the video rolled. The three stared in shock at the screen.

"We were not looking for life this time, but it found us." A cloud of dust rolled up as a ship the size of a small metro bus landed just fifty yards in front of the rover. Shortly a hatch popped open from the side of the single hulled craft and a human like creature stepped out. It was wearing an orange toned suit of sheer metallic fabric and atop it was a transparent fishbowl helmet. The creature took a few steps toward the moving rover then sped off to the left. The larboard camera followed the creature as it jogged to the top of a nearby rise where it paused a moment. Then it came straight for the rover and stood bent over it. The image of the creature close up showed it to be a humanoid probably a male. It spoke as it was bent over the rover and audio picked it up. It was a male human voice but it uttered no known human language. Then it crouched down close to the larboard camera and peered into it, smiled and waved. Audio again picked up the tinny voice, this time in perfect English; "Greetings. Pitus Peston at your service." Then the man got up and hurried away back toward the ship.

The lieutenant stopped the projector. "He is probably heading here," she said.

"He's down the hall. We've been talking to him for the past twenty minutes." Pickett smirked. "What do you say now, Agent Morgan?"

"Jesus Christ," she breathed. "I have an apology to make."

"I have some very old census records to check," said Billings.

"If he was on Mars at eleven last night," said Pickett, "He's been up all night. Let him snooze awhile. Get all you can on him and meet me back here at 1500 hours. Maybe we can get a look at that ship by then."

Pitus awoke at half past three by a knock at the door. "Come in," he yawned. Major Pickett entered and behind him another man came in dressed in a suit.

"Mr. Peston, this is Dan Henning from the Federal Bureau of Investigation." Pitus stood up. Henning offered his hand and Pitus shook it. Briefly Pitus had a twinge that they had met before. Ere he could dwell on it, the discussion began.

"If what we suspect is true," said Henning, "you are the man of the year, hell, man of the whole century!" He turned to the Major. "Is there a place where we can talk?" Pickett nodded and led them out of the room and down the corridor to a large conference room. In the center was a boardroom-size table with about twenty high backed chairs around it. On the near edge of the table was a copy of the Peregrinations. The three sat in chairs on the table end close to the door. Henning asked if coffee could be brought in. The major got up and opened the door. He gave instructions to s guard and closed the door again, returning to his seat.

They sat quietly a moment and the door opened again. A man, also in plain clothes entered with a small machine on a little stand a little less high than the table. He took a chair and plugged in the machine which looked like a small laptop computer fixed on the stand.

"This is Mr. Amos Willard," said the major. He introduced Pitus to Willard who was set up too far away to conveniently shake hands, so he made a slight bow and Pitus reciprocated. "Amos will be recording what we say here for the record. Do you object?" Pitus shook his head and the meeting began. Pickett spoke up, "Do you copy me in Washington?"

"Loud and clear with sound and video," an unidentified voice replied. Picket nodded to Henning, who pushed the book toward Pitus.

"Are you the author of this book?"

"I am," Pitus replied.

"I won't question you on whether the book is factual," said Henning. "We have ample evidence of its veracity in a hangar here on the premises."

"Then you have the orbiter," said Pitus.

"Is that what it is called," asked Pickett.

"It is an Oman made J-7 Orbiter," said Pitus.

"There is much we can learn from that craft," said Pickett. "It could enable us to reach out to the stars. Can we count on your cooperation?"

"I'll tell you what I can," said Pitus. This modest remark did not reveal his thorough knowledge of the J-7. He decided to play close to the vest, not knowing what these people had in store for him.

"May I ask you a question," said Pitus?

"Certainly," replied Henning.

"Am I your prisoner?"

"Let's just say you are an honored, though compulsory guest of the United States," said Henning.

Pitus laughed. "Very well," he said.

"You have been treated well thus far, haven't you," asked Henning?

Pitus nodded.

"V I P treatment," said the major.

"It has been confirmed you are human," said Henning, "and could easily integrate into society. If you choose to cooperate with us and permit us to extract your knowledge, I see no reason to detain you beyond the conclusion of your debriefing." Pitus again nodded. "You lying bag of shit," he thought. "If you don't kill me when you're through with me, how could you rest secure that I wouldn't 'debrief' your enemies, presuming there are some, which is likely?" He resolved at that moment to build on a plan of escape. In the meantime, he could see no reason to hold back anything. If the adage, 'keep your friends close and your enemies closer still, had any validity, then his being in the middle of repairing the orbiter was just the place to be. The vital thing was to let out the debriefing slowly enough to allow the escape plan to mature. It might be possible that they would believe his reason for returning and render some aid, but he did not disillusion himself with this.

"We are interested in your ship, of course," said Pickett. "It is a space vehicle far advanced beyond our technology. I would conservatively estimate it to be two or three centuries ahead of us.

"There is another thing of interest to us," said Henning. "You were born in Fort Edward, New York in 1787. We have actually corroborated this claim. You are listed in the New York Census of 1790 along with your parents and a brother."

"Lloyd," said Pitus

"This would make you the oldest living person in the history of mankind, yet you appear to be a man in his early thirties. Is this due to relativity?"

"I'm not familiar with that term," said Pitus.

"Time dilation at relativistic speeds has been known for more than a century since Einstein proposed it," said Henning.

Pitus thought a moment. It was back on Tonga Hinga a whole century before Einstein's revelation that he learned the concept from the lectures of Corson Loda Dilek.

"I am familiar with the phenomenon," he said. "I can tell you that it is factual. I made mention of it in the PEREGRINATIONS. Has anyone read the book?"

"I have read portions of it," said Henning. "But I don't have to read it. I Know it's true, 'old friend'," he thought.

"A fascinating book," said Pickett.

Some sandwiches sat on a platter in the middle of the table. Pitus took one and took a mouthful. During this hiatus in the conversation Pitus took stock in his situation.

"Fascinating indeed," thought Pitus, "so why haven't you started the questioning with the Omans? This was the first detailed description of extraterrestrial life and it hasn't been broached by either of you. According to The Cube, you haven't received the reply signal from Arbusko, the planetary system in Leo yet, so the Omans are the first real proof that humans of Earth are not alone in the Universe." "This is delicious," said Pitus, "What do you call it?"

"Turkey club sandwich," said Pickett. As Pitus chewed, he further assessed the two across the table.

"The existence of Oman as well as the other five inhabited planets mentioned in the PEREGRINATIONS should have been on top of the list of topics in this 'debriefing'," thought Pitus. "That is, top of the list unless the interest lies in the more parochial concerns of military advantage and dominance on this planet." He swallowed the last bit of the sandwich. The more discussion Pitus had with his captors, the more he realized that he and all these here are sons and daughters of Ewanok; Haldi to the core. He didn't like being forced into this conclusion. The session lasted for three hours, when a break was called for the day.

The next morning, Pitus was moved to another undisclosed location where his quarters were comfortable if not luxurious. His every desire was met, except the one that really counted; his liberty. All his personal effects were confiscated, including his amulet. It was time to employ some cunning with a smart quantity of patience. This last ingredient, essential in any successful endeavor was hardest to maintain. Pitus yearned to conclude his mission of ridding the world of those corstet plants where ever they were, but he knew a random search would not bear any fruit. The plants that were discovered would have to come to him, or at least the discoverer and that meant endless vigilance.

Over the next several weeks Pitus met with physicists, astronomers, computer scientists, and also linguists. He and the team assigned to him, restored function to the orbiter's computer which provided a storehouse of knowledge on propulsion and stellar cartography. These data also legitimized the information written in the PEREGRINATIONS more than a century ago. Since Pitus had hitherto showed no signs of rebellion to the long hours of work and the nightly incarcerations, the security as pertained to his person was lightened.

The main power of the ship, the artificial singularity was unfortunately beyond restoration. It had lost so much of its angular momentum, that it all but stopped rotating and no longer emanated gravitational energy waves. It was postulated to put some spin on the singularity by external means, but the object was not part of this universe, and could not be influenced directly. There was no force currently available of the necessary magnitude to do the job. The only way to recharge an inert singularity was to rapidly stream in a stupendous quantity of matter which would spiral into the void and increase angular momentum until the sufficient spin of the whole was restored. This could only be done safely in space. New science was needed for this task, and Pitus cleverly gave enough information to encourage, but not allow for success.

He did manage with one of the computer scientists, a brilliant young man of twenty-two, a download of most of the contents of the orbiter's main computer. This required a literal truckload of top of the line CPUs set in a radial configuration to hold the data. Pitus knew little about building a quantum computer like the one in the orbiter. His experience with it made it necessary only to manipulate it. "If only I had the Oman National Encyclopedia that was in Atoye's Duster," he thought. That however was literally a galaxy away.

He did, with the information in THE PEREGRINATIONS make metallic hydrogen, but the yield was far too low to attempt compressing it into a degenerate phase. Even if they could enhance the yield, it was still only the first step in producing a singularity. This task was taken over by a separate team, and would probably take years to accomplish the goal.

He taught Omanee to one of the linguists, an attractive young woman about his physical age with blue eyes and sandy blonde hair kept medium length. Shannon was shorter than he by six inches with an athletic build that did not rob her of the feminine form. She was highly intelligent, a necessity in her field, and she possessed an attitude of joy when it came to her appointed work, talking for hours in the alien tongue. She, like Pitus found languages easy to acquire and knew Greek, Latin, and many of the European tongues. This bond of language between them inevitably grew into a mutual affection which Pitus took great pains in encouraging.

Shannon and Pitus worked together on a lexicon of Oman words and syntax, which required long hours at the computer. One time when she left him for a while to compile, he used her pass code to write a small program for his future use.

He described the religion of Oman whose godhead he gave as Aldit Hor. This was a half truth since Omans knew Aldit Hor to be one of a race known as the Innovators. They were not supernatural beings in the same sense as Jehovah, Vishnu, or the residents of Mount Olympus. To the Omans they were an ancient people of legendary power, but no more. He told the scholars attached to him that the amulet was a religious symbol, a prayer talisman similar to a rosary. As such, it was given less attention than was due. In the light of day it looked like a beautiful blue diamond or topaz in a golden setting.

It was kept locked up in a vault at night, since it was believed to be worth a great deal. This was a fortunate stroke, because if one were to happen on it in the dark and see its natural blue glow, it would be taken straight to the Smithsonian and permanently out of his reach. There was only one luso stone on Earth and he would eventually need it for his escape.

Pitus wanted desperately to get his hands on the amulet once again, but didn't dare arouse suspicion by pressing the matter. He carefully nudged his way toward getting the amulet by dovetailing the spurious Oman religion into his talks on Oman history and linguistics. Eventually more questions on the Oman religion were asked and Pitus suggested a demonstration of the amulet's stations which were manifest as the symbols surrounding the stone. The amulet was brought to him and he held it up before the historians.

"The holder surrounding the stone is marked with the symbols of the four winds cited in the Book of Hibber," said Pitus. "They correspond to something like the cardinal points of our compass and the supplicant intones the following passage from the book . . ." He drew a breath instead of chanting, since he had no clue what to say next. A commotion at the back of the room shanghaied the crowd's attention a moment. A man burst into the room and shouted, "Don't let him touch the amulet. It's not a religious artifact. It's a transporter . . ." Two of the ever present guards started for Pitus, who immediately touched the two critical facets of the luso stone. Instantly a brilliant white aperture appeared and he dove through it. One of the guards had a hold of Pitus' arm and was pulled through. Pitus broke free and shoved the man back through the aperture before it closed.

A FUGITIVE

Now Pitus was a fugitive in a place far more sophisticated than when he was here in 1883. Then information was spread mainly by word of mouth, and notwithstanding the telegraph, word was still slow to disseminate. Now electronic surveillance permeated the planet and within minutes, thousands could know his description. He knew he had to act fast in these early minutes if he wanted to successfully 'integrate into society' as promised by Henning. Who did he think he was kidding? When they knew what he knew he would become a liability, and it was clear what would happen after that.

When he planned his escape, he had no set plan to find the corstet. He decided to start his search at the source in Fort Edward. The first thing on the agenda was to find a change of clothes. He was currently in a day glow orange jump suit, effective camouflage on Oman, but not in this world. He happened upon a Salvation Army collection box in the parking lot of an abandoned strip mall. The big red metal box was stuffed and boxes and bags were strewn around the base of it. He casually walked by seizing a bag from off the ground. He rounded the corner of the empty building. There was a patch of woods behind. Within the shelter of some bushes he crouched down and sorted through the clothes. He scored a pair of trousers and a flannel shirt. They were large for him and the ill fit would probably make him noticeable, but it was better than the orange. Once clad in the old clothes, he stuffed the orange suit deep in the bag and returned to the collection box. A second pass afforded him a chance to snatch a couple more bags to look through. In one of these was a pair of old sneakers which were a reasonable fit, and a better fitting long sleeve shirt. He changed into the better clothes.

A third pass yielded a brown jacket which he immediately tried on. It fit well, making him look more like a normal resident of town. He walked along the front of the empty stores looking at his reflection in the glass storefronts. He still looked like a bum, he thought, but infinitely better than when he arrived. He was satisfied with the new look and moved on.

During the time of his journey to his home world, he tried to work out a strategy for finding the corstet. Now that he was here, he realized that none of his plans were worth a damn. So much had changed over the two centuries. Pitus walked up the main street in the town in which he grew up of which nothing was familiar. But that wasn't quite so. The lay of the river was the same. He walked further up to a small park and sat down on a wooden bench that faced the river. He gazed out over the water. He couldn't shake the feeling that he was an alien.

There was an outcrop of rocks in the middle of the river he used to climb on when he was a kid. That hadn't changed. He followed with his eyes from the rocks along the opposite shore. He held his hand over his eyes as a visor in order to see the shore with better detail. Soon he saw it; the flat ledge that flanked the low spot where the boys had their late night bonfires. There was now an old gnarly maple standing in the center of the spot. The place was unrecognizable except for the stone ledge. Pitus remembered the night two centuries ago when he and Martin sat and talked about going out west. "We both made it, didn't we Marty," Pitus said softly. He thought of Leander, Allan, Ellen, and the others, now long gone. As he sat he took stock of his present condition. The orbiter was gone, but it was useless anyway. There was no way to repair it even in this time. "This place has advanced much since I was here last," he thought, "but technology is still far behind what I need to return to Oman. There is air travel but very little space travel and that with chemical rockets. That Mars probe was a worthy achievement, but it was only a crude beginning to a reach for the stars."

"This has killed my hopes of returning to Oman with a new crop of corstet," he thought. "When I find it I will have to destroy it and then secretly live out my days in this still backward place." His disappointment was acute. He came from an exciting place where he was famous and renowned. He came from a place where he mattered and could do great things. Here, he was an unknown without the tools needed to accomplish anything of importance except save the world. Pitus laughed at the irony of his last thought. If saving an entire world wasn't great, then what was . . . ?

Pitus looked around from the park bench at the village. There were buildings that were obviously old. He got up and headed toward them. "Maybe I can find the site of the shop where Lucius and I once worked," he thought. He passed a few brick houses and up ahead was an old church. "I remember that the last time I was here," he thought, but I never went into the churchyard." He looked at the lay of the land a moment and then recognized the place. That old brick church was standing on the spot of the old meeting house where he, Lloyd, Mother, Father and grandpa Jem, who was Jeremiah Peston, went to Sunday services. "Pa lies in that churchyard," he thought. He entered through a gap in the wrought iron fence and stood among the old slab grave stones. He recalled visiting Allan's grave in 1883. He was lying a mile north of where he now stood in Union Cemetery. This was a small graveyard, but no less well kept. It was but a moment before he found someone he knew. Pitus kneeled down beside the marble slab, "God, Leander, I've found you," Pitus said reverently. He touched the edge of the marker. "I hope Saint Peter didn't hold your bad language against you. He snorted a short laugh. "You doubtless won your way inside with a short game of cards." Ten feet away Leander's father, the Reverend Matthew Kincaid lay beneath a similar marker. Pitus compared the dates. Mr. Kincaid was buried in 1840. Leander's stone was dated April 21st 1836. "Fell at the Battle for Texas . . . REMEMBER THE ALAMO" was scribed beneath his name. "You're a war hero, Lea, for Chrissake."

He stood up and peered into the rows of stones. Amidst the square edged stones stood one also of marble whose top was round and ornate. A winged soul effigy was graven in the center. Pitus recognized the stone, an antique against the others, even before he reached it. "Pa," called Pitus softly as he stood before the marker of Rufus Peston. He read once again the date; July 9th, 1803 . . . in the 47th year of his age, and the stanza below;

> "Take heed stranger as you pass by
> As you are now so once was I
> As I am now so you must be
> Prepare for death and follow me."

Even though from another era, the sight of the stone, covered with lichens and worn nearly smooth in places, brought back with fresh acuteness the emotions of the day it was set. The solemnity of the moment in no wise prepared him for what he would see next. Beside the eighteenth century style stone of his father stood an incongruously plain marker of smooth gray shale. It was square with the bas relief weeping willow and urn motif of a later generation. He softly read the inscription; "Caroline Peston, wife of Rufus Peston, departed this life August 24th, 1815. AE. 41 yrs, 6 mos. 12 days . . . If it wasn't stressful enough to be seeing his mother's grave for the first time, the terse line beneath the date dealt a hammer blow; "She died of a broken heart." His own heart grew sick with blame's burden upon seeing the indictment which could have been meant only for him.

"Oh God, Mother," Pitus sobbed. He slumped against the stone, the cold smoothness of the polished shale against his cheek. "I did this to you. I should never have left you like I did. Forgive me." He suddenly realized he wasn't alone.

"Mister, are you all right," said a man who had crouched down beside him. "Have you had a heart attack? I'll call an ambulance." He whipped out a cell phone and started poking it. Pitus came back to reality and realizing what the arrival of an ambulance could mean . . .

"Stop. Don't call anyone," he said, "I am all right." Pitus hurried to his feet to prove this. The man pocketed his phone.

"Are you sure you are all right," asked the man once again. "I was coming out of the church when I saw you go down." He looked down at the stone. "Are you a descendant of the Pestons," he asked?

"Yes," said Pitus. He was now rational enough to know he couldn't be specific. Though the man didn't question him about it, he almost certainly saw him weeping before a centuries old marker with an emotional rawness of one who had just lost a close loved one. There could be no rational explanation for this conduct.

"I promise you I am all right," said Pitus. "Thank you for your concern." He hurried out of the churchyard and didn't look back.

He recalled that the meeting house was but three doors down the street from the apothecary shop. He stood at the edge of a gravel parking lot, and just ahead of him there it was . . . The stone house was still there! Now it was a tavern. The house was garbed in both old and new renovations, but the original form was still evident.

"Mike's Place," he read from the glowing neon sign over the door. He had a five-dollar bill in his pocket that he won from one of the scientists on a bet he no longer remembered, but it was a precious thing now. He was no bum as long as he had it. He looked up again at the tavern sign. A dram of rum or mead cost five cents the last time he entered Blosser's tavern just down the street from where he now stood. Now he wondered if the whole five dollars would be sufficient for the same "What's wrong with being a bum," he asked. He pushed open the door and entered.

The place was dark as most taverns were then and this had not changed over the years. Two young men were playing at a pool table while two young women were seated nearby sipping on their drinks and watching them without much apparent interest. Another young couple were seated at the bar sipping from the bottles as they talked to the bartender. Pitus took a place at the bar a few stools down. Immediately the bartender excused himself from the couple and came over to Pitus.

"What can I get you," asked Mike affably.

"Perhaps some hard cider," said Pitus.

"You have to get that at the grocery store," said Mike. "We have beer and hard booze and a limited selection of wine."

"Hard booze," repeated Pitus quizzically. "What do you mean . . . ?"

"You know hard stuff . . . whiskey, gin, rum . . ." He laughed uneasily. "You just get off the boat?" Pitus was also uneasy. He was getting snarled in an ignorance of modern idiom.

"This is pretty good," said the man at the bar who held up his bottle.

"I'll have one of those then," said Pitus. He took the "fiver" out of his pocket and laid it on the bar. Mike took it and placed a coaster, a bottle and a one-dollar bill next to it.

"Guess I won't be here long," thought Pitus. He picked up the bottle and took a drink. The cold tart carbonation roused his throat and he sighed with pleasure at the taste. By now Mike had returned to the couple who happened to be Joe and Lorraine, and continued talking.

"I'm worried about them," said Mike. "He is here almost every night with Joyce, but I haven't seen either of them for three days. Ann said Joyce hasn't been to the Library since Monday."

"Maybe they went somewhere," said Lorraine.

"I hope so, Lorraine," said Mike, "but it ain't like Johnny to go anywhere without spillin' it to me first. Joe, you look like you're thinking somethin," added Mike. "You know something we don't?"

"It must be that Peston book," said Joe. "Since the Feds took it, he has been royally pissed." Pitus looked up upon hearing this. He turned back away after realizing he might be caught staring. Till now he gulped the beer and downed half of it, intending to finish it off and be on his way. Now he pretended to drink it, intent on making it last.

"Why did the Feds confiscate the book," asked Mike?

"You read the copy of it I gave you," said Joe. "Don't you think the stuff in there should interest the Pentagon or NASA?"

"It's just a sci-fi novel, that's all," said Mike. "I'm not quite done with it yet."

"Pretty convincing sci-fi novel," declared Joe. "Some of that stuff about propulsion has been in late issues of Scientific American as futuristic speculation. It is far ahead of the time when it was written. Nobody's got an imagination like that; it must be factual."

Just then, the door flew open and in came John and Joyce.

"Well, "said Mike, "Look what the cat dragged in." The pair came up to the bar and occupied the two empty seats between Lorraine and Pitus.

"Where the hell ya' been," asked Mike. "We thought someone kidnapped you."

"Not far off," said John.

"What do you mean," asked Joe?

"Simeon Ott," said John. "I went to see him after I got out of jail to thank him for posting the bail . . . , and to get back my stuff by Pitus he stole from me."

Pitus' pulse just doubled as these words reached him. He turned slightly toward John, who sat next to him. Could it be that he providentially blundered onto the solution of his problem? He was not involved in the conversation, but he *was* the conversation. His very soul burned to break in. There was no knowing the consequences of doing this. The opportunity for solving his mission was unfolding right before his eyes, but the wrong play of it could blow the whole thing. Mike looked over at Pitus. "Ready for another beer," He asked?

Pitus shook his head. Mike returned his attention to Joyce and John.

"He held us against our will," said Joyce. She looked at John and smirked. "That might not be wholly accurate," she added. John returned the subtle nonverbal.

"He held us captive until we agreed to give him the plant. Now he has it," said John. Now Pitus was ready to explode. Jesus, and Aldit, he had to say something.

"What plant," asked Mike?

Pitus turned directly toward John and said to Mike, "I think he's referring to corstet."

Now all faces were turned to Pitus, and he was the new focus of attention. John looked at him curiously. He didn't look like an agent of the FBI or the CIA. He looked . . . like a bum.

"John Hodiak," said John.

"Pitus Peston," replied Pitus. The glass Mike had been drying went to the floor and shattered. Joe had his bottle hoisted for another pull and this went forth as a spray across the bar. Lorraine patted Joe on the back not taking her eyes of Peston. Joyce looked back and forth between John and Pitus.

"How nice to have you show up after all this time," said John, his sarcasm obvious.

"We don't have a lot of time," said Pitus sternly. "Whether you believe me or not, that corstet is the end of humanity unless we get rid of it."

"And how, may I ask, is something as beneficial to health as corstet . . ."

"Think about it," said Pitus. "It gets generally known, saves millions, becomes the desire of billions, and causes a world war over the possession of it. We have to stop it before it gets out of control."

"You expect me to just accept this doomsday scenario," asked John?

"I've seen it," said Pitus. "The year 2060 will be the last year a calendar will be printed."

"Geez Christ," said Mike. "That's when I turn seventy and can collect Social Security. You tellin' me I won't see retirement?"

"How did you *see* this happen," asked Joyce? "That's almost forty years from now."

"I saw that it would happen," said Pitus. "It was written as history in Loma's Cube." He gave the digested version of the Cube and Loma's Epic poem that described it and its location. He told them how he found it; Harnuk's Eyes and all. It made a spellbinding tale, but didn't seem to convince.

"He didn't see anything," said Joe. "He's a crackpot, a phony. Don't get suckered in by him."

"It is all true," said Pitus emphatically. "It is foretold by the Cube."

"That wasn't in your, I mean, the Peregrinations book," said John.

"When I left the book here I hadn't yet gone to the Cube," said Pitus.

"How can we believe what you say if we can't even prove you are Peston," asked John? "You'll have to admit, this is all a bit far fetched."

"You believe the corstet is real," said Pitus.

"All we've managed to do was germinate a few seeds from one of the pods. No one has had a chance to test its effects."

"I put those pods in a bottle," said Pitus, "and gave them to Ordway." This wasn't in the Peregrinations, but it was in the journals Pitus wrote. The journals had been undisturbed in John's attic for more than a century. The skepticism left John's face. Pitus, in desperation, took out his amulet. In the dark room the pale blue glow softly lit all their faces. "Now do you believe me," asked Pitus?

The pale blue glow of the luso stone was a strong sell. Joyce had it in her hands in a second and peered into it in rapt attention. "Johnny," she said, "I want one of these really bad." John gently took it from her and gazed at it a second. He knew what it was and why it glowed from the description of it in THE PEREGRINATIONS. He handed it back to Pitus.

"What do you need from me," said John.

"I need the corstet," said Pitus. "I had hopes of returning with it to Oman, but now that looks impossible. It will have to be destroyed."

"Why is returning to Oman impossible," asked Joe. He was now past his own skepticism.

"My ship crashed into Lake Huron and the army has it," said Pitus. "They also had me for eight months, till I got away."

"Then they are looking for you," asked John.

"I'm certain of that," said Pitus. "They were debriefing me, and promised to let me go when they were done, but I am no fool. Out of their hands I am a very dangerous fellow. I could see I had only two options; a life sentence or a death sentence. The technology of Oman I gladly make a gift to the people of Earth. I was disappointed to see how slow your progress is in getting out into space. The knowledge gleaned from that orbiter will accelerate things greatly. While the advanced Oman science is beneficial to mankind, the corstet will bring destruction. It must be destroyed."

"Simeon Ott has it," said John. Joyce prodded John but he grabbed her hand and squeezed it. She got the message and kept still. "He kidnapped Joyce and me. I had to give it to him as a ransom for our release."

"Who is this Simeon Ott," asked Pitus, "and where can I find him?"

"Ott lives in Clifton Park, about forty miles south of here," said John. John looked carefully at the man who claimed to be Pitus Peston and who John had some lingering doubts about. "Simeon Ott is the only son of Laura Ott," said John. He watched as Pitus' expression went blank in astonishment. Even in the dim light of the bar one could see the color drain from his face. John eyed him a few more seconds. "Only Pitus Peston would react so strongly to that particular news. I can scarcely believe it possible, but I believe it. All right Pitus, What do we do next?"

"I have to go see him," said Pitus. He was contemplative in his tone. "Jesus, I have a son . . ." To John he asked, "Does he look like an old man?"

"He might pass for *your* father, but not old looking for someone who is 207."

"Take me to him," said Pitus. "I have to get back the plant."

"He is a rich and powerful man," warned John. "He was a perfect gentleman early on in my encounter with him, but he has gotten more aggressive since the Feds have turned up the heat about your book."

"I know all about the Feds and also the military," said Pitus. "I doubt a single man can pose as great a threat . . ." Even as he said this, he recalled just how dangerous a single man could be, Ich Habine Ing being the prime example.

"He's wealthy, you say," asked Pitus?

"Loaded," replied John.

"Then I may have something to offer him," said Pitus. "I need you to take me to him."

"When," asked John?

"Now," said Pitus.

John shrugged. "He won't be happy to see me since our kidnapping," said John. He glanced at Joyce. "Is that what he did to us?"

"Kind of," said Joyce, "It was a kindly sort of kidnapping, if such a thing could be so," she added. "I don't think you should go," she warned.

"I won't take any undue chances," said John. He got up from the bar stool and led the way out of the bar to his truck. They both got in and headed west for the Northway. Pitus looked curiously at John.

"Did he kidnap you or not?" John looked straight ahead as he drove west on Route 197. "He kept Joyce at his guest house under armed guard while he and I went to my house which is actually your old house, to get the corstet. When we returned, he released us and gave us each a check for five million dollars and also made us sign an agreement to pay it back in full if either of us let it leak about the corstet. So . . . if it was a kidnapping, it was the first time ever, I'm sure, that the kidnapper paid the ransom."

Pitus didn't reply to this. He was thinking. "The plant cannot remain on Earth. If his plan for Simeon Ott fails or is rejected out of hand by him, it might become necessary for him to kill his own son. The man next to him driving the truck knows the value of the plant as well. Will he have to eliminate him and the woman? He hadn't thought of the potential stakes in the matter. He hadn't thought that saving man would cost him his own soul.

As they neared Ott's house, John asked, "What do you plan to do, just walk up and ring the bell at the gate and say, 'Let me in, I'm your ol' man?'"

"That probably wouldn't work," said Pitus. "He knows you; why don't you tell him to let you in?"

"That probably won't work either," said John. "He said not to come back or I would regret it. I took that to mean that he would have me killed."

"We could try what you said you and Joyce did," said Pitus.

"That didn't work," said John. "Repeating it might get us shot."

Planning was now a moot subject. They had arrived. They sat in the truck in front of the gate a moment. "Hell," said Pitus. "Let's try the direct approach." They both got out of the truck. Pitus stepped up to the wrought iron gate and pressed the intercom button.

"Who is it," asked a gruff voice. "Then the voice said, "Mr. Hodiak, I thought Mr. Ott was clear that you were not to come back." Pitus moved up to the intercom. "Tell Simeon his father is here and to get his ass out here and let us in." Several seconds of silence ensued, during which the two were most certainly scrutinized by camera at the gate. Then the gate started to open and they went through. They were no more than a few paces inside the gate when the two were flanked by two men holding shotguns directly on them.

One of the men motioned with the barrel of his gun toward the house. They all went up the drive in silence and entered the mansion. Pitus and John were escorted into a study. One of the men remained on guard as the other left. No one spoke. Pitus took in the room from his chair. There were lots of leather-bound books on the dark wooden shelves. The books were obviously cared for. Pitus nodded his approval, yet the guard kept still. Then Pitus noticed some familiar spines. They were all uniform in size and labeling. Pitus became curious. He turned to his captor, "May I go look at those books, he asked?"

"Go ahead," said the guard. "Just remember you are covered." Pitus got up slowly and approached the shelves. He carefully removed one of the volumes. "Universal Magazine," Pitus read from the maroon leather spine label. He opened the book. On the front pastedown was the name he expected to see; Ephas Thorne, S.J. He turned to John holding up the book. "These once belonged to me," said Pitus. "My uncle Lemuel shipped them to me from Liverpool."

"I purchased them from my Uncle Lloyd," came a reply from the entrance to the study.

Pitus turned to see Simeon Ott standing in the doorway. He looked at John as he entered the room. "Good evening, Mr. Hodiak, do you have something else of interest to me?"

"I think this should make me an associate," said John slyly sweeping his hand toward Pitus. Ott turned his gaze upon Pitus. "I don't believe we've met." He stood off several feet making no gesture to greet the newcomer in a civilized manner.

"I suppose I deserved that," said Pitus meekly. "Lloyd sold them to you?"

"In 1835," said Ott. "I gave him one hundred dollars gold. Your, or rather, Peston's entire collection is here in this room."

"This isn't going to be easy," thought Pitus. Not knowing at all how this was going to turn out, he just pressed on.

"You don't believe that I am Pitus Peston, your father?"

Ott looked at John, "How about you, Mr. Hodiak," he asked, "Do you believe him?"

"Yes," said John.

"What proof did he show you?"

"He knew about the plant," said John.

"The authorities know about corstet," said Ott. "He could be FBI or CIA."

"Proof," said Pitus. He turned back to the shelves of Universal Magazines. "Have you looked through these," he asked.

"I have," said Ott, "but not in this century or the last."

"These were once owned by a Jesuit priest named Ephas Thorne."

"He opened one of the books, Mr. Ott," said the guard.

"True," said Pitus. "I spoiled that bit of evidence by sating my curiosity." He moved toward the shelf holding the beginning of the series. "Besides the books was a letter to me by Thorne. He wrote, referring to the other books that accompanied this set, that some were not in English, to which Lemuel said, that I knew several languages besides the Mother Tongue. I kept that letter in the front of Franklin's Treatise on Electricity. Is it still there?" This moment was so poignant to John that he sat scarcely breathing, following the verbal jousting as if watching a tennis match.

Ott's expression lost its toughness. He looked at Pitus almost somberly and pointed to a quarto leather volume. Pitus move to it and plucked it off the shelf. He opened the cover and extracted the letter. He then opened the paper and, after glancing at it, laid it back in the book and returned it to the shelf.

"Why did you abandon us," asked Ott with such acerbity that John stood up. The guard raised his weapon, but John jerked his head toward the door. The guard stiffly nodded and they both left the study.

Once in the hall John said to the guard, "They may be a while. Got any coffee?"

"Kitchen," replied the guard. They both entered and John sat at a bar near a window and quietly stared out into the dark. The guard laid the shotgun on a cutting board and started a rather expensive version of a Mr. Coffee brewing a pot. After a few minutes it was done. He poured two cups. "How do you take it," he asked? Much of the adversarial tone was now gone from his voice.

"Just cream or milk," said John. The guard came over to the bar and placed the cups down, along with a cruet of cream. He then pulled up a stool to the bar a few feet from John.

"Aren't you taking a chance," asked John? He glanced over to the gun on the cutting board across the room.

"You don't seem the type," replied the guard. "Besides, I have a Walther in my pocket," he said.

"The name is Frank," said the guard. Neither moved to shake hands, but John nodded deferentially as a greeting.

"Is that guy for real," asked Frank? "How could he claim to be Mr. Ott's ol' man?"

"He is for real," said John. "That man in there with your boss is Pitus Peston, and he's been places and seen things you or I can scarcely imagine.

"Help me imagine," Frank said.

"Practically all I know of Peston's travels in space is from a visit here in 1883," said John.

"Space," asked Frank, "In 1883?"

"He printed two copies of a book about his travels and left one copy in the New York State Library and the other in the Library of Congress. I briefly had one of those copies and read it," said John.

"Had," said Frank.

"The feds took it," said John. "Actually, I had each of the copies for a short while. The bastards confiscated both of them, but not before I made a copy of my own. There is stuff in it that poses a risk to national security."

"Like Roswell stuff," asked Frank?

"Yes," said John. Pitus found a spaceship in Monument Valley back in 1811 that came from the planet Oman, which is somewhere on the opposite side of the Milky Way. He describes that planet as well as five others, with details of their societies, histories, geography, plant and animal life."

"Sounds like Jules Verne so far," said Frank.

"More than that," said John. "There's pretty specific information on propulsion and force fields, weapons and other things necessary to build a star ship. If it is all a humbug, the Pentagon, FBI, and the CIA don't see it that way."

"While I was here with my fiancée the night before last pent up in the guest house, I did some net surfing. Simeon Ott was born in 1812 in St. Louis. His mother was Laura Lee Ott, who was born in 1790 and lived till 1824. After his mother's death, Simeon started working as a cabin boy on a side-wheeler called The *Bellefleur* running between St. Louis and New Orleans. When he got older, he became an oiler, then a pilot. I even saw a daguerreotype of the crew of the Bellefleur and a young crewman stood off to the side, but still in the picture. It was him."

Frank got off the stool. "Bring your cup and come with me. I want to see." The two went down a short hallway and entered a room off of it. It was apparently Frank's quarters. Frank opened a lap top on a desk beside the bed. He motioned for John to sit at the desk. Within a minute's time John had the image on the screen. Frank bent close to the screen and breathed, "My Jesus Christ, it's him!" He read the caption beneath the photograph. "The crew of the Bellefleur taken in 1844, less than a year before its destruction at Natchez, Mississippi." Frank turned to John, "How is that possible?"

Pitus had taken an Oman herb for almost two years while he traveled in the wilderness," said John. "It made him heal quickly from wounds and recover quickly from the few diseases he contracted. But it did more than that. It altered his genes just like the medicines I dispense every day for gene therapy. When Simeon Ott was conceived, the DNA of Laura was combined with the enhanced strands of Pitus."

"So he's some sort of superman," asked Frank?

"Not like the old movies," said John. He can't leap tall buildings or anything like that, but his life force and immune system are very strong."

"I can't tell you how many times we've had colds run through the staff," said Frank thoughtfully. "Once the whole place had the flu. Mr. Ott never got so much as a sniffle any of those times. Frank stared at the photo image. "Will he live forever?"

"I'm afraid not," said John. "In fact, Ott is beginning to feel his age. That's why he wanted the plants. He hopes it will rejuvenate him."

"Will it," asked Frank?

"Unknown," said John. "What I know about the plant isn't enough to answer that question. Nobody has had a chance to test them."

They sat silent for a moment. A crash and thud traveled through the walls of the room from some place in the house. Frank sprang up taking out his Walther. He threw open the door to the hallway. In the hall the sounds were much clearer. The noise was coming from the study and it sounded like all hell was breaking loose behind those doors. They rushed to the study and Frank tried to pull open the sliding doors. They were either locked or jammed shut.

"Mr. Ott," cried Frank. There was no answer but one more crash of glass or something like it and then silence. Then of all the strange sounds to emanate from the room came a peel of laughter.

"What the hell," said Frank? "Mr. Ott, are you all right?" There was a moment of silence, then the crunch of footsteps stepping through broken glass. The doors clicked and slid open.

Pitus emerged from the study, his shirt torn nearly off his back, his face streaked with blood. John stood speechless. Frank leveled his pistol at Pitus.

"Move a finger and I'll drop your sorry ass right where you stand!" He called again to Ott.

"Put your gun away, Frank," called Simeon. He stood up from behind the large desk. He looked about the same as Pitus. Not a thing remained on top of the huge desktop where once stood a lamp, blotter, stacks of papers and a myriad of other things that desktops accumulate. There were shards from vases that once stood on plinth stands about the room. Chairs were overturned and an end table was in fragments all over the floor. Through some miracle, the books seemed for the most part untouched, quietly resting on their shelves.

Simeon came forth and stood beside Pitus. "We're all right Frank," he assured him. "We just had a good father and son discussion." He raked his hand through his hair and picked out a ceramic shard. He brought the fragment up close to examine it. "Oh shit," he said. "That was a Ming." He started laughing and cuffed Pitus on the shoulder. An amused expression grew on John's face.

"Did you accomplish anything," asked John?

Ott glanced around the room. "About seven hundred thousand dollars worth." He said to Frank, "Call Gordie. We have a lot of work to do."

Gordon Hewes, besides being Ott's unofficial muscle, shamus, and inside man, was also his business manager and accountant. These last two hats were the official ones. The former just accrued after finding that Gordie had a knack for clandestine activities. These were manifestations of Gordie's alter ego. He dutifully appeared after twenty minutes and was somewhat taken aback by the sight of John and downright shocked by the presence of Pitus whose identity he seemed to surmise. It took little convincing that Pitus was the genuine article, possibly because Gordie had been chasing Peston's shadow for years.

They were in a small conference room; Simeon, John, Pitus and Gordie. Gordie's and John's eyes were riveted on Simeon and Pitus as the meeting began.

"Thanks for coming, Gordie," said Ott. "I know it's late."

"From what Frank said, it sounded urgent," said Gordie.

"Not so urgent as important," said Ott. He motioned to his father, "Pitus has," Simeon looked sheepishly at him, "You look more like *my* son than the other way around," he interjected.

"Pitus suites me fine," he replied affably. Simeon nodded. "Pitus has evidence that the corstet I have been looking for all these years is dangerous and needs to be destroyed."

"Dangerous in what way," asked Gordie.

"If it gets out, it will cause World War Three." Gordie shrugged, "He's probably right, but who could understand what it does and still bring himself to destroy it?"

"If the proposal Pitus has can be accomplished, destroying it won't be necessary," said Ott. Gordie said nothing but laced his fingers on the table.

"Pitus assures me that he has the knowledge to construct an interstellar spacecraft, but he lacks the necessary millions to pull it off."

"The United States has spent trillions on such a thing without success," said Gordie.

"Most of their cost has gone into research," said John.

"Inasmuch as you are here," said Gordie to Pitus, "I take it that we won't need to do that."

"Just a little," said Pitus. "We will have to develop some production pathways."

"It will draw attention if we assemble money on that scale," warned Gordie."

"Can it be done secretly," asked Ott?

"It can," said Gordie, but some of it will have to be used for camouflage."

"Explain," said Ott.

"We will need a secure place in which to build it. Then we will need some top notch scientists who can be bought who can handle the technical portions of the project. If we need radioactive material . . ."

"None needed," said Pitus.

"That's a relief," said Gordie. "That would have been where millions might have become billions." He continued. "An old factory could be purchased and converted for the purpose, but again, it will stick out unless we use part of the facility for some plausible cover activity. That will take time as well as money. What about the ship you came with," he asked?

The army has it in a hangar someplace in Nevada," said Pitus.

"Can we steal it back?"

"That would probably cost more than making a new one from scratch," said Ott, "and then if it was successful, which I doubt, the military would be like a nest of hornets. Secrecy is the best hope of success."

"Especially since they are already pretty perturbed about losing track of me," said Pitus.

"How did you manage that," asked Gordie.

"With this," said Pitus, pulling his amulet out of his shirt. "I would demonstrate, but it might alert them to look for a program in their computers if I activated it." He held up the amulet and cupped his hands around it revealing the light blue glow to Gordie. "There is enough energy in this stone to power a small ship to the outer solar system, but we need to go further than that."

"How much further," asked Gordie?

"Four light years, out to Proxima Centauri."

"I know I'm asking a lot of questions," said Gordie. "That's one of my principal jobs." He smiled.

"No limit on the questions," said Ott.

"Well then," said Gordie, clearing his throat, "there is one question that should be answered before we even begin such an undertaking."

"Which is," asked Ott.

"Why are we going to do it?"

"I want to go where he's been," replied Simeon nodding at Pitus. "If Pitus knows what he's talking about, then it's an opportunity centuries ahead of its time. I know a lot of wealthy men, and what most of them do with their money is tantamount to high priced whoring. Some accumulate the world's best things, which are good for as far as it goes, but you can't take it with you. Some wax philanthropic, but the end is the same. I want a thrill and I can see no better one than going to the other side of the Milky Way," he declared. "Besides," he added, "we have something to return to Oman which they sorely need, and apparently, we shouldn't have."

The implications of this decision were enormous. If Simeon was going to do this, if indeed he could, he would be as if dead to this world. Simeon Ott was not an unencumbered man. This Gordie knew by tending his balance sheet all these years. Could Ott just walk away from his vast wealth? If so, what would become of it? Gordie had little faith that his boss would make it to his destination, let alone ever return. Something had to be done with what Ott would abandon and Gordie knew just the one who should see to it.

As Ott said, the most important thing in all of this was secrecy. The military were surely wound up over losing control of Pitus Peston. They had only begun to exploit his knowledge of the great gift he had involuntarily dumped into their laps. The orbiter had technology that would leap them ahead of the rest of the world by centuries, but the key to realizing the potential had absconded with perhaps the most strategic part, namely, the inter-dimensional transport device. For all they knew he was blabbing his secrets to the Chinese or the New Russian Confederation, either of which could make something of it. Then instead of an arms race, there would be a techno race with the winner capable of deploying its troops and materiel thousands of miles into the heart of enemy soil in an instant fully armed. They would be looking for him, and maybe the risk of losing him again to the enemy would be greater than the benefit of having him alive.

The plan of Pitus and Ott unfolded over the next few weeks. Ott went into the computer business by purchasing a large steel structure from a contractor in Menands once used to house earthmoving equipment. It was chosen because of its being close to an electrical power substation of Niagara Mohawk. The concrete floor was opened in the rear twenty feet of the building which was the size of a small airplane hangar, and a basement was excavated in this space two stories deep. While computers were assembled and sold in the front of the building, under the name of Ott Technological Solutions, the underground bunker in back was the seat of the metallic hydrogen and high energy laser experiments.

Using an auto body shop as a front in Schenectady, a middling size building at the back of the property was devoted to the construction of a clone of Atoye's original Star duster Comet, the ship that brought Atoye, Kinar and Rohab to Earth. This was larger than the J-7 and more suited for the long months of travel through Hivik's Path to the other side of the galaxy and to Oman. This required the services of a devoted assembly crew consisting of carefully selected individuals, possessing talent and as low a profile as possible. It took three months to recruit the dozen men and women needed for the various aspects of the project. The criteria were simple; the candidates had to be single or otherwise unencumbered socially. There was no desire to leave a significant other or an invalid aunt or parent suddenly without support. The pitch went something like this: "We need people for a year-long special project. It is so advanced and proprietary that whoever signs up must complete a contract of absolute secrecy and be willing to be sequestered for the term of the project which may be as little as nine months or as long as fifteen months. All room and board will be provided in comfortable quarters at no charge. All outstanding indebtedness of the enrollee will be settled by the corporation. No wages will be paid, but an off shore bank account will be established for each team member in the sum of one million tax free dollars. At the end of the project, all will be free to leave, but during the term the enrollee must remain on site."

"Any data or reports generated by team members will be released to them at the conclusion of the project. All the knowledge of the proprietary processes will become team member's property to do with as they desire." They were told that the physics they were to work on was so novel as to likely be Nobel Prize material for those who chose to pursue it. Of the fourteen candidates approached, only two of them turned down the offer. These two were paid fifty thousand dollars for their signature on a non-disclosure agreement of just the meeting for the recruitment. It would turn out to be the biggest mistake of their lives.

The team was divided into two groups with five being at the Menands facility and seven at Schenectady. All supplies were delivered to Menands as the cover of the store front computer business was more secure. No high energy components were purchased that would arouse outside interest. The equipment to build the equipment was made on site.

At the first general briefing of the scientists, Ott spelled out the purpose of the project; to build a spacecraft capable of interstellar travel. At the end of Ott's remarks, there was a lot of murmuring among the team members. Skepticism ran through them like a dose of Epsom salts. Then Pitus took the floor. He described in detail the processes involved in the project. There was more murmuring and even more skepticism. Then he booted up a computer on a desktop in front of the room and entered some code. After this, he drew out his amulet, revealing the Luso stone and pointed to a place in the back corner of the large room. He keyed the stone, bringing forth the dazzling aperture. He stepped through it and he and the aperture disappeared. From the back of the room in the place indicated, he emerged as if stepping out of the air. After that, you could have heard a pin drop in that room. Finally a young man stood up and asked, "When can we get started for Christ's Sake?"

"Any luck locating Peston," asked Major Pickett?

Henning shook his head. With Pickett was General Moses Van Cleef. "It is imperative that we find him before he gets discovered by the Russians or the Chinese. How did he get away?"

"He transported out of the facility to some unknown location," said the major.

"Transported, as in 'beam me up Scotty," asked the general?

"He was demonstrating the amulet that he represented as a religious artifact," said Henning. "It turned out to be an inter-dimensional translocator which he activated to make his escape. One of the guards grabbed him and went through with Peston, but he was shoved back out . . ."

"Did he see anything?"

"We don't know," said Pickett. He struck his head and is in sick bay."

"Get that man here if he's able," demanded Van Cleef. "I want to talk to him, and make sure that ship of his is under constant watch. He may try to get something from it or get it running."

"It is not functional," said Pickett. "The power source is depleted."

"Did you hear that from him," asked the general? He started pacing the room. "He obviously bullshitted you once. He would not be above it a second time. Clever bastard," he added. "Don't let anyone near that ship unless I say so."

"Do you have people checking the computers," asked Henning. "He may have used them to make his escape."

"We have people on the computers," said Pickett, "but there is so much data to sift through and we do not yet know what we are looking for."

"Check any atlas or mapping programs like the Google Local or the Map quest types," said Henning. "Look for any added subroutines or alterations of the original programs." This was an apparent leap of logic, since the eye witness reports of Peston's escape seemed to indicate that he used the amulet solely, but Henning knew from the distant past that the aperture needed computer guidance to select a destination. If only he was present at the so called 'prayer demonstration' he could have . . .

Van Cleef scowled, "Get every available computer guru or hacker you can find on it. The President will send a shit storm on me if we don't get him back. I need not tell you which direction that stuff slides." He turned to Henning. "What are you doing to get Peston back?"

"The FBI is using its full power on this assignment," Assured Henning.

"I mean you," said Van Cleef. "What about you?"

"I am a detective, General," replied Henning. "I will be doing what detectives do."

"Which is?"

"Asking questions, getting answers, and putting them together. I intend to start with the linguist who worked with Peston on the Omanee dictionary."

The procurement of metallic hydrogen took up a lot of time. The first method consisted of crushing liquid hydrogen at a temperature of three kelvins between pistons rammed together under low explosives. It generated sufficient pressure to metalize the samples, but the yield was too small and the product was unstable. One of the scientists suggested repeating the process under an intense magnetic field, simulating more closely the conditions on the Jovian surface where metallic hydrogen abounds. Another of the group made the added suggestion of using lasers to sustain the initial shockwave through the sample. This was tried and the yield was much larger and stabilized.

The hydrogen pellet, weighing approximately five grams, was placed in a magnetic bottle of pure gold. The vessel itself weighed about fifty kilograms representing two million dollars worth of gold bullion, but the supporting field coil bulked it up to over a ton. The bottle was studded with argon lasers positioned to further crush the hydrogen with powerful beams. With successive hammering of the pellet with the lasers, the hydrogen increased in density until it finally became a singularity with a diameter of one yocto-meter, or one-septillionth of a meter.

"Agent Henning, there's a call for you on line three," said a secretary. Henning took the call.

"Hello Mr. Henning, I am Robert McGinnis, assistant plant manager at the power authority in Niagara Falls."

"What can I do for you, Mr. McGinnis," asked Henning.

"We have detected some anomalies in the power grid during the last two days. We were concerned about a possible terrorist source, and I contacted Homeland Security about it. They gave me this number and your name."

"Tell me what you can about it," said Henning.

"The anomaly takes the form of dips in the power level, not enough to cause any permanent damage to the grid, but it once came close to shutting down a switch that would have put four million New Yorkers in the dark."

"Have you found the source," asked Henning?

"We traced it to a substation in Albany, New York."

"Any large users in the area that might account for it?"

"I called Albany Medical Center and St. Peter's asking if they had a lot of MRI machines in simultaneous use. Neither said they had more than three. Albany Med. said they have two in nearly constant use and a third for overflow, but that would not be enough consumption to cause the fluctuations." Henning had a computer connection going surfing the net as he was talking.

"I just brought up a list of schools working on high energy physics projects," said Henning. "Rensselaer Polytechnic Institute is in Troy."

"It's just across the river from Albany," said McGinnis. "I called them just before I spoke with the hospitals. They aren't currently working with any high consumptives. Besides, they are required by contract to inform us when they are about to use more than a megawatt per hour. This dip is on the order of a hundred times that."

"Maybe your billing department has the answer," said Henning.

"Afraid not," replied McGinnis. "Whoever is using this power is stealing it. So far the billable loss is more than fifty thousand dollars. We have trucks patrolling the streets," added McGinnis, "but they would have to be practically on top of the thieves to detect the drain pulses."

"Sounds more like a job for the state police," said Henning. "If the theft crosses a state line then it would be in our jurisdiction."

"This is more than a simple theft of service," said McGinnis. "The energy they are consuming is large enough for things like uranium refining."

"Jesus," said Henning. "I'll contact Homeland and tell them what you said. They'll get back to you damn quick." He got a couple of phone numbers where McGinnis could be reached and thanked him for the alert.

He got off the phone and blew out a big sigh. The conversation was on speaker. Henning looked over at the major. "Just when I thought I had enough on my place," he said.

"You think somebody could be making a bomb," asked Pickett?

"I hope not," said Henning, "but just in case, I will pass on the information." He dialed his connection with Homeland Security. After a moment of lighthearted banter with someone he apparently knew, he got down to business and delivered the information he got from McGinnis. Then he hung up the phone.

"Archie Dunn at Homeland said he would dispatch a sweeper to cruise the airspace over the suspected target area."

Pickett grimaced. "What if . . ." Just then there was a loud urgent sounding rap on the door and without further delay it flew open. The young scientist who tried to warn everyone not to let Pitus handle the amulet stood in the doorway. Both men looked up at him startled. "What's up," asked Henning?

"I overheard the conference call you had with McGinnis."

"You eavesdropped," said Pickett.

"You had it on conference call whether you planned it or not. My phone chirped and I picked it up."

"And," said Pickett.

"It has to be Peston," said the young man.

"You're Peter Sprague, the computer geek from Princeton," said Henning. "The one who warned us belatedly about the amulet," he added testily.

"That wasn't my fault," replied Sprague just as testily.

"No, it wasn't," admitted Henning.

"I read the whole book of Peston's," said Sprague. "The problem is that I'm one of the few who did. It holds the keys."

"What keys," asked Pickett?

"The keys to what Peston is trying to do and how he will do it," said Sprague.

"You have our attention," said Henning.

"He is trying to build another ship to take him back to Oman," said Sprague. "The hydrogen metalizing process is crucial to producing the black hole needed for the power source."

"Black hole," said Pickett quizzically, "as in . . ."

"Singularity," replied Sprague. "It has to be a charged singularity with spin to produce the angular momentum energy that is tapped for the ship's drive. It has to be electrically charged for it to be contained in a magnetic bottle. The magnetic field strong enough to contain it would have to be enormous."

"I'll call the general and tell him we may have located Peston," said Pickett. He picked up the phone. To Sprague he said while punching in the number, "Pete, you're a genius. From now on you report directly to me."

The conversation with General Van Cleef was short, but apparently potent in its content. Pickett hung up and immediately punched in another number.

"This is Major Morris Picket. I am operating under orders of General Van Cleef. I need a jet ready at Langley to take me and Mr. Peter Sprague to Albany, New York." He spoke a few more seconds and then disconnected.

"A car will pick us up in fifteen minutes," he said to Sprague.

Pitus and the other scientists of the 'bottle crew', as the singularity team was called, watched the monitor nervously. They had been compressing the sample with ultra powerful lasers, but the signature wave was not appearing. The metalized hydrogen inside the magnetic bottle, a mere speck of five grams of this dense material was among the most exotic substances presently on the planet. If this experiment, or rather, production attempt should succeed, then *the* most exotic substance on the planet would result. This miracle of physics would be only the beginning. If it 'went dark', as the assembler technicians on Jartic Orz would say, the little seed would then need feeding. How big a meal would this miniscule thing a billion times smaller than a virus particle require? Its first meal would have to be a mass as large than Everest. After this engorgement, its size would be still smaller than that virus particle aforementioned. The team had achieved matter degeneracy, but not nullity, and without this, there would be no engine for the ship waiting in the hangar at Schenectady.

Apprehension mounted by the second as the clock ticked away. The energy pouring into that bottle from those lasers was enormous. The power consumption was so great that it had to be time limited to prevent a catastrophic shutdown of the power grid. The laser bursts were thus limited to thirteen seconds. Any more and the whole east coast of the United States could go dark. This would be, as Atoye would say, 'sub-optimal'. The pulse was at second number ten with just three fleeting seconds to go before shutdown of the laser imploders.

The agonized anticipation of failure loomed up. With one second left before shutdown the wildly fluctuating wave on the screen suddenly calmed into a clean oscillating pulse. The hydrogen metal had collapsed into a micro black hole and stabilized.

A general cheer went up in the secret underground lab.

"Now," said Pitus, "all we need is a trillion ton mass to fatten up our little fellow in there," he said pointing to the bottle. To the scientist next to him he asked, "Is the matter stream collimator ready?"

"I believe so," replied Joshua. He was a red haired young man of twenty-two, lanky and tall, very much still a boy, but inside that head was genius. Pitus found this out while interviewing him for the bottle crew. Princeton was a bore to him. He needed some real challenge to titillate his intellect. When Pitus told him the principles behind what he wanted, Joshua's bored attitude vanished. Pitus could see that he had 110 percent of this man's attention, and that was exactly the level of interest he sought. Pitus made him crew leader, a decision he found no reason to regret.

"If what you wrote in the Peregrinations holds true, then the thing should work. The only question I have is given what is inside that flask, how the hell can we safely let it take on the matter we need? Just one slip and we are all inside a black hole. I don't think even a dead man's soul could get out of it."

"We can't get the matter here and maintain secrecy," said Pitus. "If we stole Mt. Everest, somebody's certain to notice."

"How about sea water," asked Joshua?

"That much water would make Miami Beach a mile wide and screw up the global climate," said Pitus.

"Yeah, I know that," said Joshua.

Joshua smirked. "Let's take Washington D.C. Nobody will miss that."

"Take the politicians," said Pitus. "The aggregate mass should suffice, and leave that beautiful city alone." They both laughed. Then Pitus said, "We get an asteroid."

"How do we get an asteroid?" asked Joshua. Pitus held up the amulet. "There's enough energy in here to reach escape velocity. Unfortunately, the drain will probably render it inert. If we're lucky, the energy in the Luso stone and the feeble power in the singularity can get us out to an asteroid."

"We could use the gravitation of the moon to boost velocity," said Joshua.

Pitus nodded. Once again this young man showed his worth. "Calculate the trajectory in the nav com simulator," said Pitus, "you can import the data into the ship at Schenectady."

"When will we try it," asked Joshua?

"Tonight is my plan," said Pitus. He eyed the young man curiously. "You are a wealthy man on Earth. The trip to the asteroid belt is a high risk job. If we screw it up you will either be inside a black hole or stuck out in space."

"To hell with the money," declared Joshua. "I wouldn't miss this for all the gold in Fort Knox." Pitus grinned and clapped him on the shoulder. "Then let's get on with it."

The bottle was delivered to the Schenectady site in a twenty-two foot strait job. The bottle was secured in the front of the cargo area and the last twelve feet was filled with dummy computers, in case the truck was stopped by the police for some reason. At two in the morning on a cold February night the bottle was unloaded beside the ship for installation.

"Now the interesting part starts," said Pitus.

"I don't see how anything could be more interesting than what we've done already," replied Joshua.

"Wait and see," said Pitus. "Just wait till you see the Earth as a tiny speck in the backdrop of a myriad of stars." He then recalled his own first experience of seeing his world hanging in the depths of space just after he pulled sharply on the throttle of Atoye's Duster. The impression was even more potent than his first time of making love with Lenore behind that waterfall, and that was a potent memory to be sure.

It took all night to install the bottle into the ship's engine room. The computer assembly crew, consisting of two programmers and two designers were at work all these several months building a device whose processor utilized atomic electron energy states for computation. Instead of the 'on or off' states of conventional computers, this computer utilized all thirty-two quantum states of the electron in atoms of gadolinium. This computer could perform in a nanosecond, what a conventional computer required hours to perform. The processor, a spherical object the size of a grapefruit could perform a sextillion computations in a second. Its memory block was a flawless diamond of one hundred carats. Every carbon atom in that diamond was capable of holding thirty two bits of data. It was an awesome thing. The three men and one woman of the team who built it were destined for wealth beyond the dreams of avarice.

No sooner was the power source connected than the systems booted up and went live. Besides the computers, lighting and environment, there was a force field that enshrouded the ship capable of deflecting small space objects. A graviton emitter grid built into the undercarriage supplied the artificial gravity set to terrestrial conditions. This ship, like the Duster it was patterned after, was like a flying building bearing all the comforts of home.

John came over to Pitus and Joshua. "I overheard you talking to Josh a little while ago. "Just what do you mean by 'the really interesting stuff' you promised Josh?"

"We have to bulk up the singularity," said Pitus. "It won't have the power we need as is."

"How much *bulk* does it need," asked John?

"About a trillion tons," said Pitus, "the mass of a large mountain."

"We going to rip off a mountain," asked John?

"Too dangerous," said Joshua. "We open up that bottle to suck in a mountain and we might get the whole Earth including us."

"Even the Omans never chanced filling a magnetic bottle on the planet surface," said Pitus. "They sent it out for an asteroid. We'll need one about ten miles in diameter."

"How can we get out there where the asteroids are," asked Ott, who approached as the other three were talking.

"The bottle as is will move us in space, but we'll need the power of the amulet for the power surge to break out of Earth's gravity. It will take about three days to reach the asteroid belt if our little singularity holds up."

"If," asked John.

"We will have to keep close watch of it," said Pitus. "If we overwork it, the singularity could destabilize and fizzle out. Then we would have to attempt re-entry and start all over. If we can't get back to Earth we will be stuck till NASA reaches out here in about three hundred years." He eyed the team who had now given him their full attention. "Those of you who still want to go, launch is at 0400 hours."

A chirp of a cell phone rousted Sprague out of his sleep. He grabbed the phone and glanced at the bedside clock. "One in the morning . . . what the hell . . ." he groused as he punched the answer button. McGinnis was on the other end, following instructions from Major Pickett to report any findings directly to Sprague. Ten seconds into the call Sprague was wide awake scribbling feverishly onto a note pad. Two minutes later he was dressed and out the door.

The guard at the armory gate told Sprague that both Major Pickett and Agent Henning were still on base. Sprague had a good guess where they were and wasted no time getting there. He burst into the conference room. Pickett and Henning were seated across from each other at the table. Sprague's abrupt entrance at this late hour startled the two and Pickett whipped out his side arm.

"Don't shoot," Sprague shouted. "I've got great news." Both men looked expectantly at Sprague. "What have you got for us, Pete," asked Pickett?

"McGinnis called me. The power authority has the location of the anomaly."

"Where," asked Pickett?

"Menands," said Sprague. "It's the former location of Hudson Valley Construction, now occupied by Ott's Technological Solutions."

"Sounds like computers," said Henning.

"It is," said Sprague. "At least that's what they're doing in the front part of the place. I think we'll find something else if we can get out in the back room."

"Let's go," said Henning,

"Want me to have the state cops . . ."

"No," said Henning. "They don't know what we know and there's no time to fill them in. We can't afford a screw-up. No time for a warrant either. We go in and explain later." He gave Sprague a size-up sort of look. "You ever fire a gun," he asked.

"Jesus no!" said Sprague. "I'm a physicist."

They rushed out of the armory and piled into their car. In seconds they were on interstate 787 heading toward the Hudson River. At the river the highway turned north and they followed it the three miles into the city. They took the Erie Boulevard exit and headed north on this the remaining mile to North Enterprise Drive, parking in an adjacent parking lot to the target. The building looked deserted Henning used the butt of his service pistol to break the glass in the door. He expected to trigger an alarm, but there was no sound. If it was silent, he could show the cops his creds, but this was not the first or even second choice. Henning officially was not here. In fact, the Agency didn't have the whole story. Some of the plan was only to be found inside Henning's head. They entered the building each with guns drawn. The room was dimly lit with just night lights. Other than a few scattered cartons and a big forklift the large space was empty.

"There's nothing here," said Pickett. "The bastards somehow found out."

"The other possibility," said Henning "is that this is the wrong place, in which case, we may end up in a world of shit."

"McGinnis told me this was the address," said Sprague. He looked around the room. "Hey, this is smaller inside than it is on the outside," said Sprague.

"How do you figure," asked Pickett? Sprague pointed to the wall. It was laid up with cinder block. He moved in close to it. "This is not old construction," said Sprague. He sighted down the wall to the window. "That window is about ten feet up from the wall, but I remember seeing a lot of building to the left of it; much more than would make this the back wall." He ran back outside and quickly returned. "There's thirty feet of structure to the left of that window. There's something behind this wall."

"Check outside for an entryway," said Henning. "There has to be something." They all searched the external walls but found no entrance. They circled the outside looking for a way onto the roof. There was no door secret or otherwise to be found. They re-entered the building.

"We have to keep looking," said Pickett. "There has to be a hidden entryway. They can't walk through walls." Sprague froze. "That's it!"

"They *did* walk through walls," he declared.

"The amulet," said Henning.

"That leaves only one option, said Pickett. He hurried to the forklift and started it. It was an electric propelled monster. Pickett drove it to within five yards of the cinder block wall and turned it around to face back into the room.

Then he put it in reverse and backed it full throttle into the wall, smashing it with the heavy steel counterweight. The first hit cracked the wall, but it still held. Pickett moved out from the wall and rammed into it again. This time the wall gave, leaving a man-size hole. He moved the forklift forward a couple of yards to allow access to whatever was beyond.

The three approached the break in the dimly lit wall. Beyond the breach was pitch blackness. All three again drew their weapons. Henning grabbed a sealed beam lantern off the lift and turned it into the darkness. There were strange looking apparatus all along the far wall. Directly across was an electrical panel. Henning carefully went over to it and pulled the handle. Instantly the lights came on.

"What the hell is all of this," asked Sprague?

"I was hoping you could tell me," said the Major.

"I can tell you one thing," said Henning. "We're too late."

There hopes of apprehending Peston were dashed. Finally Pickett said, "Let's get the hell out of here." Henning, with his detective instincts put up his hand. "Wait a minute," he said. He scanned the far wall of the secret annex and spied a whiteboard hanging there. There were figures written on it, unreadable from the distance. He walked over for a closer look and noticed a small desk with a blotter on top of it. In the upper right corner of the blotter were numbers. "There's a phone number here," he said. He read it off.

"That's a Schenectady number," said Sprague. "Sounds like a land phone, not a cell." Henning called on his cell phone for a trace of the number. He waited a moment, and then snapped his phone shut.

"I got it," he said. "Let's go." They once again piled into the car and sped off. On the interstate they ran full out with dome flasher going. At the Schenectady city limit they shut it off. This time Henning called in backup from the state troopers instructing them also to "code two" when they got close. Henning waited for the state police to rendezvous and then rushed in. Two dozen state police immediately surrounded the building and a S.W.A.T. team took positions on all sides.

Inside the ship Pitus was at the helm about to perform a yard high lift off. He then planned to drift it out through the hangar door for a larger test when Joshua stopped him.

"We've got trouble," he shouted. "The place is surrounded by cops." A glance at the nav com monitor confirmed a lot of activity outside which would doubtless be inside within seconds.

"Lift off is now," called Pitus, "no rehearsals." He gripped the throttle. "Grab hold of something." He pulled back on the lever and the ship rose from the floor. A gossamer shroud enveloped the ship. He redirected most of the field's strength to the dome. Gunfire erupted as the ship smashed its way through the roof of the building. "This is the second time I've seen this done," Pitus thought. The ship rose. At an altitude of two thousand feet several big flashes came from the ground. Seven surface-to-air missiles rushed toward the ship. Some serious thrust was needed right now, but could the weak power source take the strain? Pitus redirected the force field below. In the second or so that elapsed Pitus realized that the missiles singly couldn't penetrate the field, but all seven well placed might bring the ship down. He yanked on the throttle and the ship rose above the atmosphere in seconds. Way down below him he saw the tiny flashes of the self destructed missiles that the ship outran.

The crew cheered their close escape, that is, all but Pitus. He turned toward the others whose sight of Pitus's expression muffled them into silence.

"In getting away from our pursuers, I may have blown the bottle," said Pitus. An unction of shock hardened into fear throughout the crew. Joshua leaped into the seat before the monitor. The wave pattern of the singularity was erratic.

"It's unstable," declared Joshua. "It needs energy pumped in to re-stabilize it."

Pitus thought of what that could mean. The Luso stone's energy was the only source capable of restoring stability to the singularity, but to use it would almost certainly leave the stone inert. This would mean a slower velocity for the ship, perhaps not enough to reach the asteroid belt at all. The Luso stone plus a good computer meant instant travel to some useful place or away from danger. It was a hard thing to give up to be sure. Pitus thought hard, but was forced to conclude that there was nothing else to it. It had to be done. He rigged the stone to the bottle and keyed it as the magnetic field was attenuated. The electrons rushed into the bottle. The glow of the Luso stone faded and then became dark. Thus a prodigy of nature, a thing of great power and utility was snuffed out. Pitus looked expectantly at Joshua who shook his head. Pitus was about to apologize to everyone for stranding them in space when Joshua waved his hands excitedly. The singularity had become stable once again. Everyone gave a cheer of relief. Pitus said solemnly, "There is an ancient Oman legend that the light of the Luso stone bears the life force. They claimed that in the hands of a shaman, that it could revive the dead." He placed the darkened necklace on the nav com console.

"It saved all our lives, "said Joyce. Pitus nodded. "Let's get this job done and get out of here." He sat at the nav com and started the ship into a slow acceleration. "Keep your eyes on that monitor, Joshua," said Pitus. "Any change in the wave, call it out."

"How soon to the asteroids," asked John?

"Two days at ten percent of light speed," said Pitus "I feel compelled to warn you that we may not be able to maintain that velocity."

John was pensive. "Do we have to go that far," he asked? "Aren't there closer objects? NASA tracks hundreds of space rocks in near Earth orbits just in case on of them enters into a collision course. Remember the dinosaurs?"

"Good point," said Simeon. "Someone watch the scanner for blips."

John and Joyce sat before a long range scanner. Within an hour something came on the screen. "There is something at four O'clock," John announced. All eyes but Joshua's were on the screen within seconds.

"It's heading outward at thirty kilometers per second," said Pitus.

"How large is it," someone asked? Pitus took a reading.

"Twelve kilometers in diameter and nearly spherical. That's our baby!" Pitus returned to the nav com and entered an intercept course. It was six million miles away and their present speed was .01 luminal, or 1,800 miles per second.

"ETA in about fifty-five minutes," said Pitus.

While in pursuit of their quarry, Pitus had Joshua run a chemical and physical analysis of the asteroid. It turned out to be a mixture of nickel and iron dispersed in a matrix of silicate rock. It was an object with a volume of about nine hundred cubic kilometers and a specific gravity of just over six. This calculated into a mass of about three trillion metric tons. It was perfect. Pitus moved the ship to within a kilometer of the object and matched its speed.

The bottle was taken off line temporarily and ship's emergency lighting and environment were switched to battery support. The bottle was disengaged from the drive unit and secured to a tether. A compressed air drive manipulated from remote directed the bottle to contact with the asteroid. The ship was dangerously close. Half of space was now occluded by the asteroid. It looked, in fact as though the ship was poised at an altitude of a thousand feet above the barren dusty ground. The strong magnetic field of the bottle made it stretch the tether outward as if it were a plumb bob. Then it made contact.

When the field was attenuated on the contact end of the bottle, the singularity within immediately began feeding on its prey. Matter streamed into the bottle in ever increasing velocity until the stream was white hot and the shield around the bottle shimmered as a mini sun. It was all over within a minute. What was an enormous rock the size of a Cincinnati was now completely inside a football size bottle and all of it in the very center of the space no larger than a helium nucleus. The field was restored around the bottle and the tether pulled back in. Even as the newly charged bottle approached the ship, the full lighting came on strong and the ship regained full power. The bottle was replaced into the drive core.

Pitus sat at the nav com. "Shield is full," he called "and propulsion . . ." He pulled a stiff jerk on the throttle. The ship shot forth as a bolt of lightning. Within minutes they were plowing a swath through the asteroid belt, the maximum repulsive shield shoving rocks aside as though corks upon a wave of water. Pitus pushed back on the throttle and the ship came to rest. All the passengers crowded around a large observation port. Ten thousand miles below them the Great Red Spot of Jupiter churned as a disquieted crimson sea.

"For God's Sake, Pite, come see this," exclaimed Simeon. Pitus approached the window. "This is old hat for me," he said teasingly. A contagion of skepticism swept through the others. John and Joshua jeered and then laughed. "It's magnificent," said Joshua, "something a year ago I could not have imagined seeing."

"It *is* magnificent," said Pitus. "This is only the beginning." He returned to the nav com. He rubbed the console as if caressing it. "Oh you beautiful thing," he exclaimed! He turned to the others who were still drinking in the marvel of the Jovian planet. "Are you ready for the 'big trip'," he called?

"Count me in," said Joshua. "Where to?"

"We have a fully functional ship," said Pitus, "and we have all the corstet safely off the Earth. I guess it's on to Oman." He reached for the throttle. This time it was coming all the way down just to see what this ship could do.

"Does it have to be *all* of the corstet," asked Joyce? A wave of cold swept through Pitus as if someone had let the iciness of space onto the bridge. He turned to Joyce half expecting to hear a peel of laughter from some sort of prank. No one was laughing or even grinning. The blank faces of the others looked to him like so many ghosts matching the tomb-like silence that followed the clearly serious question.

"Yes," Pitus said weakly. "If corstet is discovered, it will spell doom for Earth. The main reason for my return was to retrieve all the plants to prevent it being found."

Joyce looked at John. "We've got to go back," John said.

"Do you recall how we left Earth," asked Joshua? "They were shooting missiles at us. They wanted us all dead. We're half a billion miles from Earth now where no one can touch us." No one else spoke. "This ship is in good order. Why risk going back and getting killed?"

"If a single sprig of that plant is left on Earth, it will be found and will cause a global war eventually that will bring an end to the lives of billions," said Pitus. "I've seen it." Joshua turned on Pitus.

"How can you have seen something that hasn't happened yet?"

"Someone brew some coffee and I'll tell you a tale," said Pitus.

The whole group sat around the bridge while Pitus recounted the search for Loma's Cube, explaining the efforts of Hibber, Hivik, Crolee Zem, Kinar and Orban, leaving out the still painful part of his romance with the beautiful Orinesse and her loss to him. He retold the story of finding the cube and tapping its secrets, and of the doom predicted by it for Earth. When he was done, there was a hush over the others for a moment. Again Joshua spoke.

"How can you change the outcome of Earth after what you just said? If we are in a causality loop, won't you or any of us be prevented changing it?"

"Spoken in the true tradition of Hawk's Brother," thought Pitus. That Navaho seemed to be the biggest skeptic on Earth two centuries ago when Pitus was searching the desert for what he had yet no idea of. Now, after all this time, this other young man proved a social constant distrust.

"The main problem of controlling a causality loop is not being aware you're in one," said Pitus. "I know what we are in and I intend to try changing it."

"I'm with Pitus," said Joyce. "We can't knowingly stand by and let everyone on Earth be killed." She looked to John who nodded his agreement.

"I still don't believe we have to go back and risk getting caught or killed just for a possibility," said Joshua.

"A question I have," said Simeon, "is how can we be sure we have all the plants even after we return for the ones at Joyce's apartment?" His statement had a decisive edge to it.

"Don't try putting that monkey on my back, Mr. Simeon Ott," said Joyce caustically.

"We had a bargain," retorted Ott.

"It was a ransom," said Joyce, "Not a damn bargain!"

"Never mind what it was," said Pitus. "The danger of it has just been proved on this bridge. If two can quarrel over it, you can imagine what will happen if multiplied by a million. If you want proof," he added, "We can prove it by going back in 2061," said Pitus.

"Jar Dest barg," asked Joshua?

"Yes," said Pitus.

"Isn't that something like four light years away," asked John? Pitus nodded.

"How long till we reach it," asked Joshua?

"At maximum speed, about a month," said Pitus. A general din of disapproval rose from the others.

"We have the necessary provisions," assured Pitus, "and there will be plenty to keep us occupied during the journey. Besides," he added, "I know how to shorten the travel time to five days."

Everyone called out their relief to this news except Joshua.

"To get to Proxima Centauri in five days we'll have to exceed the specifications . . ."

"It's called 'greening' by the Omans," said Pitus. "We might call it 'red-lining.'"

"Whatever you call it," said Joshua, "it holds the risk of blowing the bottle and us to hell."

"Not if we watch the monitor," said Pitus. "We push the speed till the drive core starts to flux, then shut it down to nominal and coast." Joshua looked skeptical. "I learned it from a pro," assured Pitus.

ARRIVAL AT JAR DEST BARG

There it was; Jar Dest barg. At a distance of one thousand miles it hung as a disc the size of a full moon. With the object acting as a lens funneling nearly all the star light through it, the transparent ring of gravitational energy had the appearance of a solid moon with all its brilliance. Pitus entered code into the nav com for a trajectory through the barg that would correspond with the Earth date of 2061, one year after the predicted Armageddon by Loma's Cube.

Joshua sat at the communication console listening intently.

"What are you hearing, Josh," asked Pitus?

"Lots of squelch," he replied. His right hand turned a tuner like one would find on an old fashion radio. Frequency scanning on Atoye's old Duster was accomplished by turning a gross outer knob and then a fine adjustment inner knob. This was copied in the design of the new Duster clone ship. Some ideas just couldn't be improved upon even over centuries.

"What are you listening for," asked Joyce.

"Just testing the scanner, mainly," said Joshua. "Any signal out this far will be exceedingly faint." Pitus got on a second scanner. "I'll bet five bucks I get something first." About half a minute passed with both "boys" feverishly competing. It was Pitus who announced victory.

"It sounds like a news broadcast," he said. "Janus Andropoulos, shipping tycoon died yesterday after a short illness at his Athens home . . ."

"That happened four years ago," said Simeon. "He was a friend of mine. I attended his funeral September 10, 2018." Pitus fed the rest of the transmission through the intercom. The newscast continued with Andropoulos' life accomplishments and a listing of his heirs.

"That makes sense," said Pitus. "We're out four light years. The signal is just reaching this part of space."

"God," said Simeon "It sounds strange listening to it all over again."

"It will keep going on and on for all eternity," said Pitus. The gravity of the situation weighed heavily. Joshua tried to lighten things up a bit.

"I said 'shit' once into a walkie-talkie," said Joshua. "Dad kicked my ass for it. He said the FBI would come and lock my ass up in jail for swearing on the radio. If it's still going, it seems worth the trouble it cost me. I wonder where my 'shit' is now."

"Probably it has reached the constellation Leo by now," said Pitus.

"It puts a whole new perspective on the term, 'shooting the shit' doesn't it," said John? Everyone laughed.

"It would be all too fitting if the Zoscan's first contact with Earth was something like Joshua's little communication," thought Pitus.

"Are we ready," he asked dramatically. All urged him to proceed. Pitus gently tugged the throttle and the ship closed in on the barg. The disc grew as they approached until at a hundred miles it covered half the forward visual field. All the gathered light bending through the barg lit the interior of the ship as if it was a fluorescent panel. The only palpable change in traversing the membrane was the winking out of the accumulated star light forward as they crossed it. On the other side the aft visual field glowed with the eerie brightness.

"How will we know if we reached the target date," asked Simeon.

"One way is to catch some dated outgoing radio signals like we did on the other side of the barg," said Pitus. "Failing that, I took positional readings of Neptune and Halley's comet. When we get close enough, I will take another reading and feed it through the computer. If both of them are where they belong . . ."

"When will we know if Earth is all right," asked Joyce?

"That will require either radio traffic or a direct observation," said Pitus. "We are returning with the condition that your corstet, being left behind, was found. I expect to find a dead planet if Loma's Cube is correct."

"You sound so matter-of-fact about man's greatest catastrophe," said Joyce.

"We know how to stop it," said Pitus. Joshua continued to monitor for incoming signals. Suddenly he called out, "I've got something again!" This promised to be even more interesting than the broadcasts of the past heard on the other side of the barg. These could fix the date and reveal the condition of the Earth.

"It's one of those news and commentary programs," said Joshua. "Audio and video."

"Pitus adjusted the monitor on the nav com and on the screen came the images of three men and one woman around a table in animated discussion. The moderator posed a question;

"Will the United Federation of Southeast Asia continue its program of mass euthanasia as they call it, in light of the threat of UN intervention?" Kate, you go first . . ."

"There will be no let-up. They are so overcrowded with eight billion that they will get relief from their ovens regardless of outside threats."

"Tom?"

"The UFSA has demonstrated that they have no fear of the United Nations, or the United States, for that matter."

"Bill?"

"A war with the United States would be welcome. It would accelerate a process that they haven't the capabilities to do on their own."

"One last question; "Can it happen here? This time we'll start with Bill."

"With a population in the US of one billion and a near zero death rate, I predict at least a voluntary program within the next ten years."

"Tom?"

"Our infrastructure is already taxed to the limit. Riots have already broken out in New York and Los Angeles over food supply. I believe Congress will have a 'Kevorkian Bill' by this time next year."

"Kate?"

"I agree with Tom. There was an old movie from the nineteen-seventies called Soyalent Green. We have a scenario like that in real life today."

"Well, that sort of settles the question about whether we made it into the future or not," said Pitus.

"See what else you can find, Josh," said Simeon. Joshua fingered the dial some more.

"I seem to have tapped into a weather broadcast," replied Joshua. He listened for a few more seconds. "It is January 11, 2058."

"We're four years out," said Pitus. "That means we are on time."

"For what," asked John?

"What we all expect and none of us hopes to see," said Pitus. He sat at the com and brought the ship to maximum acceleration once again. When the singularity wave started fluttering, he backed off and let the ship coast toward the Oort cloud. "Five days to Earth," he said.

On the inward journey, Joshua kept close vigil on the radio and video transmissions from Earth. The content was growing more ominous with each day's progress. As they entered the outskirts of the Oort cloud hostilities seemed immanent between the United States and the some other country in Africa. The ship slowed to one-half luminal. Joshua scrolled the frequencies for the details.

The ship made a close flyby of Halley's Comet. It was inbound between Jupiter and Mars on time for its 2061 arrival. At this point it was just an oblong object like any asteroid hurtling through space. It would start hitting the solar wind soon and take on its more familiar characteristics. Pitus verified Neptune's position against the position of Uranus. Neptune's position had changed nearly ninety degrees in its solar orbit and Uranus position was now one hundred seventy degrees from its location in 2020.

"According to the positions of Neptune and Uranus, the date should be August 28th, 2062," announced Pitus. "Close enough for our purposes."

"Any radio traffic, Josh," asked John?

"Lots of it," said Joshua. There are video transmissions . . . It sounds like all hell is breaking loose down there. Pitus stopped the ship about ten thousand miles out. The eastern seaboard of North America shimmered in the night. New York, Washington, Boston, Atlanta and Miami were twinkling smudges of brightness on the left side, and across the Atlantic, all of Western Europe was visible with London, Paris, Madrid, and Frankfort easily identifiable. Saul glowed in the background.

"It's the Seal of the United States behind the podium. The President must be going to speak." Everyone crowded around the monitor. This would likely be big news.

A question and answer session was in progress. The questions concerned accusations that the United States was preventing distribution of the universal cure needed to stop the spread of the latest flare up of Ebola virus. The United States claimed it had nowhere near enough at the present time to distribute it to anybody. The news people interrupted and attempted to talk over each other to get the President to answer their questions, when suddenly two secret servicemen flanked the President and hurried him away from the podium. The press conference was over and a stunned anchorman was trying to make sense of the abrupt termination. Then it happened. The view of the newsroom and the anchorman shook violently. The man said, "My God, it's happening." The video went to snow. Everyone but Pitus stared at the monitor in bewilderment. Pitus stood at the observation port.

"Jesus," he breathed.

"Everyone turned just in time to see small sun-like flashes erupt over both North America and Europe. Almost instantly the network of lights from the great city centers went out and all was dark. Joyce clutched John and buried her face in his chest. He instinctively closed his arms around her, but he just stared at the blackened dying world below.

"God dammit!" shouted Simeon, "The stupid bastards blew it up!" Pitus snapped a look at his son. Those were nearly the same words Pitus heard come out of Atoye on seeing the ruins of Kesst. Pitus reflected on the Oman Thirty-minutes' war. This one was even shorter. He took his seat at the nav com.

"We've got to go back," said Pitus.

"You think we can prevent this," declared John his hand gesturing at the now doomed Earth.

"We've got to try," replied Joshua. "I don't care if I ever live there again, but all of them . . ." he said, pointing out the observation port. "Deserve better than that."

Pitus looked at each of the others. "We can go back to 2020 and try to get the remaining corstet. The risk is great that we will be caught. Or . . . we can cut bait right now and head for Oman. What's the vote?" He stood up from the console. "The greatest gift a man can have is a quiet conscience. That allows me only once choice." All the others concurred and spoke in favor of returning to the Earth of forty years ago despite the risk of failure. Pitus nodded and returned to the com, punching in the course for Jar Dest Barg.

For the next five days little was said. Even though they had the means of averting the disaster in Earth's future, seeing it happen scribed its indelible mark on everyone's souls. Joshua at times seemed edgy when Pitus maneuvered the ship. He seemed in perpetual fear that something would go wrong to prevent their return to 2020 as if he was the only one who knew how vital it was. When the barg came into view once again, the angst seemed to amplify.

"Are you absolutely sure of the trajectory," Joshua asked?

"For God's sake, Josh, yes," said Pitus. "Even if it wasn't right, we could come back and correct it."

"O.K, O.K.," said Joshua, "I'm just a little keyed up . . ."

"No shit," said Pitus. Joshua laughed Pitus pulled on the throttle and they entered the barg.

The approach to Earth was once again from the dark side. This time the whole of North America was in night view. The major cities were shimmering jewels from Los Angeles to New York and from Chicago to Houston. Everyone gave a cheer at seeing the world alive again.

"Where do we land," asked John? "Joyce lives in the city, but we can't just plop down there without drawing attention."

"The decision needs to come soon," said Pitus. "When I crashed the orbiter in Lake Huron, the Coast Guard was all over me in minutes. I guarantee we're being tracked."

"There's a patch of woods behind the old Peston House," said John. "Within the wood is a clearing big enough to land this ship." Pitus set in a course.

"When is it," asked Simeon?

"About three hours later on the night of our escape," said Pitus. "I want to get the remaining corstet before someone else discovers it."

The plan was made where John and Joyce would go to Joyce's apartment, get the plants and come straight back to the ship for takeoff.

"We lost them," said Pickett. "Dammit we lost them and there's no way to go after them." He grabbed his hat from his head and threw it to the ground. He looked up at Henning. "You don't look very upset," he groused.

"We have all their equipment," Henning replied. "What they did we can do as well." I suggest we seal off this building and send some people to the Menands facility and do the same before someone else finds it. Then we can take it all to Los Alamos and really enter the Space Age."

Pickett nodded. His countenance lifted as he turned to Sprague. "You take charge of Menands," he said. "Don't even let the cops near it till we can get some of our science people in there to help you assess what we have." Sprague and six heavily armed soldiers piled into a nearby carrier. "You coming, Mr. Henning," Sprague called from the passenger window of the personnel carrier. "I'll go in my car and meet you there. The truck engine whined as the team sped away. Henning quickly moved to his car and got in.

"Once again you slipped through my fingers," he said, as he pulled onto the street behind Sprague and the others. As he drove he was deep in thought. "Why did he come back," he asked himself? "What would bring him all the way back across the parsecs? What could it be?" Then it hit him as a lightning bolt. "Corstet," he nearly shouted. He recalled reading about corstet pods in one of Kinar's journals during his last term at Holloway over eighty years before. "That tardsoon came back for the seed pods he gave Kinar. He let Sprague gain some distance on him. When the ramp came up for the Northway he took it and headed back to his room at the Dunmore in Colonie. Once in his room, he sat at his desk, plugged in his laptop and booted it up. He reviewed his notes on the case of the stolen PEREGRINATIONS. Hodiak traveled all over the country following Peston's path. Could he have found them somewhere or did he have them before his chasing after Peston?

He scrolled through his notes until he reached the spot where he interviewed Mike Briggs, the bartender. He said he sold some antique bottles and crockery to Hodiak. He scrolled further down and found where he noted that the bar was located in the building that once housed the apothecary shop of Lucius Ordway, which he knew was one of Kinar's assumed names. Hodiak was living in the house Peston lived in as a boy. He remembered the visit with Hodiak at the Warren County Jail. Hodiak said his house was broken into and some Peston related papers and books were stolen. He said he mistakenly believed Flynn and Dolph went into the house while he was away, but it also could have been his brother Ken. There was no mention of any plant specimens or bottles. If he had the corstet, would he have kept it there knowing it wasn't completely secure? Probably not, but if not there, where? It took little figuring to determine where the *where* was; his girlfriend Joyce Benton's apartment was in Glens Falls. He pulled his notebook from his coat pocket and thumbed through it. There it was; Joyce Benton, 42 Dix Avenue, Glens Falls. He shut down his computer and hurried to his car.

Forty-five minutes later he parked the car on Dix Avenue fifty yards down the street from Benton's apartment. The apartment was in a duplex and the neighbor was at home. If it came down to it he could show his badge, but he preferred to do this quietly. He crept into the vestibule and picked the front door lock. The apartment was dark but for a pale glow coming from a room at the back of the hall. He drew his pistol and crept toward the light. When he cleared the room he re-holstered the pistol and entered.

In a corner of the room in a little alcove stood a table with a small boxed in planter on it. The top of the unit held a grow light. Henning peered into the box and smiled. There were six mini pots arranged in a cluster inside the box and in four of them a tiny purple bud had broken through the surface of the soil. He took the box and turned off the light. Within three minutes he was back in his car.

Twenty minutes later he drove slowly by Hodiak's house, pulled to the side of the road and doused the lights. He grabbed a spare nine millimeter out of the glove compartment. When he got out of the car he shoved the second gun under his belt. The house was dark as he expected. He quietly moved up the driveway and into the back yard. It was only a hunch, perhaps a long shot. With some of the corstet still here Peston would come back. He had to, didn't he say the Earth was doomed if all of the plant wasn't found and destroyed? It might be days before Peston returned, maybe weeks. But return he would. Given the urgency of the situation, Henning felt it would be much sooner.

The sky was crystal clear and lit up with thousands of stars. Henning maneuvered around to the back door to gain entry to the house when he saw a blip of light swiftly moving among the stars. It was moving faster than a jet. It grew closer and then he heard the familiar whine of an inertial damper.

"Thank you for being so reliable and so prompt," thought Henning. He ran to the edge of the woods and secreted himself among some low hemlocks near the outhouse. He watched as John and Joyce left the ship. Pitus also emerged and called to them, "Get the plants and get your asses back here. This isn't safe." John ran into the house and shortly returned with his truck keys. The two jumped into the truck and sped off. When they were gone Henning checked his gun. He carefully advanced on the ship and watched. The cargo door was open.

"Mistake number two," thought Henning. "Number one was coming back here." He started toward the door and then bolted. Voices were coming from the ship. Pitus was not alone. Time for a modification of plans. He drew back into the shadows. The trip to the city and back would probably be just under thirty minutes. He didn't want the added risk of the other two returning before he was safely in the ship, so the time was now. He crept toward the open doorway once more with pistol drawn. Pitus came through the door a minute later.

"Hands up where I can see them," he barked. Pitus froze then lifted his arms. "Call your friend," he commanded. Pitus called to Simeon and he appeared at the opening.

"Henning, you bastard," growled Ott. He raised his hands and stepped out beside Pitus.

"Simeon," said Pitus, "I regret to have to introduce you to an old adversary."

"You know me," said Henning, a bit surprised.

"I never forget a face even after two hundred years," replied Pitus. To Simeon he said, "This is Mr. Rowan, alias Rohab, a Haldi mercenary who tricked Atoye and Kinar into bringing him here to steal the key to Loma's Cube left here by Ewanok."

"The first part is true," said Rohab, "but the rest is an Oman fabrication. I came here to reclaim what rightfully belongs to the people of Haldan. Because of the others' treachery I was abandoned on this barbaric planet for more than three and a half centuries."

"That is a case of one's point of view," said Pitus sarcastically.

"It matters little now," said Rohab. "All those years blending in, until my lack of aging gave rise to questions." He squatted while keeping the gun trained on Pitus and Simeon, to pick up the little box of plants. He held it out for the two to see. "I have had a little of this wonderful plant long ago while on Oman. It has extended my longevity far beyond the normal Haldi span of three score and ten. One drawback it has burdened me with here is the necessity of moving away every forty or fifty years. I changed continents six times since we last met, but one thing has never changed; my desire that we would once again cross paths so I could settle an old score." He waved the gun at the ship. "It looks like all the waiting has paid off."

"You're not taking that ship," said Simeon.

"Oh yes I am," said Rohab.

Simeon reached behind him and drew out a pistol. He fired at Rohab and missed. Pitus rolled to the side to get out of the line of fire. Simeon dove behind a tree. Rohab rolled to the side as well, dropping the corstet and drawing out his spare weapon firing both rapidly at Simeon. Then Simeon caught a bullet in the chest and went down. Pitus called "Simeon!" and rushed to him without regard to Rohab's fire. Rohab fired on Pitus and hit him in the shoulder. Then he bolted for the cargo door and closed it.

Pitus crawled to Simeon and found him still breathing. He raised his son up in his arms and the two watched as their ship rose up into the night sky and then flashed away. There was silence for a moment. Then there was the sound of John's truck returning.

"Stay with me son, John and Joyce are back. We'll get you to the hospital." Simeon let out a phlegmy sounding cough. He was drowning in his own blood. He started to speak and Pitus put his ear close to his son's lips."

"I'm done for," he gasped.

"Nonsense," said Pitus. "We're going to get you patched up and together we'll build another ship and get that son-of-a-bitch."

"You get him," said Simeon. "Get him for me. Find him wherever he's gone and say my name when you blow his brains out."

He knew Simeon was probably right. He was bleeding heavily. "I promise," said Pitus somberly. "I'll get him. Now be still and save your strength till we get you out of here."

John and Joyce pulled in and hurried into the woods. When they got nearer it was obvious that something was very wrong.

"Call an ambulance," shouted Pitus! "Simeon's shot." Joyce called on her cell phone and within minutes the sounds of sirens and flash of lights enveloped the place.

An hour later Pitus was over getting the bullet removed from his shoulder and was coming out of the anesthesia. John and Joyce were the first things he saw upon coming around.

"Simeon," Pitus croaked. His throat was dry and he could barely get out the words. He started to rise but the surgeon and an orderly forced him back down on the gurney.

"Stay still," said the surgeon. "You lost a lot of blood and I don't want to see you lose any more."

"How is Simeon," Pitus repeated? He anxiously looked around. Joyce turned away. "Simeon," called Pitus again. John put his hand on Pitus' shoulder.

"He went to surgery and seemed stable and they took him to the ICU but . . ." his voice trailed off. Pitus opened his mouth and drew in what must have been an agonizing breath and released it in a scream surly heard through the whole building.

"Lorazepam, 2 milligrams, stat," commanded the doctor!" The nurse rushed with the dose and pounded it into the IV line. Pitus let out what would have been another wail, but it came out as a sigh and then he was still.

"He was let out of the sedation the next morning. His left shoulder was bandaged and his arm in a sling. Pitus saw that John was just outside the ward room. He started to wave and then dropped his hand as he watched a guard in an army uniform give him a pat down search. John came in and smiled.

"You look better. Do you hurt?"

"Not bad," replied Pitus. "I'm glad they stopped pumping my head full of dope."

"You'll be out of here today, I'll bet," ventured John.

"Yes," said Pitus. His expression grew serious. "Listen," he said, "I'm going to be taken into custody by the army. If there is anymore of that thing you went for with Joyce, destroy it on sight. Don't stop even to think about it or you'll weaken. If you don't, you will not live to collect social security."

"Rohab took it all," said John. "When we got to Joyce's the planter was empty and the grow light was turned off."

"I thought I saw him take what he had into the ship with him," said Pitus. "Maybe we're out of danger."

"Where are you going," asked John?

"You don't expect them to tell me something like that," said Pitus.

"You have rights," said John. "I'll get a lawyer, a cat piss mean one to get you released.

"I am not being arrested. I broke no laws, except stealing some power off Niagara Mohawk. I am probably going back to Nevada or wherever the hell they stashed the orbiter. They would probably lock me up inside some mountain someplace if they didn't feel I was still useful."

"Will you go back," asked John?

"I have a promise to keep," said Pitus. "That's all I will say at the moment."

"Don't forget us," said John. "Joyce still wants to see the dawn sun strike the spires of Hibber."

"Then stay put so I can find you," said Pitus. "Give me a year or maybe two." The guard came into the room and called for John to leave.

"Till we meet again," called John as he passed through the doorway.

Immediately upon John's departure, another man entered the room.

"Major Pickett," greeted Pitus.

"The doctor has cleared you for evac," said Pickett. "Agent Henning was supposed to come with us, but he cannot be located."

"Yeah," thought Pitus. "I'd tell you, but I doubt you'd believe me even after all that has happened."

"Are you ready?"

"No time like the present," said Pitus. The guard came forward with both manacles and shackles. Pitus lifted his one hand.

"Seems ridiculous for a man in my condition . . ."

"I agree," said Pickett. He waved off the guard. "I am going out on a limb," he added. "I want your word you'll not try to escape."

"You have it," said Pitus. "Besides, I have work to do and I'm eager to get at it." Pitus swung his legs over the side of the bed and carefully stood up. He was all dressed and he stood a moment to steady himself. Then he left with the major.

THE END

104181

Edwards Brothers,Inc!
Thorofare, NJ 08086
13 December, 2010
BA2010347